HEAD CASE

Also by Michael Wiley

The Sam Kelson mysteries

TROUBLE IN MIND *
LUCKY BONES *

The Detective Daniel Turner mysteries

BLUE AVENUE *
SECOND SKIN *
BLACK HAMMOCK *

A Franky Dast mystery

MONUMENT ROAD *

The Joe Kozmarski series

LAST STRIPTEASE
THE BAD KITTY LOUNGE
A BAD NIGHT'S SLEEP

* *available from Severn House*

HEAD CASE

Michael Wiley

**SEVERN
HOUSE**

First world edition published in Great Britain and the USA in 2021
by Severn House, an imprint of Canongate Books Ltd,
14 High Street, Edinburgh EH1 1TE.

Trade paperback edition first published in Great Britain and the USA
in 2022 by Severn House, an imprint of Canongate Books Ltd.

severnhouse.com

British Library Cataloguing-in-Publication Data
A CIP catalogue record for this title is available from the British Library.

ISBN-13: 978-0-7278-8983-6 (cased)
ISBN-13: 978-1-78029-762-0 (trade paper)
ISBN-13: 978-1-4483-0500-1 (e-book)

All Severn House titles are printed on acid-free paper.

Typeset by Palimpsest Book Production Ltd.,
Falkirk, Stirlingshire, Scotland.
Printed and bound in Great Britain by
TJ Books Limited, Padstow, Cornwall.

For those who take down walls and fences

ONE

Gary Renshaw's gelled black hair jutted like a breaking wave. Ever since a guard broke his jaw during his first stint in jail, the cock of his chin matched his hair.

Sam Kelson pointed at Renshaw's head. 'You could wax a car with that thing,' he said.

Renshaw was proud of his hair and indifferent about his jaw. So he leveled his .22 Mossberg Plinkster – a kid's rifle, for shooting at squirrels if a boy wanted to give the squirrels a fighting chance – and shot Kelson clean through the arm.

The bullet popped a hole in Kelson's biceps and left another hole on its way out. Blood pulsed from the wounds and streamed down Kelson's arm.

'Ho ho,' Renshaw said. 'An artery shot.'

Kelson stared at his arm – then collapsed on the hallway floor.

Renshaw grinned down at him. 'So easy,' he said. He aimed the rifle at a scar on Kelson's forehead where a seventeen-year-old street dealer nicknamed Bicho also once shot him. 'Anything to say?'

'Oh, you're in trouble now,' Kelson said.

Renshaw grinned. He had skinny teeth.

Then a big gun fired from the end of the hallway. Renshaw seemed to lift into the air and fly away in a spray of astonishment. Kelson's friend DeMarcus Rodman had arrived.

Kelson looked toward Rodman. His eyes screwed, blurred. Rodman was six foot eight, almost three hundred pounds, but Kelson couldn't see him.

'What did you do *this* time?' the big man asked, and Kelson passed out.

Outside Renshaw's condo, the city went through the motions of a cold January day. A gray sky hung overhead. Snow, as fine as dust, fell as if it never meant to touch the earth. There was no wind. Children on school playgrounds looked up with the joy they felt. Bus drivers and cabbies hesitated before turning on the wipers.

The balding meteorologist on Midday News said the snow would stop by evening. His voice was gruff, but if you listened close, you heard the same joy you saw in the children's eyes as icy pinpricks stung their cheeks.

An ambulance siren pierced the air. The children turned their gaze back to the world. Cops flipped on their overhead lights. Bus drivers and cabbies inched to the curbs to let them by. The meteorologist *sent it back* to the anchor for a breaking story from the northside.

Kelson, his blood pooling on the hallway floor, slept the sleep of the almost dead.

TWO

'Not even close,' the surgeon told Kelson when he awoke two days later. 'I mean, another five minutes, and we'd've said *God rest his soul*. OK, it *was* close, but we got you.'

'Comedian,' Kelson said. His mouth was dry, caked with crud. 'I feel like I ate a bag of cat litter.'

'What?' the surgeon said. He rocked on his toes when he talked. He had short, curly blond hair and wire-rimmed glasses.

'You look young enough to play make-believe doctor.'

The surgeon smiled down at him. 'And *you* look like you're going to be fine after some rest and rehabilitation.' He held a clipboard with Kelson's medical information.

'Thanks for saving my life,' Kelson said. 'And my arm.' Bandages – thick as a down coat – were wrapped around the arm, from his shoulder to his elbow.

'Thank your pal for that,' the surgeon said. 'We did what we always do. He made sure you got here in time.'

'DeMarcus?'

'Great big guy? Eyes kind of funny – real close together?'

'Yeah, DeMarcus,' Kelson said. 'Is he here?'

The surgeon rocked on his toes. 'He took off when the police said they wanted to talk to him. Something about the illegal use of a weapon.'

'Could you stop doing that?' Kelson said. 'You're making me seasick.'

More rocking. 'What?'

'You look too young to use big-people scissors,' Kelson said. 'Who let you have a scalpel?'

The surgeon tapped the clipboard. 'I understand you suffer from disinhibition. Frontal lobe injury. After your previous firearm mishap. You can't help saying what's on your mind?'

'Yep, that's me.' The scar on his forehead – still pink three years after Bicho shot him – proved it. So did his drooping left eye.

'Well, it seems to be unaffected by the latest shooting.'

'Thank God for that.'

'We have a surprise for you.'

'Surprise me by standing still.'

The surgeon stepped to the door and signaled into the hall.

Kelson's twelve-year-old daughter, Sue Ellen, and his ex-wife, Nancy, came into the room.

After growing three inches in the last three months, Sue Ellen looked like a mini-Nancy, with raven black hair and a hard chin.

Nancy wore scrubs from the Healthy Smiles Dental Clinic. When she wasn't working as a dentist, she practiced mixed martial arts. Since divorcing Kelson, she mostly treated him like she wanted to head-butt him and choke him out. But now she kissed him on the forehead.

'Wow,' Kelson said. 'That close?'

'They thought you were going to die,' Nancy said.

Sue Ellen hopped on to the side of the bed. 'Mom said if you did, I could have your car.'

'Not funny,' Nancy said.

Kelson grinned. 'Funny enough.'

'Mom also said I can get a potbellied pig.'

Nancy curled her lips. 'Did not.'

Sue Ellen gave Kelson doe eyes. 'What good is having my dad get shot if I don't get presents?'

'Did you feed the cats?' Kelson asked her.

'We got them from your apartment. I'm keeping them in my room.'

'Only until they release your dad,' Nancy said.

'Or forever,' Sue Ellen said.

'Your daughter's becoming snotty in her old age,' Nancy said, and dug into her purse for a couple of bucks. 'Go be snotty at the vending machines.'

Sue Ellen snatched the bills. 'Yeah, that's subtle. If they have peanuts, I'm buying some for the pig.' She darted from the room.

'Wow,' Kelson said.

'*My* energy,' Nancy said. '*Your* lack of self-control.'

'She's tough,' Kelson said. 'Like both of us.'

Nancy looked him over. 'What the hell happened?'

'That bad?'

'You look like you crawled out of a hole.'

'A guy named Gary Renshaw ran this auto repair shop for high-end cars,' he said. 'When he had the cars in the shop, he made copies of the keys. A year or so later, he'd steal the best of them – from driveways, parking garages, restaurant parking lots. He took it slow, played the long game. He kept a list of ready buyers. Out of state. Out of country. He repainted the cars, changed the serial numbers. He was smart until he got stupid. He stole a second vintage Mercedes from the same collector in Hinsdale. I went to talk to Renshaw about it at his condo. Then he shot me.'

'Stupid to confront a man like that at his own home,' Nancy said.

'DeMarcus went with me.'

'Two stupid guys are better than one? When are you going to quit doing this?'

'*This?*'

'You had a good career – you've got disability. Yeah, it sucks that the kid shot you in the head. But it's time to take it easy.'

'I'm making a living.'

'You're going to get yourself killed. You can't help yourself, Sam. You can't shut your mouth. If you hide from a man with a gun and he calls your name, you call back, *Yo, I'm in the closet.*'

'That happened only once.'

'What happened this time? Did you tell Renshaw you were wearing a bulletproof vest so he should shoot you in your arm instead of your chest?'

'Number one, I wasn't wearing a vest. Number two, he shot me after I made fun of his hair.'

'Call this what it is, Sam. Total lack of self-control. Men with brain damage don't work as detectives.'

'It makes me better at my job.'

'In what possible sense?'

'I'm more . . . empathetic.'

'So empathetic you ridicule a man's hair? A man with a gun? A man who shoots people who ridicule him?'

'He also had skinny teeth. He looked like a chicken.'

'Sue Ellen needs a dad. A living dad.'

'Don't bring her into it.'

'Don't bring your daughter into it?'

'*Our* daughter. And she doesn't worry about me doing my job.'

'She's twelve years old. She worries about everything.'

'You think?'

'Yeah. Most of all, you.'

'When did she get started on potbellied pigs?'

'First I've heard of it. And don't change the subject.'

'I don't like *your* subject.'

A short, muscular, olive-skinned man in his late twenties came in from the corridor. He wore blue nurse's scrubs. 'Excuse me,' he said, 'you've got another visitor.'

Homicide detective Venus Johnson came into the room. Kelson knew her from two disastrous cases he'd worked since leaving the Chicago Police Department. She nodded at Nancy and raised her eyebrows as if they both knew what they were dealing with. She frowned down at him.

Kelson said, 'They put *you* on this?'

'Do you see flowers?' Johnson said. 'Do you see a teddy bear in a cute sweater?'

'Huh?'

'Do you see a get-well card? Then I guess they put me on it. I kicked and screamed but it was my bad luck.'

'Is DeMarcus in trouble for shooting Renshaw?'

'We need to talk to him is all,' she said. 'D'you know where we can find him?'

'He saved my life,' Kelson said.

'More bad luck,' she said.

'What kind of way is that to talk to a man who almost died?'

'I've been saving up especially for you.'

Nancy nodded, like she understood why.

Kelson eyed the two women. 'Didn't the doctor tell you to avoid upsetting me?'

Nancy and Johnson answered together. 'No.'

Kelson said, 'If DeMarcus is hiding, he has good reasons. You tried his apartment?'

'Yeah, dumbass, we tried his apartment. His girlfriend says she hasn't seen him.'

'Then he doesn't want you to find him. I can tell you whatever you need to know about the shooting.'

'And a lot more than I *want* to know,' Johnson said.

'Renshaw shot me in the arm. He wanted to shoot me again. DeMarcus shot him instead. That's it.'

The nurse watched their back-and-forth.

Johnson asked Kelson, 'Does he have a FOID card? I know he doesn't have a concealed carry license. I checked.'

'You want to nail him on a permit charge after he saved me from an execution?'

'We like legal heroes.'

Sue Ellen came back into the room. She had a Snickers bar and a bag of Planters peanuts. She stopped cold and stared at Kelson. She stared at Nancy. She stared at Venus Johnson. 'Are you going to arrest my dad?'

Johnson looked confused. Then she softened. 'No, honey. I'm making sure we get all the bad guys responsible for hurting him.'

Sue Ellen looked at Kelson and Nancy, then at the police detective again. 'Bullshit.'

'That's my girl,' Kelson said.

'Be polite, Sue Ellen,' Nancy said.

'Never be afraid to speak truth to power,' Kelson said.

Johnson said to him, '*You* should keep your mouth shut.'

'Never happen,' he said.

Sue Ellen nodded. 'He has disinhibition.'

The nurse laughed. His laugh was deep and easy – a strange sound in the hospital room. He said, 'You're all a bunch of messed-up *güeyes*.'

Nancy curled a lip at him. 'Don't you have somewhere else to be?'

'No, ma'am,' the nurse said. 'The doctors told me to stay close – take good care of this man.'

THREE

'**D**on't worry, I got your back,' the nurse told Kelson after Nancy, Sue Ellen, and Venus Johnson had left.

'Lately, I can't even cover my front,' Kelson said.

The nurse nodded, like he'd been through it too. The ID on his lanyard called him Jose. 'Well, I've got the human touch. I put the extra juice box on the lunch trays. I fluff the pillows. You want yours fluffed?'

'I'm good, thanks.'

'You sound like you're messed up, you want to know the truth. You a detective for real?'

'Sure. I worked undercover narcotics for five years. When a street dealer shot me in the head, the department wrote me a check and put me out. So I set up independent.'

Jose considered him. 'They let a guy with a hole in the head own a gun?'

'Two guns,' Kelson said. 'A Springfield XD-S I keep in a desk drawer and a KelTec I hide under the desktop.'

'World's gone *loco*, they let a guy like you pack, huh? You carrying when you went to see this Renshaw dude?'

'I thought he was a car thief, not a killer.'

'So you left your guns in your drawer and your secret hiding place no one knows about, except you tell anyone that asks and anyone that doesn't.'

'More or less.'

'Good thing your friend was packing. Maybe I'll talk to *him*.'

'Someone steal your luxury car?'

Jose narrowed his eyes. 'You get smart alecky with me, you see if I fluff your pillows. You don't think I have a car anybody want to steal? Because I've got brown skin and my name's Jose? You think I drive a lowrider through the barrio, that what you think?'

'I think anyone who talks and acts like you must get fired a lot. So, no, I don't think you have a car worth stealing.'

'Well, I've got bigger problems than someone stealing my

top-of-the-line. So do you, if you're in this place. That's why I've got your back. Don't want nothing to happen to you.'

Kelson said, 'I'm sure with you around, I'm in good hands.'

Jose shook his head. 'Now you get smart alecky again.'

There was a tap on the door, and a woman stepped into the room. She wore a white doctor's coat unbuttoned over a red dress. 'Ah, Mr Feliciano,' she said to the nurse, 'Dr Jacobson's looking for you.'

The nurse said to Kelson, 'When Dr Jacobson calls, I come running.'

'Wait,' Kelson said, 'your name's Jose Feliciano?'

'Yeah, what about it?'

'Like the Puerto Rican Elvis Presley?'

'First, I'm Mexican. Second, do you want an extra juice box with your lunch, *compadre*?' Without waiting for an answer, he left the room.

The doctor gave Kelson a wry smile. 'I'm Dr Madani. I've been checking in on you over the last two days. It's good to see you awake.' She parted her long hair in the middle.

Kelson shook her hand, staring at the door as if Jose Feliciano might pop back through it with a guitar.

'Quite a character, isn't he?' the doctor said. She inspected the bandage on Kelson's wounded arm. 'Did he tell you he used to be in the rodeo?'

'You're kidding.'

'He showed me the clippings. He was quite successful – a star. Are you in any pain? We can adjust the medication.'

'I'm good.'

'Well, you're a long way from good,' she said. 'But you're getting better, and we'll take it a step at a time. How's the feeling in your fingers?'

Kelson looked at the hand on the injured arm. The bruising and swelling extended from the bottom of the bandage to his fingertips. He wiggled his fingers – stiffly. 'Where's the guitar?'

She touched the fingers. 'With injuries like yours, there's often nerve damage. Your hand was without regular circulation for over an hour.' She massaged his fingers in hers. 'How does this feel?'

'Exciting,' he said.

She dropped his hand.

'I mean it feels good,' he said. 'It doesn't hurt – as much as it might.'

'Good.' She touched his fingers again. She separated them and ran her index finger up and down the inside of each, to see if he registered the touch.

'Yep,' he said, 'exciting.'

She set his hand down on the bed. 'The nerves seem fine. I don't know about the rest of you.'

A monitor showed his pulse on a screen. She used a stethoscope on his chest anyway.

'Less exciting,' he said.

'Shut up and breathe,' she said.

He breathed in deep. He breathed out.

'Again,' she said.

'You're driving me wild,' he said.

'Shut up.'

He breathed in. He breathed out.

She pulled the stethoscope away. 'No fluid. You're a remarkable man, Mr Kelson.'

'Some people say I'm a miracle,' he said.

'We'll keep you another night. Then, unless we see an infection or other problems, we'll let you go.'

He looked at her brown eyes. He considered the way her white coat fell open over her red dress. 'I wish you wouldn't.'

She smiled. 'You're pale, unshaven, and smelly. You have a gimp arm. Even before we wheeled you in, you had brain trauma that would keep you off any sane woman's list. What makes you think your come-ons will work with me?'

'My winning personality?'

'Who told you it's winning?'

'Jose likes it.'

'Ask Jose for a date.'

'You know I can't help it, right? The disinhibition. If it's in my head, it comes out of my mouth.'

'Maybe you should try harder to keep it out of your head.'

'I don't know how.'

'I have ideas.' She smiled. 'But, you know, the Hippocratic Oath.'

'Do no harm?'

'Might be hard for anyone who spent time with you.'

FOUR

Jose Feliciano brought Kelson an extra apple juice on his lunch tray. He also brought a chunk of chicken covered with brown gravy, a scoop of mashed potatoes, and a side bowl of steamed green beans and carrots. The plastic wrap on the salad hadn't kept the brown off the lettuce. Kelson prodded the square of spice cake with a swollen finger. 'You could clean a sink with it,' he said.

'It's better than it looks, amigo. But don't eat the chicken.'

Kelson shifted the food around on the tray. He offered one of the juice boxes to Jose.

'Don't mind if I do,' the nurse said. 'The coffee in the break room tastes like the chicken.'

Kelson stuck his fork into the mashed potatoes. 'I hear you used to be in the rodeo.'

Jose grinned. '*Claro*. I did the Chicago Ford Tough Series. "Toughest Sport on Dirt." I fell off a bull and broke my back. The ambulance brought me here, and the doctor fixed me. He said if I fell again, I would maybe never walk again.'

'So you became a nurse.' Kelson abandoned the mashed potatoes. He tried the green beans.

'The doctor fixed my back. But a nurse named Jill gave me a reason to live. I fell in love.'

Kelson abandoned the green beans. 'Ah, the old story. *Boy falls off bull, boy meets nurse, boy becomes nurse. Happily ever after.*'

'Not *happily ever after*. I fell in love with Jill, but she didn't want me. But I knew what she did for me. I thought maybe I could do this for someone else. Maybe even you.'

Kelson prodded the spice cake with his fork. 'If you think I'm going to fall in love with you, it isn't going to happen.'

'Sure, you laugh at the Mexican nurse. But I already found someone new. We'll get married in April.'

'Congratulations.'

Jose exposed his forearm to show Kelson a tattoo. It was the head of a long-horned bull. 'This is the one that broke my back. You should never forget someone who tries to kill you.'

Kelson forked a bite of cake into his mouth. 'Huh,' he said.

'Better than it looks, right?'

Kelson said, 'You think I should get a tattoo of the guy who shot me in the arm?'

'You laugh at me, but I think maybe you should.'

'I'm not laughing. If words come into my head, they come out of my mouth. But I think I'll try to forget Gary Renshaw.'

'What about the other man – the one who shot you in the head?'

'Bicho?'

The nurse looked confused.

'Bicho,' Kelson said. 'His street name. He was just a kid. A punk. Seventeen years old. I won't forget him. He haunts me.'

'Never get a tattoo of a ghost. But' – Jose regarded his empty juice box – 'if you respected Bicho, maybe he would stop haunting you.'

'Yeah, you're a character.'

Jose smiled. 'Only a hard man can do what I've done.' He watched Kelson eat another bite of the cake. 'And only a hard man can be a detective with a hole in the head.'

'My ex thinks I should quit.'

'What does she know?'

'She's harder than I am.'

'A hard woman is good.'

'The one you're marrying?'

'Very hard. She's from Haiti – she had it tough before she came here. A hard person should be with another hard person.'

'Sounds like you've worked it out.'

'I watch people.' He watched as Kelson finished the cake. 'How much do you cost, Mr Detective?'

Kelson eyed him. 'Depends. Usually seventy-five an hour or three hundred a day. Sometimes I charge by the job. You looking for a one-armed detective who can't keep his mouth shut?'

'You know, when I was in the rodeo, I won a lot of prize money. But you're right, I don't drive a fancy car – I drive a Yaris. I don't own a fancy house – I don't need it. I spend my money on what I see, you understand, *compadre*? I see things.'

'Ghosts.'

Jose came close to the bed. 'Can I tell you this?'

'Why not?'

'This is what I see. My sister – her name is Felicita—'

'Now you're screwing with me.'

'What?'

'Felicita Feliciano? No way.'

The nurse looked annoyed. 'I'm telling you something important, my friend.'

'I'm just saying, your mom and dad had a weird sense of humor.'

'Are you going to listen?'

'I'll try.'

'Felicita and her husband had two girls—'

Kelson grinned. 'Don't tell me their names.'

Jose gave him a hard look.

'Sorry.'

'They had two girls. When the second one was born, Carlita—'

'That's more like it,' Kelson said.

'Around this time, my sister's husband crossed the border. He's in Los Angeles now. My sister stayed in Mexico until Carlita turned one, and then she tried to cross with the girls. She paid the *coyote* to take them to LA, but the man left them in Mesa, Arizona. The police arrested them at the bus station and sent them back to Mexico. Six months later they tried again. This time they got to Palo Verde. The third time, right after they crossed the border, *La Migra* chased them – the ICE police. Listen to this now, amigo. My sister hid in a canal – an *acequia*. The border police saw her and ordered her to get out. My sister told her older girl, Alisa – she was six years old – to hold Carlita tight, to hold her and never, never let go. I don't know what she was thinking – maybe you don't think right at a time like that. This is what I'm telling you – when the police went back for the girls, Carlita was gone. Do you understand? They found her body in the canal two days later. That's why I see things. They aren't ghosts – they're the bodies of dead little girls. That's also why I became a nurse – along with love. I promised my sister.'

'I'm sorry,' Kelson said.

'I also promised myself,' Jose said. 'If I see something – if I see a person hurting – I will get justice. That's for Carlita and for my sister and for *me*.'

'That's a lot.' Kelson thought of Sue Ellen and the fights he would jump into to keep her safe, the revenge he would seek if anyone ever hurt her. 'Maybe it's all you can do.'

'You understand, *compadre*? I think you do. There are things like this – I see them. The bosses and the police don't fix them. Do you know who I blame for Carlita's death?'

'I take it, not your sister.'

'She wanted her family together. She would do anything – what's wrong with that? She wanted to go to the husband she loved.'

'But you don't blame him either.'

'I blame the men who chased my sister into the canal like she was an animal. I blame the ICE police and the police in Mesa and Palo Verde. My sister isn't an animal. Alisa isn't an animal. Carlita wasn't.'

'I'm sorry,' Kelson said again.

Jose leaned in close, as if to tell him a secret – though Kelson wouldn't keep it no matter how hard he tried. 'My friend, this place is killing people.'

Kelson looked at him uncertainly. '*This place?*'

'This hospital. Messed up, right?'

Jose was moving too fast. 'People die sometimes,' Kelson said. 'At hospitals. They do that. Sometimes.'

'I'm not stupid,' the nurse said. 'This is my job. When they die, I wipe the spit off their chins. I put Vaseline on their lips before the relatives come in. I comb their hair. I change their diapers and wipe them so they don't smell bad. Don't tell me people die.'

'Right,' Kelson said.

'But people also sometimes *don't* die. I'm talking about those people. But here they do. Two men. One woman. No reason they had to die. This lady – she came because she broke her hip. Two days later, she had a heart attack. She was seventy-three – not so old.'

'How about the men?'

'The first, he was twenty-one. Car accident messed up his legs real bad. He stopped breathing. The other, he was like a bum. Some other bums beat him up, I think. He had a thing with his kidneys.'

Kelson said, 'So three people came here with different injuries. Then they died in different ways.'

'That's right.'

'No pattern.'

'*Exactamente.*'

'No pattern means no connection,' Kelson said. 'No connection means no crime – or three unrelated crimes. Where do you see the problem?'

'How long were you a cop?'

'Fourteen years. Why?'

'You been doing the detective thing a while?'

'Going on three years.'

'How're you still an amateur then?'

'Huh?'

'You're like a *novato* – a rookie rider. OK, a bull bucks twice left, then fades, and spins right. Then the bull bucks twice left again, fades again, and spins right again. Then the bull bucks twice left again. What does he do next?'

'Fades?'

'No, *cabrón*, he bucks a third time. Maybe he bucks five times. Or ten times. Because he's a bull. The *novato* – that's *you*, Mr Detective – he thinks the bull is going to fade. Why? Because he thinks like a rookie, not like a bull. The bull throws him in the bleachers and breaks his back. The bull doesn't act like you think he acts. He isn't in your head. He acts like a bull. This killer that put down the woman and those men, he acts like a killer. Not like what you think.'

'If I remember right, a bull broke your back too,' Kelson said.

'*Sí, cabrón*. Which is why, even though you know this is a killer, you need to be very careful. He's like one of those angels of death. What do you think, will you take a look?'

'What will you pay me?'

There was a knock on the door, and Dr Madani came in, this time with her white coat buttoned over her dress. 'Ah, Mr Feliciano. Dr Jacobson needs you again.'

Jose picked up Kelson's tray. 'We'll talk about this later. Think about it, amigo. A man like you can't afford to turn down work.' He grinned at the doctor. 'Dr Jacobson calls, and I come running.'

When Jose carried Kelson's tray out, Kelson said, 'He has a lot of stories.'

The doctor had a big-toothed smile. 'I've heard most of them.'

'He thinks people are dying here.'

The doctor gazed at him, as if Kelson didn't get it. 'This *is* a hospital.'

'That's what I told him. But he thinks you're killing them – not *you* personally – I don't know what he thinks of you, though I don't see how he could object. He thinks *someone* is killing them. Intentionally.'

She looked exasperated. 'We've talked to him about this before.'

'Why do you keep him on?'

'Patients love him,' she said. 'They ask for him when he's gone.'

'He fluffs their pillows.'

'I suppose so.' She checked the monitors and wrote notes on her clipboard. 'How's the pain now? We can increase the meds.'

'You trying to make me compliant?'

She winked. 'If I want you compliant, I don't have to ask. I can roll you over and give you a shot.'

Kelson grinned. 'Jose and I were talking about women like you.'

'After he accused me of killing my patients?'

'We agreed, hard is good. Tough is.'

Dr Madani said, 'What do you say we discharge you first thing tomorrow morning? My shift starts at eight. Let's have the night staff get you out of here by seven or seven thirty at the latest.'

Kelson expected Jose Feliciano to come back, but another nurse brought dinner. Then Kelson spent the evening alone. He talked to himself about Sue Ellen. And about the cats Sue Ellen had named Payday and Painter's Lane. And about the kiss Nancy gave him on the forehead . . . Did it mean there was hope? No, it wasn't a kiss of desire. About Dr Madani . . . Why did he find her sexy? About Jose Feliciano, who found causes in suffering, as if suffering had meaning one could make sense of, though even a quick glance showed much of it was random. About Renshaw and his gelled-up hair and skinny teeth and the way he seemed to evaporate in a mist of blood and bone when Rodman shot him.

At ten p.m. Kelson was talking about Rodman's difficulties, when there was a knock on his door. Rodman himself stepped in.

Rodman carried a lot of his enormous bulk in his chest. His

eyes – small, narrowly set on his big head – might look cute on a person a third of his size. On him, they suggested a gentleness at odds with his size and apparent strength. He wore blue work-pants and an oversized parka. If he worried that the Chicago Police were looking for him, his smile didn't show it.

'Hey there,' he said. 'I heard you were back from the dead.'

'Hey,' Kelson said. 'I was just talking about you.'

Rodman glanced around the empty room. He knew better than to ask. He pulled two bottles of Red Stripe lager out of a parka pocket. 'Flower shop was closed,' he said. 'Best I could do.' He gave a bottle to Kelson, popped the cap from the other, and took a long drink.

'Venus Johnson came by this morning looking for you,' Kelson said. 'Something about being pissed off you saved my life.'

Rodman smiled that gentle smile. 'Came by my apartment too. Cindi gave her a cup of tea and sent her on her way. I was hiding in the bathtub. You know how ridiculous it is for a man like me to hide in a bathtub?'

'How did you sneak in here?'

'When you were taking your long winter's nap, I got to be friends with one of your nurses. Nice guy. He called to tell me you made it after you woke this morning. He said I could get in around now without anyone stopping me.'

'Jose?'

The smile. 'Feliciano. And the guy can't even sing. I heard him try.'

'He didn't tell me he was staying in touch with you. Funny guy.'

'You know he used to be in the rodeo?'

'He said.'

'I looked him up on my phone. He was a big name, until he wasn't.'

Kelson drank his beer. 'You need a lawyer? I can call Ed Davies.'

'I talked to him already. He set up a meeting with Johnson and her partner to talk this thing through, but they seem to have their panties tied in a knot about me.'

'Davies will convince them you could either shoot or let Renshaw commit murder.'

'Doesn't matter. When the cops look at me, they see a big black man with a gun. Scares the hell out of them.'

'Venus Johnson's black,' Kelson said.

'This matters, why? She wears the uniform. Maybe she goes home, takes a shower, and washes it off. But next morning, she puts it on, and, abracadabra, I'm a threat. She sees me with a gun, she puts one between my eyes before her white-boy partner gets his pistol out of his holster.' He drank the rest of his beer. 'Look, I've got to get going before someone here calls her. But I wanted to see you with your eyes open and hear the foolishness coming out of your mouth. When are they kicking you out of here?'

'First thing tomorrow.'

'You need anything, let me know. If I don't answer, call Cindi. She'll get the message to me.'

'Things will cool down,' Kelson said. 'Davies is good at this.'

Rodman gave him the gentle smile. 'Enjoy the beer.' Then he was gone.

Kelson lay on his bed. He sipped from the Red Stripe and felt the alcohol merge like a pleasant stream with the painkillers in his blood. Outside the slatted window shade, ice crystals formed on the glass, but Kelson felt warm. Aside from the mechanical tick of a monitor, the room was silent.

FIVE

At 7:40 the next morning, Jose brought a breakfast tray. The watery scrambled eggs tasted like soup. While Kelson lined the tater tots around the back of the plate – a battlement to keep out invading armies – Jose detached cords and tubes from the monitors, IV, and other machines. He whistled 'The Star-Spangled Banner,' badly.

A memory niggled Kelson – something he'd heard about or read. 'Didn't the real Jose Feliciano sing that at the World Series in the sixties? Did a protest thing with it?'

'Am I the *fake* Jose Feliciano now?' the nurse asked. He dropped a clamp in the garbage.

'Upset Richard Nixon or someone?'

'Did you think more about looking into the people I told you about?'

Kelson tore a corner off a piece of toast and stared at it. 'What did they make this from?' He put it in his mouth and chewed.

'Three people,' the nurse said. 'The lady. Two men.'

'No,' Kelson said. 'I'd be wasting my time and your money.'

'Sure,' the nurse said, 'but what's it hurt to look?'

A man in a white lab coat stepped into the room. He was in his late sixties, his gray hair thinning, his forehead dotted with liver spots. He had bright blue eyes and a fleshy nose. His lab coat fit his shoulders so well it could've been tailored.

He came to the bedside. 'I'm Jeremy Jacobson – chief of the ICU. Suzanne Madani asked me to stop by before we discharge you. How are you feeling this morning?'

'Like someone shot me in the arm, then pumped me up with pain meds,' Kelson said. 'More or less normal.'

The doctor's mind was elsewhere. 'Good, good.' He pressed a stethoscope to Kelson's chest. 'Breathe,' he said.

Kelson breathed. 'Less exciting when you do it,' he said.

Jose Feliciano stood by the door, watching.

Jacobson said, 'Your charts say you meet with a therapist for your head injury.'

'Once a week.'

'Keep breathing,' the doctor said.

Jose pulled out his phone and typed on it.

'Your therapist is Sheila Prentiss?' the doctor asked.

'Dr P.'

'Breathe out. You'll want to check in with her first thing. This kind of trauma – especially when it's repeat trauma – can trigger episodes.'

'I feel good,' Kelson said. 'Really.'

Jacobson pulled the stethoscope away. 'Well, your lungs sound healthy.'

'Nice to be breathing.'

Jose looked up from his phone. He started whistling the theme song to *Chico and the Man*, one of his namesake's greatest hits.

Jacobson glanced at the nurse. 'Please, Mr Feliciano, this isn't the time.'

'Sorry, Doc,' Jose said.

Jacobson nodded at Kelson as if he was used to such things. 'You may get dressed. Be careful with the bandages. You'll want to change the dressing in another forty-eight hours. I'll go over the papers with you.'

Then a female nurse peeked into the room from the corridor. 'Dr Jacobson? May I have a minute, please?'

Dr Jacobson looked resigned to interruptions. 'Excuse me,' he said, and he stepped out.

When the doctor left, Jose closed the door. He smiled at Kelson.

Kelson shook his head at him.

Jose started singing 'Light My Fire.'

'Cut it out,' Kelson said.

Jose sang louder.

'*Don't.*' Kelson slipped out of his bed and stood, shaky on his feet.

Jose kept singing.

'That's awful.' Kelson tugged at the hospital gown with his good hand. 'I'm a wounded man.'

'Three people are dead,' the nurse said. 'Think about it, *compadre.*'

Kelson undid the knot on the back of the gown. His jeans, his underwear, and a shirt and coat Nancy and Sue Ellen had brought after rescuing the cats from his apartment were folded on a tray table next to the bed. 'There's nothing to think. Three people died. I feel bad about that. But from what you tell me, there's nothing there.' He dropped the gown.

'That's because I didn't tell you all of it.'

'Look, I can't—'

The nurse started singing 'The Thrill is Gone.'

Kelson said, 'Stop it.'

Jose rocked his hips and sang.

Kelson started to sway. 'Stop. Please.'

Outside in the corridor, Dr Madani spoke to Dr Jacobson. 'Fine,' she said. 'Take care of it . . . really, it's fine. I'll finish here.'

She knocked on the door – and stepped in.

'What the hell are you doing?' she said.

Jose stopped singing.

Kelson stopped swaying. 'You've never seen a naked man dance before?'

'Is *that* what you were doing?'

'You're blushing,' he said. 'That's charming.'

She shook her head. 'Put on your street clothes. Tell me when it's safe to come in.'

'It's *his* fault,' Kelson said, as she ducked out of the room. He grabbed his underwear and jeans from the table. 'Jerk,' he said to the nurse.

'One little look?' the nurse said.

Kelson shook his jeans, opening the waist enough to put a foot in. 'Look at *what*? There's nothing to see.'

'Look. If there's nothing, stop looking.'

'You're as crazy as I am.' He zipped the jeans. 'You sure the bull didn't stomp on your head when it broke your back?'

Jose grinned. 'I'm sure that happened a time or two.'

SIX

Kelson took a cab to his apartment. The sky was clear, the sun rising bright, but the streets were gray with ice, the trash cans and fire hydrants capped with snow.

The driver glanced at Kelson in the rearview mirror, holding his eyes on the bandaged arm. 'You been away?'

Through the window Kelson watched a woman, bundled against the cold, navigate a baby stroller over an icy curb on to a crosswalk. 'On my own little island.'

'Bad place to visit, wouldn't want to live there,' the driver said.

'I hung out with a bull rider.'

The driver glanced again. 'You got any extra pills, I'll trade for the fare.'

Kelson went into his building and stood in the lobby. He smelled the familiar smells of his life. He felt the familiar heat. They made him dizzy. He stared at a security camera.

'Hi there, baby,' he said.

He rode the elevator to his floor. When he got out, he stopped again in the blue-carpeted corridor – at once familiar and disorienting. 'Huh,' he said. 'You and me against the world.'

Ever since Bicho shot him in the head three years earlier, he suffered from occasional bouts of autotopagnosia along with his disinhibition. As his therapist Dr P explained it, people with the condition don't recognize their own bodies. They see their arms and legs and wonder whose they are.

As Dr P said – and Kelson already knew – he had a peculiar form of the condition. He seemed to separate from his own appearance especially when he needed to reconcile strange events with his normal life. He would think he looked like someone else – sometimes a stranger, sometimes a person he knew well. He would look in a mirror and his reflection would startle him. 'Shooting a bullet through the frontal lobe is like jamming a screwdriver into a hard drive,' Dr P said. 'You don't know what you'll get but whatever it is, it's going to include surprises.'

Kelson had experienced fewer bouts in recent months, but now in the corridor he felt as if he stood beside himself, though the self he stood next to was invisible. He went to his door and jammed the key into the lock. Once inside, he went into the bathroom. He stared at the mirror. The reflected face – the left eye drooping under the pink scar, three days of stubble on the pale chin and cheeks – was sweating.

He laughed. He washed his face in the sink. When he looked at the mirror again, the wet face looking back still seemed strange, though less so. 'Ride 'em, cowboy,' he said.

Since Nancy divorced him, he'd lived in the studio apartment with a dining table outside the kitchenette. He went to the table and sat. Then he paged through the papers from the manila envelope Dr Madani gave him before shoving him out of the hospital. Insurance papers. Instructions about caring for his wound. Prescriptions for antibiotics and Percocet. Emergency contact numbers.

Kelson set those papers aside. He considered the remaining one – a sheet Jose had slipped in with the others, with three names on it and his own contact information.

Patricia Ruddig
Josh Templeton
Daryl Vaughn
Jose's phone number.

Kelson got his laptop from his bedside table and turned it on. 'He'll pay double,' he said. 'Or triple.'

As the computer booted up, he stared at the furniture in the apartment, dizzied again by its strange familiarity. In the first couple of years after Bicho shot him, clutter gave Kelson headaches. The headaches were rarer now, but he still kept the walls bare and he had few possessions he couldn't store in a drawer, the closet, or a cabinet. On the morning he confronted Renshaw, he'd made his bed, creasing the cover, before Rodman picked him up. Aside from two dents where the cats – now with Sue Ellen at Nancy's – had slept, the bed was neat. He made the *ntching* sound that usually brought Payday and Painter's Lane scrambling.

Then he opened Google and searched for Patricia Ruddig.

Ruddig was an unusual name, maybe Irish, and there was only one link to it when he attached it to Patricia. Her name appeared on a list of condo association members at a building on the corner of Ainslie Street and Claremont, on the city's northwest side. 'Useless,' Kelson said. He wrote the address by her name anyway.

He typed in *Josh Templeton*. He got more than eleven thousand hits. He changed *Josh* to *Joshua*. He got more than nine thousand. 'Equally useless.' He added *Chicago* to the search. Two thousand. 'Better.' He added *obituary*. Ninety-two.

He scrolled past the first four, which looked irrelevant. Then he said, 'Ha.'

According to the obituary, Josh Templeton, twenty-one, died from injuries suffered in a car accident a month and a half ago. He was a junior at DePaul University. He grew up in Fort Wayne, Indiana. Survivors of the crash included his loving mother and his fiancée Melanie. Visitation was at the Ellis Funeral Home in Fort Wayne.

Using the obituary information, Kelson dug into Josh's social media. Josh was a good-looking kid growing into a good-looking man – tall, thin, with light brown skin, his black hair done back in cornrows. His fiancée, Melanie, looked no older than seventeen or eighteen. Her skin had a creamy whiteness. 'Alabaster?' Kelson said. In one shot, she clung to Josh's arm as if she'd never let go. In another – with him standing behind her, his arms holding her close – she looked like she'd caught the biggest fish in the ocean. In a third, they sat on the hood of a brown Toyota Camry. 'Death car?' Kelson said.

He scribbled notes by Josh's name on the sheet of paper. *Fort*

Wayne. Ellis Funeral Home. DePaul. Fiancée Melanie. Brown Camry.

Then he Googled *Daryl Vaughn.* He got over seven thousand hits. Adding *Chicago* got him only four hundred. Typing in *obituary* took him down to twenty-six.

He scrolled through them without seeing anything promising. He opened the links anyway. A remote-control airplane enthusiast died at eighty-one. A north suburban banker left behind four children. A seventy-year-old retiree died after a brief illness. Kelson found no bums beaten to death by other bums.

He shut down the computer. Then he called the phone number at the bottom of the sheet of paper. The call bounced to voicemail, and Jose Feliciano's recorded voice greeted him cheerfully. *Leave a message, amigo.*

Kelson left a message. 'I looked. I didn't see anything. And what's with the *amigo* thing? Are you being ironic or are you just real friendly?' He hung up.

He went into the kitchenette, opened the refrigerator, and stared inside. He said to the refrigerator, 'Not hungry.'

Out on the dining table, his phone rang.

'Screw it.' He closed the refrigerator door.

The phone rang.

He opened the cabinet over the kitchen sink. There were boxes of cereal and crackers.

The phone rang.

'Still not hungry.' He closed the cabinet.

The phone rang.

He left the kitchen and walked past the phone, into the bathroom. He turned on the faucet. Staring in the mirror at a face he knew he should know, he shaved. Then he turned on the shower and wrapped his shoulder in a towel on the injured side. Holding his bandaged arm outside the stall, he stepped under the hot stream and cleaned himself. When he got out, he looked in the mirror and said, 'Still dirty.'

He walked out of the bathroom naked.

He looked around the apartment – at the dizzying chairs, dresser, bed.

It was eleven o'clock in the morning on a bitter January day. He climbed into bed and closed his eyes.

SEVEN

Kelson got up that evening at nine p.m., four hours after the sun set. Heat pumped from the radiator, but he shivered. He put on underwear and pants and wiggled into a shirt and an oversized sweater. He'd slept off the Percocet, and his arm ached. 'Like a pulled tooth,' he said, 'if your arm grew teeth.'

Though Dr P had mostly weaned him from the painkillers he took after getting shot in the head, he kept a vial in the medicine cabinet. He shook a pill into his hand and said, 'Hello, old friend,' then swallowed it down. He stared at his face in the mirror. 'You too.'

He rode the elevator to the lobby and went out to his Dodge Challenger in the freezing dark. The car, which he'd bought with his disability payout, was painted burnt orange.

'A muscle car,' Dr P had said. 'An orange phallus. Do you think you're trying to compensate for something?'

'Yup,' Kelson said.

Now he inched over icy streets, steering one handed, his other hand flopping by his side. He dropped off his prescriptions at a Walgreens and drove to the Golden Apple Grill.

His regular waitress knew better than to ask personal questions unless she had time for his answers. But as she handed him a menu, she gestured at the bandaged arm and said, 'Fall on the ice?'

'A car thief with a taste for vintage Mercedes shot me,' he said, then told her all about it. 'Who'd've thought – a bull rider,' he concluded.

The waitress, who'd taken a seat across from Kelson at the ten-minute mark, said, 'You live an unenviable life.'

While he waited for his food, Kelson listened to the message Jose Feliciano had left on his phone ten hours ago. The voice sounded breathless. 'It happened again, amigo. I swear to God – another lady. You've got to come back.'

'Nope,' Kelson said. 'You think it happened but it didn't.'

He deleted the message.

'You're a rodeo clown,' he said, as if Jose sat across from him. 'Too much bucking. Chuck wagons running through your head.'

The waitress set a cup of coffee in front of him and held a finger to her lips. 'You're scaring the other diners.'

'I'm an expert on delusion,' he said.

'Shh.'

So he started to call Jose – to tell him *he* was being delusional – but then he had a better idea. He dialed Sue Ellen's number instead.

'Dad.' Her voice always seemed to chime.

'Hey, kiddo. I'm calling to say goodnight.'

'Did they let you out?'

'It's not like I was in jail.'

'It's late,' she said. 'Did getting shot make you think you need to be a better dad?'

'You might be too smart for your own good. I thought phoning would be a normal dad thing.'

'But you *aren't* normal,' she said.

When they hung up, he dialed Ed Davies at his law office, where he often worked until midnight.

'Hey, hey,' Davies said, 'good to have you back among the living. You've got to stop throwing your body in front of bullets. I can't afford to lose clients.'

'Thanks, Ed. You talk with DeMarcus Rodman?'

'It's taken care of,' Davies said. 'I met with the Assistant DA. Heat's off. No commendations for heroism, but the cops'll leave him alone.'

'How did you do that?'

'A combination of superior intellect, rhetorical skill, and good looks. I also had an extra pair of tickets to the Bulls–Cavs game. The Assistant DA loves the Cavs.'

'Thanks,' Kelson said again.

'I'll bill Rodman for the tickets.'

'Send the bill to me.'

'See, that's why I'm glad you didn't die.'

They hung up, and the waitress brought Kelson's waffle and sausage. 'The world could be a better place,' he said, 'but it could also be worse.'

She raised an eyebrow. 'Yeah, *bon appétit* to you too.'

He ate half a sausage, then set down his fork and called Rodman. 'Ed Davies tells me you're clear.'

'Yeah, so he says. Sometimes I think the only good men are the hustlers. He says I owe him a steak dinner.'

'He likes the fillet at Gene & Georgetti. But after you buy him dinner, you'll be his friend. What are you up to tonight?'

'You kidding? I'm no longer a wanted man. I'm lying in bed with Cindi. You?'

'Eating a waffle. And trying to work out the answers to some questions.'

'If you think I'm going to invite you over to join us, you misread my intentions.'

Kelson laughed. 'Yeah, give Cindi a kiss for me.'

'But really, you all right?'

'Sure. I've just got the questions.'

Rodman hesitated, as if unsure of his friend's need. 'Tomorrow morning, OK? You come here for coffee. We'll talk about my saving your sorry ass from Renshaw.'

'It's a date.'

When Kelson went back out to the cold, an icy snow was falling. He raised his face to the night, letting the snow land on his cheeks. 'Where are you coming from?' he said. He looked back at the cold pavement. 'Questions.'

He got in his car, fired up the engine, and waited for the heat. 'Go home,' he said. 'Rest. Recover. Get up in the morning and drink coffee with DeMarcus.' He looked at himself in the rearview mirror.

'I don't want to go home,' he said.

'You win,' he said.

He went back to Walgreens, picked up his prescriptions, then drove to his office. The snow had started to come down harder.

'Questions,' he said, and rode the elevator to the floor he shared with a computer training company.

His office walls were bare except for a framed eight-by-ten photo of Sue Ellen and another of his cats. The desk, some chairs, and a gray file cabinet stood on gray all-weather carpet. The desktop was bare.

Kelson opened the bottom desk drawer. His Springfield XD-S

pistol was there. He checked under the desktop. His KelTec hung in its hidden rig.

'I guess that's a relief,' he said.

He went to the window and stared at the falling snow. It was turning the curbside cars as white as ash. 'What am I doing here?' he said. His reflection gleamed in the window. 'Don't get all existential on me.'

When his phone rang in his pocket, he jumped.

Caller ID said *Jose Feliciano*.

'Jerk.' He touched the answer button. 'Listen, cowboy, you've got to cut this out.'

'I need your help,' Jose said.

'No,' Kelson said. 'No you don't.'

'You don't understand. They think my fiancée did it. Wendy. I'm at Jacaranda. In La Villita. You need to come.'

'What's Jacaranda?'

'It's a bar, man. Twenty-sixth Street.'

'Are you drunk?' Kelson said.

The question seemed to surprise Jose. 'No. Are *you* high?'

Kelson did feel a little numb from the pill he took before leaving his apartment. 'I don't know.'

'You got to come. They think she did it.'

'No,' Kelson said. 'Sorry, my friend.'

For a moment, Jose was quiet. Then he said, 'You aren't a friend of mine.' He hung up.

Kelson gazed out the window. While he was on the phone, the snow had stopped. Completely. He put his face to the glass. There wasn't a flake in the air. 'Huh,' he said.

He took the KelTec from the hidden rig under the desktop. He crammed the barrel inside his belt. 'As if it'll do any good,' he said. He left his office and went down to the parking garage. When he turned the key in the ignition of his car, the roar and purr of the engine reassured him. He drove back to his apartment one handed. Faster than he should have. Sliding around corners. Once almost skidding into an intersection as other cars crossed.

He gunned the engine as he pulled from the street into the parking lot and plowed through a little snowdrift.

He got out and walked to the front of his building, where he stared up the side to his windows. The windows looked cold. 'Dead man's eyes,' he said.

He laughed at himself, went back to the parking lot, and got into his car. When he turned the key in the engine, the engine roared, then purred. He drove out of the lot and headed toward the south side of the city, where a man who was not his friend waited for him at a bar called Jacaranda.

EIGHT

J ose Feliciano had lied. He was drunk. Not so drunk he fell off his barstool. Not as long as his fiancée, Wendy Thomas, propped him up. *She* looked sober. Some nights, no matter how much you drink, you're sober.

'What do you mean, they think she did it?' Kelson stood at the bar with them.

Blue under-shelf lighting from the liquor display made the bartender's hands glow ghostlike as he served Kelson a Modelo Negra. The Jacaranda sports bar filled the ground floor of a squat two-story brick house in a rough strip of South Lawn businesses and professional offices – a sweet spot among Cash America Pawn, Gutierrez Dentistas, Boost Mobile, Centro Medico Digestivo, and Great Northern Insurance. A soccer ball hung from the ceiling in a netted bag. A bowling pin was perched above the liquor bottles. A Miller Lite poster featured a giant Chicago Bears helmet. Jacaranda was a hangout for southside working-class immigrants. Tonight, when one came or left, an icy wind blew in from the door.

'The dead lady,' Jose said, tottering on his stool. 'She came in with cramps. Appendix, right? They did the abdominal X-ray. The lady was ruptured. Emergency surgery – clean it all out.' He brought his glass to his lips and drained the drink from the ice, then signaled the bartender for another. 'But it was bad. She got an infection. Peritonitis. They shot her up with antibiotics. She responded, right? Then, this morning, she was septic. She went into shock, had a heart attack. Half an hour later, she was dead.' The bartender set a new glass on the bar. Jose blinked at the drink a couple times, then said to Kelson, 'Wendy was the lady's nurse. The doctors say she got the meds wrong.'

'I never get meds wrong,' his fiancée said. Her cheeks glistened in the soft blue light. She'd painted her lips with bright-red lipstick. Everything about her – her face, her arms, her hands, her thighs – was small and round.

'In a pleasant way,' Kelson said. She also reminded him of his breakfast at the hospital. 'Tater tots.'

'What's that?' she asked.

'With lipstick,' he said.

She shot a glance at Jose as if to ask, *Who the hell's your friend?* 'Jose says you're crazy in the head.'

'He's not the first,' Kelson said.

'This lady at the hospital,' Jose said, 'she was OK last night. This morning, she's dead. Now they want to put it on Wendy.'

'I got the meds right,' Wendy said.

Kelson asked, 'Do you think there's anything strange about her death?'

'*I* didn't kill her,' she said. 'If you're big and diabetic, sepsis'll kill you.'

'So she could've died naturally?'

'She could a lot of things,' she said. 'Dr Madani looked at the chart. She says I didn't give the lady her cefoxitin overnight.'

'Dr Madani said that? Did you record it on the chart?'

'Maybe,' she said. 'It was busy. Two ICU nurses were out.'

'So you could've forgotten the meds?'

'I never forget meds,' she said.

'Never,' Jose said.

Kelson asked him, 'What makes you think someone killed this woman?'

'Tell him, Wendy.'

'We've got the lady on monitors – heart rate, oxygen, blood pressure. One thing happens with septic shock is low blood pressure. With blood pressure too low you maybe get a heart attack. I saw the readout after she died. I've seen something like it before. When we get cocaine ODs with hypertension, we give them nitro or phentolamine. The pressure comes down fast. The lady's readout looked like that.'

'Like someone shot her up,' Jose said.

'Or maybe she just died,' Kelson said.

'I don't know,' Wendy said. 'I wanted to check inventory – see what's missing, who took it. But Dr Madani sent me home. She said they need to investigate me. I told her I gave the lady her meds. If anyone needs investigating, it's them.'

'Do you think Jose's right about the other dead people? Patricia Ruddig, Josh Templeton, Daryl Vaughn?'

'I don't know what to think,' she said.

Then, in a room behind the bar, Latin jazz started to play – horns, percussion. No one in the bar except Kelson seemed to notice.

Then Jose smiled. 'That's Proyecto Libre – a Chicago band. This is the place you come when the world feels like hell.'

'Yeah, it's nice,' Kelson said.

Jose glanced around the bar, tilting as if he sat on a bull instead of a barstool. 'You ever seen a jacaranda tree? It's Mexican – the best kind of tree for hot days. Jacaranda flowers, they look like that.' He pointed at the light around the liquor display. 'Blue. *More* than blue. What do you call that color?'

'Violet?' Kelson said.

Jose shook his head. 'The other one.'

'Lavender,' Wendy said.

'They should call that color jacaranda,' Jose said.

'It's lovely,' his fiancée said, like she meant it. Maybe she *was* drunk.

'That's what it is,' Jose said. 'It's the color of love.'

Kelson felt his resolve failing. Something about sitting in a southside bar with a bull-riding nurse and his Haitian fiancée, talking about murder and trees and love, listening to warm music while a winter wind blew outside, shook him. He said, 'I'll go back and ask around.'

Jose looked uncertain what Kelson was promising.

He said, 'I'll see what the doctors say.'

Jose grinned. 'Really, amigo? You'll take a look?'

'I know what they'll tell me. They'll say I'm imagining things. When I tell them you sent me after them, they'll think you got kicked in the skull too many times at the rodeo. And you' – he looked at Wendy – 'they'll say you made a terrible mistake with the lady who died. Maybe my talking to them about it will make it worse for you. It's harder to pretend it didn't happen once someone starts asking questions. Harder to forgive. You sure you want that?'

'She does,' Jose said.

'Jose told you about me, right?' Kelson said. 'When I start asking questions, people ask questions back. It happens every time. Then I answer. I can't help it. I tell the truth as far as I understand it. Is that what you want?'

She frowned. 'We need to know what's happening,' she said.

'Even if it means losing your job?'

'No lie, I don't know if I have a job right now.'

Jose held her hand. 'Wendy's tougher than any rider I ever knew.'

She said, 'Maybe somebody kicked my head too.'

The band in the back room started into a cover of 'Oye Como Va.'

Jose took a deep breath, as if relieved someone took his suspicions half seriously. He nodded his head to the music.

Kelson said, 'Three hundred a day or seventy-five an hour, whichever is less. Plus expenses. Do you have that kind of prize money to throw at this?'

'These are people's lives,' Jose said. He pulled a roll of twenties from a pocket and counted out enough for three days' work. 'For my sister's little girl, right?'

Kelson let him lay the money on the bar, then waved it away. 'Tell you what. I'll talk to the doctors. If I hear anything worth pursuing – and I won't – you can pay me then.'

Jose said to Wendy, 'I told you he's a good man.'

'I thought you told her I'm crazy,' Kelson said. 'I know you told *me* on the phone I'm not your friend.'

'That doesn't mean you aren't a good man.' The bull rider drained his drink to the ice and signaled the bartender.

When Kelson walked out of the bar into the freezing night, the air bit at his cheeks. He looked up at the sky, where all but a thin layer of clouds had cleared and stars shone dimly through the black. 'The hell am I doing?' he said. But for the first time since getting shot in the arm, he felt good, and he told the stars so.

NINE

At 9:30 the next morning, Kelson climbed two flights of stairs to DeMarcus Rodman's apartment. Rodman lived with his girlfriend Cindi in the Bronzeville neighborhood, across an alley from the Ebenezer Baptist Church. He answered the door in a pair of red sweatpants and a sweatshirt that looked big enough to camp in but somehow still seemed tight on him. He was barefoot. 'It's the Yeti,' Kelson said.

'The things that go through your head, man,' Rodman said. 'Come in out of the cold.'

Years ago, Rodman, Kelson, and Kelson's ex went to police academy together – Rodman and Nancy competing for the top spot in the class, Rodman usually beating her. Kelson watched them from somewhere back in the pack. Then, on a terrible evening a mile from the house where Rodman grew up, a police officer shot and killed Rodman's little brother. When the board ruled the incident accidental, Rodman bailed from the academy.

Nancy and Kelson became cops, and Rodman disappeared. Then, after Sue Ellen was born, Nancy quit and returned to school. Kelson went undercover on the narcotics squad, alone and lonely. Then Bicho shot him in the head.

So here they were. Standing in Rodman's living room, Kelson gazed at pictures of Martin Luther King Jr, Cindi, and Malcolm X hanging on the wall behind the couch. 'The consequences of our history,' he said.

'Yeah, whatever,' Rodman said. 'You want coffee?'

'You think I came for your company?'

Rodman went into the kitchen to make a pot.

Kelson followed him to the doorway. 'Cindi at work?'

'Early shift – since four a.m. How's the arm?'

'Throbbing.'

'Means you're alive. How about the rest of you?'

'Twisting and turning.'

'Glad nothing's changed.' Rodman got a bag of coffee beans

from the cabinet next to the refrigerator. 'You said last night you had questions.'

'Yeah – how're *you* doing?'

'Fine since your lawyer got his hands on me.' Rodman poured beans into the grinder. 'He's like Houdini. Cops look at me and see a big black monster. Davies puts me in a hat, pulls me back out, and makes them think I'm a little white bunny. I got a call a half-hour ago from the DA. He apologized for the trouble they put me through. A *regrettable mistake*, he said. A *misunderstanding*. I took the apology because what else am I going to do?' He pressed a button on the grinder, and the blade pulverized the beans.

As he poured the grounds into a filter, someone knocked on the door. 'Get that, will you?' he said.

Kelson went and put his eye to the peephole. 'Huh,' he said, and opened the door.

Homicide detectives Dan Peters and Venus Johnson stood on the landing.

Peters did a double take. '*You*,' he said.

'Me?' Kelson said.

'What are you doing here?' Venus Johnson said.

'Funny, I asked myself the same thing last night,' Kelson said. 'But I wasn't *here*. I was *there*. I mean, I was at my office. But it was late, and I had no reason to be there – which was *here*, at the time. So I went to a bar.'

Peters and Johnson stared at Kelson, their lips parted.

'As if that explains anything,' Kelson said.

'Where's DeMarcus Rodman?' Peters said.

'I thought Ed Davies took care of that.'

'That's not an answer,' Johnson said.

'I thought it was,' Kelson said.

Then Rodman was beside him. 'What do you want?'

Johnson gave him a thin smile. 'A quick conversation. Mind if we come in?'

'Without Davies here, I have nothing to say.'

'No need to be like that,' Peters said, and he moved toward the door.

Rodman stepped toward him, filling the doorway with his bulk. 'Uh-uh. Unless you're made of cartilage like a rat.'

'That's a myth,' Kelson said.

'Huh?' Rodman said.

'Huh?' Peters said.

'A myth. Sue Ellen did a school report. Rats have bones, like us. They're just really good at small holes.'

'What the hell are you talking about?' Peters said.

'Sue Ellen's interest in animals.'

'Not the time for this, Sam,' Rodman said. He turned back to Peters and Johnson. 'What do you want?'

Johnson said, 'The gun you shot Renshaw with. Where'd you get it?'

Rodman seemed to chew on that. 'A trade. A man I know wanted my chainsaw. He had no money. He traded me the gun for it.'

Peters kept from laughing at him. 'A chainsaw? You a ghetto lumberjack?'

'Careful,' Rodman said. His voice was calm, low.

Peters heard the danger and lost his grin.

'I got the chainsaw in another trade,' Rodman said. 'I hustle. If there's money in it, I'm interested. Is there something wrong with the gun?'

'Who'd you trade with?' Peters said.

'Uh-uh.'

Johnson said, 'Some liquor stores in Beverly got robbed a couple months ago. In the last one, the owner pulled a baseball bat. The robber shot a hole in a bottle of Patrón Silver.'

'Top shelf,' Peters said. 'I drink it, and I don't even like tequila.'

'The investigating officers ran the slug through the Ballistic Information Network,' Johnson said. 'When we pulled the slug out of Renshaw we put it in the database too. Guess what?'

'I'd prefer not to,' Rodman said.

'Perfect match,' Johnson said. 'Who'd you trade with?'

Rodman looked like he'd be sick. 'Anyone hurt in the robberies?'

Johnson shook her head. 'Thank God.'

'Who'd you get the gun from, Rodman?' Peters asked again.

Rodman sucked in a breath. 'The fact that you're asking tells me there was video at the liquor store – and I wasn't in the video.'

'Little guy about a quarter your size,' Peters said. 'Maybe an eighth. No family resemblance. But you're both too quick with a trigger finger.'

'DeMarcus saved my life,' Kelson said.

Peters and Johnson spoke at once: 'Shut up.'

'I don't know the guy,' Rodman said. 'It was someone on the street who wanted to trade.'

Now Johnson held back the laugh. 'Because what? A lot of assholes on the street want a chainsaw?'

'I don't know him,' Rodman said.

Peters looked like he would try to push past him into the apartment. 'You're lying.'

Kelson heard it too. 'Yep.'

Rodman shot him a look.

'Sorry.'

'You know how this works,' Johnson said. 'Your chainsaw friend shoots when a store owner pulls out a baseball bat, he's going to hurt someone. Maybe next time he gets unlucky and kills a clerk. I guess you're willing to live with that.'

'Time for you to leave,' Rodman said. His voice was calmer and lower than before.

'The DA made a bad decision on you,' Johnson said. 'You know this doesn't go away.'

'Nothing ever does,' Rodman said, and he closed the door.

He stood there, a big man holding it all in. He gave Peters and Johnson time to descend the stairs to the street. He caught his breath and recovered an expression of peace.

Then he said to Kelson, 'It was—'

'Don't,' Kelson said. 'I wish you could. But if you do, you know I can't keep it to myself. If they ask, I'll tell.'

Rodman shook his head and brushed past him into the kitchen. He returned with the pot of coffee, gestured at a chair for Kelson to sit, and poured the cups. His hands never shook. As if he didn't have problems of his own, he said, 'Tell me what's going on.'

'When the cops shot your brother, how close did you come to giving up?' Kelson said.

'I suppose I did give up. I quit the academy. I blew off my plans to be a cop. My life fell apart for a while. Depending on who's judging, I still don't have it back together. You planning to give up?'

'Nancy thinks I should quit. She thinks I'm going to get hurt worse – or killed. She thinks it's unfair to Sue Ellen.'

'Yeah,' Rodman said, 'it probably is.'

'You think I should quit too?'

'I didn't say that.'

'I've gotten shot twice. Feels like pushing my luck. Three times and I'm out, right? I don't even know what inning it is.'

'It's a long game,' Rodman said. He smiled. 'Unless it isn't.'

'I got out of the hospital yesterday morning, and then I slept all day. I went out last night. I went to places I know – places that know me – but everything seemed inside out.'

'You're recovering,' Rodman said. 'It takes a while. You know that.'

'What if inside really is out? What if everything that seemed to make sense makes no sense?'

'Then, I don't know,' Rodman said. 'Maybe you're screwed. Like the rest of us.'

They spent another twenty minutes drinking coffee and deciding nothing, resolving no problems, coming to no conclusions.

Then Kelson got up, and Rodman opened the door and held it for him. Winter air breathed into the apartment from the landing.

Rodman said, 'It was Cindi's baby brother, man. His gun. Sixteen years old, kid's out of control. He's going to kill someone or get himself killed. I don't know if Cindi can handle that. I don't know if I can.'

Kelson stared at his big friend's gentle face. 'I'm sorry.'

'I know. Me too. Screwed, huh?'

'Screwed.' Kelson turned and descended a stair. Then he looked back. 'What did he want with a chainsaw?'

Rodman gave a bitter laugh. 'I didn't trade him a damned chainsaw. I took the gun from him and told him if I ever saw him with another I'd beat the hell out of him.' The big man's eyes were moist.

Kelson said, 'Love's hard.'

'Yeah,' Rodman said, 'it's a bitch.'

TEN

D r Jeremy Jacobson offered Kelson a chair in his office, one floor up from the ICU at Clement Memorial Hospital. A frosty window faced the Chicago River. Stacks of manila folders rose from the desk. A bookcase looked as if someone had swept binders, medical guides, and regulation pamphlets on to the floor and then stuffed them back on the shelves in a hurry. A bunch of framed photos of the doctor's two adult sons collected dust on a bureau, on the desk, and alongside degrees and awards on the walls.

Kelson glanced at the clutter. 'Enough to give you a headache even without a brain injury.'

'Overworked and overwhelmed,' the doctor said cheerfully. He checked his watch. 'What can I do for you?'

When Kelson arrived at the hospital after leaving Rodman's apartment, he'd asked to talk to Dr Madani.

The information desk clerk made a call and told Kelson, 'She's off today.'

He asked if anyone else in the ICU was available to talk.

'Regarding?'

'Recent patient deaths,' Kelson said.

The clerk made another call and, to Kelson's surprise, sent him up to the ICU chief himself.

Kelson sat across from Dr Jacobson and said, 'Patricia Ruddig, Josh Templeton, Daryl Vaughn.'

Jacobson laced his fingers on top of the papers on his desk. 'Have you scheduled an appointment with your therapist yet?' Cheerful.

'Dr P? We're booked for tomorrow. Why?'

'I've sent the records from your stay here. I'll forward a note that you came back today.'

Kelson tried to see through the doctor's cheer. 'You say that like a threat. If so, I don't get it.'

'No threat, but concern, Mr Kelson. You spent seventy-two hours here. You were unconscious for forty-eight of those hours.

You've been out for twenty-four hours, and now here you are again, asking questions about some unfortunate patients – whose misfortunes are private and have nothing to do with you, as far as I can tell.'

'This is what I do,' Kelson said. 'Professionally.'

'You're a professional lurker? You go around asking about confidential medical matters?' Jacobson had the kind of face hospitals put on brochures. Assured. Clean. Pleasant.

'Scrubbed,' Kelson said.

'I'm sorry?'

'I ask questions. People pay me to get answers.'

'Someone paid you to ask questions about these patients?'

'Not exactly – not yet. Probably not at all. Only if you give me reason to think they should.'

'I'm afraid I don't understand.'

Kelson nodded. 'I get that a lot. What happened to the lady with the appendix?'

'What?'

'The one who died yesterday. She either got her cefoxitin or she didn't. She went into septic shock and had a heart attack.'

Jacobson's cheer fell. 'Did Wendy Thomas hire you to ask about these patients?'

'Not exactly.'

'What does *not exactly* mean?'

'It means she didn't hire me.'

The doctor sighed. 'I think you're being less than truthful.'

'Never,' Kelson said.

Jacobson unlaced his fingers, then laced them again. 'Let's say Ms Thomas administered the antibiotics. Her failure to record them on the chart opens us to charges of malpractice. We can't afford to be liable.'

'*Can't afford to be* or *aren't*?'

'The other patients suffered from a number of ailments, some of which we were aware of when we admitted them, some of which we weren't. We handled them with the best care we were capable of. Sometimes, sadly, the best care isn't enough. Patients die. If doctors tell you they get used to it, they're either liars or sociopaths. Every death hurts. But death is a fact. Patients die.'

'See,' Kelson said, 'that's all I wanted to hear you say.' He stood up.

Jacobson seemed surprised. 'That's it?'

'Is there something more?'

'No,' the doctor said. 'No, I don't think so.'

Kelson glanced around the messy office. He smiled at one of the pictures of two young men on the doctor's desk. 'Proud father.'

'What? Oh – sure. Yes.'

'Me too. A proud father. A daughter. No sons.'

'Right. Complicated family situations,' Jacobson said. He seemed distracted. 'I don't necessarily mean yours. Mine – their mother died when they were teenagers. They're all I have.'

'It's good to have something,' Kelson said. '*Somebody.*'

Jacobson smiled but with a kind of sadness. 'Hard to live otherwise.'

Kelson nodded. 'All right then.' He moved toward the door.

'The woman who died yesterday,' Jacobson said. 'She was thirty-nine. Diabetic. She suffered kidney failure two years ago. She was in very poor health – perhaps poorer than we realized when she came in.'

'OK,' Kelson said.

'If you speak with Wendy Thomas, you can tell her we'll contact her to arrange her return. She's a good nurse. We're all overworked here. Sometimes we're overwhelmed. I'm certain she did her job.'

'She'll be glad to hear that,' Kelson said.

Kelson passed a dozen closed office doors, then rode the elevator down a floor to the ICU.

In the central room, an oversized clock hung on a wall. The vinyl flooring looked like a Jackson Pollock painting. A hospital orderly with a blond ponytail sat at a circular computer station. She wore white-framed glasses on top of her head and a white sports watch on her wrist. Her desk was littered with clipboards and taped-up schedules and reminders.

Kelson asked her, 'Could you point me to the medical supply room?'

'Of course, it's—' She caught herself. 'You're kidding, right?'

'I need to check the cefoxitin register. I'll be in and out.'

She slid her glasses down to her nose and eyed him. 'Who are you?'

He reached his good hand across the desk. 'Sam Kelson.'

'Could I see ID?'

He fished out his wallet and showed her his driver's license.

'OK, Samuel Kelson,' she said, 'I need *hospital* ID.'

'Oh, I don't work here. I checked out of room sixteen C yesterday. I want to see the cefoxitin for some friends, if you can call them that.'

'I see,' she said. 'Hold on a moment.' She dialed the desk phone, then told the person on the other end, 'I have a gentleman here who needs assistance.' She smiled at Kelson as she listened. 'Yes,' she said, and 'Yes' again. She hung up and tapped a finger on the desk.

'Thank you,' Kelson said.

'You're welcome,' she said. 'I called security.'

'Oh, I wish you didn't do that. I'm doing a favor for Jose and Wendy.'

The orderly's expression changed. 'Wendy? You know her?'

'We met last night. Jose and I go back a little further.'

'What they did to her is wrong.'

'Yeah? Why is that?'

'Wendy had nothing to do with the deaths.'

'What?'

'Wendy did nothing wrong.'

'No – the death*s* part. Plural.'

'I guess there've been a couple lately. A few. Enough to worry the doctors and administrators.'

'That's not what I wanted to hear,' Kelson said.

'It happens sometimes. A cluster. But it isn't Wendy's fault.'

'Patricia Ruddig, Josh Templeton, Daryl Vaughn?' Kelson said. 'The lady yesterday morning.'

'Right – Jennifer Kowalski.' The orderly looked unhappy.

A bell rang, and the elevator doors opened. A strong-jawed man in his mid-twenties got off and headed for the computer station.

'It's OK, Rick,' the orderly said before he got to them.

Kelson gave him a look. 'I've seen you before.'

The man stared back. His eyes moved from Kelson's hands and arms – the good side and the bad – to his legs, then to his face, assessing risk.

'It's OK,' the orderly said again. 'It was my mistake.'

But the man squared off with Kelson – close enough for Kelson to read his nametag. *Richard Jacobson. Director of Security. Clement Memorial Hospital.*

Kelson said, 'The pictures in your dad's office. You're Dr Jacobson's boy?'

Richard Jacobson grimaced at the word *boy*. 'Could I see some ID, sir?'

Kelson fished out his wallet again. 'She didn't like my driver's license. You think you'll like it any better?'

The man grimaced at the license too. 'What business do you have here, Mr Kelson?'

Kelson gestured at his bandaged arm. 'My bills will probably pay your salary for the next three years.'

The orderly said again, 'It was my mistake, Rick.'

The man ignored her and handed Kelson back his license. 'Are you currently a patient?'

'Nope. You kicked me out in the cold yesterday.'

'Maybe it's time to return there?'

Kelson put his license back in his wallet, fingered a business card from it, and dropped it on the circular desk. 'Thanks,' he said to the orderly.

As Richard Jacobson escorted him to the elevator, Kelson asked, 'How's it work? Your dad's a big cheese doctor and he gets you a summer job when you're a kid – then all of a sudden you're head of hospital security?'

ELEVEN

A s the January afternoon darkened, Kelson turned on his laptop in his office. He took his Springfield pistol from the bottom drawer, popped out the magazine, checked that it was loaded, snapped it back in, and set the gun on the desktop next to the computer.

The ICU orderly said the lady who died after going into septic shock was named Jennifer Kowalski. Kelson found her with a Google search. Her Facebook profile picture showed a very large woman. 'Bigger than very large,' Kelson said. 'To tell the truth.

Which I do. Always.' Over the years, the woman had put up hundreds of photos of a bulldog named Jezebel. Now her sister and friends posted distraught remembrances of her. No one mentioned her diabetes. No one mentioned her earlier kidney failure. 'But why would they?'

Kelson wrote down the sister's name – Mary Kowalski.

He glanced at the Springfield pistol. 'The point is, what?' He fought off the impulse to check the magazine again.

Another link showed that Jennifer Kowalski worked as a dispatcher for a tow truck company called Lakeside Tow. Kelson copied the contact information.

Her name also appeared on the member roster of the Silver Bells – a hand bell ensemble – and there she was in a photo taken last month by the big Christmas tree in Daley Plaza, shaking bells with eleven other women.

Seven years ago, she was a complainant in a civil lawsuit involving a two-flat in the Andersonville neighborhood.

He called the phone number for Lakeside Tow. It rang four times and kicked to a recording. A man's gruff voice promised *speedy service twenty-four seven, three hundred sixty-five days a year, all weather – a fleet of trucks at your beck and call – leave a number and a driver will call right back.* Kelson hung up.

He returned to the Silver Bells homepage and clicked the contact link. It included no phone number but offered boxes he could check if he wanted information about auditioning, booking concerts, buying CDs, donating to the ensemble, or receiving an e-newsletter. It also had a section for comments. He typed Jennifer Kowalski's name, followed by five question marks. Then he deleted the comment and closed the page.

He glanced at his gun. He grabbed it from the desk, popped the magazine, checked it, and slapped it back in. He set the pistol down and turned to the window. Outside, the wind was blowing, and something was flapping against the building side. In another twenty minutes, the sky would be black. 'Right,' he said.

He turned off the laptop, picked up the pistol again, and said, 'Patricia Ruddig, Josh Templeton, Daryl Vaughn – and Jennifer Kowalski.' He went to the window, holding the gun.

He couldn't see what was flapping.

'Nothing,' he said.

He went back to the desk and put the pistol in its drawer. 'Start at the beginning,' he said. 'Tomorrow.'

He rode the elevator to the street and drove to Nancy's house in the dark. Sue Ellen was waiting for him in the front room when he rang the bell.

Until a year ago, already too old for such behavior, she would jump into his arms when he arrived at Nancy's.

'The divorce,' Dr P said when he'd asked if he should worry about her affection. 'And you got shot in the head. What do you expect? If we knew each other a little better, *I* would jump in your arms for reassurance.'

Lately, though, Sue Ellen had started to cool as she somersaulted toward adolescence. But when he stepped inside, she came toward him as if she would run and jump. He grinned and opened his arms – the good one, the bandaged one. A troubled look flashed across her face, and she skidded to a stop. Then she grinned. 'Dad.' Her voice expressed all the leaping joy he remembered.

Nancy came from the kitchen with a sack of cat food. 'When you drop off Sue Ellen,' she said, 'take the cats.'

'Hello, dear,' he said.

'Ha. Talk to your daughter about her math grade.'

'Bye, dear.'

'I mean it,' Nancy said. 'I don't want her out on the street.'

'Because of seventh-grade math?'

'It's a slippery slope.'

Kelson and Sue Ellen drove toward Taqueria Uptown. Plows had scraped the ice off the streets and dropped rock salt, which crunched under the tires and clicked against the bottom of the car.

'Should we get it over with?' Kelson asked at a stoplight.

'I like irrational numbers more than rational ones,' Sue Ellen said. 'I hate exponents.'

'What's to hate about exponents?'

'You don't know?' She rolled her eyes at him.

'When did you start rolling your eyes?'

'I've always rolled my eyes.'

'No you haven't.'

'Light's green.'

Kelson accelerated fast enough to spit rock salt at the car behind them. 'I'm glad we took care of that,' he said.

'I have it under control,' Sue Ellen said.

'Famous last words.'

'I'll study. Harder.'

'That'll make your mom happy.'

'And you?'

'Yeah,' he said, 'me too.'

Once a week, Kelson and Sue Ellen ate at the counter at Taqueria Uptown. The counterman – in a white apron and a black baseball cap – welcomed them like old friends. But he never told Kelson his name and gave no personal details about himself at all. He stood nearby, though, and listened in on a game called Stump Dad that Sue Ellen invented. She insisted on playing the game – which involved asking odd or uncomfortable questions that, because of his brain injury, Kelson couldn't help but answer – when they sat at the taqueria counter and often when they rode together in the car.

'*Pollo en mole*,' Kelson told the counterman.

'Guacamole and chips,' Sue Ellen said. 'And a lime soda.'

'*Claro*,' the counterman said.

When the man took the order to the cook, Sue Ellen stared at Kelson. He knew what was coming. 'Let's eat first, OK?' he said.

'You aren't ready?' She had a teasing smile.

'I think it would be nice to sit together quietly.'

'OK.' She folded her hands on the countertop.

Kelson glanced at her from the corners of his eyes.

The counterman brought her lime soda.

'Thank you,' Sue Ellen said.

As Kelson and the man watched, she opened her straw, crumpled the wrapper, and set the balled paper by her glass. She dipped the straw into the soda and drew a long drink. For a moment she looked like she would burp. Instead, she said, 'Do you like breasts?'

'Dammit,' Kelson said.

'Don't swear.'

'Yes, I like them. Very much. Now ask something less inappropriate.'

'OK. If I order a potbellied pig and have it delivered to your apartment, what will you do?'

'Pork sandwiches.'

'That's not funny.'

'It's tasty.'

'You'll upset Charlie.'

'You've named your imaginary pig?'

'The cats get lonely when you're working. They need a pig. Amber has breasts.'

'Good for her,' Kelson said. 'You're dizzying, by the way. Who's Amber?'

'A girl at school with breasts.'

'A friend of yours?'

'Not anymore.'

'Because she has breasts?'

Sue Ellen drank her soda and said nothing. A television – bracketed to the ceiling, tuned to a telenovela – played at the far end of the counter. But the counterman kept his eyes on the two of them.

Kelson said, 'What does your mother say about Amber?'

'She says it's *when*, not *if*,' Sue Ellen said. 'For most girls.'

'She's an expert on these things.'

'Breasts?'

Kelson nodded. 'Breasts.'

Sue Ellen drank her soda. 'Would you want them?'

'On me? No thank you.' He asked the counterman, 'You think our food is ready?'

'No, *señor. Pollo en mole* takes time.'

Sue Ellen said, 'Did you know potbellied pigs have sensitive skin? They can get sunburns.'

Kelson nodded. 'That's called bacon.'

'They're very social. In the wild they forage in groups. D'you know what you call a group of potbellied pigs?'

'A wienie roast?'

'Ha ha.'

'A pack?'

'Closer.'

'A pack of hotdogs?'

The counterman shook his head at him. 'Potbellied pigs are gentle creatures.'

Kelson glared at him. 'You know this, how?'

'A group of potbellied pigs is called a *herd*,' Sue Ellen said. 'They're as gentle as cows.'

Kelson still looked at the counterman. 'The two of you are in this together, aren't you?'

'No, *señor*,' the man said, and he went to the kitchen to check on the food.

'Huh,' Kelson said.

Sue Ellen drank her soda. She stared down at the counter.

'What?' Kelson said. 'I wouldn't really eat a potbellied pig. Not knowingly.'

But she surprised him. 'What happened at that house?'

'What house?'

She gestured at his bandaged arm.

'Renshaw's condo?' He screwed his mouth. 'He shot me. He shouldn't have. Obviously. But he did.'

She nodded. 'DeMarcus saved you?'

'Yeah, he did.'

She looked down again. 'How did you let it happen?'

'I didn't. I mean, I didn't mean to. I misjudged the risk – maybe.' He considered the sensation he'd felt as Renshaw's gunshot penetrated his arm. As he fell to the floor in the hallway. As Renshaw grinned at him with his skinny teeth. 'It felt like an accident,' he said. 'Like driving through an intersection and suddenly a truck comes through the side of your car. Like waking in the middle of the night to the smell of smoke.' He gazed at Sue Ellen. She held her soda straw between her fingers. Her hand trembled. 'I'm sorry,' he said.

The counterman brought out two plates and corn tortillas in a warmer. He set the food on the counter. 'What did I miss?' he said.

'Me almost dying,' Kelson said, because he had to say.

Sue Ellen looked up at the man with wet eyes.

'Oh,' the man said, and he slipped back to the kitchen.

For a while, Kelson and Sue Ellen ate without talking. Kelson tore chicken from the bone with his fork and knife. He sopped mole with a rolled tortilla. Sue Ellen ate the chips from the edges of her plate, working toward the middle. The counterman came out and silently refilled her soda.

After she ate her last chip, she watched Kelson eat. 'You know, potbellied pigs are good at sensing danger,' she said. 'They save people. A family had a pig called Lucky. They lived in a mobile home. When it caught fire, Lucky screamed and saved them.'

'The pig screamed? Where did you hear about this?'

'It's a "Fun Fact." I read it online. If we had a pig, maybe you wouldn't get hurt so much.'

Kelson stared into her eyes. 'Is this what the pig thing is about?'

Sue Ellen looked away.

'You're scared?'

Kelson forked a bite of chicken into his mouth – giving her time.

Using her knife, Sue Ellen scraped smudges of guacamole to the center of her plate.

Kelson asked, 'Is this about me?'

Staring at her plate, Sue Ellen said, 'If I say it is, can we get a pig?'

TWELVE

That night Kelson woke twice from his sleep.

The first time, shortly after midnight, Payday was standing on his pillow mewling in his ear. 'Stop screaming,' he told her, and brushed her from the bed. 'No fire.'

The second time, around four o'clock in the morning, Payday and Painter's Lane slept at the foot of the bed. The wind outside had silenced, but icy snow ticked against the windows. Kelson got up to see. The building across the street was dark, all but a high window where a single light burned. The street below was whitening again under the streetlights. He said, 'Nothing could be more beautiful.' Painter's Lane slunk down from the bed and came to him. She rubbed against his ankle. A shiver ran up his leg. 'Nothing could be,' he said.

In the morning, he wrapped his bandaged arm in a towel and showered. He fried an egg for himself and scrambled one for each of the cats, mixing it with dry kibbles. 'Who says I'm irresponsible?' he said. He set the dishes on the dining table next to his plate, picked up the cats, and put them by their food. 'Who says I take unnecessary risks?'

After he ate, he stood by the window again. The sidewalks were already shoveled clear.

He called Jose Feliciano's number. When the bull rider answered, Kelson said, 'All right, three hundred bucks a day. It doesn't get you much.'

'Yeah? I told you something's wrong.'

'Nothing's wrong – or almost nothing. I talked to a woman who said Wendy got blamed for something she shouldn't have, that's all. So I'll look into the patient who just died – Jennifer Kowalski. Anyway, the ICU chief says Wendy's off the hook. They'll take her back.'

'How about the other dead people?' Jose said. 'I got my winnings, *hombre*. You look at them and give me the bill.'

'Why do you want to spend your money on this?'

'I told you – it's what I see. It's for Carlita. You know anything better to spend it on?'

'Maybe, yeah. Why not take your worries to the cops? They work for free.'

'Never.' As if Kelson insulted him. 'You know what cops do with people like me? They dunk our heads in canals and hold us under.'

Kelson said, 'That's not fair—'

'Don't talk to me about fair. I know fair. Fair is Carlita alive with my sister and her husband. Don't talk unless you can do that.'

'I understand.'

'And don't tell me to go to the cops.'

'OK.'

'Yeah?'

'I'll give you your three hundred bucks' worth,' Kelson said.

'Yeah, do your job. I'll pay. If you treat me like a son of a *puta* in a sombrero, you're the same as them.'

'I don't know there's a job to do, though.'

'I won eighteen thousand at the Wrangler Classic. Thirty-six thousand at the Tacoma Invitational. A thousand at the Bad Boy Mowdown. I won all that in *one month* – the month before I broke my back.'

'I hear you.'

'I can pay for things I care about. I care about this.'

'How much of your earnings did the hospital bills eat up for your back?' he asked because he couldn't help himself.

'I'm a good man,' Jose said. 'I get up after I'm broken. How about you, amigo?'

'I don't know,' Kelson said. 'I'm still figuring it out.'

'Look at the hospital. Let me know what you find, OK?'

Kelson said he would call that evening.

So he zipped himself into a heavy coat and tugged on a wool hat. He went down to his car and wiped off the snow. Twenty-five minutes later, he drove up Elston Avenue toward Lakeside Tow.

The driveway into the business cut through an open gate in a chain-link fence topped with coils of barbed wire. Signs said *Lakeside Tow* in big yellow letters, *Security dogs on premises* in bigger red letters, *Towing and Recovery* in black cursive. A permanent placard said *Drivers Wanted*.

As Kelson turned toward the driveway, a green Land Rover barreled out. Kelson swerved, and his car hit a patch of ice. His rear tires slid, touched pavement again, and straightened. His car stopped just short of a curbside fire hydrant.

He yelled – then recognized the driver of the Land Rover. Rick Jacobson, Director of Security at Clement Memorial Hospital, son of Jeremy Jacobson. The man in the passenger seat looked like a younger, longer-haired version of the driver – probably the brother who appeared with Rick in the pictures in Dr Jacobson's office.

'What the hell?' Kelson said.

He started to climb out of his car. But the Land Rover sped from the driveway toward the end of the block.

'What the hell?' Kelson said again. He backed from the curb and pulled into the towing company lot.

A dozen cars were parked there – mostly beaters people had abandoned or had too little cash to spring from the pound.

At the far end of the lot, there was an old brick building. Someone long ago painted it white. In front, a thick red arrow pointed at a metal security door. Kelson got out and pushed a button on a battered intercom next to the door.

When it buzzed, he went into an office.

Faded red outdoor carpet peeled at the corners of the room. The closest thing to art was a No Smoking sign. The air smelled of cigarette smoke. 'And engine oil,' Kelson said.

'What's that?' said a squat man in a knitted turtleneck. He sat on the other side of a pass-through window. A sheet of bulletproof glass would slide across the opening if the hour got late or a customer acted spooky. At a quarter to ten on a bright January morning, the man looked at ease.

Kelson reached a hand through the window. 'Sam Kelson,' he said.

The man shook his hand vigorously. 'David Hennessey.' He laughed for no apparent reason.

Behind him, on a dirty white vinyl sofa, two old dachshunds gazed at Kelson. Their mouths and eyes drooped. 'Your security dogs?' Kelson said.

'Everyone calls them Ma and Barker,' the man said. 'If thieves can't take a joke, fuck 'em. You got a car you need to pay for?'

'No,' Kelson said. 'I have a question – a *couple* questions. Those guys who just pulled out of here?'

'Assholes,' the man said. 'Some guys got no decency. They come in here like knuckleheads when I'm in mourning.'

'For Jennifer Kowalski?'

The man's hand drifted below the pass-through counter. 'You with those guys?'

'They almost drove me into a fire hydrant,' Kelson said. 'And there's no need to shoot me.'

The man's smile turned cunning. He pulled a big revolver from under the counter, flashed it at Kelson, and tucked it away. 'Just so you know.'

'Nice,' Kelson said. 'Is it legal?'

'In Chicago? Hell no. Not for a felon. What do you want with Jennifer? A damned shame. She was a friend – my best friend.'

'The worst kind of loss.'

'It was no surprise,' he said. 'She had two heart attacks last year. Had to happen sooner or later, I guess. The third was the charm.'

'She had two heart attacks? Was this in anyone's records?'

'Not that I know. Maybe they weren't heart attacks. But she had the signs. I told her to go to the ER. I told her I'd drive her myself. She said she'd get over it. A while ago, she stopped taking her diabetes medicine. Wrecked her kidneys.'

'I heard about the kidneys,' Kelson said.

The man looked puzzled. 'Who are you? Jennifer didn't have lots of friends – just me and her music pals.'

'A couple nurses from the hospital where she died asked me to look into her.' He pulled a card from his wallet and gave it to the man.

'Those guys that were just here, they're from the hospital too,' the man said. 'Asked if Jennifer had insurance. Acted like they cared about her till I told them Lakeside Tow doesn't insure. What kind of hospital sends out guys two days after a woman dies? They never heard of a phone? They never heard of time to grieve?'

'Is that all they wanted to know about?' Kelson said. 'Insurance?'

'They asked about Jennifer's sister. Next of kin. They want to know what to do with the body. I told them the sister lives in Salt Lake City. Married a Mormon. Then they got pissy. What's *that* about?'

'That's it? Insurance and the sister?'

'Isn't that enough? At this point, I started playing with my revolver under the counter. Maybe they thought I was jerking off. The older one asked me, please don't mention they came about the money and the sister and all. I could've shot him in the nuts.' He sighed. 'What did your nurses want you to look for? They worried about their paychecks too?'

'They thought something happened to Jennifer at the hospital that shouldn't have. I guess you could say they were her friends too – at least at the end.'

'Hell, she could use a couple,' the man said. 'I don't know what anyone could've done to save her. Maybe she got fed up with it all. Makes me sad. It didn't seem she wanted to save herself.'

THIRTEEN

After lunch, Kelson went to his appointment with Sheila Prentiss at the Rehabilitation Institute. Dr P mostly did talk therapy, but today she shined a penlight into each of Kelson's eyes and measured his blood pressure.

'Remarkable,' she said.

'I take a lickin' and keep on tickin'?'

'How did you let this happen?' she asked.

'That was Sue Ellen's question too.'

'What did you tell her?'

'Something between I don't know and I screwed up.'

'You can't afford this kind of thing,' she said. 'Your brain injury – the trauma you suffered – makes you susceptible to re-injury and complications. This latest incident—'

'I slept through most of it, to tell the truth.'

'The blood loss alone could've reversed the healing you've experienced. It could've caused new damage. I want you to take an acuity test before you leave today.'

She asked him to divide fifty-four by six. She had him recite the months backwards. When she told him to touch his forefingers to his nose, he tapped his nose with the finger on his good side, then flapped his bandaged arm at her and said, '*Whose* acuity are we measuring?'

She wrote notes on his record. 'You realize your insistence on putting yourself in positions of high risk is itself evidence of reduced cognitive function?'

'I put myself in bad situations before Bicho shot me too,' he said. 'I volunteered to go undercover on the narcotics squad.'

'True.'

'And I married Nancy.'

'Ha. It does seem you've always liked the risk of pain. But that's different from pain tolerance. In your condition – with frontal lobe impairment – you might be able to tolerate far less than you think.'

'Are you telling me to quit the work I do? Because I've already heard that. But this is who I am.'

'No – no, I get that.' The warmth of her smile surprised him. 'I guess I'm telling you to avoid getting shot. Your body can't take it. Your brain definitely can't.'

'That sounds like good advice,' he said.

She gazed at him with pressed lips. 'You know, you're still riding high on the excitement from this thing. But you may crash. A little thing can trigger it. Be prepared. You'll need to adjust.'

'Except for some tics and twitches, I think I'm doing all right,' he said. 'More than all right.'

'That's what worries me,' she said.

An hour later, when Kelson arrived at the door to his office, his phone was ringing inside. Men and women – on break from classes at the computer training company – surrounded him in the hall. He fumbled with his key. Dropped it. He scooped it up and tried again. The phone rang inside. A red-haired woman with a wide, freckled face approached from across the hall. She took his key and opened the door.

'I couldn't bear watching,' she said. 'You all right now?'

'Never better.' He stepped inside. 'Which isn't quite true – but is sort of, since I wish it was.' He closed the door.

When he reached his desk, the phone stopped ringing.

He dropped into his chair.

Then his cell phone rang.

Dr Jeremy Jacobson was on the other end. 'I thought you'd like to know, the patient who died while in Wendy Thomas's care received her full antibiotic treatment. The post-mortem tests have confirmed it. Ms Thomas is in the clear. Her nursing supervisor left a message for her, but I thought inasmuch as you seem to represent her – and in light of our conversation – you might also convey the news. It's good news for her.'

'And for you and the hospital, which is why you called.'

'We're convinced Ms Thomas did her job correctly,' the doctor said. 'We've lifted her suspension. The patient also had a severely enlarged heart – and evidence of earlier heart disease.'

'I know,' Kelson said.

'You do? Well, will you also relay the message to Ms Thomas? We expect her back on her regular schedule, starting immediately.'

'I'll tell her if I can,' Kelson said. 'Did you send your boys after Jennifer Kowalski's insurance money this morning?'

If Kelson's change of subject – or his knowledge of the dead patient's name – surprised the doctor, he gave no sign of it. 'Of course not. Our collections department handles insurance payments.'

'What if a patient is uninsured? Do you send out your sons to strong-arm employers and relatives?'

'There are also contract collection services, and, as I'm sure you know, hospitals like ours swallow a lot of unpaid fees. What's this about?'

'You'll want to talk to your boys about their visit to Lakeside Tow – and about their lousy driving. There's something going on that shouldn't be.'

'I'll tell you what's going on. We're a busy hospital with a high patient load and occasional staff shortages – including a shortage of qualified nurses like Wendy Thomas. We attempt to remain personable and compassionate through all the business of making people healthy. Hence my call to you.'

'*Hence?*'

'Yes, *hence.*'

'Well,' Kelson said, 'I appreciate the call. It confirms what I thought, and it'll make Wendy Thomas happy.'

The doctor said, 'My pleasure always. I wish you well, Mr Kelson.'

Kelson had promised to call Jose Feliciano in the evening but saw no reason to wait. He took his phone to the window. The sun had broken through the clouds, and afternoon light glinted off the cars passing on the street below. 'This could be a better place,' he said. 'Or it could be worse.' He dialed.

When Jose answered, Kelson said, 'Tell Wendy she can go back.'

'Yeah, she got the message. She's already gone for an early dinner before her shift.'

'Wendy had nothing to do with the lady's death,' Kelson said. 'The woman had heart trouble and a history of ignoring her health. I never caught up with Dr Madani, but Jacobson will handle it with her.'

'What about the other people?' Jose said. 'What killed them?'

'There aren't others. I told you – no pattern. Nothing.'

'And I told you, you're looking at this wrong, amigo.'

'I'm looking at it with the only eyes I've got. I see what's there. I don't imagine it.'

'No, man, you're blind,' Jose said, and he hung up.

Kelson stared down at the street. Cars and trucks inched through afternoon traffic. Bundled men and women stood at the crosswalk, waiting for the light.

'I see everything,' he said to the world below him. He blinked. Then he closed his eyes for a count of ten and reopened them. Cars and trucks still inched through traffic. Bundled men and women gathered to cross the intersection. 'Everything.'

His phone rang and he brought it to his ear. 'Everything, amigo,' he said. '*Todos.*'

A woman spoke. 'Excuse me?'

Kelson recognized the voice but couldn't place it. 'Sorry?'

'Mr Kelson?' the woman said. 'This is Caroline Difley.'

'Still nothing.'

'We met in the ICU at Clement Memorial. When you asked about the supply room? I was at the desk. You left a card?'

'The blond orderly?'

'Right . . .' As if she regretted calling.

'Hello, Caroline Difley,' Kelson said. 'What can I do for you?'

'I looked at the inventory records. Wendy signed for the cefoxitin. She couldn't be responsible for the death.'

'Great news, but old,' Kelson said.

'Excuse me?'

'Jennifer Kowalski had a bad heart. Everyone did the right thing at the hospital. The woman had no chance.'

'Where did you hear this?'

'I pieced it together. I talked to a man she worked with at a towing company, and I talked to Dr Jacobson.'

'Oh.' Only a little disappointed. 'It was funny, because there were a bunch of flags for other medicines but none for cefoxitin and none for the time when Jennifer Kowalski was a patient.'

'Flags?' he said.

'We check inventory each month. Last month, a couple of the medicines were short. The month before, a couple of others were.'

'That's exactly what I didn't want to hear,' Kelson said. 'What were the medicines? What days were they inventoried?'

'I only paid attention to the cefoxitin,' she said.

'Can you look again?'

'I wasn't supposed to look this time. What's wrong?'

'I need to know if the medicines went missing around the time Patricia Ruddig, Josh Templeton, and Daryl Vaughn died.'

The orderly said, 'Why would you think . . .?' She stopped herself. 'The dates aren't exact. They're just when the auditor counted the totals.'

'They're something,' Kelson said. 'Look at the records. Please. Let me know what you find. Medicines and dates.'

'I can't promise,' she said.

When they hung up, Kelson swore at the phone.

Then he pulled out the notes he wrote about the other dead patients. Patricia Ruddig – seventy-three years old, broken hip,

heart attack, corner of Ainslie Street and Claremont. Josh
Templeton – twenty-one years old, girlfriend named Melanie,
car accident, stopped breathing, DePaul student from Fort Wayne.
Daryl Vaughn – homeless, kidneys, bum. He swore at the notes
too.

He spent the next two hours on his laptop, learning nothing
more about Patricia Ruddig or Daryl Vaughn but finding pictures
of Josh Templeton's accident scene among the photos on his
girlfriend's Facebook timeline. Kelson recognized the bend on
Lake Shore Drive by Diversey Parkway where the crash happened.
The brown Camry was crushed on both the driver's and the
passenger's sides. The passenger-side impact – the car wrapped
around a light pole – did the worst damage. From Melanie's
comments, Kelson learned that the accident happened in the early
morning hours of December 3, as Josh returned to school from
visiting her. *It didn't make sense*, she said. *She couldn't understand*, she said. 'Welcome to the club,' Kelson told her.

Then he realized she was right. It *didn't* make sense. Diversey
Parkway was north of the Lake Shore Drive exit to DePaul, and
Josh was returning from Fort Wayne – from the south. He over-
shot his destination by a half mile.

But then he spoke to the laptop. 'Maybe he was drifting to
sleep while he drove. Maybe he rented north of campus. Maybe
he was going to the Golden Apple for a waffle before heading
home.'

He exited Facebook.

He turned off the laptop.

While he'd been searching online, the sky outside had turned
dark.

He was hungry. 'Hunger is good,' he told the laptop, and he
put it in the top drawer.

He peeked into the bottom drawer, touching the Springfield
pistol, as if that would give him good luck.

He reached under the desktop and ran a finger along the barrel
of the KelTec.

He got up, wrestled into his heavy coat, and tugged on his
hat.

Then there was a knock at the door. Maybe the red-haired
woman who'd helped with his key had come back to help him
escape from his office. 'Maybe I'll ask her to dinner,' he said.

He opened the door.

Rick Jacobson and his younger brother stood in the hall. The younger brother's eyes were glazed. Rick planted his feet shoulder-wide. He looked as if he was daring Kelson to hit him or to give him a reason to hit back.

FOURTEEN

'You almost drove me into a fire hydrant this morning,' Kelson said when they sat across from each other at his desk. He'd pulled off his coat but left on his hat.

'You mean when you almost front-ended us?' Rick said. Everything on Rick's face was tight and hard.

'I mean when I made a controlled turn toward the driveway.'

'Without a turn signal?'

Kelson showed him his bandaged arm. 'How am I supposed to signal?'

'My point.'

Kelson felt heat in his cheeks. 'Did you come here to defend your bad driving?'

The younger brother said, 'What did Dad hire you to do?'

Kelson smiled. 'Your dad didn't hire me to do anything.'

'Bullshit,' Rick said. 'I walked into his office this afternoon when he was hanging up with you.'

'Did you ask *him* if I was working for him?'

'He said you weren't.'

'Does he usually lie to you?'

'Since my mom died, I make sure he's all right,' Rick said. 'I take care of him.'

'He seems capable of taking care of himself. He runs the ICU and all. He knows the patients – takes an interest in their histories. He seems sharp.'

'I won't let anyone take advantage of him.'

'How about you?' Kelson asked the little brother. 'Do you even have a name?'

'Scott,' he said. His inane smile suggested he found either Kelson's question or his own name funny.

'Do you work alongside Rick at the hospital, Scott? Or do the two of you just get together to shake down the employers of dead patients?'

Rick shook his head. 'When a patient passes away and the hospital has incomplete information – about insurance coverage, burial or cremation wishes, even who should receive jewelry and clothing – staff members make the necessary calls. A lot of end-of-life decisions need to be made right away. Sometimes, no one answers the numbers our people call. Sometimes, we leave messages but no one calls back. Then we need to go out and talk to the survivors personally. We can hire out that work, but we prefer to do it internally. That's sometimes me. Today Scott went with, that's all.'

'That sounds very innocent.'

'That's because it is.'

'The guy at Lakeside Tow said the two of you were assholes.'

'The guy at Lakeside Tow pulled a gun on us. *You* decide who's the asshole.'

'Burial or cremation?' Kelson said.

'What?' Rick said.

'You said that's why you rushed out to Lakeside Tow. To find out if you should bury Jennifer Kowalski or cremate her. Or are you going to wheel her out on the parking lot for the birds?'

Rick eyed him as if figuring the best angle for a punch. 'Burial,' he said. 'We tracked down her sister by phone – after several tries.'

The younger brother said, 'What did Dad hire you to do?'

Kelson gazed at him. 'You look stoned.'

Scott drew his head back.

'Or drunk,' Kelson said.

Rick said, 'What does my dad want you to do for him?'

'Nothing,' Kelson said. 'Look at my medical records. You'll see you can count on me for the truth.'

'Then what were you talking with him about?'

'Nurses,' Kelson said.

'Nurses?' Rick looked as if patience always took an effort. 'We want you to leave my dad alone.'

Kelson said, 'Why would I want to have anything to do with him?'

The brothers exchanged an uncertain glance.

'I'm glad we settled that,' Kelson said. 'Thanks for stopping by.' He stood up.

The brothers exchanged another glance and stood too. They watched as Kelson wrestled into his coat.

As they went to the door, Kelson said, 'One thing, though. What happened to Patricia Ruddig, Josh Templeton, and Daryl Vaughn?'

Rick said, 'Who?'

'Patients who died in the ICU over the last couple months.'

Rick shook his head. 'Never heard of them.'

'See,' Kelson said, 'I don't know if I believe you.'

They rode the elevator down together. When they walked from the building on to the sidewalk, they turned opposite directions without saying goodbye, Rick and Scott Jacobson to their green Land Rover, which they'd left, hazards blinking, in a loading zone, Kelson to the parking garage.

'Tired,' Kelson said, as he climbed the concrete stairs. The word echoed faintly off the stairwell walls, as if another man was confirming Kelson's fatigue. 'To be expected,' Kelson said, and the other man confirmed it.

He came out into the dimly lit third level, and his phone rang before he reached his car.

'Ignore it,' he said.

He got in.

The phone rang.

He started the engine.

The phone rang.

He looked at caller ID. It said *Nancy*.

'Huh,' he said. He touched the answer button and said, 'Hey.'

'I just got home from the clinic,' Nancy said. 'Sue Ellen isn't here.'

'Where is she?'

'That's what I mean. She didn't come back after school. This morning she said she was going by her friend Amber's house, but—'

'The one with breasts?'

'*What?*'

'Amber – the girl with breasts?'

'What the hell are you talking about?'

'I didn't think they got along any more. Did you call Sue Ellen's number?'

'Of course. I'm not an idiot.'

'Sorry, that's *me*.'

'Don't turn this into—' She stopped herself. 'I'm concerned.'

'It's early,' he said. 'Give her an hour. If it gets to dinnertime—'

'*You* should be concerned too.'

'I am. I express it differently.'

'Yeah,' she said, 'you express it wrong.' She hung up.

'Huh,' he said again.

He drove to his apartment, shifting his self-talk between his worry for Sue Ellen, the weird visit from the Jacobson brothers, and his uncertainty about Patricia Ruddig, Josh Templeton, and Daryl Vaughn. He followed a gray-haired woman in a white faux-fur coat into his building and rode up the elevator with her, managing to talk to her mostly about the bitter cold afternoon and to make only two comments about baby seals.

Upstairs, he fumbled his apartment key into his door. Most evenings, Payday and Painter's Lane greeted him as he stepped inside, meowing manically. This evening, a light was on in the kitchenette, the apartment smelled of frying meat, and he heard Sue Ellen explaining that ham was delicious.

He went to the kitchenette door. Sue Ellen held a spatula over a sizzling pan. Payday and Painter's Lane sat on the counter and watched her.

Kelson said, 'Hey, kiddo, what's up?'

She gave him a big smile. 'I'm making dinner for the cats.'

'Your mom's making *you* dinner. She thought you'd be home by now.'

'How can I be home with her if I'm here? Anyway, this is home too.'

'Good point. But you worried her.'

'Mom? She never worries.'

'She tried to call. Why didn't you answer your phone?'

'I loaned it to Amber. Amber's mom took hers away because of Ravi.'

'Ravi?'

'Amber wasn't supposed to go with Ravi, but she did, so

Amber's mom took her phone, and I loaned mine to her so she can talk with him.' She flipped a piece of ham in the pan.

'Life's confusing,' Kelson said.

She gave him that smile. 'Yep.'

FIFTEEN

The next morning, Kelson drove to the sixteen-story building at the corner of Ainslie Street and Claremont where Patricia Ruddig lived. 'And died,' he said, stepping over an ice-encrusted drift between the street and the sidewalk.

He walked past a sign that said *The Glenview, Senior Assisted Living* and through a set of automatic glass doors into a clean lobby. A man in his forties stood at a round, dark-wood reception desk. His sweater had a picture of a smiling red-nosed reindeer.

Kelson stared at the sweater. 'Really?' he said.

'It's Christmas all year around here, buddy. Whatever keeps them happy. Juanita does a Santa's elf thing every Fourth of July.' The man had friendly deep-set blue eyes.

'You're screwing with me,' Kelson said.

'Yeah, I just like reindeer. Not that the residents mind. What can I do for you?'

'I have some questions about one of your former tenants. Patricia Ruddig.'

'Patty?' He did something with his eyes, making them look forlorn. 'Sad thing. Everyone here loved Patty.'

'You knew her well?'

'Knew her and knew her husband Phil until he died a few years back. Know Dougie.'

'Dougie?'

'Her boy by her first husband. Lives in Barrington. Came every Sunday for lunch with his ma. You from the hospital?'

'No . . .'

'Insurance company?'

'No.' He gave the man a business card. 'A client asked me to find out about Ms Ruddig.'

The man slipped the card into a pocket. 'I don't know what anyone would want to find out. Patty wasn't what you'd call normal, but what's normal nowadays, right?'

'Not *me*,' Kelson said.

'You aren't into reindeer, are you?' The man winked. But then the desk phone buzzed, and he picked up. After listening for what seemed a long time, he explained the daily lunch menu for the Glenview dining room.

Kelson glanced around the lobby. The floor was hardwood, polished to a gleam. The sofas and easy chairs looked clean and expensive. A man in thick trousers, using a walker with a wicker basket buckled to the front, crossed to a set of double doors. A sign above the doors identified the next room as a lending library.

When the receptionist hung up, Kelson asked, 'What wasn't normal about Ms Ruddig?'

'Her house guests,' he said. 'Before Phil died, they had four parakeets. The day they buried him, the birds were gone. Just gone. She chased them out her window, I suppose. She looked like a parakeet herself. Maybe five feet tall. A hundred pounds. Hair dyed so blond it was almost yellow. Lipstick – always lipstick. After Phil died, she started bringing in visitors to stay. She had a two bedroom, plenty of space. She kept them until Dougie made her kick them out.'

Kelson gazed at the man. 'You're a chatty one, aren't you?'

The man leaned across the desk, confidentially. 'Number one job requirement. Talk to folks. They're lonely, most of them. Don't matter what I tell them. Truth, lies, some of both. But I talk. I make them feel connected.'

'Who were these visitors?' Kelson said.

'I don't gossip, but they say she found them at Spyner's Pub. She liked the ones you'd call downtrodden.'

'Tell me about the accident that broke Ms Ruddig's hip.'

'Can you really call it an accident?'

'I don't know, can I?'

'She was walking out of the building New Year's morning. She went out every day like that since Phil died, right at nine. She'd get a paper and a roll. Coffee in the winter, juice in the summer. Nice days, she ate the roll on a bench. Lousy days, she brought it back and ate here in the lobby. On New Year's Day, she went out to the sidewalk, and *wham*, a kid on a bike hit her. What was the kid doing riding on the sidewalk outside a place like this? He didn't stop when he hit Patty. Just pedaled away. Far as I'm concerned, that kid killed her. She stayed a week in the hospital, but the damage was done.'

'What did the police say?'

'They said bikes hit people all the time. Maybe not so much in January. They said Patty was the first for the New Year. Like that was an honor. At first it looked like Patty would be OK. An ambulance came almost before she hit the ground. They took good care of her.'

'And then she died,' Kelson said.

'That's right.'

'Did you get the accident on your security camera?'

'Uh-uh. Broken since before Christmas. I've got to get it fixed.'

'The police ever catch the kid?'

'Not that I know of.'

The phone on the man's desk buzzed again. Again, he answered and explained the lunch menu.

The man in thick trousers came from the lending library with a book in his walker basket and a look of pure pleasure on his face. He saw Kelson watching and called to him, 'Cheers.'

Kelson raised an imaginary glass. 'Cheers.'

The receptionist hung up the phone and nodded after the man, who disappeared into a corridor. 'Would you believe he had prostate surgery last week?'

'It wouldn't cross my mind,' Kelson said. 'Has Dougie cleaned out the apartment?'

'Nope. Hasn't been back since right after Patty broke her hip. He came for her magazines and prescriptions – and the pillow she liked.'

'Could I see the apartment?'

'That was Patty's home,' the man said. 'We protect the privacy of our residents.'

Kelson grinned at him.

The man didn't grin back.

'You're screwing with me again?' Kelson said. 'You just dished half the secrets of this place to me.'

'I certainly did not.'

*　*　*

Kelson went out to his car, cranked the heat high, and searched his phone for the address and hours of Spyner's Pub. It opened at 11:00 a.m., so Kelson drove a half mile north.

The pub occupied the ground floor of a two-story brick building across the street from a 7-Eleven and kitty-corner to a liquor store. Someone had painted the front blue, the entrance door schoolhouse red. A Michelob Light sign hung from a metal post over the entrance.

When Kelson walked in, a dozen women sat on bar stools or stood at the bar. The bartender wore a flannel shirt with the sleeves ripped off. Her short hair stood straight up. A skinny woman with a ponytail and a tattooed neck made small talk with her. A small, balding man swept the floor.

'Lesbian-ish,' Kelson announced.

The drinkers and bartender turned and glared at him.

'Not that I care one way or another,' he said. 'I'm just – noticing.'

The glare got colder.

'I'll shut up now,' Kelson said. 'Or try to.'

'Get the hell out,' the bartender said.

'You don't understand,' Kelson said. 'I—'

'What's to understand? Get out.'

'Right – sorry.' He ducked back out the door into the cold and stood on the sidewalk for a full minute, berating himself. Then he stepped back inside.

The bartender seemed to expect such behavior. She came around the bar and grabbed the broom from the small man, looking ready to beat Kelson to the floor. 'I said, *get out*.'

'Patricia Ruddig,' Kelson said. 'Patty.'

The bartender stopped. Her anger seemed to melt. She handed the broom back to the small man. 'Yeah, right . . . Patty.'

'I'm looking for people who knew her.'

'Who are you?'

'Sam Kelson.' He gave her a card.

'What's this about?' she said. 'Did her boy send you? 'Cause if he did, you can get the hell out again.'

'Dougie? No, I'm working for a bull rider and his fiancée.'

'A—'

'Never mind. Dougie's out of it. I never met the man.'

The bartender crumpled the card and dropped it on the floor.

'I don't know what I can tell you about Patty. She was a regular. Came in for an old fashioned in the winter, a gin and tonic in the summer. Always just one drink. Quiet until she had that drink. She took in more than a couple of women when they needed a friend – until her prick of a son stuck his nose in.'

'She took *me* in,' said a short woman. 'My wife kicked me out. I needed a place to stay. I needed to clean up. Dougie's not so bad. He watched out for his mom.'

'Dougie's a prick,' the bartender said.

'What do you know about the kid who hit her with the bike?' Kelson asked.

'Another prick,' the bartender said.

'Didn't even stop,' said the woman Patty Ruddig took in.

A tall woman, who'd gone back to her morning beer as soon as the bartender returned the broom to the small man, said, 'Patty was a tough old bird. She picked up others when they were broken. I never thought she'd break too.'

'Who dies from a broken hip?' said the woman who got taken in.

'One thing for sure,' said the tall woman, 'she wasn't gay.'

'She *thought* she wasn't,' said her companion.

'She married twice,' the tall woman said. 'Men. Wore them out, one after another. The first was poor as poor, Patty said. The second had money.'

'Phil,' Kelson said.

'Right. She liked her men and liked to talk about them after she had her drink.'

'Pricks,' the bartender said.

'You never met them,' said the one Patty Ruddig took in.

'Never needed to.'

Kelson looked from one woman to the next. 'Anything else?'

'Like I said, nothing to tell,' said the bartender.

The tall woman turned back to her beer. The small woman stared silently at Kelson. The bartender went behind the bar. The small man swept the floor.

'Thanks, then, I guess,' Kelson said.

The bartender shrugged like it was no big deal. The others didn't bother.

Kelson headed to the door. Then he stopped. 'Sorry about when I first came in. I didn't mean anything. I just – I talk.'

'What you're saying,' the bartender said, 'is you're a prick.'

'Sometimes, yeah.'

She said, 'Don't worry about it too much. You are what you are. Just keep it zipped up if you come in here.'

SIXTEEN

Early that afternoon, Kelson drove south out of Chicago, hooked east into Indiana, dropped to Valparaiso, and rode US-30 the rest of the way to Fort Wayne. As he drove past stubble fields, the temperature outside the car dropped. The sky cleared and was a pale blue, as if the cold drained it of color. Kelson notched up the heat and said, 'Snug.'

When he reached Ellis Funeral Home, he got out and kicked his legs in the freezing air. The funeral home was in the biggest, fanciest, best-kept house in its residential neighborhood. A white Victorian with a broad front porch, it had a turret built out over the porch roof and, to the side, a partial second floor with a high, dormered attic. 'Like a Scooby-Doo house,' Kelson said, and he climbed the porch steps and rang the bell.

A wide-shouldered man in an untucked teal dress shirt and black dress pants opened the door. His dark skin had a luster, as if he buffed it with a soft cloth. 'Can I help you?' he said. His voice went with the luster.

'Comforting and consoling. I can tell you're a professional.'

Nothing flickered in the man's face. 'How may I help you?'

'Right. I'm hoping to find out about a funeral you handled last month – for a college kid named Josh Templeton.'

'Yes,' the man said, 'please come in.'

Kelson said, 'I only want to know . . .' But the man started up the hall. Kelson followed him to a small sitting room with red upholstered chairs and a stiff gold-and-white sofa. A tiny crystal chandelier hung from the ceiling and, on the far wall, white curtains covered a broad window – except where they parted in the middle, exposing the afternoon sun. 'Great effect,' Kelson said. 'The bright-light-at-the-end?'

The man gestured at a chair. 'Please.'

They both sat, and the man said, 'We handled the service and

burial for Mr Templeton, yes. The flowers, the casket, the cemetery arrangements. The limousine for Ms Smithson.'

'Ms Smithson?'

'Josh Templeton's mother. Deneesa Smithson.'

'Ah, I thought—'

'I understand there was a divorce some years ago.'

'Right,' Kelson said. 'Do you have any nervous habits?'

'Excuse me?'

'Your face is remarkably still. No weird mannerisms – just
right for the job.'

'Thank you.'

'Would it be possible to get Deneesa Smithson's address?'

The man excused himself and, after a minute, returned with
a gilt-edged card on which he'd written an address.

Kelson said, 'When I die, you're the man for me.'

The funeral director showed him out.

Kelson drove to a little single-story pink house, built shoulder
to shoulder with two other little single-story pink houses. No
trees grew in the front yards. No trees grew in the back or side
yards. 'The great Indiana wasteland,' Kelson said as he pulled
to the curb. The sun was lowering in the west.

When Kelson knocked, a dog barked deep in the house, and
then a woman in a yellow pantsuit opened the door. She had the
same light-brown skin as her son in the online pictures Kelson
had seen. But unlike Josh's neat cornrows, her hair looked as if
she'd spent the day running her fingers through it. 'Yes?' She
lifted a hand toward her hair but stopped without touching it.
The dog barked and scratched at a door in another room. 'Is this
about—?'

'Your son,' Kelson said. 'It's probably nothing. I feel bad for
intruding . . .'

'Then why are you here?'

'Unanswered questions. Not mine. Not so much. Other
people's. Fascinating people. I tried to convince them there's
nothing here, but they insisted.'

'Look, I just came in from work. My dog is frantic. I—'

'Could I come in for a few minutes? I have a couple questions
– then I'll leave you alone.'

'No,' she said. 'Just tell me what you want to know.'

'Maybe it's only one question. Was there anything strange about how Josh died?'

'Anything?' She looked as frantic as the yapping dog sounded. 'Yeah, everything was strange. It was strange he was driving back to Chicago from Melanie's at three in the morning. I didn't even know he was here. It was strange a car ran him off the road when no one in their right mind would be out. It was strange he broke his leg but then stopped breathing. Nothing *wasn't* strange.'

'A car ran him off the road?'

'Of course it did. Have you seen pictures of the wreck? Damage on both sides.'

'What did the police say?'

'They said Josh shouldn't have been drinking and driving. They said he shouldn't have been speeding. They didn't say Josh got what he deserved, but they meant it.'

'I didn't know he was drinking – or speeding.'

'Josh and Melanie shared a bottle of wine before he drove back to Chicago. A three-hour drive. He wasn't drunk. The police say that for the car to be so badly damaged, he had to be moving fast.' She ran her fingers through her hair. 'Look, I spend my days with troubled boys. Josh wasn't like them. I left my husband when Josh was fourteen. I work long hours. Josh had every opportunity to go wrong. He was by himself most of the time as a teenager. But you know what? He turned out good. He was a *good* kid.' She twisted her hair in her fingers. 'Sometimes on holidays, I brought kids home on passes from Lutheran – the ones whose parents couldn't visit for legal reasons or chose not to—'

'Lutheran?' Kelson said.

'Lutheran Center for Boys. Where I work. A place for kids who can't be placed through the foster system.' She forced a smile. 'High risk. It's us or the warehouse.' The smile fell. 'I brought them home, and Josh shared the holidays with them – he shared *me*, even though there was too little of me to share. That's who he was. A smart, generous child. Not a reckless drunk. Some things you don't get over.' She wiped her eyes. 'Some things you never will.'

'Nothing's worse,' Kelson said.

'No,' she said, 'nothing.'

In the back room, the dog stopped barking. Deneesa Smithson glanced, as if concerned by the silence. Then the dog barked again.

'One other thing,' Kelson said. 'When Josh died, how did the hospital explain it?'

'They told me it was a blood clot. Pulmonary embolism.' She wiped her eyes again, ran her fingers through her hair. She forced another smile. 'Honestly, I feel fortunate the ambulance took him to Clement Memorial. If Josh had a chance, he got it there. I have insurance but not enough. They kept him comfortable and operated on his leg without demanding proof he could pay.' For a moment the smile became easy. 'There was one nurse – he used to be a rodeo clown or something – he took care of Josh real good. I know how hard it is to treat kids in need.'

'Yeah,' Kelson said, 'they've got some good people at that hospital.' Since he said it, he realized he must think it was true.

When Deneesa Smithson closed the door and went to quiet her dog, Kelson got back in his car. Before he could pull away from the curb, a girl approached on the sidewalk. She wore white leggings, a white down coat, a white hat over her bleach-blond hair, and red mittens. Her skin was as white as— 'Alabaster,' Kelson said aloud.

Kelson rolled down the window on the passenger side. As the girl turned on to the concrete path to Deneesa Smithson's house, he called out, 'Did anyone ever tell you that you look like alabaster?'

She kept walking. 'They told me never to talk to jagoffs.'

'Alabaster,' he called out.

She was almost to the front door.

He said, 'You're Melanie?'

'And you're a spooky man who talks to girls.'

'Could I ask you a couple questions about Josh?'

'So you like boys, not girls?'

'You're too quick for a kid.'

'I've grown up a lot in the last month. What do you know about Josh?'

'I'm looking into how he died.'

The girl came back down the path. She hesitated, then leaned into the passenger window. Up close, the effect of her skin was stronger. 'You could be made of soap.'

She stepped back from the window. 'Keep it in your pants, creep. Are you a cop?'

'Ex-cop. Now people pay me to look into things the cops aren't interested in. Or things people don't want to go to the cops about. Not that I'm very good at keeping secrets from the cops – or anyone else. You know, I can almost see through your skin. It's unearthly. In a good way.'

The girl snapped. 'What's *wrong* with you?'

'I got shot in the head,' Kelson said. 'Three years ago. And the arm. Recently. But when people ask, they usually mean the head.'

As if she didn't hear him, she said, 'My boyfriend died. I'm *seventeen* – I'm a *kid* – and now I'm visiting my dead boyfriend's mom because she's even more fucked up than I am. My mom and dad won't talk to me since they found out where I was that night. And you sit in a car and tell me I look like a fucking alien.'

'I didn't say—'

'And you make creepy comments as if I'd ever, *ever*—'

'I didn't,' he said. 'I wouldn't. I didn't mean it like that. I—'

'Fuck you, old man. Fuck you.'

Kelson stared at her. 'Was Josh drunk?'

As if his words took the last energy from her, her knees bent. She sank to the concrete and sat. 'No,' she said. 'He wasn't drunk. I brought the wine. I stole it from my mom and dad when I snuck out. We had, like, two sips at the Econo Lodge. To celebrate. We'd been dating a year. I just wanted to celebrate being together.'

'I'm sorry,' Kelson said.

She looked at him, teary-eyed. 'Yeah. But what good does that do?'

SEVENTEEN

K elson drove back into the city at 9:30 that night. He knew better than to call Dan Peters or Venus Johnson in the CPD homicide room. Before he could ask for information, they would start quizzing him – and he would talk and talk and talk. Not that dealing with them in person was much better, but when they went face to face, he tended to annoy them and short-circuit their questions. He couldn't hang up on them in the middle of an in-the-flesh conversation, but they couldn't hang up on him either.

He parked outside the Harrison Street station, went in, and asked the man at the front desk if Dan Peters was on duty.

He wasn't.

'Venus Johnson?'

The man called the homicide room, then printed a pass, and sent Kelson in through security.

Johnson was eating a hamburger in the cubicle she shared with Peters. An open green binder, scattered papers, and a Styrofoam cup littered her desk. The air smelled of stale sweat. Johnson looked as if she'd survived on that air for a long, long time. Her desktop computer – the volume muted – showed a YouTube video of waves breaking on a tropical beach.

'Wishful thinking,' Kelson said.

'What do you want, Kelson?'

'Daryl Vaughn.'

'Who?' she said.

'Homeless guy. Got beaten up by a bunch of other homeless guys a few days before Christmas. Died in the hospital – maybe from unrelated causes.'

She bit into the burger and asked through her mouthful, 'What about him?'

'Tell me what you have on him?'

She drew a long drink from a bottle of Coke. 'Nope.'

'I'm trying to find out—'

'One, does this look like an information desk? Two, even if it did, we wouldn't have your guy in the homicide database unless he died because of the assault. Even *you're* smart enough to work that out.'

'Take a look at general records?'

'Dammit, Kelson, this is my dinner break.' To prove it, she bit into her burger again.

'But you're eating at your desk.'

'Yeah, I am.' She chewed. 'As if I don't see enough of it when I'm on the clock.'

'By your computer.'

'Which is helping me achieve mindfulness – or was until I made the mistake of telling the desk officer to send you back.'

'I promised to look into the guy.'

'I care?'

'I've put in twelve hours today.'

'Still don't care.'

'I just got back from Fort Wayne, Indiana. Six-hour round trip.'

'Jesus Christ. If I check, will you shut up and leave me alone?'

'I'll try.'

'Forever and ever?'

'For as long as I can control myself.'

She slapped the remainder of the hamburger on to her desk. She exited the tropical video. 'Spell the name.'

Kelson spelled *Daryl Vaughn* and added, 'Died at Clement Memorial. End of December.'

She typed Vaughn's name on the keyboard. She stared at the screen. She said, 'Nope. He's got trespassing and vagrancy violations two or three times a year going back four years, petty stuff before that. But nothing in December.'

'How can that be?' Kelson said. 'If he was beaten that bad—'

'Don't know, don't care.' She picked up the hamburger and bit into it. Kelson watched her chew, watched her swallow. She said, 'Look, if a squad responded, there's a good chance he had no ID. They'd shove him into an ambulance as a John Doe. No reason he'd show in the database.'

'Can you look at EMT records?'

'No.'

'Can't or won't?'

'Won't. I've got one bite of dinner left, and I'm going to enjoy it while watching waves breaking on the bright white sands of Cornwall Beach in Montego Bay.'

'Then will you look up two other names? Patricia Ruddig and Josh Templeton?'

Johnson's eyes got big with fury.

'Or just the EMT records,' Kelson said. 'And I'll get the hell out of here.'

'Dammit,' Johnson said. 'I'm going to give a shoot-on-sight order to the desk officer.' She slapped the hamburger back on the desk. She brought up a new database. She searched for Daryl Vaughn's name. She sighed. 'Fine. December twenty-three.

Unconscious male, later identified as Daryl B. Vaughn. Transported from South Wacker at Monroe. Paramedics took him to Northwestern Medical.'

'You mean Clement Memorial.'

'No' – she tapped the screen like she meant to break the glass – 'I mean Northwestern.'

'He died at Clement Memorial.'

She exited the database. She started the tropical video again. She said, 'Don't care.' She shoved the last bite of hamburger into her mouth.

When Kelson got home, he fed Payday and Painter's Lane, then boiled spaghetti for a late dinner. He ate alone at the dining table, glancing now and then across the apartment at the window. Nothing happened outside the window – nothing he saw. 'Probably for the best,' he said. Payday rubbed against his ankle, then leaped into his lap. She sniffed at the table, sniffed at the marinara at the edge of the plate, and gave Kelson a dirty look. 'Probably for the best,' he said again.

After he scraped his plate into the garbage, he carried his phone to the window. The bitter cold kept most people inside, though a pickup truck idled at the curb across the street, its exhaust half obscuring it under the streetlights. 'The best,' he said.

Then he dialed Jose Feliciano.

'*Hola*,' the bull rider said after the third ring.

'I did it,' Kelson said. 'I went to Patricia Ruddig's building. I drove to Fort Wayne. I made an enemy of a cop I wasn't friends with to begin with. I asked the kind of questions a lot of people won't answer. This time they answered. They mostly told me nothing. Yeah, there's some strange stuff, but strange stuff happens all the time and that's all it is – strange stuff.'

'OK,' Jose said, sounding only a little discouraged. 'What's next?'

'Nothing's next. We're done. *I'm* done. You can send me the three hundred for a long day's work. It'll about cover gas and meals.'

'What's the "strange stuff," amigo?'

Kelson told him. The hit-and-run bicyclist and Patricia Ruddig's houseguests. Josh Templeton overshooting the exit for DePaul and the evidence of impact on both sides of his old Camry. The record showing Daryl Vaughn going to Northwestern Medical instead of Clement Memorial.

'*Muy bien*,' Jose said.

'*Muy* nothing.'

'This is what I thought. The same for all three.'

'No.' Kelson kept his voice low. 'It's not. It's totally different for each one. There wasn't a pattern before. There isn't a pattern now.'

'I think you aren't so smart, amigo. With all of them, something happened that shouldn't have.'

'That's why we call these things accidents,' Kelson said. 'No one means for them to happen, but they happen. Except with Daryl Vaughn. Someone meant to beat him up. Then, someone made a mistake with the records. Another accident.'

'Those weren't accidents,' Jose said. 'Who rides a bike on a sidewalk on New Year's Day? Who leaves a lady lying on the ground? Who hits a car and makes it crash? Who beats up a bum?'

'Jerks,' Kelson said. 'There're a lot of them around.'

'I'll come to your office in the morning,' Jose said.

'Why?'

'To bring your money. Three hundred dollars. And another nine hundred so you can keep asking questions. In the morning, you can tell me what's next.'

Kelson sighed. 'You're as exasperating as I am. I still don't get it. Why do you want this so much?'

'You'll never break the spirit of a bull that's worth riding, you understand?'

'No,' Kelson said. 'Not at all. I don't, and I don't appreciate your getting metaphorical with me.'

'If you have talent, you ride him eight seconds and you walk away without dying.'

'I'm sure that means something.'

'A man should always ride an animal bigger and meaner than he is. That's what the police who killed my sister's daughter were, but I can't fight them. That's what Clement Memorial is too. A great big bull. And we can do something about it. I rode some rank bulls – some of the meanest God ever made. You looked at their faces and you saw fire. I think Clement Memorial is a rank bull. You know why? It's almost invisible. How does a man ride a bull he can't see? I'm going to figure out how to ride it. You can be my flank man.'

'I think you're full of shit,' Kelson said.

Shortly before midnight, he turned out the lights. He went to the window again and looked down at the street. The exhaust-spewing pickup was gone. The streetlights shined on empty pavement.

He went to his bed and climbed in. Payday and Painter's Lane jumped on to the foot of the bed, kneaded the covers with their claws, and curled up to sleep.

He closed his eyes.

Then, outside in the freezing night, a green Land Rover turned the corner and drove toward Kelson's building.

Eyes closed in his bed, Kelson said, 'Goodnight, Payday. Goodnight, Painter's Lane. Goodnight, goodnight.'

The Land Rover paused in front of the building. A man gazed up through the windshield at Kelson's window. Then the Land Rover accelerated into the dark.

EIGHTEEN

In the morning, Jose Feliciano laid a roll of twenties on Kelson's desk.

'I can't take your money,' Kelson said.

'Mine to spend,' Jose said.

'Mine to refuse. I don't like robbing you or anyone else – no matter how deluded they are.'

'I have an idea, my friend. You take the money. You spend three more days asking questions. If you find out I'm right, you keep the money. If I'm wrong, you give the money back because you don't want to rob me.'

'Sounds like the risk is all mine.'

'Or you can keep the money. I don't mind risk.'

Kelson stared at him. Jose grinned back. Kelson picked up the roll of twenties. He slipped the rubber band off it and divided the money in two. He put the rubber band back around half of the bills and set them in front of Jose. He slid the others into his top drawer with the laptop. 'I'll put in one more day,' he said. 'If I find anything worth going after, you can pay me the rest, and I'll be on the job. If I don't find anything, I quit. You can throw your money at some other lost cause.'

'This time, you should get your partner to help.'

'DeMarcus? Now you're telling me how to do my job?'

'If he asked me a question, I would answer. That's all I'm saying. I'll pay him too.'

'Leave,' Kelson said. 'Let me give you a full day's work.'

'OK, amigo.' Jose stood up. 'I think today you'll get lucky.'

When Jose was gone, Kelson opened the top desk drawer again and stared at the twenties – money he didn't know how he would earn. Then he opened the bottom drawer and removed his Springfield. He popped out the magazine, checked that it was loaded, and snapped it back in place. He put the gun in the drawer.

Then his phone rang. He touched the answer button and said, 'I don't know.'

'Know what?' The caller was Caroline Difley, the blond orderly from Clement Memorial.

'Sorry,' Kelson said. 'What can I do for you?'

'I got the records.'

'What—?'

'The records,' she said. 'The supply room inventory. The missing medications.'

'Wow,' he said. 'Do you believe in magic?'

'What are you talking about?'

'Three minutes ago, I was told I would get lucky today.'

'I've had the records since yesterday afternoon. I didn't know if I should let you see them. You don't seem entirely dependable.'

'What made you decide?'

'The patient deaths. There's a problem. Can you meet me?'

'Right – yeah, of course.'

'In an hour,' she said. 'A restaurant called Kiko's, on Lincoln Avenue. Do you know it?'

'I can find it.'

'An hour,' she said.

'I don't believe in magic either. In case you're wondering.'

An hour later, Kelson walked into Kiko's Meat Market & Restaurant. Caroline Difley sat in a green vinyl booth across from a tall, round-shouldered man in his forties. The orderly had a cup of coffee, the tall man coffee and a plate with a meat pastry on it. The man slid to make room for Kelson, but Kelson pulled a chair from a nearby table and sat at the end of the booth. 'Because it's a little strange,' he said. 'With strangers.'

Caroline Difley glanced at the tall man and said, 'I told you.'

The man offered to shake Kelson's hand. 'Aleksandar Kovacic,' he said. He had an Eastern European accent.

'Aleksandar is head custodian at Clement Memorial,' the woman said. 'He got the records for me.'

Kovacic had a broad face. 'I have keys to every room.'

'Before he came from Bosnia,' the woman said, 'he studied medicine.'

'In Sarajevo,' he said. He touched his left arm at the same spot where Kelson wore a bandage over his gunshot wound. 'I have one of these also. From the fighting. Since then, I will not be a doctor. I have bloody dreams.' He smiled. 'I don't even like knives. I'm like a monk.'

'A monk who knows pharmacology,' the orderly said.

The man turned his broad face to her. 'I pay attention. That's all.'

A waitress came. She set a cup of coffee in front of Kelson without his asking and refilled the other cups. Kelson pointed at Kovacic's pastry and said, 'One of those, please.'

'Yes, sir,' the waitress said, with the same accent as Kovacic's.

The orderly said to Kovacic, 'Tell him what you found.'

'What I did *not* find,' he said. 'I did not find epinephrine. Twelve vials last August. Ten vials in September. Thirteen in November. All missing.'

Kelson considered that. 'One medicine? From what I hear, the people died different ways. Patricia Ruddig had a heart attack. Josh Templeton stopped breathing. Daryl Vaughn had something with the kidneys.'

'Renal failure,' the tall man said. 'Also a heart attack. Epinephrine overdose can do these things.'

'I thought doctors used it to save people,' Kelson said. 'EpiPens and all.'

'Yes, but too much can stop a heart. It can cause edema – the lung drowns. All the missing vials. It's enough.'

'Wouldn't the hospital detect the drug afterward?' Kelson said.

'Maybe.' Kovacic drank his coffee. 'Epinephrine is adrenaline. When bodies are hurt, they make adrenaline. When people have heart attacks or cannot breathe, doctors inject epinephrine. These dead people, they might have a lot of adrenaline, a lot of epinephrine. Maybe no one is surprised.'

The waitress brought Kelson his lamb *borek*. He forked a bite into his mouth. He said, 'The three of them would've had way too much in their blood, right?'

'Maybe,' Kovacic said. 'But doctors make mistakes. If the mistakes look like they happened when the doctors tried to save a life, maybe no one chooses to notice.'

Kelson wasn't convinced. 'Do *you* think someone killed these people?'

Kovacic raised his round shoulders. 'Maybe.'

Caroline Difley said, 'That's his way of saying yes.'

For twenty minutes, Kovacic explained his thinking. Epinephrine starts a heart after a heart attack, but can also damage the heart muscle. It relaxes airways and keeps a person from suffocating, but can also fill lung tissue with fluid. It makes blood vessels constrict, stopping kidney-destroying anaphylaxis, but in big enough doses can cause veins and arteries to collapse, injuring the kidneys or worse.

'Who'd've thought it?' Kelson said.

'There are other ways,' Kovacic said. 'Dilantin. It is for seizures. Heparin. It is a blood thinner.'

'Spooky stuff to know so much about,' Kelson said. 'You ever hear about arsonists who hang around to watch the fires they start? Or killers who volunteer their help as cops investigate a murder?'

'No, I have not heard of this.'

Caroline Difley looked angry. 'Aleksandar is the best person I know at the hospital. He's also one of the smartest. Don't accuse him. Don't even suggest—'

Kovacic gave Kelson a broad, confused look. 'Do you accuse me?'

'I'm just paying attention,' Kelson said. 'I'm not accusing anyone. I'm only starting to think there's anything to accuse someone of.'

The orderly said, 'Aleksandar could get in a lot of trouble for helping me – and you.'

Kelson acknowledged that with a nod.

'We could both lose our jobs,' she said.

'Thank you,' he said.

'It is nothing,' Kovacic said.

'No,' she said, 'it's a lot.'

After they paid their bills, they stepped outside together. An icy breeze blew down Lincoln Avenue. Kovacic wore a thick wool shirt but no sweater or coat.

'You need a ride?' Kelson said.

Kovacic shook his head. He didn't look at all cold. 'I live near here. By the Rosehill Cemetery. I like to walk in the cemetery before I go to work. I – what is your word? I *commune* with the people.'

'Sounds cold,' Kelson said. 'Do you have a friend or family there?'

Kovacic gave him a funny look. 'Why would I?'

'You commune with dead strangers?'

'The dead are never strangers,' Kovacic said.

NINETEEN

Kelson drove back to Clement Memorial talking to himself about Aleksandar Kovacic, epinephrine, lamb *borek*, angel-of-death killings, and the big black chunks of smoked beef called *suho meso* hanging from strings behind Kiko's meat counter. 'You could dangle it from a tree to catch a grizzly,' he said.

The hospital complex was mostly concrete and glass, built at a bend in the Chicago River. A circular helipad rose on spiderlike legs from the roof of the central building. Eight floors down, a circular drive led to a parking garage, the ER, and the main hospital entrance. In the middle of the drive, a fountain jetted water in the summer and sat empty the rest of the year.

Kelson cut from the drive into the parking garage, took a spot marked for families of patients, and walked the halls to the information desk.

'No,' the attendant said after calling the ICU, Dr Jacobson wasn't available. 'No,' Dr Madani wasn't either.

Kelson took the elevator to Jacobson's office anyway.

When he knocked, no one answered.

So he tried the knob – and the door opened.

Jeremy Jacobson sat at his desk, reviewing a chart. He had earbuds in his fleshy ears, and for a moment seemed lost in whatever he was listening to. Then he looked up, alarmed, and tugged the earbuds off. Before he could say anything, Kelson stepped inside and said, 'Epinephrine.'

'I'm – *what?*'

'Thirty-five vials missing since last summer.'

'What—?'

'Do the math.' Kelson closed the door.

'I'm sorry – I don't understand. Missing from where? And what are you doing here?'

'Medical supply. Missing from the hospital.'

'You know this, how?'

'Confidential sources – Caroline Difley and Aleksandar Kovacic.' He caught his breath. 'Dammit.'

Jacobson stared at Kelson. 'I honestly don't know what to make of you, Mr Kelson. We released you. We *discharged* you. We judged you well enough to send you home. And yet, you return day after day. There's really nothing more we can do for you.'

'Epinephrine.'

'I heard you the first time. And, like the first time, I have no idea what I'm supposed to do with that.'

'Patricia Ruddig, Josh Templeton, and Daryl Vaughn all died in ways that could have been caused by overdoses of epinephrine.'

'I doubt that very much,' the doctor said. He looked at his earbuds as if they might have an answer to the problem Kelson presented. 'Do you know what the most common cause of death from epinephrine is?'

'Heart attack?'

'Not even close. It's something you may know a little about after your brain trauma. It's cerebral hemorrhage.'

'Huh,' Kelson said.

Jacobson looped the cord on the earbuds and laid the coil on the chart. 'It used to be when new medical students toured the hospital, we asked them to diagnose patients after giving them a little information. The smartest and the least intelligent among them were quickest to offer their opinions. They were almost always wrong, the smart ones as often as the unintelligent ones. They drew conclusions too fast from too little information and after too little training. The smart ones would eventually learn better. The others failed out or, if they hung on and earned a degree, became incompetent and dangerous doctors. I emphasize the word dangerous. Now – and this is how what I'm telling you applies to you – it's not only the new doctors. It's everyone with access to the Internet, which is to say, nearly everyone. Smart people and dumb people think they know better than trained physicians. The smart ones eventually learn better. The dumb ones behave irresponsibly, even dangerously. They leap to conclusions. These conclusions can harm themselves and others.'

'Huh,' Kelson said again.

'Which are you, Mr Kelson – smart or dumb?'

'So you're saying heart attacks, asphyxiation, and kidney failure can't happen with epinephrine?'

'I'm afraid that was the wrong answer,' Jacobson said. 'I run a very busy part of this hospital. I don't have time to educate the uneducable.'

'Which is your way of saying all those things can happen.'

'Goodbye, Mr Kelson. I'd prefer you leave on your own instead of making me call security.'

'You mean, your son, Rick.'

'Rick doesn't tend to small problems. I'm sure he would send an assistant.'

'No need to bother,' Kelson said. 'But I was hoping you'd be concerned about what I told you.'

The doctor sighed. 'I don't mean to be harsh. I appreciate your concern' – he smiled, a little – 'at a certain level. But you must understand. You barge into my office. You don't know what you're talking about. You insinuate that on my watch—'

'I'm not insinuating.'

'You *are* insinuating.' He eyed Kelson as if he knew more about him than Kelson wanted him to know. He gave him

more of the smile. 'Sometimes when one's life has . . .' He
hesitated. 'What I'm saying is I sympathize. I understand what
it means to fall into the deep end, better than you might guess.
But you also need to understand, the way to get out isn't by
pulling others under with you.'

'You have a great smile,' Kelson said. 'Sympathetic.'

Jacobson looked unsure what to do. 'Goodbye, Mr Kelson.'

'You managed to duck my questions.'

'Perhaps there were no answers,' the doctor said. 'Perhaps
next time, before you walk uninvited into a man's office, you
should think about what you want to know more thoroughly.'

Two hours later, as Kelson sat in his own office with his KelTec
and Springfield on the desktop, his phone rang.

He answered, and Caroline Difley said, 'What did you say to
him?'

'What do you mean?'

'What did you *do*? Aleksandar and I just got fired.'

'Dammit,' Kelson said, 'I didn't mean to.'

'You didn't *mean* to? You just wrecked my life. And Aleksandar
– do you know what he's been through? Do you know what you
did to him?'

'I'm sorry – I couldn't help it.'

'*No*.' She sounded as if only her anger kept her from crying.
'That was unforgivable.' She hung up.

'Dammit, dammit, dammit,' Kelson said. He hated nothing
more than hurting people who loved him or did him good.

He drove home in the middle of the afternoon. He let himself
into the apartment, went into the bathroom, and stripped off his
clothes. He stared at the naked man in the mirror.

Then he peeled back the adhesive tape from the edges of the
bandage on his arm.

His arm was bruised and bloody and stained with antiseptic.
His guilt over Caroline Difley and Aleksandar Kovacic hurt more
than the gunshot wound.

He bent and straightened his fingers. 'The feeling is mostly back,'
he told his reflection. He bent and straightened his elbow. The motion
tugged at his sutures. 'Tingling. A little pain.' Payday came into the
bathroom, leaped on to the closed toilet seat, and watched him.

He wet a bath towel in the sink and washed the wounds on both sides of his arm. When the blood crust was gone from the surrounding skin, he dabbed the wounds until pink showed through the scabs. He stared at the mirror and let his arm dry. Then he bandaged himself with pads of cotton gauze and wrapped a strip of medical tape around them.

He pulled on his underwear and pants. Before putting on a T-shirt, he stared at his reflection. Blood showed on the cotton pads. 'Good for you, you bastard,' he said. 'Two down – how many to go?' He put on the T-shirt and a sweater.

Then he went down to the lobby and out into the cold. The sun hung bright in the winter sky. He went to his car, drove south through the city and, a half-hour later, pulled into the alley between the Ebenezer Baptist Church and DeMarcus Rodman's building.

TWENTY

Rodman's girlfriend Cindi gave Kelson a cup of tea. 'You're shivering, baby,' she said.

'I'm not cold.' He sat on the couch under the portraits of Malcolm X, Cindi, and Martin Luther King, Jr.

'That's worse,' she said. When he knocked at the door fifteen minutes earlier, she told him, 'DeMarcus is on a job with Marty LeCoeur – won't be back until midnight.' But she saw something in his eyes and invited him in. Now she said, 'I go to work in an hour. You can stay as long as you want, you know that, but maybe you should be with someone when you feel this way.'

'I'm all right,' he said.

'I've seen all right, and you aren't it.'

Cindi worked in maternity at Rush University Hospital. Lately they had her in neonatal with the preemies. She taped snapshots of the tiniest of them on the fridge. The babies were hooked to sensors and monitors, as helpless as chicks in incubators.

'I'm hoping you can do something for me,' Kelson said. 'I know a couple people who just got fired from hospital jobs. Could you put in a word for them at Rush?'

'What kind of jobs?'

'She was an ICU orderly. He was head custodian.'

'Kind of out of my area. What did they do to get fired?'

'Nothing,' Kelson said. 'I did it.'

She didn't look surprised. 'Are you sure they want you to do them any more favors?'

'I hate when I do this.'

'You can't help yourself, though, right?' she said. 'It's not your fault.'

'Whose is it? It shakes me. I hurt people.'

'Sure, but you do it while trying to do good.'

'Does that make a difference?'

'I guess it's better than trying to hurt them.'

For the next forty minutes, he told her the whole thing, from Jose Feliciano's belief that something terrible was happening at Clement Memorial, to the visits to Patricia Ruddig's and Josh Templeton's homes, to the conversation with Caroline Difley and Aleksandar Kovacic at Kiko's. He said, 'After I betrayed them, Jeremy Jacobson treated me like a sorry fool, which is what I deserved.'

Cindi never interrupted. Now she said, 'Good doctors go to the most likely cause first. Usually they're right, and to look in any other direction would be bad medicine. But sometimes, the most likely cause isn't the real cause. Then they need to keep poking at a problem until they get it.'

'You're saying you think Jacobson screwed up?'

She shook her head. 'I'm saying he did what he's supposed to do – he went to the obvious answer. But that doesn't mean the obvious one is the right one. Still, he'd be stupid to do anything else.'

'And me?'

'You'd be stupid to accept his answer if you think it's wrong.'

'He had a story about dumbasses like me jumping to conclusions.'

'He's wrong about that. You say a lot of stupid stuff – stuff you should keep to yourself – but when it comes down to it, you do the smart thing.'

Kelson thought about that. 'Have you heard about how I got banned from Big Pie Pizza for dancing naked on a table?'

'*Most* of the time, you do the smart thing.' She stood up. 'I've got to go. You want to hang out and wait for DeMarcus?'

Kelson stood too. 'I'll walk down with you.'

'If this woman and the custodian want, you can have them call me. I'll put them in touch with HR.'

'Thanks, Cindi,' he said. 'I'll spend an hour with you anytime.'

Kelson drove back through downtown. Cars, buses, and trucks – filthy with the spray of road salt and the greasy crud of winter – inched through the rush-hour streets. The sky was dark now, and the pavement glowed orange under the street-lights. 'Could be better,' Kelson said as he jammed the brakes to keep from rear-ending a van that stopped short of an intersection. Talking with Cindi had helped, but he still felt rotten.

He drove past his apartment building. 'I should be with someone,' he said. 'As if that ever mattered.'

The front porch lights were on at Nancy's house. 'As if she . . .' he said, and angled his car to the curb, walked up the front path, and rang the bell.

When Nancy opened the door, she seemed confused.

'Thought I'd stop by,' he said.

'You know you need to call first.' She gave him a second look. 'Are you all right?'

'*Daad.*' Sue Ellen ran from the kitchen.

Nancy spoke under her breath. 'Always call first.' She opened the door and let him in.

Sue Ellen saw he had both arms through his coat sleeves – and so she leaped.

He caught her with his good arm. 'I needed that,' he said.

'You,' Nancy said to her, 'are way too big to do that.'

Sue Ellen grinned at Kelson. 'I'm exponentially big.'

'Good math,' he said.

'Nonsense,' Nancy said. 'That's a complete misuse of the term.'

'I'm rationally irrationally too big,' Sue Ellen said.

'Works for me,' Kelson said.

'What do you need, Sam?' Nancy asked.

He lowered Sue Ellen to the floor. 'I was hoping we all might have dinner together.'

'*Yes*,' Sue Ellen said.

'You came, hoping I would feed you?' Nancy said.

'No – well, I guess, kind of. I thought it would be nice.'

'Nope,' she said. 'Not nice. Not nice to come without calling. Not nice to create false expectations.'

'She means me,' Sue Ellen said.

'Of course I mean you,' Nancy said.

'What false expectations?' Kelson said. 'I came because I had a hard day, and I thought—'

'You need to take your hard days elsewhere,' she said. 'That's the nature of – *this*.'

'She means being divorced,' Sue Ellen said.

Nancy shot her a warning look, then said to Kelson, 'Don't you get that?'

'Yeah,' he said. 'I get it.'

'Mom?' Sue Ellen gave Nancy a look of her own.

'I'll go,' Kelson said.

'*Mom?*' Sue Ellen said. Nancy would suffer repercussions.

'Jesus Christ,' Nancy said. 'Stay.'

'No,' Kelson said, 'I'll—'

'Goddammit, you'll stay for dinner,' she said. 'If you think you can set me up this way and then leave, you're wrong.'

Kelson stayed for dinner. He sat at one end of the table, Nancy at the other. Sue Ellen sat between them and acted as if they did this all the time.

Nancy knew better than to ask Kelson about his troubles. He told her about them anyway.

Then Sue Ellen said, 'What do you get if you teach a Vietnamese potbelly pig to lift weights?'

'Extra-strength bacon?' Kelson said.

She shook her head. 'Arnold Schwarzepigger.'

'You made that up,' Kelson said.

'What do you get if you cross a potbelly with an eighteen wheeler?' she said.

'Stop,' Nancy said.

'An oinker trailer,' Sue Ellen said.

Kelson and Nancy looked at her, blank faced.

Sue Ellen rolled her eyes. 'Like a *tanker* trailer?'

'I'll bet it's a road hog,' Kelson said.

'No dessert for anyone who says another word,' Nancy said.

Sue Ellen and Kelson both missed dessert.

When Sue Ellen went upstairs to do her homework, Kelson put on his coat and hat. 'Thank you,' he said. 'That meant a lot to me.'

'Let's not make a habit of it,' Nancy said. But she added, 'It was nice. Sue Ellen liked it.'

'Yeah,' Kelson said. 'Me too. I loved it.'

'We won't start that talk again,' she said.

'I wasn't – I just meant I liked it. No, I loved it. It. I know we can't have it.'

Nancy looked exhausted. 'Maybe now and then, we could. Not often. Dinner.'

'Yeah,' Kelson said. 'Dinner. Why not?'

'Now and then. For Sue Ellen.'

Kelson wanted to kiss her. 'It would be a terrible idea,' he said.

Nancy looked confused. 'Dinner would?'

'No,' he said, 'dinner would be great. Whenever. Wherever.' He rushed out into the cold night.

As he drove back to his apartment, he glanced in the mirror. His face smiled back. 'You son of a bitch,' he told it. But by the time he pulled into the parking lot behind his building, the letdown started. 'Never could,' he said. 'Not even now and then – because it's the time between that matters.'

He drove slowly over the icy pavement, turned at the end of a row, and slid his car into his space. For a minute, he left the engine running. He stared up through the dark windshield. He saw no moon. He saw no stars. 'For better or worse,' he said.

He cut the engine and got out.

Then, as he closed the door, an enormous weight hit him.

His body slammed against the side of his car. Pain shot down his injured arm into his fingers, radiated into his neck and chest.

Hands were on him. They held him against the freezing metal. They wrenched his arms behind him. He felt the stitches rip from his wounds. He cried out in pain. A thick-gloved hand slapped over his mouth.

A voice said, 'Shut the fuck up.'

The hands turned Kelson around, holding him against the car. Rick Jacobson gazed at him with fascinated anger.

Scott Jacobson stood a few feet away. He stared at the dark sky.

'I told you not to hassle my dad,' Rick said. 'And what do you do? You break into his office.'

'I didn't break—'

'I said, shut up. Don't make my job harder.'

'What *is* your job?' Kelson asked.

Rick Jacobson punched him in the ribs. It wasn't the punch of a professional or even an especially skilled fighter. It knocked the wind out of Kelson anyway.

'Please,' Rick said. 'Please don't ignore me.'

He turned his back on Kelson. If Kelson had been able to breathe – if he'd been able to use both of his arms and was clear-headed – turning away from him like that would've been a mistake. The brothers walked three cars down the row to their Land Rover. They got in and started the engine, and the car eased over the icy pavement to the exit.

TWENTY-ONE

K elson watched the tail lights as they moved to the end of the parking lot. He straightened his body – as much as he could without vomiting – and stumbled toward his building entrance. The warm liquid of his open wound snaked down his arm. 'The hell if I'll . . .' he said, and he turned around and stumbled back to his car.

When he pulled from his parking spot, the Land Rover was already at the stop sign at the end of the street. It turned and was gone.

Kelson hit the gas. His tires skidded on the ice and parking lot gravel. He nearly skinned the side of an Audi. He straightened the wheels, cut them the other way when the car slid again, and headed for the exit. He rounded on to the street without slowing. He hardly paused at the stop sign.

Three sets of tail lights shone in the distance. One vanished as a car turned at a corner. 'Play the odds,' Kelson said and, blowing through a red light, followed the other two.

The trickle from his wounds spread around his arm. The wet sleeve was tacky against his elbow. He flapped his arm to free it, and pain shot into his shoulder. 'Stupid, stupid, stupid.'

The cars he was following stopped at the next red light. He closed the gap. In front of him there was a silver Honda Accord. The car in front of it was the Land Rover.

When the light turned green, Kelson dropped back. No one who paid attention could miss his burnt orange Dodge Challenger. But the Jacobsons apparently weren't paying attention. 'Screwballs,' Kelson said. 'The stupid leading the stupid.'

He followed the Land Rover south and then west through the city. When other cars merged between them, he closed the distance. When the cars turned away, he dropped back a half block or more.

When the Land Rover turned on to West Carroll and drove into an area of empty warehouses and loft buildings, all other traffic disappeared. Kelson dropped back farther. The Land Rover slowed, and Kelson slowed. It stopped, and Kelson stopped. It sped forward for a half block before slowing again.

'Uh-oh,' Kelson said, and rolled forward. Had the Jacobson brothers spotted him?

Then the tail lights on the Land Rover went out.

Kelson stopped.

He turned off his headlights.

He turned his headlights on again.

He rolled down his window and cut his engine. Listened. Music – a bass beat, something electronic – floated over the sounds of the city.

'Huh.'

He started the car and rolled forward.

At the side of the street where the Land Rover first slowed, there was a dark-fronted brick building. In a recessed doorway, above a black door, a red cursive neon sign shined dully – visible only directly outside the entranceway. It said *Club Richelieu*.

The music was loud, clear – a techno beat. 'Shake, shake, shake,' Kelson said, 'enough to make hair stand on end.'

A half block farther, he passed the Land Rover. It was parked in the shadow of a dumpster. He turned the corner and pulled to the curb before a freight dock.

He touched his ribs – winced. He pinched his coat sleeve and sweater from his bloody arm. 'Who says I have bad judgment?' he said, and got out of the car.

As he walked back to the black door, blood spread like a stain across his wrist and on to his hand. So he stuck the hand into his coat pocket and kept it there.

He went into the recessed entrance, paid a twenty-dollar cover charge, and moved into an eddy of sound and ultraviolet light.

The waitresses and bartenders were women, all young, all with long hair, all dressed in white – white leather shorts, white halters, one in a weird white backless turtleneck dress. The DJ – in a tight white leather bikini bottom, a tiny white leather bikini top, and five-inch white stilettos – danced like she was on ecstasy. 'Look at that,' Kelson shouted to the waitress in the turtleneck. The waitress had dark hair, a square face, big lips with white lipstick, and painted-on eyebrows. 'How does she do that in those shoes? Like stilts.'

'Drink?' the waitress said.

'Anything with bourbon in it,' Kelson said.

'Woodford?' One of her dark eyes tilted inward, but they were great eyes.

'You have great eyes,' he said.

She went to the bar, and he scanned the room. The dance floor was painted with a black-and-white zigzag design, like static on an old TV. Couples – men with women, women with women, men with men, none of them older than thirty – danced as if they were internalizing the zig and the zag. A thick carpet of long white tassels hung from the ceiling over the bar. The liquor bottles glittered. The bartenders shook cocktail shakers.

Kelson scanned the men at the bar, the men on the dance floor. He didn't see Rick or Scott Jacobson. But at one end of the dance floor, a corridor led to VIP party rooms.

As he started toward it, the waitress returned. 'Hey, where're you going?' She had his bourbon on a little white tray.

He fished out his wallet. 'A question,' he said. 'Do you know who Rick Jacobson is?'

For unclear reasons, that made her laugh. 'Everyone knows Rick. He's the medicine man.'

'Is he? And his brother?'

'Scott? I'm not sure what *he* is.'

'Have you seen them tonight?'

She nodded at the corridor. 'You were going the right way.'

So he handed her a twenty and took his drink.

'Frida,' she said.

'What?'

'Frida. My name.'

'Oh,' he said. 'Thanks, Frida-with-the-great-eyes.'

'*You* have a screwy eye.' She wiggled a finger, tipped with white polish, at his drooping eye. 'But so do I and, anyway, you're cute.'

'No one ever calls me cute,' he said.

'You've got the Napoleon thing going with your hand and pocket.'

'I didn't know Napoleon was cute either.'

'I have a dog named Napoleon. A Maltese.'

'Lucky dog.'

She smiled. 'Let me know when you want another drink.'

Kelson went to the corridor.

The first doorway opened into a room where a single red-shaded lamp hung from the ceiling. A sectional couch extended around the walls. Couples were making out, reaching up each other's shirts, down each other's pants. 'The night is young,' Kelson said, and moved on.

The second doorway led into a room where groups of men and women talked and drank. A bar, smaller than the one in front, stood in a corner. The bartender – a flat-chested woman in a white halter top and white cowboy hat – mixed cocktails for a man who wore his shirt untucked and unbuttoned. A red, white and blue neon motorcycle hung on a wall across from the bar.

The Jacobson brothers stood in a group with four other men. They'd gotten rid of their coats and both brothers wore bright white shirts as if to play into the theme. Rick seemed to be telling the others a story. Kelson stepped behind him and slapped his bloody hand flat on his back.

Rick turned, grinning, seemingly expecting a friend. When he saw Kelson, he said, 'What the—?'

'I try not to miss a good party. What are you shielding your dad from?'

Rick managed to keep most of the grin. 'I don't know what you're—'

'What the hell, Rick?' one of the other men said. He and the others stared at the bloody print on the back of Rick's shirt.

Rick turned to them, like a dog chasing its tail. 'What?'

Scott saw Kelson's hand itself and looked distressed. 'I'm so sorry . . .'

Still unaware, Rick said to Kelson, 'I don't know where you get off coming in here.' He glanced at his friends, forcing the grin. 'This guy – *this guy* . . .' He seemed unsure what to say about him.

'I'm sorry,' Scott said again and he moved toward Kelson as if he meant to help.

Now Rick saw Kelson's hand. 'What the hell did you do to yourself?'

'Why are you protecting your dad? Why's it so important to keep me away from him?'

Rick sensed the opening and grinned at his friends. 'Because you're a sicko. Coming here all bloodied up—'

'I'm so sorry,' Scott said.

'Shut up,' Rick said to him.

The other men looked unsure what to make of the confrontation. One of them said, 'You've got blood on you, Rick.' He pointed at the back of Rick's shirt.

Rick tugged the fabric to see. 'Ah, shit. Why'd you do that?'

'Are these your friends, Rick?' Kelson said. 'Or do they hang around with you because you hand out pills? How much time do you spend in the hospital supply room?'

For a moment, Rick was speechless. Then he said, 'This guy – is insane. What the hell are you talking about?'

'Why do they call you the medicine man?'

Rick let out a long breath. He was back in control. 'Um – because my dad's a doctor.' He glanced at the others. 'And when this place was about to go out of business last year I told him it was a good investment. He listened to me.' He quieted as if he knew the confrontation was over and he'd won it. 'And now look around. Profitable for seven out of the last eight months. I made it feel all better. I got it the medicine it needed – cash.'

'Oh,' Kelson said.

'Yeah,' Rick said. 'But what do I do with *oh*? *Oh* won't do me any good. It won't clean my shirt. It won't buy me a drink. It won't get me laid.' He nodded at a thick-shouldered man who'd watched from a spot by the bar. 'Want to know one of the benefits of being the medicine man?'

The thick-shouldered man sauntered over. He wore white jeans and a tight white T-shirt.

Rick said, 'Would you please escort this gentleman the hell out of here?'

'No problem,' the thick-shouldered man said.

'Hands off,' Kelson said to the man, and they walked together out the corridor and across the dance floor.

When Kelson reached the hostess stand, he glanced back into the room. Frida was staring at him from the bar. He waved at her with his good hand, and she gave him a long, funny smile. The thick-shouldered man shoved him, and he was back out in the cold.

TWENTY-TWO

Kelson called Jose Feliciano from his car. It was eleven p.m., and Jose was an hour into a night shift. Kelson said, 'How are you with stitches?'

'I don't know, man. I got seventy-eight in my leg after the rankest bull in Shiprock, New Mexico, hung me up on its horns. Never liked stitches much after that – getting them or taking them out – but I've done both. What's up?'

'I need some patching. If I can, I need it without a lot of questions – because I'll answer everything I'm asked.'

'You find out something?'

'Yeah, I found out it's a bad idea to get your arm twisted when you have stitches in it. I found out it's bad to get punched in the ribs – anytime. I found out Rick Jacobson has serious daddy issues.'

'I don't know about that. How bad are you?'

'I've been better. Mostly I look like a mess.'

'I've got a break at midnight. Meet me downstairs at the hospital. We'll fix you up.'

* * *

At midnight, Kelson and Jose rode an elevator up past the ICU. They got out at a floor of offices and went through a series of corridors. They walked past a lounge with a half-dozen empty armchairs, a sink, a refrigerator, and a microwave. Deep in the hospital, it was neither day nor night, neither summer nor winter, neither Chicago nor elsewhere.

Jose stopped at a door and knocked gently.

Dr Madani opened it. Her eyes had the startled look of a person who rarely saw direct light. She shook her head at Jose, looked at Kelson, and shook it some more. She glanced at Kelson's hand and sighed.

When they were inside with the door closed, she told Kelson to take off his coat. Framed photographs of canyons and mountains from the American Southwest hung on the walls. On one side of the office, there was a daybed with an airline pillow and a blue and white crocheted blanket for naps when the doctor had double shifts.

Kelson pulled his coat off. 'Thanks for—'

She held a finger to her lips. 'No. I don't want to hear it. I'm insane for doing this.'

There was a suture tray on her desk. She used a pair of scissors to cut off Kelson's sweater and shirtsleeve. His arm looked dyed red from his shoulder to his fingertips.

'If Jose didn't convince me it was necessary,' the doctor said, 'you'd be nowhere near here.'

'Jose's persistent if not persuasive,' Kelson said.

She pointed at an office chair. 'Sit. Don't get blood on the desk.'

He sat, raising his arm.

She considered his bloody hand, then peeled the bandage from his upper arm. She inspected the wounds. 'In general, when we discharge patients, we expect them to take care of themselves.' Using toothed forceps, she plucked out bits of broken suture.

'Ouch,' Kelson said.

'You want the battlefield treatment, you get it.' She used gauze and antiseptic to clean the wounds. She irrigated them with a syringe and saline. She dried them with more gauze.

'Ouch,' he said again.

'We expect people to follow our protocols. When they don't

. . .' She took a length of fresh suture and drove the needle into Kelson's arm.

'Ouch.'

'Have you been taking your antibiotics?'

'Ouch. Yes.'

When she finished stitching his wounds, she dressed them with sterile pads and wrapped the pads in gauze tape. 'Not as bad as it could've been,' she said. 'Worse than it should be. Do yourself a favor. Take care of yourself this time.'

Kelson lifted and lowered his arm. He bent and unbent his elbow. The sutures tugged.

Dr Madani handed him his coat.

'Tell me about the Jacobsons,' he said.

'Jeremy's family? What about them?' she said.

'What's up with them? His boys are sensitive about him. I can set off Rick Jacobson by walking into the same room where his dad's been breathing.'

'You don't know his story?' she said. 'He lost his wife eight years ago. It was in the news. Bad circumstances – an accident involving Scott. Jeremy broke down for a while. The whole family did – Rick was nineteen, I think, Scott fifteen. It hit Scott hardest, of course. I don't know all the details, but I know Rick held them together through the worst of it.'

'Huh,' Kelson said, 'and I was thinking of ways to break his nose.'

She gave him a look.

'I mean, after my arm heals.'

'Terry Ann – Jeremy's wife – was twenty years younger than he was. He was in his early forties when they met, and I think she was his first love. I didn't know him before they were together, but I understand he was hard to work with. I don't know that she *completed* him, but once he was with her and they had their boys, he softened. What you see now is quite different from what he was when they were together.'

'I was pretty impressed by him when we talked,' Kelson said.

'I started here ten years ago. You should've seen him then.'

'Before he fell into the deep end,' he said.

'Exactly.'

*　*　*

'What do you think, amigo?' Jose said, as he and Kelson rode the elevator down.

'I think my arm aches and my ribs hurt. And I'm starting to get a nasty headache.'

Jose said, '*I* think I'll pay you the rest of the money and you can keep looking.'

'I think I'm wiped out and I'm going home to sleep. I'll put in a little more time. Something isn't right, though I don't know it's wrong the way you think it is. I'll call you tomorrow and let you know how things stand. In the meantime, if you see Rick Jacobson, punch him in the nose for me.'

'I want to keep my job, *compadre*,' Jose said, and he wished him a good night.

Kelson walked alone to the parking garage, taking the stairs to the second level.

When he came out of the stairwell, Scott Jacobson was standing by his Dodge Challenger.

'Really?' Kelson scanned the shadows between the other cars. He didn't see Rick Jacobson. He moved sideways to get another perspective. Still no Rick Jacobson.

'I'm alone,' Scott said.

Kelson ducked low and looked under a van near his car.

'Rick stayed at Richelieu,' Scott said. 'I had to get out of there.'

'How'd you know I was here?' Kelson stayed in the open space.

'I didn't. When I pulled into the garage, I saw your car.'

'Then why'd you come here – if not for me?'

'I'm sorry – for tonight – for Rick,' Scott said. 'He does that. I wish he wouldn't. He makes things worse – most of the time. You asked what he's protecting our dad from.'

'Right. But I just heard about it—'

'He's protecting Dad from himself. If you want the truth. Dad's his own worst enemy.'

Kelson nodded. 'I sympathize.'

Scott gave him a simple smile. 'He takes everything personally. Even if he has no control over it.'

'*I* talk when I should shut up,' Kelson said. 'And sometimes when I look in a mirror, I'm surprised by the face that looks back.'

'That's unusual.' Scott moved out from between the cars.

Kelson took a step back before realizing Scott meant to go to the stairwell.

'I'm sorry about Rick,' Scott said again.

'I'll get over it.'

Scott stopped in front of him, almost shyly. 'But you impressed your server. Frida. No one at Richelieu ever takes on Rick.'

'I think he came out on top.'

'I hope you feel better. I honestly do.' His eyes were vacant – but pleasant.

Kelson said, 'After your mom died, what did they do to you? Or were you always this way?'

Scott gave him a soft-lipped smile. Then he walked to the stairwell and disappeared through the door.

TWENTY-THREE

The next morning, Kelson called Rodman and filled him in on what he'd done since they last talked.

'Busy boy,' Rodman said. 'Some men go from trouble to trouble like it's the only air they breathe. Anything I can do?'

'D'you want to help canvass the streets around Wacker where Daryl Vaughn hung out? I want to know what he did to get himself beat up.'

'Sure. Maybe I can keep you from talking too much and getting beat up again too.'

'Fat chance. One other thing. Jose Feliciano says he'll pay both of us. He says he's thick with prize money from his rodeo days, but I don't know. If he doesn't pay, I'll split whatever I get with you – mostly nickels and dimes so far.'

'Maybe we could rethink our business model.'

'Also, Rick Jacobson worries me. Maybe we could visit him together.'

'Trouble to trouble,' Rodman said.

Forty minutes later, Kelson picked him up at his Bronzeville apartment. As they drove to the Loop, Kelson asked about his night with their friend Marty LeCoeur.

'We did an intervention with Cindi's baby brother,' Rodman said. 'No more guns and liquor store robberies for him. I tried talking to the kid myself and he blew me off. But I put him in a room with Marty, and I swear to God the kid came out terrified.'

Marty had been a bookkeeper at Westside Aluminum until he came into big money the previous spring. *Illegal money, technically*, he said if you asked, *but anyone who says dirty money stinks never smelled dirty money*. He was tiny and had only one arm after goofing around in a railyard as a kid. But he was the most vicious man Kelson had ever met, capable of taking apart a roomful of men three times his size. Which supposedly he'd done once or twice.

'Marty's like if a wasp climbs inside your ear,' Rodman said. 'What're you going to do but pray it flies out on its own? Cindi's brother whimpered after they talked. He asked me to take him home – like he'd lock himself in his room and play with toys. I asked if he had any weapons he wanted to give me. He said, "Yes, sir," and he brought out two pistols and a sonofabitch semi-automatic Barrett carbine.'

'Did he use them in his liquor store robberies?'

'I didn't ask and didn't want to know.'

'If the cops find you with any more hot guns, Ed Davies won't be able to talk you out of jail.'

'How're they going to find guns at the bottom of the river?'

'Good call.'

'Except the carbine. I need to study that baby before ditching it.'

'Bad call.'

'Yeah, and tell me again how *you* spent the night?'

'Sure, but I'm brain damaged – I have an excuse.'

They left Kelson's car at a self-park garage at Clark and Wacker and split up, Rodman heading east toward Michigan Avenue, Kelson toward the West Loop.

On a cold January morning, most homeless men and women huddled by vents and warm grates on the lower level streets. But Kelson started up in the sunlight.

He stopped by a woman, wrapped in layers of rags, who panhandled under the El tracks at Wells and Wacker. 'Do you know Daryl Vaughn?' he asked.

She stared without seeming to see him.

'Daryl Vaughn?' he said again. 'Got hurt last month. Beat up. Went to the hospital. Never came back.'

Her gaze drifted up and off, as if she watched a bird fly out of his head.

He dropped a five-dollar bill in her box of change.

'Bless you,' she said.

Kelson walked onward, crossing under the El tracks at Franklin Street as a train roared past.

He turned around and went back to Wells Street, where he descended a set of slick concrete stairs to Lower Wacker. On the lower level, Wacker divided into three sections – fast westbound lanes, fast eastbound lanes, and, inside a concrete barrier that opened only at intersections, a slow eastbound lane with street-side parking. The cars shooting along the echoing street and the sound of trucks rumbling overhead on Upper Wacker disoriented Kelson, and he stood for a moment in the concrete cavern with eyes as lost as the panhandler's.

Then he rushed across the fast lanes and stepped between parked cars to the basement wall of a building that rose into a sky he couldn't see. He edged along the wall, moving east again.

He came to an encampment where two men had arranged sleeping bags and plastic sacks of their possessions. They wintered here in the thick of the cavernous fumes, mostly out of sight from drivers. One of the men – dark skinned, with a long, tangled beard – lay in a sleeping bag with his eyes wide open, watching the other. The other – crouching, pale, beardless, younger than the man in the sleeping bag – tore the side of a large cardboard box into shreds, dropping the pieces into a mound on the oily pavement.

'Yep,' Kelson said. 'I know the feeling.'

The pale man said, 'I don't do it with white men.'

'Fine with me,' Kelson said.

'Entitled bastards.'

'You seem to know what you're talking about.'

The man snatched another side of cardboard and tore it. 'What do you want?'

'Do you know Daryl Vaughn?'

'Black or white?'

'To tell the truth, I don't know,' Kelson said.

'I don't do it with white men.'

'Right. He lived around here. Then some guys beat him up.'

The man said nothing. He tore and tore.

'He died,' Kelson said.

The man stopped tearing. He stared at the mound of ripped cardboard.

'At the hospital,' Kelson said. 'Not here. He died there.'

The man dug a blue Bic lighter from his pocket. He flicked it with his thumb. He held the flame to the mound. When a piece of cardboard caught fire, he held the flame to another, and then another. Then he held his hands over the flames to warm them.

'That makes sense,' Kelson said. 'I guess.'

The man in the sleeping bag said, 'I knew Daryl.'

'Yeah?'

'Black.' He nodded at the man who started the fire. 'But Jimmy never did him.'

'I don't do everyone,' the pale man said.

'That would be asking a lot,' Kelson said. He asked the man in the sleeping bag, 'Were you around when he got beaten up?'

'Nah. Heard about it. A couple punks.'

'Guys who live down here?'

'Why would guys who live here shit in their own bed? A couple white kids with baseball bats. Sixteen, seventeen years old. Probably took their mom's car and drove in from the suburbs. Went hunting for black men in the city.'

'It's not *all* about black and white,' said the one at the fire. 'I would do a white guy if the situation was right.'

The one in the sleeping bag said, 'The kids with baseball bats always go after us black guys.'

'You're obsessed with racism,' said the other.

The one in the sleeping bag sat up. 'That's like telling a man who's on fire he's obsessed with water. These white kids come in to get their rocks off. Happens every couple months. Happened to Brianna.'

'Brianna?' Kelson said.

'My wife till she died.'

The one at the fire said, 'You never had a wife, faggot.'

'Common law,' the other said.

'You never had anything in law.'

'Who saw the kids beating Daryl Vaughn?' Kelson asked.

'The professor,' said the man in the sleeping bag.

'The who?' Kelson said.

'The professor. Him and Daryl hung out.'

An enthusiastic voice spoke behind Kelson. 'Speak of the devil.'

Three more people approached.

A stout, round-faced, red-haired man with bad skin and wire-rimmed glasses pushed a shopping cart. A waiflike woman with bowl-cut hair shuffled behind him in black Converse high tops. Behind them both, Rodman showed Kelson his hands as if to say, *Who'd've thought?*

The man in the sleeping bag nodded at the stout one and said, 'Meet the professor.'

After the introductions, Kelson asked about Daryl Vaughn.

The stout man said, 'Do you ever worry you're only a character in someone else's book?'

Kelson shook his head. 'Nope. One of the few things I don't get.'

'It happened to Daryl,' the professor said, as a truck rumbled over them on Upper Wacker. 'Daryl could be very convincing in his narratives. Like a talented mime. People credit Marcel Marceau as the best, but I refer to Jean-Gaspard Deburau in his time with *Le Théâtre des Funambules*. You could almost see the walls he believed in – Daryl, not Deburau. You could almost hear imaginary people talking back to him.'

'Was he schizophrenic?' Kelson said.

The professor laughed. 'Who isn't, a little? In a time of late capitalism. Who *isn't* divided from himself or herself?'

Kelson said, 'You're confusing me.'

'These are the dangers,' the professor said.

'Whose story did Daryl think he was part of?' Rodman asked.

'One need not be a Freudian to know the answer,' the professor said.

The waifish woman spoke. 'A father figure.'

'The father figure of Daryl's dreams ran the whole show,' the professor said. 'Daryl believed he was a scripted character in this man's story. In this sense, he might have been more enlightened than most people. Who's to say who's schizophrenic when the mad men run the asylum?'

'You'd be a lot of fun at a party,' Kelson said.

The professor bowed. 'After the young men beat Daryl, I went to see him at Northwestern, but he was already—'

'Not at Clement Memorial?' Kelson said.

'That's where Northwestern sent him when they kicked him out.'

'Huh. Why'd they kick him out?'

'I can't answer that,' the professor said, 'other than to note the obvious about corporate health care. I also can't tell you why Clement Memorial took him, other than to surmise that they have a policy.' He said *policy* with a flourish.

'Huh.'

The professor leaned in. 'Did you know that "huh" is a universal word?'

'A what?'

'Almost every language has it or a variant of it.'

'Nope,' Kelson said, 'I didn't know that.'

'It's a good word,' the professor said. 'A word for a universal man.'

TWENTY-FOUR

K elson and Rodman went to Kelson's office and told each other the stories they'd heard as they canvassed the streets. 'That was one whacky dude,' Rodman said.

'I'm not a universal man?'

'No, you're pretty much one of a kind.'

'You think there's anything to what those guys said?'

'I believe the thing about the white kids coming in with baseball bats,' Rodman said. 'Every word of it. Why'd they go after Daryl Vaughn instead of someone else? A black man's a target for scum like them. A *homeless* black man's a powerful magnet. A homeless black man who's talking with imaginary friends? Irresistible. I wish his getting beat up meant more than that we live in the world we live in. But you know what's weird?'

'Changing hospitals like he did?' Kelson said.

'Yeah. Who ever heard of a hospital inviting in a charity case like Daryl Vaughn? He wasn't a baby with a cleft lip. Wasn't a damned Siamese twin. No good press – just a dirty bum. How'd Northwestern convince Clement Memorial to take him off their hands? How'd he even get from one place to the other? You think he stumbled across the city all broken up the way he was? You think he called a cab or an Uber? He must've cost a lot of money in the shape he was in – money he wouldn't repay.'

'My thinking too,' Kelson said. So he took his phone and dialed.

The line rang four times and bounced to voicemail.

He hung up and dialed the same number again.

'What're you doing?' Rodman said.

'Waking up a bull rider. He worked the nightshift.'

This time, on the third ring, Jose picked up. *'Hola.'*

'Did I wake you?' Kelson said.

'Yeah, amigo.'

Kelson held the phone away and told Rodman, 'He was sleeping.'

'What's that?' Jose said.

'How did Daryl Vaughn get to Clement Memorial?' Kelson said.

'I don't know, man – in an ambulance, I guess. His legs were wrecked. His hip was shattered. He came in on a gurney.'

'How does that make sense? Northwestern Medical had him first. Why would they send him to you?'

'I don't know about that. Northwestern does trauma. We do trauma. Never heard of them sending us anyone.'

'Who would arrange to bring him over?'

'I don't know,' he said again. 'Could be a doctor. But they'd need to get the approvals. No one wants a poor man.'

'Is there anyone at the hospital I could talk to and find out?'

'It's all paperwork. Admissions. Insurance. I know a girl in Transport Services. They do the helipad and work with AZT.'

'What's AZT?'

'Ambulance company we contract with. If, like, we need to take a burn victim to the unit at Cook County, we fly them or call AZT.'

'Can you talk to your friend in Transport Services or put me in touch with her?'

'Yeah, maybe I better do it – I heard about Caroline and

Aleksandar. I'll see what I can find out about admissions too.'
He sounded like he wanted to go back to sleep.

'One more thing,' Kelson said. 'How did Patricia Ruddig and
Josh Templeton end up at Clement Memorial? Patricia Ruddig
got hit by the bike in Ravenswood, and Josh Templeton crashed
in Lincoln Park. That's five or six miles apart – and another six
or seven miles from the hospital. Do you usually get patients
from those neighborhoods?'

'That's not how it works. If a hospital does a special thing
– like burns at Cook County – the ambulances maybe try to take
you there. If it's a big emergency, they take you to whatever's
closest. If you've got time, they take you where you want to go.
If this was a big emergency, we might get Ravenswood. Lincoln
Park would probably go somewhere else.'

'When I talked to the deskman in the building where Patricia
Ruddig lived, he said an ambulance came fast – almost before
she hit the ground.'

'I don't know about that,' Jose said again. 'Usually it's like
ten or fifteen minutes. Maybe it was coming from another job.'

'Ask your friend about Patricia Ruddig and Josh Templeton
too?'

'Sure thing.'

They hung up, and Kelson told Rodman, 'He'll let me know.'

'You ready to talk to your pal Rick?'

'Talking isn't my first impulse.'

'That's why you have a friend like me – to keep you from
your impulses.'

A half-hour later, they walked into the Clement Memorial
lobby and checked the directory. They rode an escalator down
to the basement and walked past an imaging lab and a cafeteria.
A double set of gray industrial doors led to a hallway with signs
for Physical Facilities, Laundry, and Security.

They passed Physical Facilities, passed a long interior window
inlaid with wire mesh, and came to the security office.

A woman in jeans and a yellow sweatshirt sat at a reception
desk. She looked up from her phone when Kelson and Rodman
came in.

'Could we see Rick Jacobson?' Kelson said.

She had an expression that made her look as if she was used
to being disappointed. 'I'm afraid he's in a meeting.'

'Until?'

'He didn't say. Sorry.' She didn't look sorry.

'Where?' Rodman said.

'Out of the hospital. He's attending to another business interest.'

'Yeah? What kind of business interest?' Rodman asked.

'I'm afraid I can't share that information,' she said.

'Never mind,' Kelson said. 'I think I know his business.'

Even in the bright light of winter noon, the warehouse district around Carroll Street was bleak. The red neon sign at Club Richelieu was off. With its dark, yawning entranceway, the building looked bored by its own existence.

Four cars were parked outside – the Jacobsons' green Land Rover, a silver Porsche, a little red BMW, and a banged-up red Ford Fiesta. Kelson pulled into a space by the Land Rover.

Rodman followed him into the entranceway and through the black door into the nightclub. The all-white bar and furniture, which had glowed ultraviolet the previous night, looked dingy under regular lighting. Two standing fans, positioned at the doorway to the corridor leading to the VIP party rooms, blew across the big main room, but the air still stank of spilled drinks, sweaty bodies, and piney floor detergent.

Three people sat together at the bar. A skinny, black-haired woman nursed an iced drink with a lime in it. She laid a hand on the leg of the man next to her – a Sean Penn lookalike but with jet-black hair. As she kneaded his thigh with her fingertips, he drank a Coke and talked with Rick Jacobson, who drank beer from a glass. On the other side of the bar, Frida the waitress arranged glasses on a white shelf.

She looked up when Kelson and Rodman walked in. She smiled in surprise and started to speak, then seemed to realize Kelson had come for someone other than her. Kelson said, 'Hey there,' then remembered why he'd come.

Rodman moved in. 'Rick Jacobson?' His voice couldn't be gentler.

The skinny woman kept nursing her drink. The two men turned. Neither seemed intimidated by Rodman.

'Which is a mistake,' Kelson said.

Jacobson frowned. 'Who wants to know?'

'I'm DeMarcus Rodman.' He offered to shake hands. Usually, his soft voice made people want to lean in. Usually, his enormous hands made them recoil.

Jacobson showed no reaction.

The black-haired Sean Penn, watching with lips parted, offered to shake hands too. 'I'm Jeffrey Vargas. I own this place. What can I do for you?' His teeth looked expensive.

'My ex is a dentist,' Kelson said.

'I'm sorry?'

'Your teeth – whitened, right? I've been tempted. But whenever a dentist sticks fingers in my mouth, I think of Nancy – and it gets complicated. Plus, whitening might be working it too hard for a guy like you. Too obvious. Like walking around with your zipper down. Is the Porsche yours?'

Rodman put a hand on Kelson's shoulder. 'Sam . . .'

'Right – sorry. So,' he said to the man, 'Rick's daddy saved you by investing in the nightclub?'

Vargas looked amused. 'We have a financial agreement.'

'Well, congratulations on your success. Great looking place when you dim the lights.'

The man looked at Rodman. 'What can I do for you? We don't open until nine tonight, but if you'd like a drink . . .' He signaled Frida, who drifted over.

Rodman gazed at Rick Jacobson. 'We came by so I could meet *this* man. Sam told me about him – made me curious. We went to the hospital looking for him, but they said he was at a meeting off site. Sam knew right away where to look next. Sam's smart that way.'

Frida eyed Kelson. 'What can I get you to drink, Sam?'

'Huh,' Kelson said.

'Yeah, he's smart, all right,' Jacobson said.

'I should warn you,' Kelson said to the waitress, 'I have few inhibitions.'

Most women retreated when Kelson started talking. The waitress smiled, as if she got a kick out of him. 'D'you promise?'

'None, really,' he said. 'No inhibitions, to tell the truth – as I do.'

'Sounds exciting,' she said.

Rodman said, 'That's one word for it.'

'Who names a kid *Frida*?' Kelson asked.

The waitress looked used to the question. 'My mom digs Frida Kahlo's paintings.'

'You don't look like a Frida.'

'What my mom says too. I'm a disappointment.'

'Then, a Sprite, please,' he said. 'How about you, DeMarcus?'

'Not what we came for,' Rodman said. 'Smart, but easily distracted.'

Kelson turned back to Jacobson. 'What are the rules about contracting with an ambulance company?'

That unsettled Jacobson more than Rodman's handshake. 'The rules – about what?'

'Come on, you're Director of Security. You deal with rules all the time. Maybe a mom and dad go bonkers because their kid died. What's the rule? Do you calm them down or get the cops to take them away? Maybe an upstanding citizen ODs and you need to keep it quiet. Maybe a dying gangbanger wants one last good time with his girlfriend, no nurses peeking. You must face hard questions every day. What are the rules? What counts as right and wrong when you contract with an ambulance company?'

'You're a bewildering man,' Jacobson said.

'Let's say it's a burn victim,' Kelson said. 'Since you have a contract, the ambulance brings the victim to you first instead of the burn unit at Cook County – because the victim is rich, and the company knows you'll get insurance money. Then maybe you pay the company a second time later for a ride to Cook County if the burn victim needs it.'

'That would never happen,' Jacobson said.

'Or let's say the company is named AZT, and you pay them to bring in a patient who it makes no sense to have – for reasons I, for one, can't figure out. But what's good for AZT is good for Clement Memorial and what's good for Clement Memorial is good for AZT.'

Jacobson stared until Kelson finished. 'I'm not sure what you're accusing Clement Memorial of.'

'Me either, to tell the truth,' Kelson said. 'Which, as I told Frida, I do – I tell the truth. Which might be my point.'

Frida set a glass on the bar. 'Your Sprite.'

He asked, 'Do *you* paint?'

She showed him her fingernail polish. 'I did body paint once at a contest in Key West. I got third prize. Jell-O shots for the night. I ended up having my stomach pumped. I can't win.'

'I know the feeling. We should get together sometime.'

Vargas stared at Rodman. 'What the hell?'

Rodman shrugged and said to Jacobson, 'From now on, keep your hands off Sam.'

Jacobson smirked. 'So this is an intimidation visit?'

'That's about it,' Rodman said.

'As long as your boy stays away from my family, we've got no problem,' Jacobson said.

'No, we've got no problem unless you make a problem.'

Jacobson turned away and handed Frida his glass for a refill.

The black-haired Sean Penn frowned at Rodman. 'Let's keep trouble out of my club, OK?'

Ninety-nine percent of the time, Rodman lumbered away from a conflict. The other one percent, there would be blood, bodies, and crime scene tape. If the cops learned about his involvement, he might need to go into hiding until the blood was washed away.

This time, he said, 'C'mon, Sam – let's get out of here,' and he lumbered toward the door.

Kelson said to Frida, 'I'll come by.'

'Do,' she said.

He followed Rodman out into the cold. When he started the car, he realized Rodman was grinning at him. 'What?' he asked.

Rodman shook his head. 'I love going places with you.'

TWENTY-FIVE

'Yeah,' Rodman said as they drove back toward his apartment, 'something's screwy with Rick Jacobson.'

'I don't think you scared him.' The early-afternoon sky shimmered as if ice crystals hung high toward the sun. But the streets were gray, the exhaust from the bus they followed thick and brown.

'Some guys you meet and you know they're off,' Rodman said. 'Nothing particular stands out. They look normal. They talk normal. They act normal. But you know it.'

Kelson said, 'Vargas seems OK, though.'

'You see what his girlfriend was doing to him?'

'No.'

''Cause you were too busy getting it on with Frida.'

'I like her.'

'The girlfriend was kneading Vargas's thigh with her finger-nails. Weird kink or something. He didn't seem to mind.'

'I didn't see.'

'Pay attention next time.'

'I paid attention.'

'To Frida.'

'I like her.'

When they climbed the stairs to Rodman's apartment, Marty LeCoeur was lying on the couch with his eyes closed. The paintings of Malcolm X, Cindi, and Martin Luther King Jr watched over him. Before coming into money, Marty shopped at TJ Maxx. Now he bought designer – Ralph Lauren pants, Versace socks, and a variety of Nat Nast bowling shirts.

'Who ever heard of a one-armed bowler?' Kelson asked a week before Renshaw shot him.

'Woody Harrelson,' Marty said.

'What?'

'You never seen *Kingpin*? Woody Harrelson's a one-handed bowler. Hooks up with this Amish guy—'

'A pretend role, Marty. Woody Harrelson's got both hands.'

'Doesn't.'

Kelson looked for help. 'DeMarcus?'

'Don't put me in the middle.'

Now, lying on the couch, Marty opened his eyes and let his gaze wander from Kelson's good arm to his wounded one. 'Hey, gimp,' he said, 'who's laughing now?'

'I never laughed at you, Marty,' Kelson said. 'Never would.'

'You lacked sensitivity.' He sat up, wiggled his toes in his socks, and slid his tiny feet into a pair of Gucci loafers. 'When I heard about Renshaw, I hoped you'd lose your arm too. With the problems you got with your head, it would be nice to look down on someone.'

'You already do more with one arm than most men could do with four,' Kelson said.

'Who ever heard of a four-armed man?' Marty said.

'Woody Harrelson?'

Marty grinned at him with his little teeth. Which meant they were friends and he wouldn't kill him.

'Which is good,' Kelson said.

'It's all good,' Marty said, then told Rodman, 'I took apart the Barrett carbine and put it together again.'

Kelson mumbled, 'One-handed.'

'That's a fucking killing machine,' Marty said. 'What did Cindi's brother want with it? Young kid, his balls don't drop yet – what's he think, this gun's going to make him a man?'

'I think that explains it,' Rodman said.

'If he pulls the trigger on that motherfucker, his balls'll shrink like he's swimming in ice. The kid's misguided.'

'You didn't know that when you talked to him last night?' Rodman said.

'I just thought you wanted me to scare the fuck out of him.'

'By explaining to him how misguided he was.'

'You do it your way, I do it mine. Hey, I hope it's OK I crashed on your couch while I waited. Cindi said it was no problem.'

'You know you're always welcome, Marty. What's up?'

'Janet and me had a disagreement. She's having second thoughts. Doesn't like my lifestyle.'

'Coming in at three in the morning after hanging out with me?' Rodman said.

'Right? What's not to like? I tell her, this is the way I am. I've got self-esteem. I tell her if she don't like it, she knows what she can do.'

'Kick you out.'

'I guess that's what she figures.'

'Well, you've got a place here any time you need it.'

'Thanks,' the little man said – then eyed Kelson. 'How about you? If it's late at night and I'm in the neighborhood?'

'I have a studio,' Kelson said. 'My daughter sometimes sleeps over.'

'You don't think I'm good with kids?'

'I think you're good at scaring them.'

'Now I'm insulted.' He looked it.

'OK, Marty,' Kelson said, 'any time day or night, if you don't mind sleeping on the floor.'

The insult vanished from the little man's face. 'Thanks, gimp.'

*　　*　　*

The three of them sat at Rodman's dining table for the rest of the afternoon. Marty showed how he took apart and put back together the Barrett assault rifle. 'Now, do it blindfolded,' Kelson said.

'That's just stupid,' Marty said.

'Anyone hungry?' Rodman said.

'I'm always hungry,' Marty said.

They ordered in Chinese and ate with the Barrett carbine in the middle of the table.

Then, a few minutes after five, Kelson's cell phone rang.

Jose Feliciano was on the other end. 'I got it, but I don't like it, amigo,' he said.

Kelson chewed a bite of General Tso's chicken. 'What've you got, and what's not to like?'

'The girl I know in Transport Services is on vacation. But I talked to the guy in Admissions. He showed me the file for Daryl Vaughn.'

'Does it say who brought him over from Northwestern?'

'Why d'you think I'm calling? The name on the file was Suzanne Madani.'

'Wow – Dr Madani?'

'It's worse than that, man. You know how that ambulance picked up Patricia Ruddig before she hit the ground? It was an AZT ambulance. You know where the AZT depot is? A mile south of the hospital – other way than Patricia Ruddig. You know why the ambulance was two blocks from Patricia Ruddig's building when the bike hit her?'

'Don't tell me Dr Madani was involved.'

'Her name's on the order. The records say the ambulance was supposed to pick up a bariatric patient. It was one of the big rigs – for heavy people. But no emergency, so it redirected and picked up Patricia Ruddig. Thing is, I don't see they ever rescheduled the fat guy.'

'Huh. How about the file for Josh Templeton?'

'That's what hurts me. There's no transport file for Josh Templeton. The record starts when he came in the door.'

'Is that unusual?'

'Not unusual if a patient walks into the ER. Not unusual if a friend carries him in. But Josh Templeton came in at four in the morning. He couldn't walk in himself, and no one brought him in. Yeah, it's unusual. No one gets paid if there's no record. Everyone wants to get paid.'

'Is Dr Madani's name anywhere in his file?'
'Nowhere, my friend.'

So, after eating a fortune cookie, Kelson drove to Clement Memorial, rode the elevator, and knocked on Dr Madani's door. 'Because this is what I do,' he said.

No one answered.

He tried the knob. 'Though I shouldn't do some things I do.' The door was unlocked. He opened it and stepped inside.

'Holy shit,' he said.

Suzanne Madani lay on the daybed. Her head rested on the airline pillow. Her bare feet rested on the folded crochet blanket. It was the stuff in between that bothered Kelson. Her red dress was hiked up to her waist, exposing a pair of underwear decorated with little red hearts. A syringe stuck from her left thigh. Two empty fifty-milliliter vials, each labeled fentanyl citrate, lay on the rug by the daybed. Another vial, full, lay in her left hand. Some dead people look like they're sleeping. Not Suzanne Madani. She looked dead.

'Some things I never want to see,' Kelson said. 'Some things I never want to know.'

He eased the door closed and went to her body. He touched her forehead and wrist. Cold and cold. He wanted to pull her dress down over her legs but stopped himself.

He moved around the office without touching anything.

He considered the photographs of canyons and mountains on the walls. 'Arizona,' he said.

Dr Madani's white medical coat hung from a hook on the back of the door.

Her shoes lay side by side under her desk.

Three neat stacks of paper rested on the desktop. Kelson leafed through them. None of the papers mentioned Patricia Ruddig, Josh Templeton, or Daryl Vaughn.

Kelson kept his fingers off the desktop computer. The screen showed a picture of Madani and another woman, wearing hiking boots and backpacks, smiling into a camera on a mountain trail where the rocks and soil were burnt red and the sunlight soft. 'Once upon a time,' Kelson said.

He pulled out his phone and dialed Venus Johnson at the Harrison Street police station.

She picked up and said, 'What?'

'I've got something for you,' he said.

TWENTY-SIX

'Stay where you are,' Venus Johnson said.

'Right,' Kelson said, and hung up.

He left the office, clicking the lock on the door, and rode the elevator down. 'I don't need it,' he told a Pakistani man who rode with him between the fifth and third floors. 'I don't like it. I don't want it.'

That night, when Kelson turned off his phone and got in bed, sleep seemed to slam into him. But he dreamed that thousands of insects bit and stung his face, and he snapped awake in a panic. Payday was kneading his cheek. 'Dammit,' he said, and swept her off the bed.

He lay in the dark and listened to the sounds of the building – the tap and hiss of plumbing, a deep, quiet hum in some invisible shaft, the refrigerator motor in the kitchenette.

A soft rush and hush of distant traffic came through the walls – and then a far-off siren whined like a locust busy in a summer tree, unconcerned with men lying awake in their beds.

Kelson slept again – and dreamed of the skinny, black-haired woman kneading Vargas's thigh with her clawed fingernails.

Look at that, Rodman said in the dream. *You see what she's doing?*

Kelson stared. *She looks like a knife.*

Shh, Rodman said.

Then *She looks like a knife* became *She has a knife* – though she didn't have one, not even in the crazy logic of the dream.

He snapped awake again. Payday and Painter's Lane were cowering elsewhere, as they did when Kelson had bad dreams.

Kelson got out of bed and went to the window. It was four o'clock in the morning, and the neighborhood was quiet.

He left the window and sat on the carpet, leaning against his bed.

Painter's Lane came first, emerging from the kitchenette. She rubbed against Kelson's arm, purring. She climbed on to his lap. He petted her, and the purr became a gentle roar.

Payday came from under the dining table. She rubbed. He petted. She purred. She leaped on to the bed and settled close enough to Kelson that he could rest his head against her.

With the cats purring in front and behind, he closed his eyes. Now he slept until the winter sun brightened the apartment and his neighbors passed noisily in the hall outside his door. Then Payday meowed behind him.

'All right, all right,' he said.

He showered and fed the cats. Then he turned his phone back on.

There were seven voicemail messages from Venus Johnson and one from her partner Dan Peters.

Johnson's messages played a single tune. *Where the hell are you? Where the hell did you go? Get the hell back here.* Dan Peters' message summed up her words. *We expect you to give a statement at the station at eight a.m.*

Kelson looked at the clock. It was 7:48. 'Expect away.'

He rode the elevator downstairs and drove to AZT Emergency Services instead. The company sent out ambulances from a single-story gray-brick building a block from the tangle of on- and off-ramps where the Dan Ryan Expressway met the Eisenhower. A sign in front said A Z T in big red block letters and *We're there when you need us* in smaller cursive.

'Or when you don't,' Kelson said. 'As the case may be.'

Kelson went into the office through a glass door. No one was at the reception desk, but behind a glass wall, a dispatcher wearing a telephone headset sat at a desk, waiting for any emergencies the morning might bring.

When Kelson tapped on the glass, the dispatcher raised his eyebrows. 'Yeah?'

'Could I talk with whoever's in charge?' Kelson said.

The dispatcher hit a button and spoke into a mouthpiece. 'Mrs Erichsen – office, please.' His voice reverberated through the building from an intercom. Then he said to Kelson, 'Behind you.'

A squat woman in jeans and a floral jacket came through a door from the ambulance garage. 'Yes?'

'Yes.' Kelson offered her a card. 'I'm looking into the deaths of some people you took to Clement Memorial.'

She studied the card. 'Are you working for an insurance company?'

'Nope – a bull rider.'

'A *bull rider*?'

'He's a nurse now – though I sense he misses the rodeo. The dead people are Patricia Ruddig and Daryl Vaughn. There's a third person too, though I don't know if you transported him – Josh Templeton.'

'None of those names means a thing to me. Our service transports dozens of people every day. Aside from the paperwork, we know little about them.'

'That's why I'm hoping you'll check the paperwork,' he said.

'Can you tell me why we would want to do that for you and your bull-riding client?'

'Can you tell me why you wouldn't?'

'As you can see, we're very busy.'

Kelson glanced into the dispatch room. The dispatcher sat listening to them, his headphones slack around his neck.

'One of the Clement Memorial doctors died last night. She arranged for AZT ambulances to pick up Patricia Ruddig and Daryl Vaughn. She died of an overdose. Fentanyl. I found her when I went to ask her about the ambulances. Was the overdose accidental? Was it suicide? Was it something else?'

The woman's face fell. 'Suzanne is dead?'

'I thought you didn't know about any of this.'

She stared into the dispatch room, then pursed her lips and gestured for Kelson to follow her into a conference room, where she closed the door. She offered Kelson a chair and took one herself. She seemed to need to sit. 'Yes, I knew about Daryl Vaughn,' she said. 'And yes, Suzanne asked me to bring him over from Northwestern Medical.' She stared into Kelson's eyes as if looking for something to keep her afloat as a current drew her down. 'Suzanne did this kind of thing a couple times a year – bringing in a man from one of the shelters or from the street. This was the first time she got one from another hospital. I told her it might raise flags. She reassured me. She died last night?'

'I found her yesterday evening,' Kelson said. 'She'd already been dead a couple hours.'

The woman looked down at the conference table. 'This was Suzanne's secret thing. *Our* secret thing.'

'Sorry, but the secret's out now. The hospital will check everything she had her hands on. They'll have to.'

'Suzanne would be mortified.'

'Yeah, I would think so,' Kelson said. 'How did it work? You gave her kickbacks?'

'What? *No.* You don't get it – the men were injured or sick. She found them and brought them to the hospital for care they couldn't afford and wouldn't get without her. Once they were at Clement Memorial, the hospital was legally required to treat them, but they never would have gotten there without her. The hospital would fire her if anyone found out, but she did it because she cared about the men. She didn't do it for money.'

'Saint Suzanne?'

The woman looked angry. 'If you want the truth – yes.'

'How about you?'

'Me?'

'You billed the hospital, right? You earned money from the deal.'

'Because if I didn't submit a bill, the hospital would know something was funny about the admissions. I stood to lose more than I gained. Without the Clement Memorial contract, my company would be in trouble. But Suzanne approached me – she persuaded me . . .'

'Did you talk to her lately?'

'Last week,' she said. 'We became friends, you know – over the years.'

'Did you sense she ever worried about someone discovering your secret deal?'

'She always worried. So did I. We reassured each other, I guess.'

'Did you know about her using fentanyl?'

'No – but it seems like most of the people I know use something.' The sadness in the woman's face looked deeper than tears. 'Suzanne said she set up the admissions so no one would understand them for what they were.'

'Would you check the paperwork?'

'I suppose so.'

They went out of the conference room and through the door into the ambulance garage. Four gleaming yellow and white ambulances stood on a polished concrete floor. In a break room, paramedics watched TV, played cards, or read their phones.

Kelson followed the woman into a little windowless office.

She sat at a desk and typed on a keyboard. When the results came up, she read the screen, touched another key, and read a new screen. 'Yes,' she said then. 'We scheduled a pickup for January first, nine a.m. A bariatric patient named Clarence Viabhav. Probably to prep him for surgery the following day. An unusual date for an elective pickup, mostly because of doctor schedules over the holidays, but not unheard of. Then a nine-one-one call came in, and we grabbed it since we were close by. The elective pickup could wait.'

'Was it ever rescheduled?'

'No. That's unusual too.'

'I heard Dr Madani's name is on the order.'

'She was the physician on record for Clarence Viabhav's transportation request.'

'Did she do bariatric surgery?'

'No, no. Sometimes orders come through with the name of any physician available for a signature. Her name on the order means nothing.'

'How about Josh Templeton?'

She typed on the keyboard, then read a screen, a second, and a third. 'OK, this one is odd too. But Suzanne's name doesn't appear on it.'

'So, what's odd?' Kelson asked.

'When people report car accidents, they call nine-one-one. If we're closest or have an ambulance nearby, we respond. This accident happened on Lake Shore Drive in an area usually serviced by other companies. But we got a direct call – which almost never happens for emergencies. And the caller asked us to take the victim to Clement Memorial – not the closest hospital.'

'Who reported the accident?'

'Someone identified in our records only as a witness.'

'Any phone number?'

'No.'

'Anything else unusual?'

'That's all,' she said. 'Does any of it help?'

'I don't know,' he said.

Now there were tears in her eyes. 'Suzanne did this for years without getting caught. Maybe no one will see it now.'

'Maybe . . .'

'Please don't tell anyone,' she said.

'I wish that was an option,' he said.

TWENTY-SEVEN

As Kelson drove toward his office, his phone rang. He checked caller ID, then answered. 'Get it over with.'

'Where the hell did you go last night?' Venus Johnson said.

'Home to sleep.'

'Why did you leave when I told you to stay?'

'I'd had enough. Too much.'

'Dan Peters told you to come down and give a statement.'

'I was sleeping.'

'Do you know what I want to do to guys like you?'

'I have a pretty good idea. I try to keep a step in front of you.'

'Kelson, you're so far behind you can't see my tail lights.'

'As long as we keep our distance.'

'Most of the time, I'd like that. Right now, I want you here telling me everything you know about Suzanne Madani.'

'How about ten minutes?'

'How about five?'

Twenty minutes later, he walked through security at the Harrison Street station and went to the homicide room. Johnson and Peters sat in their cubicle.

'Good morning,' Kelson said.

Peters snatched a digital recorder from his desk and said, 'Let's go.'

They went to an interview room – air conditioned even in the middle of January. 'If you're not already shivering with fear?' Kelson said, and sat on a metal chair.

Peters switched on the recorder and stated the time, the date, Kelson's name, and the officers present. Then Johnson said, 'Tell it.'

Kelson told it. All of it. Including what he'd just learned from the woman at AZT. When he started to explain how he felt excited as Dr Madani massaged his fingers to check for sensation after he woke from his gunshot wound, Johnson switched off the recorder.

'When you spill, you spill everything,' she said.

'No levees on this river,' Kelson said. 'No sandbags around this foundation. No—'

'Got it,' she said.

'No drains in this tub.'

'*Got it*,' she said.

'Was the death accidental or a suicide?' he asked.

Dan Peters shook his head. 'You were a narcotics cop for, what, eight years? You know better than that.'

'You mean because there weren't old needle marks on her thigh? I tried not to look. You mean because if you're killing yourself, you load it all into the syringe – you don't go to sleep with a full vial of fentanyl in your hand?'

'Yeah, I mean that and more,' Peters said.

'What's the *more*?'

'The *more* is her prints were on the empty vials and syringe – close to but not quite where they'd make sense if she was injecting herself. The *more* is why would a successful doctor who's so good-looking she can turn on a screwball like you just by touching his hand want to kill herself?'

'A lot of suicides make little sense, though, right? Besides, she was afraid her charity deal with the homeless men was about to go public.'

'Yeah, there's that. But except for one set of prints on the doorknob – yours – the place was clean. *Her* prints weren't on the knob. Someone wiped it down and then you touched it. Personally, I kind of wish we could nail you for the killing.'

'Sorry to disappoint you,' Kelson said.

Peters said, 'Do you think there's anything to this idea about the three deaths at the hospital being funny?'

'I didn't worry much about them at first,' Kelson said. 'No pattern. No connection. I can still explain away each of the circumstances. But add them together and there's a lot to explain.'

'Madani is a connection,' Peters said.

'And now she's dead,' Kelson said. 'A broken connection.'

Johnson said, 'We'll need to talk to your bull rider.'

'You can try,' Kelson said. 'You'll find him working at the hospital. But he distrusts cops. He has a big, bad history with you guys. What else did you find out about Suzanne Madani?'

'Nothing we can share,' Peters said.

'I tell you everything I know, and you give me nothing?'

'That's the way it works,' Peters said. 'We're the cops. You're the not-cop. We ask questions. You give answers.'

'*Long* answers,' Johnson said.

Kelson said, 'Don't expect me to come running when you need help.'

'You didn't come running,' Peters said. 'You went home and slept.'

'I'd had enough.'

'Go home again now,' Peters said. 'Go back to sleep.'

'Funny thing.' Kelson stood up. 'I woke full of energy.'

Before he got to the door, Johnson said, 'We think Madani might've been unconscious when she was injected. No signs of struggle. We're testing for Rohypnol. She went down to the hospital cafeteria an hour and a half before you found her. Eating alone, we think. But people stop by a table when you eat alone – colleagues, families of patients. One of them could've slipped her something. Or maybe someone gave it to her afterward in her office.'

'How about security video?'

Johnson glanced at Peters, who shook his head. She told Kelson anyway. 'No cameras in Madani's hallway. Plenty around the rest of the hospital. We're looking at recordings to see if we can identify a trail.'

'Do her files tie her to the dead patients?'

'We haven't touched them,' Johnson said. 'We need a court order to get around doctor–patient confidentiality. We haven't even started into her computer.'

'Will you tell me if anything turns up?'

'I've already told you more than I should,' she said.

'But—'

'You push too hard,' she said. 'You need to learn when to shut up and be grateful.'

'Don't get your hopes up,' he said.

TWENTY-EIGHT

When Kelson got back to his office, he pulled his Springfield pistol from the bottom desk drawer and checked the magazine. He put the gun away, took the KelTec from its under-the-desk rig, and checked it too.

He took his laptop from the top drawer. 'Circle back,' he told it.

As it booted up, he called Jose Feliciano. The call bounced to voicemail, and he said, 'You must know about Suzanne Madani by now. A couple of homicide cops are coming to talk with you about – well, everything. Sorry.'

He hung up and opened Google. 'Circle,' he said, and typed the name Dougie Ruddig – Patricia Ruddig's son. He got no hits. He tried Douglas Ruddig and then Doug Ruddig. Nothing and nothing.

He stared at the computer. Then he said, 'First husband.' The deskman at Patricia Ruddig's building told him Dougie was her son by her first marriage. 'Not Ruddig.'

Kelson got the building phone number and called it.

'Y'hello,' said the deskman.

'As cheerful as a guy who wears reindeer sweaters in January,' Kelson said, then told him what he wanted.

The deskman said, 'Tomlinson. Dougie Tomlinson.'

'You said before that he lives in Barrington?'

'Yeah, works at a bank there.'

Kelson Googled Dougie Tomlinson. He got a couple hundred hits, and so he added *Barrington* – and got nothing. But *Douglas* Tomlinson was a Wells Fargo branch manager in Barrington. Kelson found Tomlinson's Facebook page. It included a profile picture of a round-faced man in his forties with thinning black hair and glasses. 'The unassuming type,' Kelson said. The posts – mostly from the summer months – showed Tomlinson racing a little Sunfish sailboat. In those pictures, he wore Ray-Bans. 'Nope, Dougie,' Kelson said, 'you don't sell it.'

*   *   *

An hour after Kelson tucked his computer back into the desk drawer, he drove into Barrington, a moneyed suburb forty miles northwest of the city. He went past a wine bar, turned at a jeweler's, and swung into the Wells Fargo parking lot. He edged into a space made skinny by a mound of ice and walked into a lobby where a single teller stood behind a bank counter designed for three. The teller brightened as Kelson came in and asked how she could help.

'Mr Tomlinson, please?' he said.

She nodded at an open door, where Dougie Tomlinson, dressed in a gray business suit, sat at a desk. 'He's with another customer. But he should only be a few minutes.'

Kelson sat in one of the vinyl armchairs in the waiting area. 'Sleepy town,' he said to the teller.

'No one comes in,' she said, quietly, as if the secret could get her fired.

By the time the customer stepped out of Tomlinson's office twenty minutes later, Kelson had explained his compulsion to tell strangers about himself ever since Bicho shot him in the head. The teller had told him about her plans to backpack through southern Europe when she quit her job next summer – *please say nothing about that to Mr Tomlinson.*

When the customer left the bank, Tomlinson put on a practiced smile, adjusted his glasses, and welcomed Kelson into his office. His hands looked soft and well scrubbed, and when he sat at his desk, he crossed his fingers as if he liked to display them. 'What can we do for you?' he asked.

Kelson gave him a card and said, 'I have a few questions about your mom's death.'

Tomlinson stared blankly at Kelson, then wiped the back of a well-scrubbed hand across his lips. 'It's been hard. She was all I had. She was difficult at times – always involved in my business – but now that she's gone . . .'

'I'm sorry,' Kelson said.

'I took care of her in the last few years – after Phil died. If nothing else, I gave her that. I took care of her.'

'The women at Spyner's Pub have mixed feelings about how you handled it. One of them thinks you're a prick, though another says you aren't so bad.'

That startled him. 'I worried about people taking advantage of Mom.'

'Did those women do that?'

'I couldn't be with her all the time. I don't know what went on when I wasn't there. You have to understand, Mom liked to involve herself in other people's lives.'

'From what everyone says, she sounds like a good woman.'

'She lived on a fixed income and couldn't afford some of what she did,' he said. 'She always needed a cause – and she'd make one up if she couldn't find one. If she wasn't saving people, she bugged the heck out of them.'

'What did you think when you heard about the bike hitting her?'

'The news flattened me. Look, my mom was old, but not *old* old. I didn't see this coming.'

'What do you get now that she's dead?'

Kelson's question made the man hesitate. 'You mean, what do I inherit?'

'Sure.'

'You're really asking that?' But he shook off his irritation. 'Phil's money goes to his daughters from his first marriage. He owned the apartment – it goes to them too. I get Mom's photographs and jewelry. There's not much of it and there's not much else. Satisfied?'

'I was never unsatisfied,' Kelson said. 'What do you think about the care your mom got at the hospital?'

'What's this about anyway?' Tomlinson said. 'Why are you asking these questions?'

'A nurse at Clement Memorial thinks some deaths at the hospital look strange. Your mom's death is one of them. He hired me to look into them.'

'Strange, how?'

'Based on your mom's injuries, he thinks she shouldn't have died. He thinks someone helped her along.'

'Really?' Tomlinson readjusted his glasses. 'I was there with her as much as I could be. I liked her doctor – and her nurses.'

'Do you remember the doctor's name?'

'Of course. Dr Madani. And the nurse who was mainly with Mom was Wendy.'

'Wendy Thomas?'

'That's right.' A real smile flickered and faded. 'The stories she told about her fiancé made Mom laugh.'

'Did the head of the ICU treat her at all?'

'I don't know – I don't think so.'

'Jeremy Jacobson?'

Again Tomlinson looked startled. 'Jeremy Jacobson is at Clement Memorial? I thought he retired after his wife died.'

Now Kelson was startled. 'He took time off but came back. How do you know about him?'

Tomlinson looked ashen. 'From my mom. My damned busybody mom. She saw Terry Ann Jacobson get run over. She swore an affidavit. She was going to go to court, but the trial never happened. They worked out a deal. If you want to know the truth, I think that disappointed Mom. She wanted to testify.'

'What did she see happen?'

'A bad accident. Terry Ann Jacobson's son was backing out of their driveway. He was only a kid – barely old enough to drive – maybe he only had a learner's permit. Mrs Jacobson was on the driveway talking on her phone. She didn't see him coming. I guess he didn't see her either. He hit her and panicked. The police found him a couple hours later, sitting in the car in one of the lakefront parks.'

'Scott Jacobson?'

'That's right. Just a kid. Mom felt as bad for him as for his mother and the rest of the family. Jeremy Jacobson hushed it up. He kept the details out of the news. His lawyers talked to Mom and tried to keep her quiet too. But she insisted on at least swearing the affidavit. She sure would've liked to testify.'

TWENTY-NINE

As Kelson drove back toward the city, he called Rodman and told him what he'd learned.

'Wow,' Rodman said.

'Yeah, that's pretty much what I said. I'm going back to Patricia Ruddig's apartment. I'll get more out of the deskman if I have to twist him out of his reindeer sweater.'

'What if he has nothing more to give?'

'Then I feel bad for his sweater.'

The deskman took no twisting – and he wasn't wearing the reindeer sweater. Now his sweater was bright green. So was his hat.

'Let me guess,' Kelson said. 'St Patrick's Day early?'

'Every day's a holiday around here. I've got something for you.' He peeled a Post-it note from a pad and slapped it on the desk. 'There you go.'

Kelson read it. '*Ken.*'

'He's the doorman across the street. When you came before, you asked about video of the bike hitting Patty, and I told you our security camera was broken. But today I'm thinking I should ask who Ken's boss got to fix the camera at his building when it broke last October. That was around Halloween – because I was wearing my pumpkin sweater – but it could've also been July. Long story short, the building across the street might have video of Patty getting hit.'

Kelson picked up the Post-it note. 'I *almost* like you.'

'Give it some time,' the deskman said. 'I'm very popular with the eighty- and ninety-year-olds.'

Kelson crossed the street. Ken stood inside the automatic doors, wearing thick olive-green pants, a blue wool coat with epaulettes, and a plastic-visored bellman's cap. He needed a shave and had the complexion of a man who'd crawled out of bed after sleeping off a hangover.

The doors slid open under Kelson's weight. 'Morning,' he said.

The man nodded hello.

'Taciturn,' Kelson said.

'Sorry?'

'I would call you taciturn.'

'Sticks and stones.'

'Right,' Kelson said. 'What's the point?'

'The point of what?' His voice was flat.

'Of having a doorman when you have automatic doors.'

'Don't know.'

'Santa from across the street sent me to talk with you.'

Ken's eyes were uncomprehending.

'Mr Lucky Charms. The Great Pumpkin.'

'You mean Jerry the Sweater?'

'Is that what people call him?'

'It's what I call him.' Flat.

'Jerry the Sweater says you might have video of Patricia Ruddig getting hit by a bike.'

At her name, the doorman's eyes showed sudden warmth. 'Poor Patty.'

'Heat wave in the tundra,' Kelson said. He handed him a card. 'If you have video, I'd like to see it.'

Ken stared out the glass doors as if a rush of residents might need his services. 'I guess so.' He led Kelson across the lobby to a utilities room. He went to a computer desk and accessed the date-stamped video files for the first week of the month.

'Do you sleep in that hat?' Kelson said.

'No.' He clicked the January 1 video.

'I'm kidding,' Kelson said.

The doorman watched the video load.

'Sort of,' Kelson said.

The doorman started the video playing at 08:57.

The camera pointed at the area outside the automatic doors, extending across the circular driveway to the sidewalk and street.

From 08:57 until 08:59, nothing moved. Then two cars passed. At 09:00, a van rolled by. Then the door to Patricia Ruddig's building opened, and a small woman in an overcoat stepped outside.

The doorman said, 'Patty.'

She moved with the cautious steps of an explorer venturing on to thin ice.

A dark bicycle shot toward her from the right side of the screen. As she edged out, the rider – a tall man in black leggings, a dark jacket, a black bike helmet, and bike goggles – swerved, as if to avoid a patch of uneven pavement, a piece of garbage, a pothole. He slammed into her.

She hit the pavement with a force that seemed to burst from the computer screen. The bicycle skidded, the rider barely holding on.

Patricia Ruddig lay on the pavement.

The rider stopped. He got off the bicycle. He approached Patricia Ruddig as you might go to a wild animal you hit with your car. You want to help it, to hold it, but you're terrified it will tear you apart with all the fury of its pain.

Patricia Ruddig didn't move.

The rider seemed to speak to her. Obscured by the distance from the camera and by his helmet and goggles, he might have apologized to her – or accused her of carelessness – or sworn at her – or said nothing at all. He went back to his bicycle. He climbed on and rode away.

A moment later, Jerry the Sweater came from the building. Patricia Ruddig raised her head as he squatted beside her, touching her shoulder, her ribs, with the gentleness of a lover.

'Damn,' Kelson said.

'The rider hit her on purpose,' the doorman said.

'I don't think so,' Kelson said.

The doorman restarted the video at the moment when the bicyclist flashed on to the screen. 'Why's he riding on the side-walk?' he said. He adjusted a knob and started the video again, in slow motion. The bicyclist inched toward the building entrance. Patricia Ruddig inched out. The bicyclist swerved toward her. 'Why'd he do that?' the doorman said. The rider seemed to have time to swerve away. He drove head-on into her – lowering himself over the bike frame and bracing his shoulders before the impact – though he might've done that to keep from flying off the bike when he saw a crash as inevitable.

'I don't know,' Kelson said.

The doorman restarted the video and watched the collision at regular speed. Then he did it again. Kelson let himself out of the utility room as he restarted it once more.

Kelson got in his car and turned the heat high. He called Rodman and told him the latest.

'Well, that sucks,' Rodman said. 'What're you going to do now?'

'Keep circling,' Kelson said. 'You want to go back to the underworld?'

Rodman did.

Through the afternoon, they breathed exhaust fumes in the shadowy lower-level streets fingering from Lower Wacker into underground Chicago.

They met dozens of homeless men and women huddling over warm grates, shoving stuffed shopping carts along the narrow street sides as cars flew by, sharing Schlitz tallboys or crusty bottles of vodka. None of them admitted to knowing Daryl Vaughn. Most knew the professor and his waifish friend, though no one had seen them in a couple days. Kelson and Rodman went back to the encampment they visited the last time they came. It was vacant. Except for burnt scraps of cardboard, a cruddy blue Bic lighter, and a grimy T-shirt, Kelson would've thought they'd come to the wrong place.

'People don't just disappear,' he said.

'Sure they do,' Rodman said. 'In so many ways.' He crushed the plastic lighter with his boot.

They climbed three flights of metal stairs and came out into the evening dark. A cold, wet wind wrapped around their necks, and Rodman pulled up his coat collar.

Kelson took him to dinner at Bella Bacinos. They talked about the uncertainty of almost everything Kelson had learned – about the way they could explain it as meaningless, adding up to nothing at all, *or* as evidence of murder.

'Except for Patricia Ruddig seeing the Jacobson lady's death,' Rodman said. 'That's something. Those coincidences don't happen.'

They agreed they would drive to Fort Wayne in the morning to see Josh Templeton's mother – *circling back*.

Then they talked about other screwed-up families.

Cindi's brother and the whirlpool of trouble pulling him down.

Rodman's brother, whose death made another whirlpool when the police shot him years ago.

Kelson's divorce from Nancy.

Kelson's divorce led them to talk about Sue Ellen. Maybe it was that last change of topic – or maybe it was the warmth of the five-meat penne Bolognese – or maybe it was some of each – but when Kelson and Rodman stepped out of the restaurant into the cold, wet wind, they looked satisfied with the world.

So much so that instead of driving straight home, Kelson headed back to his office. 'When you're on a roll,' he said to himself.

The computer training school was closed for the day, and the cleaning staff had already come through. His heels clacked down the empty hallway, and when he came to his door, he stopped and listened to the silence.

He went in and, since the warmth of dinner was starting to

fade, locked the door. He peeked at the KelTec pistol under the desktop. He checked the Springfield in the bottom drawer. Then he went to his window and dialed Jose Feliciano's number.

When the call bounced to voicemail, he repeated what Jerry the Sweater had told him when he arrived at Patricia Ruddig's. 'I've got something for you.'

He hung up and walked around the office, stopping by the framed photos of Sue Ellen and the cats. 'Could be worse,' he told them. He circled again, then sat at his desk. The building around him was silent. He tapped a finger on his desk – and stopped. The office was silent. He was silent.

He found his own silence intolerable. It seemed to squeeze his body.

'And where do I go from here?' he said.

As if in answer, there was a knock at the door.

It made him jump. He stared at the door.

Another knock.

'Yes?' he asked.

Another.

Kelson considered his Springfield and KelTec.

He went to the door and opened it.

Frida, the waitress from Club Richelieu, stood in the hallway. She wore jeans and a flannel shirt, no coat, and her dark hair looked as if she'd spent a long time in the wind.

'Hey,' she said.

'Hey.'

She shivered, as if she'd carried the cold air in from outside the building. She said, 'I can't get you out of my head.'

THIRTY

'Christ, you've got great eyes,' Kelson said. 'By which I mean, come in – warm up.'

'I didn't know if I should come,' Frida said, her right eye cocking the tiniest bit inward.

'Intimate,' he said. 'You have intimate eyes.'

'I almost froze,' she said, and sat on one of the client chairs.

'How long were you outside?'

'I saw you go in about twenty minutes ago. I was there a while before that.'

'Kind of stalkery,' Kelson said.

She let her eyes rest on his.

'Smoky and intimate,' he said. 'Why aren't you wearing a coat?'

'Do you ever *not* say what you're thinking?'

'I talk most when I'm nervous or scared or with someone I find attractive.'

'Which is it with me – nervous, scared, or attractive?'

'A little nervous, a lot of attractive. You have a great smile.'

'I'm not wearing a coat because I left it at Richelieu. Rick Jacobson came in and started bullying Mr Vargas – Jeffrey – the way he does. Jeffrey got upset, and when he's upset, he takes it out on the bartenders and servers. So I scooted out when everything started to fly.'

'I thought Rick and Vargas were pals.'

'Jeffrey needs cash – he *always* needs cash. Rick doesn't always want to give it to him.'

'He said the club makes a profit.'

'Weekends are good. Thursdays if we have a hot DJ. Richelieu's still open, so they must work something out. Jeffrey gets his money, and Rick plays the big man. Anyway, seeing Rick get all uptight again made me think of you. Thinking of you made me wonder . . . well, here I am.' She gave him more of the great smile. 'I'm sort of impulsive.'

He smiled back. 'Have you ever had a brain injury?'

She gazed over his shoulder at the framed picture of Sue Ellen. 'Is that your daughter?'

'My one and only.'

She glanced at the other picture. 'And cats.'

'Payday and Painter's Lane.'

'Either you hang out at the racetrack, or your daughter named them.'

'She originally wanted a horse. Now she wants a potbellied pig.'

'Kids,' Frida said.

'Kids.'

'Do you need to get back to her tonight?'

'She's with her mother.'

She gazed at him with her cocked eye. 'It's a shame to be alone on a cold night.'

'You move quick,' he said.

'Too quick?'

'I like quick. Do you do this kind of thing often?'

'Would it bother you if I did?'

'I once sat butt-naked on a woman's dinner at Big Pie Pizza.'

'Your point is?'

'My point is, who am I to judge?'

Frida said her Maltese, Napoleon, peed on the couch out of jealousy when she brought men home, so they drove to Kelson's apartment. The wind buffeted the car and made street signs flutter on their posts. Kelson notched the heat high, and Frida held her hands over the vent like it was a tiny campfire.

They came to a red light, and three cars crossed the intersection, followed by a motorcycle ridden by a man in snow pants and a parka, a woman in a matching outfit clutching him from behind. 'The things we do for love,' Frida said.

'I know an ex-bull rider who's in love with a little round nurse. They're going to get married.'

'See?' she said. 'I like couples like that.'

'Sure, what's not to like? Or your boss and his girlfriend.'

'Jeffrey? He's gay.'

'What about the woman he was with at the club – the one kneading his thigh with her fingernails?'

'Darla? She's his cousin.'

'You're kidding . . .'

'The girl has issues. She hooks up with Rick. A funny couple, but it seems to works for them.'

'Do you know much about the Jacobsons?' Kelson asked.

'Just what Darla tells me. I think they're into each other for the pain.'

'The things we do for love.'

She laid a hand on his thigh. She kept her fingernails to herself. 'Yeah.'

At his building, they ran from the car to the entrance. 'The elevator's slow,' he said.

'Quick is good. Slow is OK.'

The elevator came and they got in. 'Go, go, go,' Kelson said.

So Frida put her lips on his, and they rose to his floor in a long kiss.

'Yeah, you're quick,' he said when the doors opened. They rushed down the hall to his apartment.

He fumbled with the key, crammed it into the lock – and stopped.

A voice spoke inside the apartment.

'Oh, no,' he said.

Frida didn't hear it. 'Oh, yes,' she said.

'Oh, no, no, no.' He peeled her hands off and opened the door.

Sue Ellen sat on the carpet at one end of the room. She was struggling to position Payday and Painter's Lane in front of her. Between her and the far wall, she'd set up a straight two-lane course made out of soup cans, bed covers, and most of Kelson's shirts. At the end of the lanes, there were two plates, each with a slice of salami. Payday mewled as Sue Ellen grappled with her.

'*What* are you doing?' Kelson said.

'Cat drag racing,' she said. 'I saw it on YouTube.'

'No, no, no,' Kelson said.

Frida laughed. 'That's the greatest thing – ever.'

For the next hour, Sue Ellen and Frida raced cats. Kelson lay on his bed and rocked. Then he went to the kitchen and got more salami for the finish line.

A little after eleven p.m. Kelson and Frida drove Sue Ellen back to Nancy's house.

'Cool kid,' Frida said as Sue Ellen disappeared inside the house.

'The best,' Kelson said.

He drove Frida to her apartment in a courtyard complex in the Edgewater neighborhood. At the curb, he said, 'That didn't work out how I expected.'

'Yeah,' Frida said. 'It was pretty great.'

'I suppose so.'

'Come in?'

'What about Napoleon?'

'Screw Napoleon,' she said.

Kelson went in.

Napoleon peed on the couch all night long.

THIRTY-ONE

Kelson and Rodman drove to Fort Wayne the next morning. Overnight, the wind rose, and now the sky hung thick with clouds. The radio said snow would start falling by mid-afternoon, up to a foot before it stopped.

'Frida,' Kelson said to his friend.

'What?'

'Just saying.'

As they crossed the border from Illinois to Indiana, Kelson called Josh Templeton's mother. He got no answer – not even a recording.

'Could be love,' he said when he hung up.

'Frida?' Rodman said.

'Who else?'

'Or could be good sex,' Rodman said.

'Sure was. She makes *me* look level-headed.'

'Careful, or you'll hurt yourself.'

'What she said too.'

Thirty miles later, Kelson tried calling again. No answer. No recording.

'Could be a waste of a trip,' Rodman said.

'If she isn't home, we'll look for her at her job at Lutheran Center.'

'Could be we get trapped there when the snow starts,' Rodman said. 'Like in *The Shining*.'

'No one I'd rather have by my side if Jack Nicholson comes after me with an axe.'

'Except Frida?'

'Take out the axe part, and then OK.'

'You fall hard, man.'

'I'm not falling – I'm flying.'

'Watch out you don't get too high.'

'What she said.'

* * *

When Kelson stopped outside Deneesa Smithson's little pink house, Rodman gazed at the bare lot around it and the surrounding little houses on their bare lots. 'Worth keeping in mind when I think I've got it tough.'

'This isn't so bad,' Kelson said.

'Yeah, you could tear down the houses and then there'd be nothing.'

They went up the path and Kelson knocked.

No one answered.

Rodman knocked – harder.

Silence.

'Lutheran?' Rodman said.

Kelson stared at the door. 'Last time I came, there was a dog.'

'Another Maltese?'

'Uh-uh.' Kelson stepped off the side of the concrete porch, went to a window, and peered in.

'What're you doing?' Rodman said.

Kelson stepped back on to the porch and tried the door handle. Locked.

He kicked the door.

'What are you doing?' Rodman said.

'Stronger than it looks.' Kelson kicked again.

'Why the—?'

'Kick it in, will you?'

'No – what do you—?'

'Just kick the damn door,' Kelson said. 'Please.'

Whatever Rodman saw in Kelson's face was enough to persuade him. 'OK, man.' He kicked it. The door broke into the house, splintering from the top hinge.

Kelson stepped inside, Rodman behind him.

In a little front room, on a little gray couch, Deneesa Smithson sat with her skirt pulled up to her waist. A syringe stuck out from her thigh. Three empty vials of fentanyl lay on the floor. She was dead – Kelson and Rodman didn't need to feel for a pulse to know that. The room was unnaturally warm, as if she'd turned the heat high before shooting up. On a round wooden table by the couch, there was a shrine to her son – Josh's baby photos, school awards, a high-school diploma, a pack of playing cards, a pair of toddler-sized gym shoes, a king-size pack of Reese's peanut butter cups.

Rodman went to the dead woman. He held his enormous hands above her, as if he could make her rise. He said, 'I would've preferred Jack Nicholson with an axe.' He plucked the syringe from her thigh and threw it across the room.

'Don't touch her,' Kelson said. 'Don't . . .'

Rodman pulled her skirt down over her legs.

'Don't touch *anything*,' Kelson said.

'It's indecent,' Rodman said.

'Don't.'

'You have me kick in her door and then you'd leave her like that?'

'From outside I thought she might be alive,' Kelson said.

'You thought wrong.'

Kelson picked up the syringe. '*I'm* the one who's supposed to be irresponsible.' He wiped Rodman's prints off with his sleeve and set the syringe on the couch by the dead woman. 'Jesus.'

They searched the rest of the house, keeping their fingers to themselves. In the kitchen, there were two empty glasses in the sink. Kelson smelled them. 'Nothing,' he said.

There were two bedrooms. Josh's had a skinny bed, a banged-up dresser, and a set of shelves. On the shelves there were old schoolbooks, a stack of DC comics, sports trophies, and a strip of picture-booth photos of Josh and his girlfriend Melanie dressed for prom. In Deneesa Smithson's room, the bed was made neatly with a threadbare cover. There was a polished wooden bureau and a matching bench where a person could sit while getting dressed. The bathroom was as neat as the bedroom, with a single towel creased over a towel bar.

'Nothing,' Kelson said.

The door at the end of the hall was open a couple inches. Kelson nudged it with an elbow.

The room smelled like a combination of laundry and kennel. A stacked washer and dryer stood against one wall. The other walls were marked with divots and scars from a dog scratching and chewing. A plastic water bowl and an empty food dish rested on the floor by a back door.

'Where's the dog?' Rodman said.

Using his sleeve again, Kelson opened the back door.

In the yard, there was a dog chain linked to a metal post. But there was no dog.

'I guess we should call the cops,' Kelson said.

'And tell them what? We kicked in the lady's door, fixed her skirt, and toured the premises? I don't know how that goes for white guys, but I call it asking for trouble. Let's phone it in from the road.'

'You've got inconsistent ideas about decency.'

They went back through the house. When they reached the front door, Kelson glanced into the front room again.

'Huh,' he said.

Josh's alabaster-skinned girlfriend, Melanie, in white leggings and a white down coat, stood staring at Deneesa Smithson. She was reaching to touch the woman's face when she heard Kelson and Rodman. She glanced at Kelson, stepped back from the body involuntarily, and said, 'What did you do to her?'

THIRTY-TWO

Kelson and Rodman spent the next two hours explaining to the Fort Wayne police why they came to Deneesa Smithson's house, why they kicked in the door, why Rodman adjusted the woman's skirt, why they touched evidence and wiped it down afterward. The Fort Wayne police didn't like it.

'At least you stuck around,' said Judy Blanchard, the lead detective. 'Good choice.'

'Not really,' Kelson said. 'We were skipping out when we got caught.'

She gave him a look that might mean twenty-to-life.

'Call Venus Johnson or Dan Peters at the CPD. They'll vouch for us.'

Blanchard made the call, stepping out in the cold to talk. When she came back, she told Kelson, 'Venus Johnson vouches that you're a screwball. And you' – she meant Rodman – 'she knows you mostly by reputation.'

'Which is?'

'Academy dropout. Street hustler. Suborner of justice. *Suborner* is her word – I don't talk so fancy. Borderline criminal. Does that about describe you?'

'Depends on what you mean by *justice* and *criminal*,' he said.

'She also says you're all right – if I'm willing to ignore all the other stuff. Should I ignore all the other stuff?'

'Depends on what you mean by *justice* and *criminal*,' he said.

'I'll have to think about that,' she said. 'Meantime, both of you can put your hands behind your backs.'

She handcuffed them and seated them at the kitchen table while the Fort Wayne Police worked the scene.

'What do you make of it?' Rodman asked Kelson when they were alone.

The twist of Kelson's arms tugged at his stitches. 'I'm willing to bet the next inventory check at Clement Memorial shows a bunch of missing fentanyl.'

'The Jacobsons, right?'

'Maybe, but which one? Why would any of them kill these people?'

'We've got to talk to Scott,' Rodman said. 'Patricia Ruddig saw him run over his mother. Everything else must tie to him.'

A uniformed cop came into the kitchen and went to the sink.

'You'll want to bag those glasses before you turn it on,' Kelson said.

'Shut the hell up,' the cop said. But he left without touching the faucet, and an evidence technician came in and bagged them.

Kelson said, 'Check them for Rohypnol.'

'Shut the hell up,' the tech said.

Then Detective Blanchard came in and sat at the table. 'The only question now is what we do with you.'

'I like *catch and release*,' Kelson said. 'Humane.'

'I like *get out of town by midnight*,' Rodman said. '*Or else.*'

'Because this is funny?' she said. 'I like *breaking and entry*. Two to eight years.'

'We broke in because we thought we could save her,' Rodman said.

'And you waited to call nine-one-one until you were sneaking out, because . . .?' she said.

'Because we didn't want to deal with a tight-ass like you,'
Kelson said.

'*Sam* . . .' Rodman said.

Blanchard stood up. 'Just to show you how tight-assed I am,
I'm going to let you go for now. This is a bad, sad situation,
but I see no criminal intent. So, get out of town by midnight,
or' – she glanced at her wristwatch – 'maybe you could manage
it by six o'clock.'

'Thank you,' Rodman said.

'Do you have any sense who did it?' Kelson asked.

'Yeah, a pretty good one,' she said. 'Most likely accidental.
Could be suicide.'

'Bullshit,' he said.

'Pardon me?'

'Not again,' Kelson said. 'Maybe you aren't a tight-ass. Maybe
you're just stupid.'

Rodman shook his head.

Blanchard said, 'The woman's son died a month ago. She's
got mega-dose Xanax in the medicine cabinet. She was hurting.'

'Her death looks exactly the same as the death of a doctor in
Chicago two nights ago,' Kelson said. 'It isn't suicide, and it
sure isn't accidental.'

'You know how many overdoses we had in this county last
year?'

'You don't get what I'm saying . . .'

She poked her finger at his chest. 'Nine hundred eighty-eight.
Don't tell me about a dead doctor two days ago in Chicago. I
see this right here three times a day.'

'You don't get it.'

She leaned to the hallway and called to a cop by the front
room. 'Hey, cut these two clowns loose. If I spend another minute
with them, I might go rogue.'

Just before Plymouth, Indiana, Kelson and Rodman drove head-on
into a blizzard. One moment they were barreling through dark
bare fields, and the next they hit a wall of falling snow.

'Holy crap,' Rodman said, though his voice was calm.

Kelson took his foot from the accelerator. He tapped the brakes
– once, twice. The car slipped to the side. He took his foot from
the brakes. He steered out of the slide, and for several moments

the car seemed to glide through an airy space between the tires and the road.

As the car slowed, it touched down, and Kelson tapped the brakes again – once, twice – and the wheels gripped pavement. They drove at twenty miles an hour through a white vortex. They passed the off- and on-ramps for Plymouth, the glimmer of a Days Inn, an ice-blasted sign thanking drivers for visiting Plymouth and encouraging them to return soon.

'Just goes to show,' Kelson said.

'Sure,' Rodman said, and he eased his eyes shut, 'just goes to show.'

The next ninety miles back into the city took three hours. When Kelson dropped Rodman off in Bronzeville, the big man stepped through drifts to his building. Kelson cut back to the interstate and followed a snowplow to the northside.

He went up to his apartment and fed Payday and Painter's Lane a late dinner. He boiled a pot of frozen ravioli for himself. As he spooned a second helping on to his plate, he remained silent. The wind-blown snow seemed to have whirled in his head as well as the air outside, confusing his thoughts, making them unspeakable. 'Just goes to show – what?' he said to Painter's Lane.

She cocked her head, as if she thought he would offer her a ravioli.

'Which just goes to show.' He took his plate into the kitchenette, scraped it.

Payday came into the kitchenette, rubbing against the door molding. She meowed at him.

'You're right,' he told her. 'Love the one you're with.'

What would Frida be serving to the few customers who fought through the storm to reach Club Richelieu? He got his phone and texted her one word. *Tomorrow?*

Then he dialed Nancy's number. When she picked up, he said, 'Love the one you're with.'

'Excuse me?'

'Not that I still love you,' he said, 'which isn't to say I don't. But that isn't why I'm calling – which is only partly true.'

'Why *are* you calling, Sam?' she said.

'To make sure you and Sue Ellen got home safe in the storm.'

'First, we were both home when the snow started. Second, you don't need to check up on me now that we're apart.'

'How about Sue Ellen? Do I get to check on her?'
'Sue Ellen's fine,' she said. 'Goodnight, Sam.' She hung up.
Kelson held the phone to his ear. 'Me too. Home safe.'

THIRTY-THREE

Kelson fell asleep with his phone by his ear. When it rang
the next morning, he jolted from a dream in which his
therapist, Dr P, was shaking him by the shoulders and
refusing to stop.

He grabbed the phone, read the time – 5:24 a.m. –
and answered. *'Cut it out.'*

'Mr Kelson?' The voice was shaky.

'Yeah, right.'

'This is Jeremy Jacobson – from Clement Memorial—'

'A call from a doctor at five in the morning – always bad
news. Like cops knocking on the door in the middle of the night.'

'I'm afraid I need your help. I learned about a situation twenty
minutes ago. It's urgent.'

'A *situation*?'

'Yes.' Nothing more.

'Meet you at your office?'

'If you could come to my house . . .'

'Hold on a second.' Kelson got out of bed, went to the window,
and stared down through the dark. Snow was still falling, but a
plow had come through, and under the streetlights the street
looked passable. 'Eight o'clock?'

'Sooner, if you can, please.' Jacobson gave him an address on
North Orchard.

'I'll be there around seven.'

Kelson showered and shaved. He fried an egg. Payday jumped
on the counter and watched him. 'Yeah, what the hell,' he said.
He slid the egg from the pan to a plate, tore a strip of egg white,
laid it on the counter for the cat, and ate standing by the sink.

As he rinsed his plate, his phone rang again. Caller ID said
Jose Feliciano. Kelson answered, 'Howdy, partner.'

'They busted her,' Jose said, his voice as shaky as Jacobson's.

'What? Who busted who?'

'The cops came two hours ago. They arrested Wendy. You've got to help, man.'

'Why? What did she do?'

'She didn't do anything.'

'What did the cops say she did?'

'They told her her rights like that, and they put her in the squad car. They didn't tell me anything. Wendy needs your help.'

'You have a pen and paper?' Kelson gave him his lawyer's contact information. 'Ed can find out what's up as fast as anyone in the city. If there's a way to get her out, he'll do that too.'

'You've got to come over here,' Jose said. 'I need to show you – it's messed up, man.'

'What aren't you telling me?'

'You've got to see it. It doesn't make sense.'

'Give me an address. I'll be there at nine or ten.'

Jose gave him the address in South Lawndale, where he and Wendy lived. 'Hurry, my friend.'

'Nine or ten,' Kelson said.

The morning sky was still dark, the snow falling gently, when he left his building. He trudged to the parking lot and wiped the car windows.

As he sat, warming the engine, his phone rang again.

He answered, 'On my way.'

But a woman's voice spoke. 'I need to see you.' It was Caroline Difley, who got fired along with Aleksandar Kovacic when Kelson revealed their leaks to Jacobson.

'You're kidding,' Kelson said.

'Can I meet you at your office?' she said.

'Hell, the way it's going, let's schedule for next week.'

'I'll be there in an hour – waiting.'

'No, look, give me till noon. What's this about?'

'Aleksandar.'

'The genius custodian.'

'I don't think so,' she said.

'Tell me,' he said.

'It's lies – most of it. I'll show you at your office.'

*　　*　　*

The 1800 block of North Orchard ran one-way northbound past multi-million dollar houses built in a mix of styles, early twentieth century to futuristic. Jeremy Jacobson owned one of the oldest and best kept – a three-story greystone with a basement garage, narrow windows, and a high front door. A black wrought-iron fence, piled high with snow, enclosed the front steps. On either side of the driveway, where Scott Jacobson had backed over his mom six years before, tall hedges, draped with snow, reached toward the sky. 'Ghosts,' Kelson said, and pulled in.

Jeremy Jacobson opened the front door and watched as Kelson came through the gate. He wore khakis and a yellow V-neck cashmere sweater. His fleshy face looked heavy and tired, but his eyes were alert. 'Thank you,' he said. 'Thank you so much.'

Kelson kicked the ice off his shoes and stepped into a high-ceilinged front hall. 'What's this about?'

'Please,' the doctor said, and he led Kelson to a kitchen, where his son Rick sat by an open laptop. 'Please take a look.' Rick turned the laptop so Kelson could see.

Kelson stared at a spreadsheet with six columns, each topped with three or four capital letters – which meant nothing to him. 'Very impressive,' he said.

'Look,' Rick said, and brought up another spreadsheet. 'That's last month.'

'That sure is a bunch of numbers.'

The father and son exchanged a glance. 'We've known there's a problem for several months,' the doctor said. 'We do internal checks. Even if we weren't required to, we—'

'Epinephrine,' Rick said. 'Fentanyl. See that? And that?' He tapped the screen. 'It's missing.'

'Where's Scott?' Kelson said.

'At his apartment,' the doctor said. 'Why?'

'He should be here for this.'

'He has nothing to do with it,' the doctor said, 'no connection to the hospital.'

'And enough problems of his own,' Rick said.

'Five to one, he stole the drugs,' Kelson said,

'Nonsense.' The doctor looked flushed.

'Last night, I would've spread the odds evenly between the three of you, maybe tipping toward him, but since you two called me, let's throw the money on Scott.'

The father and son exchanged another glance. Then Rick exited the spreadsheet and opened a video file. 'Watch,' he said.

In grainy color, a woman in a red dress and open medical coat walked into the Clement Memorial pharmacy supply room. Suzanne Madani. For several seconds, she stood still, as if she forgot why she'd come. Then she moved into one of the aisles, took a large plastic-wrapped box from a metal shelf, and broke it open.

'Epinephrine,' Rick said.

Madani took a handful of vials and put them in her coat pocket, then took another handful, and another.

'She had no good reason to do that,' the doctor said.

'Even if she did, she'd record it in the computer log,' Rick said.

'Huh.'

'Then, this.' Rick opened another video. 'This was four days ago, the morning before she died.'

Madani came into the room again, her medical coat buttoned. Her movements were jerky. She took another box from the shelf – this one already unsealed. She took a handful of vials, pocketed them, and returned the box to the shelf.

'Fentanyl?' Kelson asked.

'Yes,' the doctor said.

'How much did she steal?'

'Three or four units.'

'That makes no sense,' Kelson said.

'If it made sense, I wouldn't have called you,' the doctor said.

Rick opened a third video. 'This was two nights ago,' he said. 'Late. After Madani was dead.'

A small, round woman in thick lipstick came into the room.

'That can't be right,' Kelson said.

The woman took the box of fentanyl from the shelf. She plunged her hand in, just as Madani did in the previous video. She put the box back on the shelf. As she left, she turned her face straight to the camera as if posing for a mugshot.

'Wendy Thomas,' Rick said.

'Huh,' Kelson said.

'I wish you wouldn't say that,' the doctor said. 'It makes me question whether you're the right man for the job.'

'What job?'

'When Rick suspected thefts, he put in new cameras – hidden – aligned with each aisle in the supply room. Rick wanted to handle the situation internally. The hospital directors much prefer to deal with this kind of thing discreetly – partly out of concern for employees suffering from addictions but, as you might guess, mostly because they worry about the hospital's name and profitability. Rick had the situation under control until Dr Madani's death.' He gave his son a tight-lipped nod before continuing. 'He may have thought he still had it under control even after the videos of Dr Madani. But now we have the video of Wendy Thomas. You understand this is very delicate.'

The doctor went to a cabinet and opened it. Next to the china, there was a white envelope. He gave it to Kelson.

Kelson opened it and riffled a stack of fifties.

'Five thousand dollars,' the doctor said. 'We can draw up a contract as soon as there's time.'

'What's the job?' Kelson said.

'We understand you're working for Wendy Thomas's fiancé. She appears in only the one video. We need to account for the fentanyl – which means creating a plausible medical reason for her removing the drug, a reason she agrees to sign off on. We need to head this off immediately and quietly.'

'You're at least a few hours too late.' Kelson handed the envelope back to the doctor. 'The police arrested Wendy Thomas last night.'

THIRTY-FOUR

Kelson drove to South Lawndale, where Jose Feliciano and Wendy Thomas lived in a brick bungalow, a few houses in from 31st and Albany. The couple could look out their front window, across La Villita Park, to a towering industrial smokestack and, next to it, a Department of Corrections Division IX maximum-security dormitory. But on summer evenings when the wind blew warm, families grilled and picnicked in the park, and the air would smell of charcoal smoke and cooking meat and the sugary sweetness of *churro* carts. Today, when

Kelson got out of the car, the park was a blanket of untrammeled white, and the air smelled of snow.

Kelson rang the doorbell, and Jose let him in to a bright little living room. A framed poster for the Atlantic City Bull Riding Invitational hung on one wall. In the middle of the poster, under the word *CHAMPIONSHIP*, Jose rode an enormous white bull, his right hand gripping a braided bull rope, his left hand raised to the sky as if praising God, the bull bucking its hind quarters as if it meant to send Jose to the God he praised.

The man who stood in the living room with Kelson looked angry enough to climb off that bull and throw it to the dirt. 'They say Wendy stole drugs from the hospital,' he said.

'She did,' Kelson said.

As if he didn't hear: 'Wendy never, *never* . . .' Jose caught his breath. 'Wendy's the most honest – the *most* honest—'

'The hospital installed cameras,' Kelson said. 'I saw the video. She went into the supply room two nights ago, grabbed a bunch of fentanyl, and walked out.'

Now the words penetrated. 'She *what*?'

'Then, yesterday, Josh Templeton's mom died of a fentanyl overdose. I'm guessing the drug that killed her is the same that Wendy stole. I doubt the cops have connected her to it yet, but they'll get there. Then they'll charge Wendy with murder.'

'What the hell are you talking about, *cabrón*?' Now Jose looked ready to throw Kelson to the dirt.

'I'm telling you what I saw. I'm telling you the way it's going to be – unless Wendy can explain her way out of this.'

'She stole nothing,' Jose said.

'I *saw* her.'

'If she took anything, a doctor told her to. How did she get into the supply room?'

'She walked through the door.'

'She doesn't have a key. Nurses aren't allowed. Somebody let her in.'

'Not on the video. Did you call Ed Davies?'

Jose shook his head, like the whole world sickened him. 'He said he was busy. He'll get to Wendy this afternoon. I told him, this is my fiancée – she's never been in jail. He needs to get her out.'

Kelson checked his watch. Ten fifteen. He phoned Davies.

The lawyer picked up on the fourth ring. 'Don't tell me I need to bail you out too.'

'I'm one step ahead of trouble, or behind it, or—'

'What d'you need?'

'I'm standing here with Wendy Thomas's fiancé. Any chance you can get to her before this afternoon?'

'I've been waiting on her at Harrison Street since nine,' Davies said.

Kelson gave Jose a thumbs-up. 'It'll be a narcotics charge,' he told Davies. 'Maybe theft in there too.'

'Yeah, I knew that at nine-oh-five. But something's funny about this. Usually, I see a client within a half-hour of arriving, unless the client refuses counsel – or agrees to talk without me – or the police hold off on the interview because whatever's happening is happening fast. Whatever it is, someone usually tells me, because they know I'll bust their balls in court if they don't.'

Kelson gave Jose a thumbs-down. He told Davies, 'Get her out now, or else she'll be facing a murder charge.'

'Do you want to explain that?'

'My *wanting* to explain it has nothing to do with my explaining it.' He told him about finding Deneesa Smithson dead in Fort Wayne and about the videos the Jacobsons showed him.

'Answer this without letting the fiancé know I'm asking,' Davies said. 'Would Wendy Thomas be better off in jail? For her own safety – or others'?'

Kelson held the phone away and, because he couldn't help himself, asked Jose, 'Would Wendy be better off in jail?'

'No,' Jose said.

'No,' Kelson told Davies.

'I'll see what I can do. One more question, and *don't* tell him I'm asking. Do *you* think she's responsible for this woman's death?'

Kelson stared at Jose but told Davies, 'I don't know. I can't see why she would be, but I really don't know.'

'I'll call as soon as I have something,' Davies said, and hung up.

When Kelson relayed the message, Jose didn't look like that would be enough. Kelson said, 'He can do more than just about anyone else.' Still not enough. 'He's done it for me. More than once.' Still. 'You need to tell me everything you know.'

'What can I say? I told you, Wendy wouldn't do this.'

'Tell me what you know about the Jacobsons. Especially Scott.'

'Why? What's up with them?'

Kelson told him about Patricia Ruddig witnessing the accident that killed Terry Ann Jacobson.

'I don't know, man,' Jose said. 'I hear the gossip, you know. The doctor – him and his wife was like a love story. They say he was mean before her. Then they met, and she's something special. They say he became like a new man with her and his kids. You know, caring.'

'I looked her up online but didn't find much,' Kelson said.

'When they met, she was a pharmaceutical salesperson, you know. Or medical equipment. This was a while ago – like thirty years. Long time before I started at the hospital. She and Jacobson got married and they had the boys. Rick, then Scott. I don't know about them when they were kids. But everyone around the ICU knows them now. Rick wants to be a big man – a playboy with all the girls. You know what we call men like him at the rodeo. *Gunsels*. They dress like big boys – they have pride – but everyone laughs at them. A proud little man who wants people to think he's a big man – that's dangerous. His brother, Scott – he's another thing. Too bad about him and his mom.'

'What are the stories about that?' Kelson asked.

'Stories, that's all. Some say Scott argued with her. Some say that's a lie. She was on the driveway – I know that much – talking on the phone with Dr Jacobson. Scott backed out of the garage and hit her. Some say he meant to do it. Anyway, he kept driving. Maybe he panicked. He ran her over. Then he drove away.'

'The police found him by the lake?'

'That's what they say. Story is he tried to kill himself. After that, they sent him away for a while. You know, these rich people, they tell the cops to close their eyes and put their fingers in their ears, and the cops do it – I see it at the hospital. The people say they'll send their son or daughter to rehab. They say they'll get a psychologist. Family wishes. Dr Jacobson already lost his wife. The cops left Scott alone, the way it always is.'

'Not if Scott meant to kill his mom,' Kelson said. 'That would be too much for them.'

'You don't know cops the way I do.'

'I used to be one.'

'That's what I'm saying. Anyway, no one really knows what happened.'

'Patricia Ruddig knew. She wanted to testify.'

'A long time ago, man.'

'How well does Wendy know Scott?'

'No reason she should know him more than I do. He comes around because of his dad and Rick. Mostly, we try to avoid him.'

'Does Wendy get along with the other Jacobsons?'

'Until Dr Madani got her in trouble when that lady Jennifer Kowalski died. The hospital took Wendy back, but she thinks Dr Jacobson's looking for her to make a mistake.'

'How well did she know Dr Madani?'

'It hurt her when the doctor blamed her for Jennifer Kowalski. Wendy always liked her. You know, respected her. She thought Dr Madani respected her too.'

'Madani seems to have had a complicated life,' Kelson said. 'Can you think of any reason Wendy would steal the fentanyl?'

'No.' Again, Jose looked like he was getting ready to wrestle a bull. 'She wouldn't. Whatever you saw on that video, it's a lie.'

'Love sucks that way, doesn't it?' Kelson said.

'What do you mean?'

'You see evidence that someone you love did something wrong. You know it's a fact. But you deny it anyway.'

'The evidence is a lie,' Jose said.

'Yeah, love sucks that way.'

THIRTY-FIVE

Kelson arrived at his office at a quarter to noon. Caroline Difley stood outside his door, a camelhair coat draped over her arm, a manila folder in her hand.

He stuck his key in the lock, and said, 'Before you tell me what you have, tell me about Suzanne Madani.'

'Sad,' she said.

'Yeah, sad,' he said.

'What's to tell? Out to save the world, even if the world doesn't want to be saved.' They went in, and she laid her coat over one of the client chairs and sat on the other. 'She was from Connecticut. Got married when she was in med school at Temple. Divorced when she was doing her residency. Came out as gay six, seven years ago. Dated a veterinarian named Liz for three years – the vet got the dog when they broke up. Athletic, but not obsessive about it. Tried vegetarianism, missed Chicago hotdogs, gave up vegetarianism.'

'What's to tell?' Kelson said.

'Sitting at the orderly desk, you don't have to try to listen – you just hear.'

'What have you heard about the Jacobsons?'

'Which one?'

'Start with Scott.'

'Sad, too,' she said, then repeated much of what Jose had told Kelson, but as fact, not rumor. Scott and his mom argued. He killed her. He attempted suicide. His dad managed a cover-up. Scott spent time institutionalized somewhere in Wisconsin.

'How do you know all this?' Kelson asked.

'I worked at that desk for eleven years. I heard *everything*.' She opened the manila folder and laid three sheets of paper on his desk. The top sheet was a photocopy of a page from a high-school yearbook. It included a picture of Aleksandar Kovacic at eighteen years old – only it named him Alex in the margin.

'Lane Tech High School,' she said. 'On Addison? Aleksandar grew up in Chicago – not in Bosnia.'

She pulled away the page. The next was a transcript of Kovacic's freshman year at University of Chicago. The grades ranged from C to F, averaging around D-minus.

'Failed out,' she said.

'You've been busy,' Kelson said.

'I'm not working any more.' She laid her eyes on him. 'I have spare time.' She showed him the final sheet of paper, a printout from a company called Checkpeople.com. It said that Alex Kovacic was arrested twice for shoplifting – first when he was eighteen and again when he was nineteen.

'What the hell, right?' She was turning red.

Kelson asked, 'How did you get the Bosnian med student story to begin with?'

'Aleksandar told me. Why would he make up a story like this?'

'How good of friends are you?'

'We're work friends, that's all – or we were. You know, we got along. We'd have coffee. Sometimes we'd eat at the cafeteria.'

'Did you ever think he wanted to be more than work buddies?'

'Aleksandar? He's like fifteen years older.'

'Yeah, enough to make a guy tell stories to impress a woman he thinks is out of reach. There's a certain heroism in a man who suffered through a war and sacrificed so much, just to push a mop over a hospital floor. Kind of makes you want to take him in your arms.'

'I don't know what you're talking about.'

'A lonely refugee in a big country like this?'

'No,' she said. Then, more quietly, 'No. He lied. Why should I believe anything he said about the drugs? Why should *you*?'

'He still seems pretty smart. So maybe he tells a good story to impress a woman he works with. Maybe he tells the story to others so he can live with himself and his failures. Everything he said about the missing epinephrine checked out. He may be a liar, but he knows the hospital and he knows drugs.'

'I don't trust him,' she said.

'Probably a good idea. But I'll tell you something. After getting shot in the head, I tell the truth all the time. No filters. I'm totally trustworthy. But my wife divorced me. The police department kicked me out. Sometimes a good story might be better than the truth.'

'A good story is different from a lie. Aleksandar lied.'

'Ask him about it. Call him out. See what he says.'

She shook her head.

'You seemed to like him,' Kelson said.

'I liked the man he said he was.'

'Your loss. And his.'

'What if *he* stole the epinephrine?'

'Then it was pretty crowded in the supply room,' Kelson said. 'Plus, he told you – and me – about the thefts. And the two of you were gone from the hospital before Suzanne Madani died. Do you have any reason to think he was involved?'

'You mean aside from his lies and his arrest record?'

'A record that's thirty years old.'

'And the way he goes for walks in the cemetery?' she said.

'OK, that's spooky.'

She sighed. 'I've always liked him. He's always been smart and funny and kind.'

'Talk with him,' Kelson said. 'See what he tells you – how he explains the lies. But if he asks you to walk in a cemetery, suggest a coffee shop instead.'

She eyed Kelson. 'Will you come with me?'

'Don't you think you'll have a better conversation without me?'

'I don't know *what* I'll have.'

When she left, Kelson considered all he'd learned during the morning. He tried to prioritize the information according to importance. 'Useless,' he said. But he turned on his laptop and said, 'Begin at the beginning – or in the middle – or . . .'

He Googled Suzanne Madani.

Three hundred twelve hits.

The doctor appeared on the membership lists of the AMA, the Society of Critical Care Medicine, and the Chicago Medical Society. She attended a Labor Day benefit for the Childhood Leukemia Foundation. She belonged to a softball league run by the Chicago Metropolitan Sports Association. Nothing indicated she was an opioid addict or hung out with other addicts or was suicidal or liked sticking needles in her leg.

'But maybe nothing would,' Kelson said.

She was an undergraduate at Swarthmore before going to Temple Med.

'La-di-da,' Kelson said.

Her Facebook photos showed her at crowded bars, with her softball teammates, hand in hand with a blond woman.

'Sometimes what one hears is true,' Kelson said.

He exited Google and took his KelTec from under the desktop. He popped the magazine, saw it was loaded, and popped it back in. He laid the pistol on his desk. He nudged the barrel. The gun spun a quarter turn. He started to nudge it again – and his phone rang.

He jumped – then answered, '*What?*'

'*What* yourself,' Ed Davies said.

'Sorry. I almost shot myself in the balls.'

'You . . . never mind. I just met with Wendy Thomas. Can't say I know what to think.'

'Did she admit she stole the fentanyl?'

'Anything but. She says she was putting the fentanyl back. What exactly did you see on the video?'

'No way. She went into the room – where she wasn't allowed. She waited a moment, like she knew what she was doing was wrong. Then she dug into the box of fentanyl.'

'Did you actually see her take the vials?'

'I don't know . . . No. But why else would she reach into the box?'

'She says she found a bunch of vials in her work locker the day before Suzanne Madani died. Says someone must've put them there, but she doesn't know who. Says her supervisor cracked down on her since the questions about the cefoxitin and Jennifer Kowalski's death. She thought someone was setting her up. She had the bright idea she could return the drugs.'

'Sounds ridiculous,' Kelson said.

'That's what I told her. She insists it's true.'

'Who let her into the supply room?'

'She won't say. I told her that knowing who it was could make a big difference to what happens to her. She still wouldn't tell.'

'So did you get her out?'

'No – they charged her with killing Deneesa Smithson. With aggravating circumstances.'

THIRTY-SIX

At two o'clock that afternoon, when Kelson walked through the homicide room at the Harrison Street police station, Venus Johnson and Dan Peters were sitting in their cubicle.

'Howdy,' Kelson said.

'How did you get in here?' Johnson asked.

'Sounds like he rode a goddamned horse,' Peters said.

'The guy at security recognized me from when I was a cop – waved me through. Funny, it's three years and I don't remember his name, but he said, "Afternoon, Kelson," like we were pals.'

'Heartwarming,' Johnson said. 'What d'you want?'

'Everything you've got on the Wendy Thomas case.'

'Get out,' she said.

'I—'

'I mean it. Leave. Or I'll call your pal at security and tell him to drag you out.'

'Wendy Thomas says she didn't steal the fentanyl. She says she was putting it back.'

Peters stood, as if he would drag Kelson out himself. 'You don't think she told us that? You don't think her lawyer told us again? Do you realize how stupid that sounds?'

'Yes.'

'Then get out,' Peters said.

'She had no reason to steal the fentanyl.'

Johnson gave him a disappointed smile. 'No reason to shoot up a woman who got her suspended from her job a week ago?'

'Suzanne Madani? She died before Wendy Thomas appeared on the supply room video.'

'Appeared *this* time,' Peters said. 'The cameras went in only a month ago. Who knows how many times she snuck in before?'

'Zero. She had no reason to.'

'Prove it,' Johnson said.

'You can't prove something like that.'

'Exactly,' she said.

'You haven't charged her with Madani's death.'

'Yet,' Peters said.

'What about Deneesa Smithson?' Kelson said. 'Why would Thomas want to kill her?'

Peters moved toward him, signaling it was time to go. 'Open investigation.'

'Which means, you don't have an answer.'

'No – it means it's not your problem.'

'You've got nothing,' Kelson said.

'Now you sound as stupid as she does,' Johnson said.

'C'mon, scoot,' Peters said.

'Do me a favor first.'

Peters took him by the wounded arm. 'Only favor we'll do is if we don't kick you in the ass.'

Kelson peeled Peters' fingers off, one at a time. 'Tell me about the investigation into Terry Ann Jacobson's death six years ago. It got filed as accidental. One of her sons drove over her with her car on their driveway. What do the notes say? Who investigated?'

Venus Johnson yelled at him. 'Out!'

But Peters moved back to his desk chair and sat, heavily enough to get a glance from Johnson.

'Something there?' Kelson said to him.

Now Johnson rose from her chair. 'Out. Go on.' She shoved Kelson from the cubicle.

'Hold on.' Peters was standing again. 'Get back in here a minute.'

They found an empty interview room. Peters looked at the camera mounted by the ceiling to make sure the recording light was off.

'I was secondary,' he said. 'This was before me and Venus partnered. I was with an old guy named Freddy DeVos – you ever know him when you were on the Narcotics squad?'

'Never heard of him,' Kelson said.

'Sure. He was a quiet guy. On Homicide since forever – retired a couple months after the Terry Ann Jacobson thing. Bought a place outside Tucson. He was always thorough. He taught me a lot. A lot of good lessons.'

'But with Terry Ann Jacobson?'

'Not so good,' Peters said. 'The woman's son needed help. No question about it. Freddy said that when he first joined Homicide – before you and me were even born – that boy would've gone straight to the nuthouse. No investigation – because the mind of a kid like that, it was outside of what we could do. Freddy was old school. He took care of it old school.'

'Scott Jacobson meant to run over his mom?'

'Sure looked like it. Look, Freddy wasn't a bad guy—'

'What did Jeremy Jacobson pay him?'

'He's in Arizona, isn't he? I hear it's a nice house. Pool. Pretty fountain in the cactus garden.'

'Shit,' Venus Johnson said.

'Jeremy Jacobson runs the ICU where Wendy Thomas works,' Kelson said. 'Scott is in and out all the time. You don't want to get too confident that Thomas did this.'

'Shit,' Johnson said again. 'Shit, shit, shit.'

THIRTY-SEVEN

Kelson drove back to Jose Feliciano's house. The plows had cleared the streets, and cars sped over the salted pavement.

Jose answered the doorbell, looking ragged.

'Davies told you about the charges?' Kelson said.

'Yeah – and it's on TV.' He seemed smaller, hunched, as if pain bent him inward. 'The picture they're showing. It doesn't look like Wendy.'

'That's good. Keep your own idea of her in your head. It'll be easier afterward.'

'You think?' They walked to the kitchen. 'Break my bones, man. But not this.'

'I just came from the police,' Kelson said. 'They know there's more going on than Wendy. It'll work out if they do their job.'

Jose didn't seem to hear. He opened the refrigerator, stared at the juice, the eggs. He closed the refrigerator and stared at the teapot on the stove. 'You want something, man?'

'No,' Kelson said.

'Me neither.'

'Someone let Wendy into the supply room. She won't tell Davies who. She won't tell the cops. D'you have any idea who might let her in? Could she have gotten a key?'

'She never told me about any of this,' Jose said. 'You live with a person, you know? You look in her eyes when you eat. You kiss her. You make love to her in your bed. But you don't see it. She's got a secret. It makes me angry – and sad. It makes me real sad.'

'Could we look through her things?' Kelson said.

Jose shook his head. 'That's crossing a line.'

'The cops will come as soon as they get a search warrant. They'll look for a key to the supply room. They'll look for drugs or anything else Wendy might've taken from the hospital, anything connecting her to Madani or Deneesa Smithson. It's better if we find it first.'

Jose still shook his head, but he walked from the kitchen to the bedroom.

Kelson went to the dresser and opened the top drawer. It was full of Wendy's underwear and bras.

'You punch me in the heart,' Jose said.

Kelson touched nothing. He closed the drawer and opened the one under it. Jose's underwear and socks.

'Next one down,' Jose said.

Wendy's other drawers contained T-shirts and shorts, sweatpants and pajamas. At the front of the bottom drawer, there was a jewelry box. It contained hoop earrings, necklaces, a thin gold bracelet.

Kelson found nothing interesting in the closet. He found no unmarked or mismarked medicine vials in the bathroom cabinets, no stolen or borrowed medical equipment of any kind.

'Where do the two of you keep bills, deeds, that kind of thing?' he asked.

They went back to the kitchen and Jose opened a door into a room with a washer and dryer. Next to the ironing board, there was a table, and next to the table, a scuffed wooden cabinet, stacked with papers.

Kelson thumbed through the papers. Nothing worth knowing.

He walked back through the house, opening doors, drawers, and cabinets, fingering the things on the shelves.

'I got pride, you know,' Jose said, as if unsure how much he should resent Kelson.

'You want boundaries or you want Wendy?' Kelson went back into the bedroom and dug through the underwear and bras.

'I got pride,' Jose said again.

'Never give it up.' Kelson held up the red camisole by the straps like he was inspecting a flag. Then he opened the drawer of T-shirts and shorts.

'Stop,' Jose said.

'What?'

Jose pulled out his phone. He opened his photos. 'Two nights ago, I looked in her purse when she was in the shower.'

'You snooping bastard,' Kelson said.

'She acted funny, you know? Nervous.' He gave the phone to Kelson. 'She had a letter. I took a picture.'

The picture was of a notice, printed on letterhead, from the

Human Resources department at Clement Memorial. The notice listed three violations of hospital policy over the past six months.

Wendy failed to show up for a scheduled shift on August 9. She was overly familiar and demonstrated a lack of professional etiquette with a patient named Tamara Adma during the days of December 6–9. In connection with that incident, she failed to follow the directives of a Dr Robert Clerey and showed insubordination when reprimanded by Jeremy Jacobson. Then she failed to respond fully and accurately when asked about administering cefoxitin to Jennifer Kowalski on January 17. The notice warned that any further disciplinary problems would result in her firing.

'She didn't tell you about this?' Kelson said.

'She has pride too. The day when she didn't go to work, her car wouldn't start. She called the supervisor. The problem with Tamara Adma – that old lady was Haitian. She didn't speak English. She was scared.'

'What was the thing with the doctor?'

'Clerey was new. Wendy thought he made a mistake on a medical order.'

'Did he?'

'Clerey said he didn't. He shouted at Wendy. Wendy didn't like that. She called him a *tet zozo*. It's the same as dickhead. He didn't know what she said, but Tamara Adma did, and the way that old lady laughed at him – he reported Wendy to Dr Jacobson. Then Dr Jacobson shouted at her too. She called him a *zozo santi*. Stinky dick.'

'Nice,' Kelson said.

'Look at the next one. It's a picture I got from Wendy's phone.'

Kelson swiped the screen.

'What the hell?' he said.

The picture was of Kelson himself. He recognized the place and time. He was coming out of Dr Madani's office on the night he found her dead – turning from the door toward the elevator bank. Wendy Thomas must have been thirty or forty feet away, standing in another office doorway or at the corner to the next corridor.

'I didn't see her,' he said. 'Was she there when I came or was she following me?'

'She doesn't trust you so much, my friend. One more picture.'

Kelson swiped. 'Huh.' Rick Jacobson stood at Madani's door.
'She took that picture after she took the one of you.'

'Why didn't you show this to me before?'

Again, Jose looked unsure. 'Wendy didn't work on the night
Dr Madani died. She shouldn't have been at the hospital. I don't
know why she was in that hall.'

'How sure are you she had nothing to do with the killings?'

Jose shook his head. 'All my life, I've had a feeling I know
what's true. When I ride a bull, I sense what he will do next. In
my legs. In my chest – do you understand? In my arms. I don't
think about it, but I *know*. I can feel how it is with Wendy. The
way she moves. The way she talks. I know.'

'But then a bull breaks your back – and Wendy has secrets.'

Jose looked sad again. 'Yes.'

'So, that's all you have? This *feeling*?'

Now resentment spread across the bull rider's face. 'Yes. But
it's the right feeling.'

'You'd put your neck on the line for it?'

'I'd put all of me.'

'OK.'

'Yeah?'

'For now,' Kelson said. 'When the police come with their
search warrant, maybe you should keep your phone out of
their hands. Maybe Wendy's phone and the HR letter could go
missing too.'

THIRTY-EIGHT

In the basement at Clement Memorial, Rick Jacobson sat on
the corner of the front desk. The receptionist, in a Chicago
Bears sweatshirt, was blushing. Rick looked pleased with
himself.

When Kelson stepped into the security office, they straightened
their faces as if he'd caught them misbehaving. But when Rick
asked how he could help Kelson, the receptionist giggled as if
she and her boss had been telling jokes about him.

'When I found Suzanne Madani in her office, you showed up

right after I left,' Kelson said. 'Before the police came.' As if the joke was on Rick.

'Uh-huh?'

'Why?'

Rick glanced at the receptionist. 'Because . . . I'm Director of Security?'

'But why would you go to her office right then?'

'A homicide detective called and asked me to check. Venus Johnson. She said you phoned in a crazy story about Dr Madani OD'ing. She wanted me to take a look before she wasted her time and resources.'

'Oh,' Kelson said.

'I guess you wasted her time and resources before?'

'That might be a matter of opinion.'

'You aren't so bright, are you?'

'I have better days and worse.'

'Looks like this might be one of the bad ones.'

The receptionist let out a little laugh, though she didn't seem sure she knew what she was laughing at.

'What about Scott?' Kelson said.

'What about him?'

'I talked to Venus Johnson again this morning. I heard some stories about him and your mom. D'you know if he also went to Suzanne Madani's office on the night she died?'

Rick slid off the desk. 'Out.'

'That's what Venus Johnson said this morning. Then we sat down for a long talk. You used a master key to get into Madani's office, right? Did you ever lend it to Scott?'

Rick grabbed Kelson and steered him out of the office. 'C'mon.' He took him past the cafeteria and imaging lab toward the elevator bank.

'I hear Dr Madani ate dinner down here on the night she died,' Kelson said. 'Does Scott spend time with you in your office? Maybe he ran into her and decided she needed a kill-shot of fentanyl.'

'Shut your damn mouth.' Rick steered him around a bend.

'But what would Scott have against her? I know why he might hurt Patricia Ruddig – with the whole witnessing thing. I don't know about Josh Templeton or Daryl Vaughn. Or Josh's mom or Suzanne Madani. What's your theory?'

Rick's fist seemed to come from nowhere. His knuckles cracked against Kelson's jaw, and Kelson fell to the floor. He sat on the tile, stunned. Rick looked like he was thinking of kicking him. 'Stay the fuck away,' he said, and went back down the hall toward the security office.

Two nurses, coming from the cafeteria, gazed at Kelson as if they might offer help. Instead they scurried toward the elevators.

Kelson went up to his car and cranked the heat high. As warm air spilled from the vents, he inspected his chin in the mirror. It was red and painful to the touch, but the skin was unbroken. 'Joke's on me,' he told the man in the mirror, 'after all.'

So he pulled out his phone and dialed.

The number rang twice, and Sue Ellen's voicemail picked up. Her recorded voice – which always made Kelson think of bells – said, 'Mom says I can't tell you my name because you might be a scumbag, but if you aren't, please leave a message.' The *please* dripping with twelve-year-old irony. She added, 'If this is Dad, two words. *Potbellied pig.*' The message signal beeped.

'Is *potbellied* one or two words?' Kelson asked. Then he said, 'It's about four o'clock. I just called to say hello. Love you.'

He hung up and cocked his head so he could see his chin in the mirror. 'Going to be nasty,' he said.

He started to dial another number – but the phone rang in his hand. Caller ID said it was Sue Ellen.

'Hey, kiddo.'

'Oink,' she said.

'Ha. Why weren't you answering your phone?'

'I'm meeting with my math tutor.'

'Since when do you have a math tutor?'

'Since Mom saw what I got on my algebraic expressions test.'

'What are you doing calling back while you're in a tutoring session?'

'It's boring.' As if the *r* in *boring* went on forever.

'Is he at least cute?' Kelson said.

'Who?'

'Your math tutor.'

Sue Ellen held the phone away, and Kelson heard her ask,

'Mrs Christensen, my dad wants to know if you're cute.' She came back to the phone. 'Mrs Christensen is glaring at you.'

'She can't even see me.'

'A math tutor can see everything.' Then, 'Now she's smiling at you.'

'It's good to hear your voice, honey,' he said.

'*Potbellied* is one word. A compound. Now, Mrs Christensen is smiling at *me*. Kind of creepy.'

'Love you, kiddo,' Kelson said.

'Love you too.' She hung up.

He looked at the mirror. 'See?'

Then he dialed a second number.

Frida picked up. 'Hi there.'

'Hi there,' he said. 'Sorry I didn't call earlier. Can we get together after work?'

'Uh-huh. Pick me up when Richelieu closes?'

He glanced at the mirror. 'What do you think of bruises?'

'Spanking's my limit. Maybe candle wax on the nipples.'

'Huh – I mean, not you. Me.'

'What're you into? Paddles? Riding crops?'

'Not if I can help it,' he said. 'But bruises happen sometimes – to me. As in twenty minutes ago.'

'Visible?'

'On the face.'

'If I don't like them, we'll turn out the lights.'

'That works for me.'

Kelson drove home. In the early evening, he lay on his bed with an icepack on his chin. Payday jumped on to the mattress, and then Painter's Lane joined them. The cats kneaded Kelson's chest. After a while, he dozed. He woke at nine p.m., then slept again. When he woke at midnight, the cats were gone, and he got up and stumbled to the kitchen. The cats were waiting at the refrigerator. 'Right,' he said, 'I'm nothing but a meal ticket.' He asked Painter's Lane, 'And if I don't feed you?'

She meowed.

'Right – you'll eat me.'

He fed them, topping each of their bowls with sliced ham.

Then he went into the bathroom, looked at the mirror, and ran his finger down his jawline. 'Not so bad,' he said.

He shaved, dragging the razor gently over the spot where Rick Jacobson had hit him.

At 1:30 in the morning, he sat at the Golden Apple Grill and told his regular waitress about taking a punch in the face.

She poured him a refill. 'Next time, keep your mouth shut, Rocky, and maybe the man won't stick his fist in it.'

'Next time, I'll take you along to remind me,' he said.

At three o'clock, Kelson picked up Frida at Club Richelieu. She didn't mind his bruises. At 3:45, back at his apartment, they kept the lights on.

THIRTY-NINE

As the sun rose the next morning, Kelson drove to Lower Wacker and walked the streets, looking for the professor. A woman with a sore on her lip said she saw him the previous evening on Lower Randolph. A man smoking a cigarette on a milk crate on Lower Randolph said he saw him in the middle of the night sitting in a cloud of vent steam by a lower-level garage entrance on North Columbus. 'Like a wizard,' the man said, and spat.

A half-hour later, Kelson found the professor on South Water Street, standing by his shopping cart, staring at a shaft of daylight that fell from between the upper-level roads. His red hair was filthy, but the lenses on his wire-rimmed glasses shone clean. Somewhere along the way, he'd lost his waifish companion. 'Like the gleam in God's eyes,' he said, as Kelson approached, 'if God had eyes to see.'

'It'll blind you if you keep staring,' Kelson said.

The professor kept staring. 'Do you know what Derrida said about death? It's "the possibility of the impossible." He died nastily – pancreatic cancer – and he never accepted his mortality. He said he was "uneducable about the wisdom of learning to die." For Heidegger, on the other hand, death, or what he called "being-toward-death," was liberating. On this point, I think Derrida had it right and Heidegger was full of shit.'

'Where's the girlfriend?'

The professor lowered his eyes to him. 'You haven't listened to a word I said. Mycobacterium tuberculosis.'

'What?'

'My assistant has TB. Drug resistant. The clinic put her in a house where they can monitor her. She'll die. They always do.'

'*They?*'

'The people I love.'

'I'm sorry.'

'Yes.' He stared at the beam of sunlight.

Kelson tried looking at it. He managed three seconds before he felt a searing. 'I need to know more about Daryl Vaughn.'

'Dead too.'

'The thing is, I'm confused by his death.'

'We all suffer from the "non-access to death,"' the professor said. 'Unless we're Heidegger.'

'You were with Daryl when the kids beat him with the baseball bats?'

The professor was still staring at the sunbeam. 'It was a moment of cowardice on my part – mitigated only by the fact that I was protecting my assistant, lest the boys attack her too. But my protection was unnecessary. The boys were interested only in beating Daryl.'

'Did they say anything?'

The professor turned his eyes back to Kelson. 'They made it clear they meant to thrash him to death.'

'Did they say why?'

'I refer you to Foucault's reinterpretation of Galtung's conception of structural violence.'

'Please don't.'

'The boys used all the usual epithets for an African American. They insinuated that Daryl engaged in non-normative sexual activities. In short, they seemed interested in demonstrating domination. They beat him with wooden sticks. It's an ancient ritual.'

'Last time we talked, you said Daryl thought he was living out part of someone's story. He felt like a puppet, a character in a book. Did the kids who beat him say anything connected to that? Did Daryl say anything afterward that made you think of it?'

'The boys broke his jaw. They beat him unconscious. He said

nothing.' The professor jerked his head away and stared at the sunbeam again, as if a strange bird flew through the light. Then he looked back at Kelson. 'But you know what Foucault says about power.'

'What does Foucault say about insane professors?'

'Foucault and madness? Surely you're joking.'

'Am I?'

'He wrote the definitive account.'

'What do you know about Daryl and a family named Jacobson?'

'What *don't* I know?'

'I'm sorry?'

'The Jacobsons figured centrally in his stories.'

Kelson felt the rush he felt at moments like this. 'Careful,' he said. 'Did he mention a doctor? Jeremy Jacobson?'

The professor smiled nervously, as if Kelson was jiggling his sense of reality. 'Yes, Dr Jacobson was the teller of the story, the author of the book, the spinner of the dream. How do you know this?'

'Two sons?'

'At least two. With Daryl, it was sometimes hard to tell.'

'The boys' mother?'

'A tragic figure. Like all tragic figures, as Derrida taught us, she had a hole in the middle, an absence – the *O* in Ophelia.'

'Do you realize how annoying you are?'

'I lost my career because of it.'

'Me too,' Kelson said.

The professor gazed at Kelson as if he was a vaguely interesting critical problem. 'How do you know Daryl's story?'

'I don't. Or I only know part of it. Tell me what he told you.'

The professor eyed him suspiciously. 'Which version? He told it a hundred different ways. You know the distinction between story and plot, of course?'

'Uh-uh.'

The professor frowned. 'Story is *everything* that happened, every detail – events, actions, how much water was in the toilet, the design of the tire treads. Plot is how you tell it.'

'Just tell it,' Kelson said.

The professor's suspicion seemed to evaporate. He gave Kelson the look of a very smart man talking to a very stupid student.

'In most versions, Daryl worked for the Jacobson family and others like them, who hired him to do odd jobs.'

'He worked for them?'

'I'm *trying* to tell you. Daryl claimed to have been a handyman before his troubles. While he was doing one of his jobs for the Jacobsons – retiling a bathroom or scraping wallpaper from a bedroom, depending on the account – Mrs Jacobson accused him of stealing money from her purse. Daryl claimed one of her sons stole it. But she called the police and insisted on pressing charges. After Daryl got out of jail, he never worked again.'

'A simple plot,' Kelson said.

'A tale of injustice, as Daryl told it. He swore he didn't take the money. But, as in many retold folktales, the plot took various forms depending on the telling. In some versions, Daryl, distraught over the false accusation, went back and killed Mrs Jacobson. In others, one of her sons killed her. All versions converged at the end. Mrs Jacobson was wrong in believing Daryl was a thief. The injustice of her death echoed the injustice of Daryl's jailing.'

'Scott,' Kelson said.

The man's thoughtful face seemed to crack, replaced again by nervousness and a kind of crazed suspicion. 'What?'

'The name of one of the sons in Daryl's story. The one who killed his mom.'

For a moment, the professor looked distressed. Then, as if triggered by an invisible switch, he said, 'What does one understand under "the name of a name"? This is Derrida's question. "What occurs when one gives a name? One does not offer a thing, one delivers *nothing*, and still something comes to be."'

'Right,' Kelson said. 'I need you to talk to a couple of homicide cops.'

Another crack. 'No, no, no.'

'They're all right. They don't know this Derrida guy – or Foucault or the rest – but they're smarter than I am. You'll like them OK.'

'Uh-uh . . .' His philosophy abandoned him. He grabbed his shopping cart and shoved it into the traffic on South Water Street. A rusted white van swerved to avoid hitting him. The drivers in the cars behind the van slammed on their brakes.

Kelson started after him – jerked back when a VW cut around

another car and accelerated. 'What did Foucault say about playing in traffic?' he yelled at the professor.

As the professor rushed into the farther lanes, a ComEd truck smashed into his shopping cart, ripping it from his fingers, tumbling it down the pavement. For a moment, the professor froze. Then he darted between cars to the other side.

He turned – outraged, frantic – and yelled at Kelson. 'Coward!'

FORTY

K elson picked up Rodman forty minutes later at the head of the alley beside the Ebenezer Baptist Church. They drove through the mid-morning traffic, cut into the Loop, and returned to Clement Memorial.

They rode the elevator to the basement, passed through the cafeteria fumes, and went into the security office.

As they walked past the front desk, the receptionist said, 'Hey – you can't . . .' and then fumbled with her desk phone.

'Go ahead,' Rodman said, 'call security.'

He and Kelson went to Rick Jacobson's office, where the door was open and three men in blue security uniforms sat across the desk from their boss.

'Out,' Rodman said to them – and they stood like little soldiers.

'Hey,' Rick Jacobson said, 'you can't—'

'Oh, yes, I can. Meeting's over.'

The men moved toward the door.

Rick Jacobson said, 'Don't go anywhere.'

But Rodman cocked his head at them, and they slipped out.

Kelson smiled at Rick. 'I brought my big brother again.'

Rodman settled his narrow eyes on the security director. 'Did you hit my friend in the face?' His voice was gentle, terrifying.

'I'm calling the police.' Rick grabbed his phone.

Kelson sat on one of the chairs abandoned by the security men. 'Tell them you want to give them a statement about your family's old handyman, Daryl Vaughn. Tell them they might want to talk to Scott too.'

Rick set the phone back on the desk. He looked like he might get sick. 'What do you want?'

Kelson said, 'Wendy Thomas is in jail for stealing drugs from you and using them to kill the mother of one of the patients who died here. She didn't do it.'

'We have video that says she did,' Rick said. 'At least she stole the fentanyl—'

'Two patients who died here in the last six weeks had histories with your family,' Kelson said. 'Patricia Ruddig saw your brother run over your mom. Daryl Vaughn worked for you until your family fired him. Josh Templeton – whose mom Wendy Thomas is charged with killing – must have a connection to you too. You want to tell us about it?'

'I don't know what you're talking about.'

'And then, there's Suzanne Madani. What's that all about?'

'Dr Madani was troubled,' Rick said.

'You're grabbing anything that floats, aren't you?'

'She had an opioid problem. We were investigating her for admitting unauthorized patients. She—'

'The homeless guys she carted in from the streets and shelters.'

Rick looked unsurprised that Kelson knew. 'Yes. Eight of them over a period of three years. Do you know what that cost the hospital?'

'You're going to tell me, aren't you?'

'Upwards of a million dollars. These were terminal patients, many of them. Men who needed extensive and expensive care.'

'Stupid of her to bring them to a hospital for it.'

'You know it doesn't work that way.'

'Yeah, I guess that's my point.'

'The hospital would go bankrupt if everyone did what Dr Madani did.'

'Well, it looks like you took care of that problem.'

'*I* took care of nothing. I liked Dr Madani as far as I knew her. I think she must have had a good heart. But it didn't make her honest, and it didn't make her a victim.'

'What are you going to do about Wendy Thomas?'

The man was sweating. 'There's nothing I can do. We're cooperating with the—'

'Bullshit.' Rodman said it softly.

'Scott killed them,' Kelson said.

Rick rose from his chair as if he meant to punch him again. 'That's a hell of a thing to say.'

Kelson rose too. 'I can't prove it yet, but I will.'

'Get out,' Rick said.

'Sit down,' Rodman said.

But Rick was beyond fear. He came around the desk and said, 'Out. You don't come here and accuse – you don't—'

Rodman showed his palms, letting the other man know he didn't want to hurt him but could knock him across the office if he needed to. 'We're talking,' he said, 'just talking.'

Rick stopped. 'Not any more, we aren't.'

Kelson backed toward the door. 'You know it's only starting. The cops will come soon enough. They take longer than we do – they want to make sure they line everything right before moving against a family like yours – but they'll figure it out and they'll come. You can talk to us now, and we'll listen and maybe we can make things a little better, or—'

'Out,' Rick said, and he went after Kelson.

'OK,' Rodman said, stepping in front of him. 'No problem.'

'Too late to clean up,' Kelson said. 'Too late to buy your way out of this.'

Rodman took him by the arm and guided him from the office, past the receptionist, past the cafeteria, to the elevator bank.

When they got on, instead of heading back to the parking garage, Kelson touched the button for the floor above the ICU. 'Start at the bottom and work our way up,' he said.

Jeremy Jacobson was at his desk when Kelson knocked on his office door. The doctor told him to come in, then looked past him to Rodman – seemingly more curious than concerned about the big man.

'Did Rick tell you we were here?' Kelson asked.

The doctor looked confused. 'Did Rick tell me what?'

'No?' Kelson said. 'And that's interesting.'

The doctor looked more confused. 'I'm sorry – what is?'

'Rick,' Kelson said. 'And you. You and Rick – and Scott. The whole Jacobson family. Interesting.'

The doctor tried a smile. 'I'm glad you think so. What can I do for you?'

'Tell us about the day Scott killed your wife.'

Jacobson recoiled as if Kelson had slapped him. 'Jesus . . .'

'It must've been terrible,' Kelson said.

'Yes – terrible.'

'Your wife dead. Your son trying to off himself. I can only imagine what—'

'Why are you saying this?' The doctor looked stricken. 'What could possibly—'

'I can only imagine what you'd be willing to do to try to put it all back together again.'

The doctor ran his fingers through his thinning hair. 'There was no putting it together.'

'Exactly,' Kelson said. 'When I got shot in the head, I told the doctors I wanted everything back the way it was before. It was a bad joke, though I didn't know it then. Some things don't go back together. But d'you know what they said? They said, "We'll do the best we can." Sometimes that's all you can do – the best you can.'

Jeremy Jacobson stared at him, dumbfounded.

Rodman put a hand on Kelson's shoulder. 'What Sam's saying, I think, is it's understandable – whatever's going on. That doesn't make it right, but it's understandable.'

The doctor looked from Kelson to Rodman and back. 'I have no idea what you're talking about.'

'Tell us about the day Scott killed your wife,' Kelson said again.

'No,' the doctor said. '*No*. Why would I? Why would *you* want—?'

'What were they arguing about? We've heard she was on the driveway, talking to you on the phone. What was she telling you? Where were you? When you found out that Scott drove away after running her over, what did you do? What about when you found out he tried to kill himself? Did you talk to the police first – or your lawyer?'

The doctor started to cry.

'Oh, don't do that,' Kelson said.

Rodman said, 'How'd you work out the deal to put Scott in treatment instead of the lockup? I'm truly curious, because a guy who looks like me, it's straight to the joint. Hell, I don't have to kill my mom to get there – I can have a broken tail light.'

Tears shone in the doctor's eyes. 'Why are you doing this?' Kelson breathed out. 'You really don't know?'

'I know that one day I had a family and the next I didn't. I know I've tried to heal myself and my sons—'

'On that part,' Rodman said, 'you've come up short.'

The doctor looked from him to Kelson and back. 'I don't know what to say.'

'You'd better figure it out quick,' Kelson said. 'The truth hasn't always worked out so well for me, but *you* might want to try it.'

'I'm not sure I even know what the truth is,' the doctor said.

'That never stops me,' Kelson said. 'Talk with Rick. For Christ's sake, talk with Scott. Whatever happened – why ever it happened – you all are going to be owning it real soon.'

FORTY-ONE

Back in the Dodge Challenger, Kelson said, 'Go see Venus Johnson and Dan Peters?'

Rodman sank in the seat. 'You know I don't like going to the station.'

'Face your fears,' Kelson said.

'No fear,' Rodman said. 'I just hate the smell of that place.'

'You know how I wanted you with me here in case Rick Jacobson started playing Floyd Mayweather? I'm pretty sure Venus Johnson's been fantasizing about gut punching me too.'

'Ah, you're just trying to make me feel needed. Look, if you tell Johnson and Peters what this professor guy told you, what're they going to do with it? You've got a homeless man who talks crap. He's a crazy dude, and even *he* thinks Daryl Vaughn's stories about the Jacobsons were schizophrenic delusions. On the other side, you've got a big-name doctor in charge of an ICU – and his son, who runs a security unit. Who're they going to believe?'

'Me.'

'A pest with a brain injury telling a story about an insane man's memory of another insane man's dream. Sorry, but you know better than that.'

'You saw how Rick Jacobson acted when we talked to him.'

'Sure, but we surprised him. Now the surprise is gone. The moment the cops walk in, he'll tell a good tale – or he'll shut his mouth and call a lawyer.'

So Kelson dropped Rodman back in Bronzeville, then re-crossed the city and parked by his office. After spending the night with Frida and the morning searching subterranean streets for the professor and holding a flame to Rick Jacobson, he was exhausted. He bought lunch from Ricky's Red Hots, rode up to his floor, and laid the food out on his desk. 'Energy,' he told the French fries, then unwrapped the waxed paper from the hotdog. 'She's a little wild for me, isn't she?' he said. He drew a mouthful of Coke. 'Wild seems the only kind who'll tolerate me.'

He ate, then spent the next two hours on the phone.

He got Fort Wayne homicide detective Judy Blanchard to tell him that one of the drinking glasses in the sink at Deneesa Smithson's house tested positive for Rohypnol.

He bugged Dan Peters to tell him if Suzanne Madani's blood also tested positive, and though Peters hung up on him, he never denied Madani was knocked out by the date-rape drug before taking a fatal hit of fentanyl.

Jose needed twenty minutes of calming down before he would answer Kelson's questions about Scott Jacobson and Wendy. 'No,' he said, 'why would he want to hurt her? No.'

Frida said she had a great time last night. She was working again at eight p.m. – did he want to pick her up at three when she got off?

'I'm so wiped out, I'm getting sloppy,' Kelson said.

She said, 'Sloppy is fun.'

He said, 'See you at three.'

When he told Nancy he thought he might be falling in love, she said, 'Congratulations – why are you calling to tell me this?'

'I thought you'd be happy for me,' he said, 'since you broke my heart.'

'Uh-uh,' she said. 'Divorcing you meant I didn't have to be happy, or sad – or feel any way about you at all. But good for you, Sam. Good for you.'

Venus Johnson wasn't interested in his love life, so he force-fed her an account of his talks with Rick and Jeremy Jacobson and asked if she'd drop the charges against Wendy. 'Um . . . no,' Johnson said.

Kelson said, 'Show some feeling. You've got a bull rider freaking out about his fiancée.'

Johnson hung up.

In the middle of the afternoon, he turned off the office light, leaned back in his chair, and closed his eyes.

His mind raced – Rick Jacobson punching him in the jaw, Jeremy Jacobson crying silently at his desk, Frida doing that thing she did with her tongue. 'Screw it,' he said. He put on his coat, locked the office, and rode the elevator down to the lobby.

He drove halfway back to his apartment before he spotted the green Land Rover behind him.

'Sloppy,' he said.

He slowed until the Land Rover came close behind. Scott Jacobson was driving it. He looked serene, out for an afternoon cruise.

Kelson waved at him.

Scott waved back.

'Asshole,' Kelson said.

Scott waved some more.

Kelson drove to his apartment and parked in the lot. Scott parked beside him, and they got out of their cars together.

'What?' Kelson said.

Scott drew a pistol from inside his coat.

'Oh, *that*,' Kelson said.

'Let's go inside,' Scott said.

'What'll the neighbors think?' Kelson walked to the building entrance, and Scott slipped the pistol into his coat pocket, leaving a hand on it. When they got on the elevator, he slipped it back out.

'What I want to know,' Kelson said, 'is why Josh Templeton? Why his mom?'

'*Who?*' Scott said.

'Yeah, right. What did you and your mom argue about on the day you killed her?'

Scott held the barrel of the pistol against Kelson's ribs. 'Please be quiet.'

'If you know anything about me at all, you know that's impossible – especially when I'm nervous.'

'Do your best.'

The doors opened at Kelson's floor. 'Are you going to shoot me?' he said. 'Because I should warn you – others have tried, and it didn't work out for them. A seventeen-year-old drug dealer named Bicho – dead. A car thief named Gary Renshaw – dead.'

'Please,' Scott said, 'shut up.'

At his apartment, Kelson got out his key. 'So, what's the plan? Will you hold the gun against my head and stick me in the leg with fentanyl?'

Scott said nothing.

'Oh,' Kelson said.

He turned the key in the door lock and stepped inside.

He stopped. 'Huh,' he said.

Alex Kovacic sat at the dining table. He held a revolver. He aimed it at Kelson and Scott Jacobson.

FORTY-TWO

'You don't get enough thrills walking in the cemetery, you've got to break into my apartment?' Kelson said.

But Kovacic had his eyes on Scott Jacobson's gun. 'Drop it.'

Scott aimed at Kovacic's chest. 'No, sir.'

'I've got to say I'm with Scott on this one,' Kelson said. 'You have the Bosnian thug act going, but you look jittery. Have you turned the safety off?'

'Shut up,' Kovacic said. He signaled Scott to lower his gun. 'Go on.'

'You might as well,' Kelson told Scott. 'He doesn't look like he knows what he's doing, but he seems committed, and he might get lucky.' Then to Kovacic, 'Where are my cats? I swear to God I'll—'

'I locked them in the bathroom,' Kovacic said. 'I have an allergy.'

'A thug with a cat allergy?'

Kovacic glared at Scott – who gave no sign he'd lower his gun but also none that he meant to shoot it – then said to Kelson, 'Why'd you tell Caroline about me?'

'Ha, is that why you're here?' Kelson walked toward the dining table. Kovacic and Scott swung their guns and, fingers on the triggers, aimed at him. 'Whoa,' he said – and to Kovacic, 'You know, don't you, that she's into you? You pissed her off with your Bosnian refugee lies, but she likes you. If she didn't, she wouldn't be so pissed off.'

'Why'd you tell her?' The accent was gone.

'She Googled you, you idiot. How long did you think you'd get away with this?'

'She thinks I drugged and killed those people.'

'Ah, so *that's* why you're here. Well, breaking into a man's home is a great way to show your innocence.' Kelson went to the bathroom door and opened it. 'Do you mind?' Payday and Painter's Lane came out, and Payday went straight to Kovacic and rubbed against his legs.

'Look,' Kelson said, 'you're in love with her, right?'

Kovacic shrugged.

'Tell her,' Kelson said. 'Come clean. Be honest with her – maybe she'll go for it. Even if she doesn't, she'll think you're just a pathetic schmuck instead of a murderer. And don't break into any more apartments.' He made *ntching* noises to draw Payday from the other man, but she seemed happy where she was.

Kovacic, his eyes watering, waved his revolver at Payday to shoo her away.

'*Careful,*' Kelson said, and moved toward him.

Kovacic yanked the revolver up and aimed at him.

So Payday hissed at the man.

Kovacic aimed at her again, and Kelson yelled and rushed him.

A gun blasted. Once. Not Kovacic's. Scott Jacobson shot a bullet into the ceiling. A chunk of plaster fell to the carpet. A look crossed his face – no one was more surprised or scared by the gunshot than Scott himself, except Payday and Painter's Lane, who disappeared under Kelson's bed.

In the stunned silence after the blast, Kelson looked from Scott to Kovacic. '*Amazing,*' he said.

Kovacic got up and drifted toward the door. 'I'm so sorry,' he said. 'I didn't mean it to turn into this – I can't be here . . .' He went out into the corridor.

When he was gone, Kelson said to Scott, 'How about you?

Are you going to stick around? This isn't the best building, but gunshots upset the neighbors. If you're staying, you should figure out what you're going to tell the cops when they come. If *I* tell it, I'll tell the truth, and that won't look so good for you.'

'I just want to talk to you,' Scott said. 'I need to explain—'

'Unless the neighbors all went deaf, in about five minutes you can explain to a bunch of nice cops. Maybe a SWAT team.'

Scott edged toward the door. 'Maybe not.'

'You aren't going to kill me?'

'You've got me wrong.'

'I doubt that. Stick around and tell me.'

Scott stepped into the corridor. 'Meet me at your office in an hour.' He closed the door behind him.

'You've got to be kidding,' Kelson said. Then, after waiting enough time for Scott to clear out, he left the apartment too. The police could pound on his door. They could break it down or get the building super to let them in. They could bag the bullet casing and the plaster chunk. They could do all that without Kelson's help.

''Cause I'm gone,' he said, and ran down the corridor to the elevator. 'Gone, gone, gone.'

FORTY-THREE

B y *gone*, Kelson meant south through the city to Bronzeville, where he climbed two flights of stairs and knocked on Rodman's door.

Marty LeCoeur answered. He was wearing skinny jeans and a red sleeveless T-shirt with the word GUCCI in gold across the front. He pointed the stump of his missing arm at Kelson and said, 'I know what you're thinking.'

Kelson stepped inside. '*I* don't even know what I'm thinking. If I did, I'd say it.'

'You're thinking, why would I spend four hundred ninety bucks on this T-shirt?'

'You paid four hundred ninety for that?'

'Don't start. Janet busted my balls about it this morning. So I walked out. Then I'm outside in the fucking cold. I knock so Janet'll let me back inside. She says, not unless I apologize. Fucking cute, right? I came here again. A shelter in a storm is what this is.'

'So why'd you pay four hundred ninety bucks for it?'

He gave Kelson a look like he was measuring his neck to knock his head off. 'I bought it 'cause I fucking could. Why are *you* here?'

'Shelter from a storm.'

The answer seemed to calm Marty. 'DeMarcus and Cindi went out. What's your storm?'

Kelson told him about Scott Jacobson confronting him with a gun in the parking lot and then Kovacic greeting him with another gun in his apartment.

When he finished, Marty said, 'Kovacic's a jackass, but sounds like Scott's a real fuckwad.'

'He thinks I'm meeting him at my office in about ten minutes. If I read him right, he does bad things when someone upsets him – he runs over his mom, maybe shoots people up with killer doses of drugs.'

'You want me to beat him up?' At five feet tall and missing an arm, Marty got a lot of laughs when he talked that way. But Kelson had seen the damage he could do, and Rodman told hard-to-believe stories of Marty's outrageous violence, swearing they were true.

Kelson said, 'I was thinking I'd hide here for the evening and hope Scott doesn't burn down my office when I don't show up.'

'Sure, if you want to be a coward.'

'You're the second man to call me that today.'

'First one must've been smart.'

'His friends call him Professor.'

'Doesn't surprise me.'

Kelson lay down on the couch under the portraits of Malcolm X, Cindi, and Martin Luther King Jr, and soon he slept. He dreamed of a dozen men holding guns to his head. Only six of those men were Scott Jacobson.

When Marty started doing one-armed push-ups on the living-room floor, Kelson woke and buried his face in the couch cushions. He woke again – sort of – when Rodman and Cindi came in laughing like they'd figured out that the whole universe was a crazy joke. He drifted off and then opened his eyes again when Marty and Rodman left the apartment together. He slept and woke once more at midnight.

He sat up on the couch, suddenly alert.

Rodman and Marty were still gone.

Cindi was sleeping in the bedroom.

He went into the kitchen and made a pot of coffee, then opened a couple cabinets and found a jar of peanuts and a box of Cheerios. He was standing at the counter, chewing, when Cindi came in. Her hair looked like she'd been sleeping hard.

'You keep weird hours,' she said.

He chased a mouthful with coffee. 'I've got a date in a little while.'

She raised her eyebrows. 'Vampire or stripper?'

'*You* work plenty of nights yourself. A lot of nice people do.'

'Yeah, but when was the last time you dated a nice person?' She yawned big.

'Maybe *nice* is overrated. Anyway, I might be in love.'

'Good for you, Sam. We all need some of that.' She glanced at the coffee pot, decided against it.

'Thanks for the couch,' he said. 'Did I wake you?'

'From bad dreams,' she said.

'It's that kind of night. Where did DeMarcus and Marty go?'

'Marty told DeMarcus about some guy waving a gun at you in your parking lot. He said you wanted them to talk sense into him.'

'That can't be good,' Kelson said. He pulled out his phone and dialed DeMarcus. The number rang four times and bounced to voicemail. 'Marty's exaggerating about me being a coward,' Kelson told the recording. 'And I don't want you to go after Scott Jacobson.' He hung up.

Cindi shook her head at him. 'I'm going back to bed.'

Kelson dialed Marty's cell number. It rang twice, and a woman's voice answered. Kelson almost recognized it. 'Marty?' he said.

The woman said, 'This is Lieutenant-Detective Venus Johnson—'

'What the hell?' Kelson said.

'Right,' she said. 'Who is this?'

'Sam Kelson.'

'What the hell?' she said.

'Why are you answering Marty's phone?'

'Whose?'

'Marty LeCoeur's.'

'I have a better question,' she said. 'Why's Marty LeCoeur's phone covered in blood?'

FORTY-FOUR

Thirty-five minutes later, Kelson arrived at an alley across Lincoln Avenue from Kiko's Meat Market & Restaurant. A strip of yellow crime-scene tape closed the alley from the street. Emergency lights glowed hot on the pavement.

Kelson told a uniformed cop that Venus Johnson had summoned him. The cop lifted the tape and said, 'Have at it.'

Kelson stepped past a half-dozen little evidence flags.

The freezing wind bottled in the alley. Johnson and the other officers stood around a kidney-shaped bloodstain. Around them, the walls were covered with black and green graffiti.

'We got a bunch of nine-one-ones about shots fired,' Johnson said to Kelson. 'Reports of a man hit. All we found was this' – she pointed at the blood – 'and your buddy's phone. Any bright ideas?'

'Sure. Track down a man named Alex Kovacic.' He nodded toward Kiko's. 'That's his hangout.'

'Who?'

'He's allergic to cats.'

'What?'

'Cats. His eyes tear up like he's leaking.'

Johnson kept her patience. 'Who is he?'

'A liar in love. Used to be a hospital custodian. Lives a couple blocks from here.'

'Any idea why your buddy's phone would end up here?'

'None I like. Marty LeCoeur and DeMarcus Rodman were trying to teach me how to be brave. I didn't think they were coming here to do it. Did you check the call history on Marty's phone?'

'Ten calls today to a number he's got ID'ed as *Janet*.'

'His girlfriend. They're fighting.'

'The last call's a partial number,' Johnson said. 'It lines up with the phone you called from. Seems he wanted to talk to you when he lost the phone. Any idea why?'

'Sure, he went out hunting because of me.'

'Hunting?'

'Not *hunting* hunting. Marty's good at convincing people to behave nicely.'

'Does he have a gun?' Johnson asked.

'A bunch of them – big, small, you name it. For a while he had a machine gun. Not that he needs them. He can kill a man without.'

'I see.'

'Not that he did kill anyone,' Kelson said. 'Not that he would.' He stared at the blood, which was congealing in the cold. 'Not that that's what this is about.'

'You don't think he maybe talked sense into someone here tonight? Maybe this Alex Kovacic? Or is this Marty's blood?'

'Don't even think it.'

'So he was just cruising by and decided to leave his phone? D'you want to explain what happened here?'

'I want to, and I would if I could.'

'Not even a theory?'

'None *you'd* like.'

'Spill it,' she said.

'You know when you hung up on me for telling you about Scott Jacobson and why you should drop the charges against Wendy Thomas?'

'You're going to stir *this* into that pot of crap?'

'I wouldn't call it a pot of crap,' he said.

'Second thought, keep the theory to yourself.'

'I thought so. I take it you're done with me?'

She shook her head. 'We've got another problem.' She moved close, as if she'd grab him if he ran. 'When I checked in with the department on how this was playing out – with you calling the mysterious phone and all – they put your name in the system. Guess what they told me?'

'Do I have to?'

'Exactly. They came back with an incident report from your

apartment this evening. Responding officers went in, and there was evidence of a shot fired. Does that surprise you?'

'Huh,' he said.

'It gets worse. When a man reached under your bed for the shell casing, your cat clawed his arm. He went to get a tetanus shot.'

'Which one?'

'I've no idea – probably an evidence tech.'

'Which *cat*? Is she OK?'

Instead of answering, Johnson nodded to another cop. 'Take Mr Kelson to the station. Put him in an interview room. Get him coffee. Give him a sweet roll.'

'Are you arresting me?' Kelson said.

Johnson gave him a dry smile. 'Did you shoot up your apartment?'

'No.'

'Did you shoot up this alley and leave a little skating rink of blood just for me?'

'*No*.'

'Then let's call this a midnight snack. Call it a talk between friends. A friend you can't brush off. A talk where you tell me everything I want to know.'

Kelson gestured at the bloody pavement. 'Do you think *I* have something to do with this?'

'Gunfire in your apartment and gunfire here.'

'So?'

'And you called Marty LeCoeur's phone, didn't you? Why would you do that?'

'To tell him I'm not a coward – even if the professor says so.'

Johnson started to ask but shook her head and stopped herself. She said to the other cop, 'Get him out of here.'

FORTY-FIVE

In the back seat of the cruiser, Kelson called Rodman's number. It rang through to voicemail again. 'What happened?' he said to the recording. 'And what's going on with Marty? Are you guys OK? Venus Johnson has his phone. She sort of arrested me.'

'*Not* arrested,' the cop said from the front.

Kelson hung up and dialed Rodman's apartment. He woke Cindi. 'Have you heard from DeMarcus?'

'You know how much I dread questions like that. What happened?'

Kelson told her. 'If you hear from him, tell him Venus Johnson's got the hots for Marty. He might be hurt. If he isn't, he needs to stay low unless he likes jailhouse food.'

The cop in the front said, 'Don't say that.'

Kelson told Cindi, 'Johnson's got the hots for me too – thinks I've got something to do with the shooting. She semi-arrested me.'

'Cut it out,' said the cop.

Kelson called Marty's girlfriend Janet. 'Have you heard from Marty?'

'I never want to talk to him again,' Janet said.

'He might be hurt,' he said again. 'He's at least in bad trouble. The cops found his phone in an alley where someone got shot.'

Janet burst into tears.

'Wow – don't do that,' Kelson said.

She cried harder.

'He'll take care of himself,' Kelson said. 'He's always fine. He's strong.'

'He's' – she caught her breath – 'a tough' – she blew her nose – 'little motherfucker.'

'That's more like it,' Kelson said.

'I love him. But he can be' – she blew her nose again – 'such a fucking bastard.'

'You're starting to talk like him.'

'No fucking way.'

'If you see him, tell him to keep his head down. If he needs a lawyer, he should call Ed Davies.'

'Thank you, Sam,' she said.

'Any time.' He hung up.

'Huh,' said the cop in the front.

'Yep.'

Kelson texted Frida from the back seat of the cruiser. *Sorry – I can't tonight – I wish I could.*

Then he called Ed Davies. Davies picked up on the first ring. 'Two in the morning, Sam. What the hell?'

Kelson told him.

'Keep your mouth shut till I get there,' he said when Kelson finished.

'Now you're mocking me.'

'Ah, shit – I'll get there soon as I can.'

'Thanks,' Kelson said. 'I'm not worried I'll say anything I shouldn't.'

'Yeah,' Davies said, *'that's* what worries me.'

The cop took Kelson in through the back of the Harrison Street station, then upstairs to the homicide room. He opened one of the interview rooms, flipped on an overhead light, and told Kelson to sit. The room was freezing, the aluminum chair icy.

When the cop started to leave, Kelson said, 'I could use that coffee.'

'Johnson was screwing with you about that – you know that, don't you?' The cop locked the door.

Kelson burned through most of his phone battery looking at pictures of Sue Ellen and the cats. Then he laid his head on the bolted-down metal table and tried to sleep, but the chill kept waking him. He paced the room. The video camera mounted at a corner of the ceiling might've been on or might've been off, but he told it how much he'd rather be with Frida at the moment and described that thing she did with her tongue.

Two hours after the cop locked the door, Venus Johnson unlocked it and came in. She looked blown out with fatigue.

'You look haggard,' he told her.

'You know how much time I waste with your shit?' she said. He started to answer, but she cut him off. 'Begin with the gunshot in your apartment tonight. Finish with how the gunshot ties to the blood in the alley. I swear to God if you spend more than ten minutes telling it, I'll put another hole in you.'

'You make me wait two hours and then want it all in ten minutes?'

'Nine minutes, fifty-five seconds.'

'But it started before the shooting in my apartment.'

'Nine minutes, fifty.'

'OK. I thought Alex Kovacic was going to shoot Painter's Lane.'

'I swear to God, Kelson.'

'I'm telling it, I'm telling it. Kovacic broke into my apartment, and—'

'Report says nothing about damage to your door. A bullet in your ceiling, yeah, but nothing about the door.'

'Kovacic was like this super-custodian. I'm sure he knows how to get into places when people lose their keys.'

'So you've got a super-custodian cat murderer—'

'I don't think he was really going to shoot her, as it turns out. I might've over-reacted.'

'Dammit, Kelson.'

'You *sound* haggard too.'

'Nine minutes.'

'I walked into my apartment. Scott Jacobson had his gun in my ribs.'

'*Wait* – where did Scott Jacobson come from?'

'The parking lot. He followed me home from my office.'

'Why'd he do that?'

'I guess to stick a gun in my ribs.'

'When I talk to you, I get woozy,' she said. 'It's not a good feeling.'

'I get that too. Not from you talking – from hearing myself. Scott Jacobson had his gun in my ribs. Kovacic pointed a gun at me too. Then they pointed them at each other. Then me again. Then I let the cats out of the bathroom and Kovacic looked like he'd shoot Painter's Lane. I tried to stop him and Scott Jacobson shot a hole in the ceiling.'

'Why was Kovacic in your apartment to begin with?'

'He fell in love with a hospital orderly named Caroline Difley—'

'I should just kill you now.'

There was a knock on the interview room door.

Johnson shook her head. 'What's this about Scott Jacobson?' Another knock.

'What I've been telling you,' Kelson said. 'His mom's death when he was a teenager connects to what's happening now. Check out Patricia Ruddig. Check Daryl Vaughn. Check Josh Templeton and Deneesa Smithson – and Suzanne Madani.'

A pounding.

Johnson went to the door and opened it.

Ed Davies burst in, followed by a cop. 'What the hell?' Davies said to Johnson. 'I get here an hour and a half ago and they send me to the Wentworth station. At Wentworth, they send me to Englewood. At Englewood, they send me back here.'

Johnson bristled. 'Bureaucratic tangle? Happens all the time.'

'Nothing he's said can be used,' Davies said.

'It's all right,' Kelson said. 'We were just talking.'

Davies stared at Johnson. 'He's free to go?'

'Uh-uh.' Then she told Kelson, 'We're holding you for unlawful discharge of a weapon in your apartment.'

'*I* didn't shoot,' Kelson said.

'So you say.'

'I didn't even have a gun.'

'It was *your* apartment,' she said. 'It was your failure to report it. You thoroughly pissed off your neighbors. I don't know why anyone would rent to you in the first place.'

FORTY-SIX

Ed Davies bailed Kelson out at nine in the morning. Whenever Davies did a job, he sent Kelson an itemized bill – and demanded dinner at one of Chicago's steakhouses. This morning, Kelson offered to buy him steak and eggs at Miss Ricky's Diner.

'Hell no,' Davies said, 'you call at two in the morning, you're buying me a center-cut at Morton's – after a starter of bacon-wrapped scallops. Did I mention a bottle of wine?'

'I owe you that and more,' Kelson said.

'Oh, you'll pay it.'

'Thanks, Ed.'

'Hey, what else am I going to do at two in the morning?'

Kelson took a cab to Lincoln and Winona, where he'd left his car when Venus Johnson put him in the back of the cruiser. A coat of ice glazed his windshield. He sat on the cold front seat, with the defroster notched high, and stared at the glass like a cataract. 'Story of my life,' he said. The heat melted the glaze, and he wiped it with the wipers. 'If only it was that easy.'

He drove to his office and rode the elevator up with a bunch of junior accountants from Ernst & Young, who'd come for computer classes at the training school. He followed them through the hall, went into his office, and closed the door. The sun through the window was warm, the light on the walls golden. He stared at the framed picture of Sue Ellen. 'Sorry, kiddo,' he said, though he didn't know exactly what he was sorry for. 'Maybe for being me. Yeah, it's dizzying being me.'

He went to his desk and took the KelTec pistol from the hidden rig. He popped the magazine and checked that it was fully loaded. He snapped it in place again and tucked the barrel into his belt. 'Because I'm not an idiot,' he said.

He paced his office, from the sunny window to the closed door. Then he phoned Rodman's cell number. It rang through to voicemail. 'Where the hell are you?' he said and hung up.

He dialed Rodman's apartment.

Cindi picked up and said, 'I'm worried.'

'DeMarcus handles situations no one else can,' Kelson said.

'That's what worries me. He thinks he can handle anything. What's going on with him and Marty?'

Kelson felt the question like a pain in his belly. 'I don't know.'

'Find them,' she said.

'Yeah, I'm working on it.'

When they hung up, he called Janet.

She hadn't heard from Marty either, but she no longer sounded weepy. She sounded drunk. 'When you find him, tell him I love him,' she said.

'Sure,' Kelson said.

'Tell him we *all* love him.'

'I will.'

'Tell him I don't care if he's a fucking bastard. Tell him he looks cute in Gucci.'

'Are you drunk?' he said.

'Fuck you, Sam,' she said.

They hung up, and he called Caroline Difley. 'I need to talk to Alex,' he said.

'He called and explained the thing about Bosnia,' she said, as if that's what he asked. 'He said he's attracted to me. When we met, he was ashamed to admit who he was.'

'No news to me.'

'It's incredibly sweet,' she said.

'Or not.'

'You clearly don't know anything about romance.'

'I take it you didn't tell him to get lost.'

'I'm having lunch with him today.'

'That's good news. Where's the big date?'

'Don't be silly – Kiko's.'

'Silly me – be careful not to track in blood.'

'What?'

'Be careful, that's all.'

'One should never be careful in love,' she said.

At eleven o'clock, Kelson drove back to Kiko's Meat Market & Restaurant, parked by the alley, and waited. The crime-scene tape was down and the only evidence of the previous night's shooting was a sprinkling of sawdust over the stain on the alley pavement. The winter wind channeled down Lincoln Avenue, and thin clouds tore across the sky. Kelson tried Rodman's number again and hung up before the end of the voicemail recording. He dialed Rodman's apartment but ended the call before the first ring.

At 11:30, he listened to the news on the radio. There was no mention of a night of unexplained gunfire on the northwest side of the city. The weather would continue cold, cold, and colder.

Kelson used his phone to search online for any mention of the shooting. He found none.

He checked the weather. Still cold and colder.

He watched the entrance to Kiko's.

Strangers came and left.

At 11:55, Caroline Difley, wearing her camelhair coat and a pair of brown leather boots, walked down the sidewalk and went into the restaurant.

Kelson looked at himself in the rearview mirror. 'One should never be careful in love?' He considered Frida. She'd never responded to his text from the back of the police cruiser. He considered his phone, as if Frida lived inside it. He brought up the string of text messages he'd exchanged with her. He typed, *Hey* . . .

He almost missed Kovacic crossing the street and disappearing into Kiko's.

He brushed his fingertips over the grip of his KelTec, got out of the car, and jogged across the street. He caught his breath and pushed through the door into the restaurant.

Kovacic and Caroline Difley sat in the same green booth where they'd sat on the day she introduced him to Kelson. They weren't holding hands yet, but they were smiling at each other in a way that said they would be soon.

Kelson slid on to the bench next to Caroline Difley.

She and Kovacic looked startled, but Kovacic gave Kelson a shy smile. 'I followed your advice. I admitted my feelings to Caroline. Thank you.'

Kelson drew the pistol from his belt. He flashed it at Kovacic, then lowered it under the tabletop and aimed it at the man's belly. 'Keep your hands where I can see them, OK?'

Caroline Difley made a squeaking noise.

Kovacic said, 'Please, Caroline, it's all right.' An Eastern European accent tinged his voice again. He stared, unblinking, at Kelson. 'What do you want?'

'Tell me what happened in the alley across the street last night. Tell me where DeMarcus Rodman and Marty LeCoeur are.'

'*Alex?*' Caroline Difley said.

'I'm sorry, Caroline.' Kovacic held his eyes on Kelson, as if looking for a signal whether Kelson meant to shoot him. 'Maybe we can talk in another place.'

'I'm not going anywhere until I get answers,' Kelson said, 'and neither are you.'

'I can take you to Rodman and LeCoeur.'

'Where?'

'Come,' he said, standing. 'Nothing about you scares me.'

FORTY-SEVEN

Kelson drove with Kovacic beside him and Caroline Difley in the back seat.

'I'm sorry, Caroline,' Kovacic said again. 'I lied to you.'

She pulled her coat close around her. 'The old lies, or new ones?'

He shrugged.

'But why?'

'You know why – what would you think of me?'

'Don't get carried away with that, Romeo,' Kelson said.

'Tell me the truth,' Caroline said. 'All of it. Now.'

'I can't,' Kovacic said.

'Why?'

'It would be unsafe – for you.'

'Bullshit,' Kelson said under his breath.

'I can't be with you unless I know who you are,' Caroline said.

'I can't . . .' Kovacic said.

'Let me out,' she said to Kelson.

Kelson slowed, pulled to the curb.

Before she could climb out, Kovacic said, 'When I was a senior in high school, I did a project on Bosnia. I became obsessed with the war – the rapes, the killings. My mom and dad came from there, and I grew up with stories about it before the war. My mom's parents and sisters still lived in Vitez. Later, her mom and dad – my *baka* and *deda* – died, and one of her sisters disappeared – just disappeared. After I finished the project, I couldn't get Bosnia out of my head. I started college, but it didn't mean anything to me. I spent all my time trying to find out what was happening in the war. I wanted to be part of it, you know? The fighting. Nothing else mattered. I left school and went to Bosnia.'

'Bullshit,' Kelson said.

'I went to Bosnia,' Kovacic said again. 'My cousins were there. My uncle was a captain. I joined them.'

'I'd get out, if I were you,' Kelson told Caroline Difley.

So Kovacic unbuttoned his shirt.

'What are you doing, Sugar Shack?' Kelson said.

Kovacic peeled off the shirt. Over his right nipple he had a tattoo of a ringed cross with three pine-like branches sticking from the top. Over his left nipple he had a tattoo of a three-striped flag. Extending from the base of his left shoulder to his elbow, he had the rips and divots of a terrible scar.

He touched the scar. 'Like you,' he said to Kelson, 'I was shot. Like you, I lived. I spent a year in my uncle's house, recovering.'

He turned to Caroline. 'If you want to know all of the truth, during that year, I fell in love. She fell in love with me too. I planned to stay. Then they killed her. They killed the girl I loved.'

'Huh,' Kelson said.

'I came home – if you can call this home. That's the truth.'

Caroline said, 'If it is, why wouldn't you tell me before?'

'I broke the law by fighting. I would've been arrested when I came back if anyone knew what I did.'

'That was a long time ago,' she said. 'Why lie about it now?'

Kovacic tilted his head back, exposing his chin to her, as if her question poked a painful part of him and he was readying himself for another blow. 'No,' he said. 'You should go.'

She gazed at him. 'Uh-uh.' She slid to the middle of the back seat. 'Tell me.'

Kovacic shook his head.

'*Tell* me,' she said.

Kovacic put back on his shirt. He did the buttons. He screwed his mouth. He put his hand on the door handle as if he would get out and force Caroline Difley out too.

'Please,' she said.

Kovacic let go. He sighed as if breathing tore at his insides. 'Terrible things were done to my family – my grand-parents, my aunt, the girl I wanted to marry. So I did terrible things too. That's the truth. I was at the Ahmići massacre – you can look it up. After the war, I came home. But the things I did don't go away. There are still people in Bosnia who would kill me for what I did – families who want revenge for their sisters and brothers the way I wanted revenge for the people I loved.'

'What did you do?' Caroline Difley said. She sounded more sympathetic than disturbed by the confession.

'No,' Kovacic said. 'Some things, no. I was a soldier, but in Bosnia there was no innocence in that.'

'How the hell do DeMarcus and Marty tie in?' Kelson said.

Kovacic sighed. 'Last night, I ate dinner at Kiko's. When I left and was crossing the street, someone started shooting at me. I couldn't see the shooter. I ran into the alley and hid.'

'What about DeMarcus and Marty?'

'I knew for a long time this might happen,' Kovacic said. 'Someone would come for me, or someone would hire a killer.

The shooter fired at me five or six times from a car. I had my revolver' – he glanced uneasily at Caroline Difley – 'so I shot back once, and then I hid in the alley. The first lesson I learned in Bosnia was to never leave a hiding spot if a sniper stops shooting. I hid a few minutes, and then Rodman and LeCoeur walked into the alley. I thought they must be the ones who shot at me from the car. They were careless – the little one was on his phone. Foolish.'

'No one gets the better of them,' Kelson said.

'I shot the big one in the leg,' Kovacic said.

Kelson jabbed the KelTec at him. 'You shot DeMarcus?'

'He's all right,' Kovacic said. 'Some blood. But he's got a lot of blood in him.'

'If he isn't OK, I'll kill you,' Kelson said.

Kovacic shook his head at him. 'You're as foolish as they are.'

'Where are they?'

'A friend of mine is watching them at my apartment. You understand, I needed to talk to them – to find out what they were doing. The little one just kept telling me to fuck myself. I had to gag him.'

'Why were they even in the alley?'

'The big one – Rodman – said they were following someone – he wouldn't say who. He said they were circling the neighborhood and heard the gunshots. They saw casings on the street. That's all he would say and it sounded like a lie. I needed to figure out who they were.'

'And then you thought you'd just slip out for a date?'

Kovacic gazed at him coolly. 'I needed to act as if everything was normal in case anyone was watching. I've been doing this for a long time. Also, I really wanted to see Caroline.'

'Take me to them,' Kelson said.

Kovacic turned to Caroline. 'You can get out now – if you want.'

She had tears in her eyes, but she shook her head and sank deep into the back seat.

FORTY-EIGHT

Kovacic's friend – a thick-necked man with a graying buzz cut – was watching a soccer game on TV when Kovacic, Kelson, and Caroline walked in. He'd positioned his chair so he could also keep an eye on Rodman and Marty, who sat on an old brown fabric couch. Duct tape bound their ankles. Marty was gagged with a cloth and more tape. Rodman, stripped of his pants, wore red boxers and, over his right thigh, a section of gauze was wrapped to his leg with medical tape. His wrists were tied behind his back. Marty's one hand was cuffed to a bike cable extending from a radiator. The room was hot and smelled of sweat and stale cigarette smoke. Venetian blinds hung over the windows.

When Kovacic's friend saw Kelson and Caroline, he leaped from the chair and aimed a black revolver at Kelson's chest.

Kelson pointed his KelTec back at the man.

'It's OK, Tomo,' Kovacic said.

Tomo lowered the revolver.

But Kelson held his own gun steady. 'Put it all the way down.'

A faint smile formed on Tomo's lips and he raised the gun again.

'Ne, Tomo.' Kovacic spoke some more in another language – calming the other man or strategizing with him, Kelson didn't know which.

Still smiling, Tomo sat again and set the revolver on the floor.

'How quick could he snap that up?' Kelson asked Kovacic.

'You wouldn't even see it. But that's as much of a compromise as you'll get.'

Kelson smiled at Tomo too and tucked the KelTec in his belt. Then he turned to his friends, frowning at the patch on Rodman's leg where Kovacic shot him.

'How's tricks?' Rodman said.

'Cindi's worried.'

'She gets worked up about little things.'

'How bad is it?' He kept his fingers near the butt of the KelTec.

'Blood and muscle. No bone. I can walk.'

Kelson glanced at Kovacic and Tomo. Then he ripped the tape from Marty's mouth and pulled out the rag.

Marty spat – tried to speak – choked.

'Water?' Kelson asked.

Kovacic went into the kitchen and returned with a cup.

Marty sipped – spat again – choked – drank more – tried to speak. He rasped: 'I fucking hate soccer. Ten fucking hours. D'you know there's a Fox fucking Soccer Plus channel? Soccer twenty-four fucking hours a day – except, get *this*, when they have *fucking* rugby. I'm going to go home and kick a fucking hole in my TV.'

Kovacic said, 'Who's winning?'

Marty jerked his taped-up legs. 'Unhook me and I'll cram the TV down your fucking throat.' He said to Kelson, 'This guy shot DeMarcus. And then, you know what they made me eat? Goulash.'

'No one makes you eat,' Tomo said, sullen.

'If I didn't want to fucking starve.'

Kovacic said, 'Will you please put the gag back on?'

'Marty, shut up,' Kelson said.

Marty turned his fire to him. 'Don't *ever*—'

'Be quiet, Marty,' Rodman said.

Marty looked stung. 'DeMarcus? No one talks to me like that.'

'Yeah, but this isn't the time. I'm kind of hurting.'

'It's whatever fucking time I say it is.' But Rodman's reprimand quieted him.

Kelson stripped the tape from Rodman's legs and untied his wrists.

Kovacic and Tomo exchanged looks as Rodman stood up and tried his leg. 'Thanks, man,' he said to Kelson. 'All this time I thought I was saving you from yourself, and you ride in on your little pony and rescue me.'

'Fuck that,' Marty said. 'We wouldn't be here to begin with except for him.'

'You want to explain what happened?' Kelson said.

'Yeah,' Rodman said. 'We were going after Scott Jacobson for you, and—'

'You want to unhook me first?' Marty said.

'You promise to play nice?' Rodman said.

'I don't promise a fucking thing.'

Kelson tore the tape off Marty's ankles anyway. He said to Kovacic, 'Key?'

Kovacic gave him the key to the handcuffs.

'Was this a mistake?' Tomo asked Kovacic.

'*They* didn't try to kill me,' Kovacic said.

'That's what we fucking told you,' Marty said.

'But,' Kovacic's friend said, 'we thought you are a fucking liar.'

Which made Kovacic laugh.

'Don't fucking laugh at me,' Marty said.

'What happened?' Kelson asked Rodman.

'We caught up with Scott Jacobson at Clement Memorial,' he said. 'I don't know what he was doing there. Visiting his dad or brother maybe. Or stealing drugs from the supply room. He drove from the hospital to your office building. He slowed long enough to check if there was light in the window. Maybe he still thought you'd keep your appointment. I don't think he knew Marty and I were following him at this point. He drove to Club Richelieu and went inside. We figured we'd grab him and have a talk when he left, so we parked by his car and waited. Forty-five minutes later, he came out with Jeffrey Vargas – the guy who owns the place, right? They got into Vargas's Porsche and took off. We took off after them, and now they knew we were following them. I mean it was a Porsche, and Vargas drives fast.'

As Rodman told the story, Tomo got up and drifted over to Kovacic and Caroline Difley, leaving the revolver on the floor.

'We followed the Porsche most of the way back to the hospital,' Rodman said. 'Then they seemed to change their mind – or maybe they got tired of us following them. They headed north. We thought they were going to your office again, and we let them get a little ahead, figuring we'd catch them when they got there. But then they cut over to Lincoln Avenue, and we lost them at a light. We were looking for them when we heard gunshots over by Kiko's Restaurant. We figured it had to be Scott Jacobson – who else but your ceiling shooter would be blasting at the neighborhood on a freezing night? So we took a look. That's when this guy' – he meant Kovacic – 'decided I'd look good as a peg leg.'

Kovacic and Tomo were whispering to each other – heatedly.

Then Kovacic went back to Tomo's chair and picked up the revolver.

Kelson fumbled with the KelTec.

But Kovacic turned to Rodman. 'Thank you. That's what I needed to know. I'm very sorry about the misunderstanding.'

'A misunderstanding is what you call shooting a guy in the fucking leg?' Marty said.

Kovacic took Caroline's hands in his. 'I'm sorry,' he said again. He kissed her cheek. 'Maybe – but not now.' He walked out of the apartment.

She looked stunned.

'What the fuck?' Marty said.

FORTY-NINE

At three o'clock that afternoon, Rodman and Marty met Kelson at his office.

Rodman limped through the door with a duffel bag on his shoulder. He had a gentle smile.

'You're a beast,' Kelson said. 'The Terminator. The Energizer Bunny. The—'

Rodman set the bag on a client chair. 'I grind my teeth every time I put weight on it.'

'You should get it looked at,' Kelson said.

'Cindi took a peek. She says it's as pretty and clean as anything she's seen a doctor do.'

'Did you tell her a janitor bandaged it?'

'I told her it was a guy with field experience.' He pulled a Walther semi-automatic from the duffel and laid it on the desk.

While students in the neighboring classrooms learned Advanced Web Design and Adobe Photoshop, the three men set five other guns next to the semi-automatic.

Kelson's KelTec and Springfield XD-S.

Rodman's Beretta and snub-nose Colt.

Marty's 'Dirty Harry' .44 Magnum Smith & Wesson.

'Might be a bit much for the circumstances,' Kelson said.

'Fuck if it is,' Marty said. Inside his unzipped parka, he wore a bright-yellow bulletproof vest.

'We can keep the big firepower in the trunk,' Rodman said, 'but what's it hurt to have it with?'

They stuffed the guns into their coats and rode the elevator to the lobby. Marty clambered into the back seat of Kelson's Dodge Challenger, and Rodman eased into the front passenger seat. Twenty-five minutes later, they parked outside of Club Richelieu.

The lights inside the club were bright and made the white furnishings look cheap and grimy. The air smelled of stale alcohol and bleach.

The main room was empty except for Jeffrey Vargas, who sat on a white barstool at a white high-top table. He was dressed all in black and had a little glass of ice and whiskey.

'It's Johnny Cash,' Kelson said.

'More like fucking Hamlet,' Marty said.

'Sometimes you surprise me,' Kelson said to Marty.

'*'Tis not alone my inky cloak nor customary suits of solemn black*,' Marty said, and pulled the Magnum from inside his parka. He pressed the barrel against Vargas's head. 'Give me the keys to your Porsche,' he said, '*and* to your house.'

Vargas should have looked more terrified. Mostly he looked angry. He reached – slowly, as if he'd done this before – into his pocket and removed a set of keys, which he put on the table.

Rodman said, 'What were you doing with Scott Jacobson last night? Did it include shooting at a man named Alex Kovacic?'

'Screw you,' Vargas said.

Rodman slipped the snub-nose Colt from his pocket. He set the barrel next to Marty's on Vargas's skull.

'Why not?' Kelson said. He pressed the KelTec against Vargas's head too. 'What'll we find in your car and house?' he said. 'What if we tear this place apart?'

'See,' Rodman said, 'we're pretty sure Scott is causing a lot of damage, hurting a lot of people. And last night, you were his sidekick. You were with him when someone shot up an alley.'

'I don't know what you're talking about.' Vargas was calm as calm.

Then a door from a storeroom behind the bar swung open, and Frida came in, carrying a twelve pack of Dos Equis. She wore little white leather boots, a white miniskirt, and a fuzzy

white top that exposed her belly. She stopped sharp at the sight
of the men. She stared at Kelson.

'Sam?'

Rodman said, 'It isn't quite what it looks like.'

Marty said, 'It's exactly what it fucking looks like.'

'I wish it weren't,' Kelson said, 'and sorry about last
night.'

'Keep your eyes on the prize,' Rodman said to him.

'I wanted to be with you,' Kelson told her.

'Jeffrey?' Frida said to Vargas.

'It's all right,' Vargas said. 'Everything's under control – you
get out of here now.'

But she set the twelve pack on the bar and stared hard at
Kelson.

'I'm sorry,' he said.

'You didn't show up when you said you would,' she said.

'I know.'

'Oh, no, the girl's high maintenance,' Marty said. 'Take it from
me – never ignore her. You should hear Janet when I fuck up.'

'*Guys*,' Rodman said.

'Go on, Frida, get out of here,' Vargas said.

Frida looked at her boss uncertainly – looked at Kelson the
same way. Then she went back into the storeroom and returned
with a white winter coat.

She pointed at Kelson with a long fingernail and said, 'I don't
understand you.'

She crossed the bar and went out into the cold.

'I'll call,' Kelson yelled after her.

Marty lowered his gun and scooped up Vargas's keys from the
table. 'We'll see about this,' he said.

Vargas said, 'If you touch my car . . .'

Rodman said, 'You get one chance. What were you doing with
Scott Jacobson?'

Vargas said nothing – so Marty went out to the street.

They listened.

An engine raced outside.

'Uh-oh,' Rodman said.

'Goddammit,' Vargas said.

The tires screeched, and the Porsche roared away.

Vargas said, 'If he so much as . . .'

Tires screeched again in the near distance – then the car roared past, going the other way.

'He's an excellent driver for only one hand,' Rodman said.

Tires screeched – screeched – screeched.

'Is he doing donuts?' Kelson asked.

'Goddammit,' Vargas said.

The car roared past again. Then, down the street, there was a terrific, metallic crash.

Vargas was speechless.

'I hope he wore a seatbelt,' Rodman said.

They listened – for twenty seconds, thirty.

Then the door to the club opened and Marty came in, dangling the keys.

'Sorry.' He waved his empty coat sleeve at Vargas. 'I lost control.' He told Kelson and Rodman, 'The car's clean. No gun, no blood, nothing. Want to check his house?'

'*No,*' Vargas said.

'No?' Rodman said.

Marty said, 'But this is getting good.'

'Scott didn't shoot at anyone,' Vargas said. 'We passed right after it happened.'

Rodman pulled his gun an inch from Vargas's scalp. 'You passed? You didn't think to stop?'

'Why would we?'

'A man in need? Good Samaritan? All of that?'

Vargas scowled. 'Bullets flying. I like my skin without bullets in it.'

'Why were you there?'

'Uh-uh,' Vargas said.

Rodman touched the Colt barrel to his head again.

'Ready for a house party?' Marty said, like it was all good fun.

'All I'll say is, you got it wrong about Scott,' Vargas said. 'He didn't shoot at anyone. He's had it hard – harder than anyone I know. You won't hear a lot of people say they respect him, but I do. He's loyal to the people he loves. I respect that loyalty.'

'That kind of attitude gets you a club like this, I suppose,' Kelson said. 'It gets you a Porsche. Only you don't have the Porsche any more. I wonder how long you'll have the club.'

'I'm for ripping down his house,' Marty said.

'You've got to watch out for the little ones,' Rodman told Vargas. 'Always have something to prove.'

'*Me?*' Marty said.

'I've told you all I can,' Vargas said.

So Kelson hit him with a question from the side. 'Who were Josh Templeton and Deneesa Smithson?'

'You haven't already figured that out?' Vargas seemed almost relieved he didn't get something harder. 'You must not know the right questions or the right people to ask.'

'I guess you're the right people, then,' Kelson said.

Marty drew his .44 Magnum as if he would set the barrel against Vargas's head again.

Vargas glared at him. But he said, 'When Scott's mom died, Jeremy Jacobson sent him away for treatment. Deneesa Smithson worked at the clinic.'

'Nope,' Kelson said. 'Deneesa Smithson lived in Indiana and worked with foster kids. Scott Jacobson went to a fancy place outside Milwaukee.'

Vargas turned the glare to him. 'She divorced Josh's dad in Milwaukee and moved to Fort Wayne. For Christ's sake, she's not that hard to find.'

'Huh,' Kelson said. 'So, why did she die?'

Vargas said, 'You're asking the wrong person.'

'And how would Scott even know about Josh Templeton?'

'Do you have kids?' Vargas said. 'D'you keep pictures in your office? Josh's mom did.'

Kelson said, 'Right.'

'Christ, you're stupid,' Vargas said.

'Cut that,' Marty told him.

'But why kill Josh?' Kelson asked.

Again Vargas said, 'I'm the wrong person to ask.'

'But he's asking *you*,' Marty said. He raised his gun now and held the barrel a couple inches from Vargas's nose. 'I'm out of patience.'

Vargas paled but he said, 'You're a mean little bastard, aren't you?'

'You know who calls me that?' Marty said. 'My girlfriend. So leave that the fuck alone, OK?'

'What's the story with Alex Kovacic?' Kelson asked. 'What else aren't you telling?'

'Uh-uh,' Vargas said. He kept his eyes on Marty.

Marty moved the gun barrel closer.

'I'll lose everything I have,' Vargas said, 'everything I *am.*'

'If Marty goes off on you, you're lost too,' Kelson said. 'There'll be nothing left.'

To prove the point, Marty touched the gun barrel to Vargas's nose.

'Uh-uh.' Vargas's voice sounded hollow.

'You take chances,' Marty said. He exchanged looks with Kelson and Rodman.

Then, he pulled his gun from the man and stuffed it inside his parka. Rodman dropped his snub-nose into his coat pocket. Kelson stuck his KelTec in his belt.

Marty stared at Vargas with the kind of admiration brutal men sometimes show those who resist them. 'You didn't even sweat.'

But Marty overestimated him. Vargas took his glass from the high-top table and downed his drink. It hit his belly wrong. As Kelson, Rodman, and Marty left the club, he was on the floor retching.

FIFTY

'That's enough to act on,' Rodman said, as they sat in Kelson's car outside the club. A half block down, Vargas's Porsche was wrapped around a utility box. 'More than enough.'

'You think he told the truth about Scott not shooting at Kovacic?' Kelson asked.

'I think he was puking up his lies.' Marty settled into the back seat.

'There's something else going on,' Kelson said.

'One guy can tell us for sure,' Rodman said.

'Scotty?' Marty said.

Kelson turned the key in the ignition and pulled from the curb. 'Thoughts about where to find him?'

'Family first,' Rodman said.

* * *

The receptionist in the security office at Clement Memorial shoved her chair back and stood when the three men entered. 'Not this time,' she said.

Marty reached into his parka.

'No, Marty, no,' Rodman said.

Kelson said, 'We need to see Rick.'

The receptionist shook her head. 'Unless you schedule—'

'Let's schedule right now,' Rodman said, and gave her the nicest smile. 'Please.'

The receptionist looked from him to Kelson and back. She looked at Marty. He tried to imitate Rodman's smile.

'Where is he?' Rodman asked.

She hesitated. 'On the third floor?'

'We'll wait,' Kelson said.

They waited. The receptionist radioed her boss, telling him Kelson had returned with two friends. Five minutes later he came into the office, accompanied by two uniformed security guards. The guards, working hard to look tough, squared off with Rodman and Marty.

'Fun and games,' Marty said.

Rick asked Kelson, 'What do you want?'

'Where can we find your brother?'

Rick glanced at the receptionist. He glanced at the others. 'You two stay here,' he said to Rodman and Marty. He walked toward his office door.

Kelson followed him, closing the door behind him.

Rick leaned against his desk but looked ready to fight. 'What do you want with Scott?'

'Mostly I want to lock him up where he can't hurt anyone else.'

'What are you talking about?'

'Patricia Ruddig. Josh Templeton. Daryl Vaughn. Suzanne Madani.'

'He has nothing to do with them.'

'Deneesa Smithson—'

'Stay away from him.'

'One way or another, I'm going to get him,' Kelson said.

'If you ever do anything to hurt him—'

'I just had a conversation with a friend of yours who talked the same way about his car.'

Rick wavered between anger and confusion. 'What are you talking about?'

'Totaled. The utility box it hit too – beyond repair. Where's Scott?'

'Stay away from my family.'

'Which is your way of saying, you don't know where he is?'

'Which is my way of saying that my dad has connections in this city – political and legal – and he'll use them if he needs too. Stay away.'

'Do you really think that's possible?'

The men went back down to the parking garage, then drove through the late-afternoon traffic to Jeremy Jacobson's North Orchard Street greystone. Under the darkening sky, the green Land Rover, which was wedged between the tall hedges on the driveway, looked like a black shell. Kelson pulled to the side, blocking it in.

He popped the trunk, and the men got out.

Marty grabbed Rodman's Walther semi-automatic. 'D'you mind?'

'Be my guest,' Rodman said. He took the Beretta.

Kelson grabbed the Springfield, released the magazine, checked that it was loaded tight, and snapped it back in place. 'All right then.'

The men went up the stone path, and Kelson rang the doorbell.

No one came.

Kelson rang again.

No one.

He tried the knob.

Locked.

'Fuck it,' Marty said, and booted the door.

The door held.

'Fuck fucking it,' Marty said, and aimed the Walther at the lock.

'Marty?' Rodman said.

Marty lowered the gun.

Rodman hit the door with the palm of his hand.

The door pushed inward an eighth of an inch or so from the frame.

Rodman hit it again.

The door swung open.

'Honey, I'm home,' Marty said, and stepped inside.

Kelson followed him. Rodman limped in and eased the door shut.

Kelson called out, 'Scott?' His voice echoed in the high-ceilinged hall.

They looked into the living room. The chairs and sofa were plush and floral. A set of bay windows, sided by golden drapes, faced the street in front.

On the other side of the front hall, the men looked into a formal dining room – its table and sideboard gleaming with polish.

Rodman called out now. 'Scott?'

They went up the hall to the kitchen. A freezing wind blew in from a door that opened into the backyard. Someone had knocked it in too.

'What the fuck?' Marty said.

Then two gunshots blasted from inside a large pantry. One hit the doorframe next to Marty. The other shattered the glass front of a kitchen cabinet.

Alex Kovacic appeared at the front of the pantry. 'Ah, shit,' he said, ducking back inside. Then he stepped into the kitchen. He held his hands in the air, one of them gripping a revolver – pointing it at the ceiling, a finger on the trigger. He said, 'I thought you were him.'

'Who?' Marty almost squeaked he was so angry. 'Scott Jacobson? What the fuck? I mean, Jesus fucking—'

A siren interrupted – sounding from in front of the house.

Then another siren, also in front.

A third seemed to be approaching.

Kovacic lowered his revolver and stuck it in a hip holster. He slid toward the back door.

Marty squared the Walther on him. 'Where d'you think you're going?'

Kovacic reached the door. 'I can't be here. I . . .' Then he was gone.

More sirens sounded in front. Car doors slammed.

Marty followed Rodman and Kelson to the living room, where they stared out through the bay windows. On the street, there were six police cars and a tactical van. Five cops stood on the pavement with their guns drawn. Venus Johnson climbed out of one of the cars.

'Wreck my fucking day,' Marty said.

'Maybe for the best,' Kelson said.

Marty gave a look like Kelson was insane. 'You've got strange ideas of best.' He drifted back toward the hallway. He asked Rodman, 'D'you mind?'

'Go on,' Rodman said.

Clasping the semi-automatic, Marty went down the hall and out the back door.

'Huh,' Kelson said.

The cops outside were coming up the stone path.

Rodman set the Beretta on the living-room floor. He stepped away, where no one could mistake his intentions.

Kelson put his Springfield beside Rodman's gun. But then he went back into the hallway and climbed the stairs to the second floor.

As the cops waited for orders on the front porch, Rodman went up the stairs after him.

They stopped at the landing. Six doors branched into separate rooms. A light was on in one of those rooms, and Kelson moved toward it.

It was a bathroom. On the tile floor, there was a pair of khaki pants, folded neatly. Next to the pants, there were a blue crewneck sweater and a white long-sleeve T-shirt. In the tub, there was a man in white underwear and blue argyle socks. Scott Jacobson. Next to him, on the tub side, was a bloody razor blade. His wrists were slashed. He also had a single cut on the right side of his neck. His skin was pale, his eyes glassy. He was breathing – a very little bit.

Kelson reached for him, but Rodman pulled him back and said, 'No.'

Footsteps charged up the stairs. Low voices spoke on the landing. Loud voices shouted downstairs.

Venus Johnson stepped into the bathroom. Her eyes were wild. She gripped her service pistol in both hands. She aimed it at Kelson, then Rodman.

Their eyes were wild too. They raised their hands above their heads.

'Hell, no,' she said. She looked down at the unconscious man in the tub. She aimed her pistol at him and said, 'You're under arrest, you asshole.'

FIFTY-ONE

'What – you thought we had our heads up our asses?' Venus Johnson said. She sat with Kelson in the icy interview room at the Harrison Street station.

Kelson said, 'I didn't think you—'

'No,' she said, 'you didn't think. I hear stories about you. *Sam Kelson, the miracle man* – shot through the head but still sharp. Still able to work out the hardest problems. You know what I call those stories?'

'Bullshit?' Kelson said.

'*Now* you're thinking.'

'Tell me what happened,' he said.

'No,' she said, 'it wasn't your job then, and it isn't your job now.'

'Technically, that's not true. Technically, Jose Feliciano hired me. My job.'

She glared at him.

'By definition,' he said.

'By definition, I should string you up by your balls,' she said.

'How did you figure Scott Jacobson did it?'

Johnson sighed. 'Jesus Christ. How long after you got shot in the head did your wife divorce you?'

'About eighteen months.'

'She's a saint, putting up with you that long.'

'How'd you figure it?'

She shook her head – more at herself than at him. 'Mostly it was the dead kid.'

'Josh Templeton?'

'And the doctor too – Suzanne Madani. But mostly the kid.' She considered Kelson, and went on. 'Nothing added up right about the car accident. Why was there damage on both sides of his car? Then the driver who called it in disappeared. Maybe that wasn't so strange, but along with the damage, it pointed at least to a hit-and-run – and *maybe* to someone who intentionally ran Josh Templeton off the road.'

'I told you that,' Kelson said. 'A week ago, I told you.'

'It's how it comes out of your mouth. It sounds like crap. But I checked. Give yourself that much credit – I looked into it because of what you said. Then there's the fact that the ambulance took him to Clement Memorial. No sense in that – the ambulance had to pass two other hospitals.'

'I *told* you.'

'Crap. It sounded like crap. But I admit, it was interesting crap. Then Deneesa Smithson died. Now it was seriously interesting crap. We did the background checks, personal histories, everything. And we found out Deneesa Smithson handled Scott Jacobson's case when he got sent away for what they called behavioral issues but I prefer to think of as offing his mom. And we found out Scott and Deneesa didn't work out so well. She had pictures of her boy Josh in her office, and she came in one afternoon to meet with Scott, and he'd broken the pictures out of the frames. Do you want to know what he was doing to them?'

'Probably not.'

'I'm not supposed to know either. Medical records. Confidentiality. But you can't put photos in the wash, and some images you never get out of your memory. There was a blowup, and they held some meetings with the clinic directors and Scott's dad. They decided Scott could stay but with a new set of counselors and therapists. There were further incidents between Deneesa Smithson and Scott, though the people who assessed him thought he'd resolved everything before they discharged him.'

'Yeah, they were wrong.'

'We think Suzanne Madani gave Scott the epinephrine he used to kill Josh, Patricia Ruddig, and Daryl Vaughn – most likely without any idea why he wanted it. She was running that little operation on the side, taking in patients she shouldn't have been. Scott lurked around the hospital without anything better to do than watch the goings-on. Maybe he blackmailed her for the drugs – his silence, her epinephrine. We're also checking the signature on the order to transfer Daryl Vaughn to Clement Memorial. We expect Scott forged it.'

'Huh,' Kelson said.

'That's what I said too – about a hundred times in the last

week. You satisfied now? Did I tell you everything the curious little part of your pinprick brain wanted to know?'

'You're a good person,' he said.

'In spite of what they say?'

'I've never heard anything different.'

'Get out of here before you make me cry – though more likely I'll break your balls.'

He stood up. 'What do the doctors say about Scott now?'

She stayed in her chair, looking tired enough to sleep there. 'He's stable. They'll transfer him to jail in the next twenty-four to forty-eight. Suicide watch. I hear his daddy has lined up about ten lawyers.'

'Are you going to release Wendy Thomas?'

Johnson managed an exhausted smile. 'She rode out of here with her bull rider an hour ago.'

'I'll bet that made the bull rider happy.'

Johnson shrugged. 'Yee-haw.'

Kelson went home.

He vacuumed the carpet under the hole where Scott Jacobson shot the ceiling.

He fed Payday and Painter's Lane.

He stood in the shower for an hour.

In the chaos of the afternoon and evening, he'd missed dinner.

'I don't care,' he said.

At 9:15, he climbed into bed.

The reporters started calling a half-hour later. The police statement about Scott Jacobson's arrest barely mentioned Kelson, but he'd been a human interest story in the past – the badly wounded cop who reinvented himself as a private investigator – so the reporters were alert to his name.

When the first one called, Kelson said too much, as he always did – answering every question, as he always did. Eventually he started talking about Payday, who was sleeping on his chest as he talked, and the reporter ended the interview. When the second called, more or less the same thing happened. After the third called, Kelson said, '*Enough.*' But before he could turn off the phone, it rang again.

It was Frida.

'Wow,' she said.

'Yeah,' he said.

'I mean . . .' She didn't say what she meant.

'I know.'

'Are you all right?'

'I think so. Tired. Real tired.'

'I want to be with you,' she said.

'I'm glad,' he said.

She said nothing.

He asked, 'Are you working?'

'Uh-uh.'

'Can you come over?'

'Uh-huh,' she said.

Forty-five minutes later, Kelson buzzed her in.

He was exhausted, close to breaking. They slept in each other's arms.

FIFTY-TWO

In the morning, after kissing Frida goodbye and promising he'd find a way to call her even if Venus Johnson locked him up again, Kelson drove to Kovacic's apartment. He touched the buzzer on the intercom outside, and Kovacic answered with a thick '*Da?*'

'You've got to cut that out,' Kelson said.

Kovacic dropped the accent. 'What do you want?'

'Let me in.'

'Do you have a gun?'

'I'm stripped naked and harmless,' Kelson said, 'and it's freezing out here.'

Kovacic buzzed him in.

The apartment smelled like sweat. 'You were going to kill Scott?' Kelson said, when Kovacic closed the door.

'I wanted to talk to him, but I would've killed him before I let him kill *me*. He tried once. I wouldn't let him try again.'

'At first, you thought DeMarcus and Marty tried to shoot you in the alley. You only figured out Scott did it when I came here for them, didn't you?'

Kovacic did something noncommittal with his lips, then turned away and went into the kitchen. 'Would you like tea?'

Kelson followed him. 'Why would Scott even try to shoot you?'

Kovacic filled a metal teapot at the kitchen tap, set it on the stove, and turned on a gas burner. 'Revenge? The same reason he killed the others? He must have known Dr Jacobson fired me because I checked the drug supply records – and that's when this thing started to break open.'

'Maybe,' Kelson said. 'You know the police will want to talk to you. Sooner or later they'll track you down.'

'Not if no one tells them who I am.'

'Yeah, sorry about that,' Kelson said.

When the tea was ready, they carried their cups back into the living room. Kovacic sat on the couch, his revolver on the couch cushion next to him. He didn't touch the gun – didn't seem to notice it was there.

Kelson took a worn armchair across from him and frowned at the weapon.

'No,' Kovacic said, 'you're no threat to me. You aren't especially brave. Or strong.' He gave Kelson the thinnest smile. 'You aren't even good-looking. But you mean well.'

'Damning praise,' Kelson said.

'You helped me find Caroline. That's something.'

'You'd already found her. You just didn't know it.'

Kovacic's big round shoulders looked soft, comfortable. 'We're all fools,' he said. 'Amazing we don't fall off the end of the earth.'

FIFTY-THREE

Over the next three days, the story came out in pieces. Scott Jacobson was conscious and recovering from his suicide attempt in the medical ward at the Cook County Jail. At the advice of his lawyers, he wasn't speaking. But the police believed he ran Josh Templeton into the guardrail on Lake Shore Drive. Then he reported the accident to the AZT ambulance company, telling them to take Josh to Clement Memorial, where he gave him a fatal dose of epinephrine.

According to new witnesses – rounded up from the subterranean streets where the homeless camped through the winter – the teenagers who beat Daryl Vaughn seemed to think they'd killed him. The police believed Scott hired the kids for the job. Daryl Vaughn's survival and transportation to Northwestern Medical were mistakes Scott tried to fix by transferring him to Clement Memorial. The police were publicizing pictures of a bat broken in the attack and asking for help from the public as they tried to identify the teenagers.

Reporters followed Jeremy Jacobson through the public areas at Clement Memorial and once – when he parked on his driveway instead of in his garage – from his car to his front door. Then the hospital announced he would take a temporary leave from his medical duties as he dealt with his family crisis.

The police reclassified Suzanne Madani's death as a homicide. Wendy Thomas admitted – only to Jose, who told Kelson, who, in spite of himself, told anyone who'd listen – that on the day before Madani's death she swiped the doctor's key to the pharmaceutical supply room so she could return the fentanyl she found in her work locker. She was planning to come clean to Madani about swiping it on the evening when Kelson found the doctor's body. Admitting she had Madani's key after the police charged her with Deneesa Smithson's death seemed like a terrible idea.

The police believed they had a lead on the bicyclist who ran down Patricia Ruddig on New Year's morning – a man who hung out with the crowd at Club Richelieu.

Scott seemingly had decided to kill off people related to the trauma of his mom's death – and then Suzanne Madani when the doctor threatened to expose him – and then Alex Kovacic because he saw Kovacic as a threat or he already had momentum or just for fun or who really knew when dealing with the insane logic of a man like him?

On the night after Scott's arrest, Kelson had dinner with Sue Ellen. While he waited for her to come downstairs, Nancy said, 'We've been watching you on the news.'

'Yep.'

'Again.'

'Sure.'

'Jesus Christ, Sam.'

'I know.'

'Sue Ellen looks up to you. Are you trying to wreck that even before she gets there on her own?'

'I'm doing my job.'

'You're impulsive. You're reckless. How can someone with a hole in his brain be so headstrong? You know the word for a man who acts the way you do?'

Kelson said, 'Frida says it's sexy – and frisky.'

'Frida.' As if the name was a turd. 'The word is *idiotic.*'

'I try to be smart.'

'A man who thinks he's being smart by doing idiotic things? That's doubly idiotic. How many times do you have to get hurt before you stop? You stick your fingers in a spinning blade. It cuts off your fingers. So you stick in your hand.'

Sue Ellen came down the stairs two at a time, looking as if she'd leap into Kelson's arms. But she skidded to a stop. She smiled at him.

'One day that smile's going to be dangerous,' Kelson said.

'It already is. Logan thinks so.'

Kelson and Nancy asked at once, 'Who's Logan?'

'Gotcha.' Sue Ellen's smile broadened, and she was a little girl again. 'Mom and I saw you on the news.'

'I know,' Kelson said.

'Mom says you're being idiotic.'

'I know.'

'I think you're being . . . admirable,' she said.

'Then you're idiotic too,' Nancy said.

'Can I have guacamole?' Sue Ellen asked Kelson.

'Always,' he said.

'*Tres leches* for dessert?'

'Of course.'

'And *flan*?'

'Sure.'

'And coffee?' she asked as she and Kelson went out the door.

'No coffee,' Nancy shouted after them.

*   *   *

The next morning, at his therapy appointment, Kelson told Dr P, 'Nancy says I'm idiotic.'

'What do *you* think?' Dr P asked.

'I think I make mistakes. Bad ones. But I fix them when I can. Everything seems to work out OK.'

'OK for everyone?'

'No.'

'Even for you?' she asked.

'Maybe not completely.'

'But you seem pretty content anyway.'

'Is that strange?'

She set down her pen and notepad. 'For some people, every moment of happiness is also a loss. It's a moment they'll never experience again. You aren't one of those people. For you, it's mostly more and more. You don't look for subtraction. Whenever you can, you see *extra*. That's nice. Enviable even.'

'Huh.'

'But dangerous too – if you don't recognize the damage you do to yourself and others.'

'Sometimes I wonder if it's all too much.'

'You'll know when it is,' she said.

On the third evening after Scott Jacobson's arrest, Kelson held a gathering of five couples in his studio apartment.

Frida came early to help clean and set up.

Rodman and Cindy came next, with bags of empress chicken, Yu-Shang pork, bok choy, and Hawaiian fried rice from the House of Wah Sun. 'And this is for the two of you to share later,' Cindi said, handing Frida a bottle of red.

Marty and Janet came at seven o'clock on the dot. 'It's the fucking accountant in me,' Marty said, and Kelson explained to Frida that the little man used to keep books at Westside Aluminum until he got rich *not exactly legally*.

'But always while maintaining my principles,' Marty said.

He and Janet also brought wine – six bottles of it, which Marty said he got off a friend of a friend, as if that made it better than buying it from a store.

Jose and Wendy came twenty minutes later. 'You look reborn,' Kelson told them when they came in, and everyone agreed they seemed to sparkle.

Jose gave Kelson a bottle of champagne. 'A celebration,' he said. 'Thank you, amigo.' He kissed Kelson on each cheek.

Wendy kissed his cheeks too, then said, 'What the hell,' and kissed him on the mouth.

They all laughed and popped the corks and were half-drunk by the time Kovacic and Caroline Difley arrived.

With Rodman limping from Kovacic's mistaken gunshot, the couple were a last-minute invitation – made only because Rodman himself insisted. Still, Caroline looked spooked.

Rodman gave them his gentle smile and said, 'No hard feelings.'

She said, 'No, no . . .' She wasn't afraid of *him*. She worried because she felt certain a car had been following her for the past two days. Four times her phone had rung, and when she answered, no one was there.

'Telemarketers,' Frida said. Which seemed right to the others.

'Drink,' Marty said, filling the wine glasses, 'and the world's a beautiful place. Drink more and you'll pass out and won't see when it turns ugly.'

Kovacic and Caroline drank – taking a wine bottle each and swallowing away their fears.

'Good news for me,' Wendy said then. 'Northwestern Medical called. I start training in the MRI department tomorrow.'

So everyone drank to celebrate her new job.

They partied until the building super came with a noise complaint from Kelson's next-door neighbor. Frida invited the super in, Rodman loaded a plate of empress chicken and fried rice for him, and Kelson poured him a glass of wine, then talked with him about patching the hole in the ceiling.

Then the neighbor knocked too. Frida invited her in, Rodman put together a plate, and Kelson poured wine.

The party broke up at two a.m. The super and the neighbor stuck around to scrape plates and carry the garbage to the trash chute.

Then Kelson and Frida locked the door, turned off the lights, and fell into bed.

They got up the next day at noon, showered together, then found themselves in bed again. At three in the afternoon, they decided to have breakfast at the Golden Apple Grill.

They rode the elevator to the lobby, holding hands. Holding hands, they crossed to the door, which, in the bright winter-afternoon sunlight, glared like a portal to another world. Out on the sidewalk, the freezing air had a scraped-blood smell, so clear and harsh it took their breath away. They gasped, and laughed together.

Laughing, Kelson didn't hear the gunshot.

They were stepping from the sidewalk on to the frozen grit of the parking lot – hand in hand – and then Frida dropped to the pavement.

Kelson thought she was joking – thought she pretended the cold air swept her feet from under her.

Which – he realized later – made no sense.

Still, a laugh escaped from his mouth – even as he saw the blood.

It sprayed through the afternoon sunlight.

Its liquid warmth stung the skin on his face.

The joke wasn't funny.

In his confusion, he thought the blood was his own. A half-formed thought passed through his head – *not again* – and he felt *he* should fall to the ground – *again*. But gravity kept its fingers off him.

And Frida was already crumbling, already lying on the pavement. *Her blood.* The thought formed – half-formed – and the sound that came out of his mouth was incoherent. It was a whine, a groan, a sound that registered that he'd *fucked up and fucked up badly*, or maybe he had nothing to do with it – and that made it worse – maybe the world, the whole universe, was *fucked and fucked forever.* He could laugh all he liked – he could see beyond the loss-after-loss and could love what remained – but everything was *totally fucked.*

He sank to the pavement by Frida – he let himself sink, which was worse than having his legs blown out from under him – and the noise from his mouth stopped. He touched Frida's bloody forehead, where a bullet – fired from an unseen point between the parked cars or from the window of a neighboring building or from somewhere else – had cracked through her skin and her bone, blasting the inside of her skull, exiting from the back. He felt her heat, her amazing heat. But she had no miracle to match his own from when he took a bullet in his head on a night as black as this day was bright.

She was dead.

FIFTY-FOUR

'You were the intended target,' Venus Johnson said.

Kelson sat in the back of an ambulance on the parking lot outside his building. When the paramedics came, they guided him over and strapped an oxygen mask to his face.

'Breathe,' the EMT woman said. '*Breeeathe.*'

He breathed.

Now the oxygen mask lay on the bench next to him, and Johnson said, 'Your apartment. Your job. Your background. No reason anyone would pick on the girl, right? Must've been you.'

'One bullet,' Kelson said. 'Why?'

'Dumb luck?' Johnson said.

The police combed the parking lot, the street, the pathways around nearby buildings. They found no bullet casing.

'This can't be true,' Kelson said.

'Easy now,' Johnson said.

'Scott Jacobson's in jail. It doesn't work this way.'

Johnson touched his arm, as if to reassure him he was solid.

'Christ,' Kelson said.

'You want that oxygen again?'

When Kelson refused to go to the hospital, the paramedics kicked him out of the ambulance. Now he sat in his Dodge Challenger with the door open, his eyes on the white heap where Frida lay under a body sheet.

Someone must've called Rodman. When he arrived, he climbed in on the passenger side and for a long time said nothing. Then he said, 'It's a bastard.'

Kelson's mind was empty, cold.

'I'm sorry,' Rodman said.

Uniformed officers, detectives, and evidence technicians moved across the parking lot or stood waiting for orders, exhaling steam into the freezing afternoon. It seemed nothing could come of such methodical slowness.

'Nothing,' Kelson said.

Already the bright afternoon was darkening as the sun bent toward the high building tops.

'Who?' Rodman said.

'Does it matter?' Kelson said.

'Of course it does. It's *all* that matters.'

A half-hour later, four men put Frida's body in the back of a white van, and she was gone. Still, the officers and detectives swarmed, ringing buzzers of apartments with windows facing the parking lot, measuring possible angles of incidence for the gunshot. Still, everyone moved with maddening slowness.

An icy wind blew across the lot, and the sky went black.

'Let's go in,' Rodman said.

They went in. Kelson lay down on his bed. Payday leaped on to the mattress and kneaded his belly. He swatted her off the mattress. 'Jesus,' he said, as guilt flooded him.

Rodman went into the kitchen. He made coffee, poured a cup, drank it, and poured another, as if it would prepare him to do what needed to be done.

He stood next to Kelson's bed. 'How?' he said. 'Can't be Scott Jacobson.'

'Stating the obvious.' As if anger at his friend could ease the guilt – as if *he* hadn't said the same to Venus Johnson.

'What did you miss?' Rodman said.

'Me.'

'What did . . .?' The big man could tear other men apart but mostly kept that ferocity inside, like a personal heat. 'Get up.' He said it gently.

Kelson didn't move.

Rodman said, 'The thing is—'

Kelson's phone rang in his pocket.

He let it ring.

'The thing is,' Rodman said, 'it's happening now. If Johnson's right and you were the target, whoever did this is stumbling, trying to regroup. That gives us an opening.'

Kelson barely breathed.

'*If* we take it,' Rodman said.

Kelson's eyes were unblinking.

'*If* we move fast – before whoever did this tries to kill you again.'

Kelson sat up on the bed.

Rodman stared at him.

Kelson stood up next to the bed.

'Thatta boy,' Rodman said, and watched as if Kelson might fall.

Payday approached and leaned against Kelson's leg. She seemed to have no fear he would fall.

He swept her into his arms and held her to his chest. She purred.

His tears came then – hard and hot. He clutched the cat and cried.

'Yeah,' Rodman said, 'that's right. Do that for a while.'

Later, they sat at the dining table.

'Not Scott Jacobson?' Kelson said.

'Looks that way,' Rodman said. 'Or Scott Jacobson and a partner. Or someone picked up where he left off.'

'Most likely not him.'

'Looks that way.'

Kelson's phone rang in his pocket again. He fished it out and checked caller ID.

Unidentified.

He answered. No one responded to his voice. 'Hello?' he said again – and again. 'Hello?'

Silence.

He hung up and checked his call history. The call he'd ignored while lying on his bed also came from an unidentified number. 'Same thing's happening to Caroline Difley.'

'Could mean nothing,' Rodman said.

Kelson felt an impulse to shrink inward. Tears pressed against his eyes.

Rodman said, 'Maybe we should—'

The phone rang.

Kelson snatched it, answered, 'What the hell?'

'You're on TV again.' Sue Ellen's voice had none of its usual bounce.

'I'm sorry, kiddo.'

'Are you OK?'

'No,' he told her, 'I'm not.'

'Oh,' she said.

Nancy took the phone from her. 'Sam?'

'Hey.'

'At least you could reassure her. Tell her a lie.'

'I wish. Tell her what you want – whatever you think is best.'

'I think it would be best if you learned some common sense.'

'Thanks for the concern,' he said.

'What good would it do?'

They hung up.

Rodman let him stare at the phone, then said, 'Maybe we should check on Kovacic and Caroline Difley.'

Kelson got up and went into the bathroom. He turned on the water and stared at the mirror. He watched himself breathe – deep in, hard out, a man struggling for air. He willed himself to cry again, but the face staring back at him was strange and dry-eyed. 'Rip myself to pieces,' he said, then turned off the water and went back out to Rodman. 'We should check on Jose and Wendy too,' he said.

They put on their coats and rode the elevator down. In the lobby, Kelson hesitated before the glass door.

'Hold on,' Rodman said, and went outside alone. A minute later, his van pulled up at the building entrance.

Kelson went out and ran to the passenger side.

'Back to the rodeo,' Rodman said quietly when Kelson settled low in his seat. As the big man steered into the evening dark, Kelson's phone rang and rang.

FIFTY-FIVE

When Kelson and Rodman arrived at the apartment, Kovacic opened the door with a bottle of Bacardi Limón in his hand, black boxer shorts on his tattooed body, and the heat in his apartment dialed high. Caroline lay on the couch in a pink terrycloth robe, smoking a joint.

'Can't afford Miami right now, so we're doing the best we can,' Kovacic said, and offered Kelson the bottle.

Kelson stepped past it. 'Are you watching the news?'

'We're on vacation,' Caroline said from the couch. 'Nothing

but tropical drinks and delivery from Royal Caribbean Jerk. Want a hit?'

Rodman told Kovacic, 'Scott Jacobson didn't do it – at least not alone.'

Like a cold wind through the room. 'What happened?'

'Frida's dead,' Kelson said. 'Shot outside my building.'

'Ah shit,' Kovacic said.

Caroline looked stricken. 'I'm so, so sorry.'

Rodman asked her, 'Are you still getting calls? Do you still think someone's following you?'

She looked as if she would be sick. 'We came straight here last night after the party. We wanted to take a couple days for ourselves. I turned off my phone.'

'Check it,' Rodman said.

She crushed the joint and went into another room, returned with the phone. 'Four calls since last night. Unidentified. No messages.'

'Stay inside if you can,' Rodman said. 'Keep away from windows.' He asked Kovacic, 'Still got the revolver?'

'Of course.'

'Keep it loaded. Keep it close.'

As Rodman and Kelson drove through the dark from Kovacic's apartment to Jose Feliciano's house, Rodman called Marty and said, 'I might need that firepower you took out the back of the Jacobsons' house.'

'I saw on TV,' Marty said. 'The fuck happened?'

'That's what we're trying to find out.'

'If it gets bad, I'm ready. How's Kelson?'

Rodman said to Kelson, 'Marty wants to know how you are.'

'Hurting. Hurting real bad.'

Rodman told Marty.

'And pissed off,' Kelson said.

Rodman told Marty that too.

'Fucking right,' Marty said. 'Tell him that shit about him being a coward was just shit.'

'He'll appreciate that.'

'It might even be true.'

*   *   *

When Kelson rang Jose and Wendy's doorbell, light showed through the front shades from a deeper room. No one answered, and the house was silent.

Rodman tried the knob.

Locked.

'Go in anyway?' he asked.

Kelson pulled out his phone and dialed Jose. The call bounced to voicemail. 'We've got a problem,' he said to the recording.

Rodman drew his arm back, as if he would punch the door off its frame.

'No,' Kelson said.

He went down off the porch and around the side of the house, Rodman limping after him through the snow.

In the back, Kelson tried the screen door.

It opened stiffly.

He tried the wooden door inside it.

Locked, snug in its frame.

Rodman went to a back window and peered in. 'Not good,' he said.

Kelson joined him and looked. The kitchen table and chairs were tumbled on their sides. The cabinet doors were open, the contents swept from the shelves. The drawers were yanked off their tracks.

'That's more than a search job,' Kelson said. 'That's fury.'

Rodman went to the back porch, cocked his arm, and broke the door off its hinges.

The furniture throughout the house was knocked over, the drawers, cabinets, and closets emptied.

But there was no sign of Jose or Wendy, no evidence they were present or hurt when the house was wrecked.

'The doors were locked, though,' Kelson said. 'Jose or Wendy let in whoever did this, or the person had a key.'

He and Rodman stepped through the mess of broken plates, the tossed silverware, the plastic, metal, and broken glass. 'What's it tell you?' Rodman asked.

'Nothing,' Kelson said, 'and more nothing.'

'Someone wanted to destroy them,' Rodman said, and went to the front door. 'Let's get out of here.' He opened the door – as Wendy walked up the front path.

She was smiling until she saw the big man in her house.

'What . . .?' she started.

Rodman stepped backward into the room. 'We didn't do this,' he said. 'Except the back door – sorry.'

'Where's Jose?' Wendy asked.

'No one was here,' Rodman said. 'The doors were locked. Where were you?'

'Northwestern Medical – training for the last six hours.'

Rodman glanced at the mess. 'Would Jose have any reason to . . .?'

'No,' she said. '*No*. We were going to go out tonight – because of the new job.' She looked frightened. She pulled out her phone, dialed.

'He's not answering,' Kelson said.

She let it ring anyway.

'This was a smashup,' Rodman said. 'If someone was searching for something, what would it be?'

She went to the bedroom. She picked up clothes from the floor and piled them on the bed. She stood in the middle of the room and stared at the rest of the wreckage. She tried a couple of the half-open drawers. She said, 'The notes Ed Davies told me to keep are gone.'

'What notes?' Kelson asked.

'About wrongful termination. Harassment.'

'Who did you name in them?' he asked.

'Everybody. My supervisor fired me without cause. Dr Jacobson approved the firing. Rick Jacobson always treated me like I was guilty of something.'

'Did any of them know you were keeping the notes?' Rodman asked.

'I didn't hide it. They deserved to worry. I wanted them to know.' She gazed around the room. 'I wrote plenty. I used to love that hospital. But the people who run it are too close to each other. Much too close.'

'You need to report this,' Kelson said.

She nudged a yanked-out drawer with the toe of her shoe. 'Uh-uh. Jose would never forgive me. You know how he is. Cops either arrest us or hassle us like they want us out of the city.'

Kelson and Rodman helped her pick up the worst of the mess. They nailed the back door into its frame and promised to replace it as soon as they got clear of the confusion and chaos.

They stepped out into the dark at 10:30, and Rodman drove back to Kelson's apartment building. Kelson dashed from the van to the entrance door and ducked inside. He stood for a long time in the lobby, listening to the sounds of the building. Then he rode up to his floor and stood outside the elevator – listening again.

He went down the hall and stopped at his door.

A cat meowed from the other side.

Kelson felt a charge of fear. 'Christ,' he said. He slipped his key into the lock and went in.

The quiet in the room felt like a human presence. 'Like Frida,' he said, and though he thought again that he should cry, he felt only anger.

Payday and Painter's Lane meowed together.

Kelson fed them. He eyed the windows, eyed the bullet-pocked ceiling. Then he pulled back his blanket and climbed under. 'Stupid,' he said. 'Always stupid. A step behind. A minute late. Eyes closed when they should be open.'

He closed his eyes, opened them. Closed and opened them again. After an hour of that, he slept.

FIFTY-SIX

I n the morning, Kelson made two false starts from his building, then ran out, climbed into his car, and drove to the Harrison Street police station. He asked to talk to Venus Johnson and got sent to the homicide room.

She was sitting back-to-back with Dan Peters in their cubicle. They stared at him like he was a wandering war refugee.

'I'm sorry about your girlfriend,' Johnson said.

'About everything,' Peters said.

'Do you know anything new?' Kelson asked.

'It's early,' Peters said,

Johnson gave her partner a look. 'Based on the wound, we think the shooter was street level – maybe a drive-by.'

'That's more than she should tell you,' Peters said. 'Did you see anything?'

Kelson shook his head. 'I had my eyes on Frida.'

'We're reviewing security video from the buildings around yours,' Johnson said. 'So far, nothing. None of the neighbors saw anything.'

'There's got to be something,' Kelson said.

'We recovered the bullet,' Johnson said.

'It's *early*,' Peters said, this time to her.

'Yeah, it's early,' she said, 'but it looks like it matches the ones we found in the Lincoln Avenue alley. We put a rush on, but it'll take some time.'

Kelson suffered fewer headaches lately than he did in the first months after he got shot above his eye, but the connection between the shootings jabbed him like a needle.

'You all right?' Peters said.

Kelson fought it. 'What's the latest on Scott Jacobson?'

Again, Johnson and Peters exchanged a look.

Peters sighed. 'He tried to hang himself last night.'

'Didn't get very far,' Johnson said. 'A guard cut him down. We have him in a suicide smock now. But there's more—'

Now Peters warned her. 'Uh-uh.'

'We got records from the place where Scott Jacobson was put after his mother's death. They gave us something we shouldn't technically have.'

'Not *legally*,' Peters said.

'Nothing that'll ever go in front of a jury, but maybe it helps. Seems, when Scott was a kid, someone maybe abused him.'

'Who?' Kelson said.

'Records didn't say. This was in a note on an assessment the place did before they released him. It said the abuser was "immediate family." No way they'll tell us more. No way we'll ask.'

'We won't even admit we got the information,' Peters said. 'It could make everything from the facility inadmissible.'

The needle jabbed deeper – and twisted. Kelson squeezed his eyes. 'If Rick or Jeremy abused him and his mom found out, that might tie to her death.'

'It might tie to a lot of things,' Johnson said. 'Whatever else, it would've screwed him up bad.'

'How about you?' Peters said to Kelson. 'Can you tell us anything we can use?'

Kelson told them about the ransacking of Jose Feliciano and Wendy Thomas's house – and Jose going missing – about how Wendy wouldn't report the break-in because talking to the police would betray Jose, even though Jose might be in danger. As he talked, the needle seemed to pull out of his head, millimeter by millimeter.

Johnson said, 'D'you think we have the wrong guy in jail?'

'As you say, Scott Jacobson's screwed up,' Kelson said. 'I don't see how he's not involved. But whoever's out there now is cranking it up.'

'Yeah,' Johnson said, 'and playing it dumb. With Scott in jail, the smart thing would be to lie low, let things cool. The latest stuff is emotional. Whoever's doing it is angry or scared – or both. My guess is this person'll try to get you again, no matter the risk. You need to stay out of sight.'

'I'm OK,' he said.

She considered him and didn't seem impressed. 'What part of you can take care of yourself?'

'I have a pistol strapped under my desk. I have friends who are quicker with a trigger than I am.'

'You're the kind of guy who dies,' she said. 'You know that, don't you? You hear gunfire, and you run toward it. I feel sorry for you, Kelson, but if you insist on diving in front of bullets, there's not much we can do for you.'

Kelson went out to his car and drove north through the city. He pulled into a spot in the parking garage by his office and went down to the sidewalk. 'Diving in front of bullets?' Then he asked a man coming out of his building, 'Do I look like I have a death wish?' Without waiting for an answer, he went in and pushed the call button for the elevator. 'No,' he said, 'I have a life wish.' He rode up to his office, and as the doors opened, he added, 'For me, it's all *extra*.' He went down the corridor.

Where he stopped hard.

His door was open a crack.

'On second thought,' he said, and pushed inside.

Jeffrey Vargas, dressed in the all-black suit he wore at Club Richelieu, looked up, startled, from one of the client chairs.

Kelson walked past him and pulled his KelTec pistol from under his desktop. He pointed it at Vargas.

The other man shrank back. 'What?'

'How did you get in here?'

'The door was open.'

'Why?' Kelson said.

'How do I know?'

Kelson opened the desk drawer with the laptop. Had someone broken in and checked it? He went to the file cabinet. Had someone thumbed through the folders?

'What are you doing here?' he asked.

'Frida . . .' Vargas said. He looked like he was hurting.

Kelson breathed out. 'Yeah, Frida.' The fear and anger sucked from him.

'She liked you,' Vargas said.

'I think so.'

'I've been waiting here – to talk to you – to tell you that . . .'

Kelson laid the pistol on his desk. 'Thank you.'

'She loved – men,' Vargas said. 'Not all men. Broken men. You. Me. She didn't love me the way she loved you, but she loved me.'

The gun looked obscene on the desk. Kelson wanted to put it out of sight. He left it. 'I don't know.'

'She also was broken,' Vargas said. 'But you know what they say about broken bones.'

'No.'

'They get stronger when they heal – at the point of the break. She saw that in others. Strong broken people.'

'You knew her well,' Kelson said.

'I loved her.'

'Oh,' Kelson said.

'I wasn't with her,' Vargas said. 'Not like that.' He looked at Kelson to see if he understood.

Kelson didn't.

'I'm with Scott,' Vargas said.

'Oh?'

'Yes.'

'Oh.'

'We keep it quiet. Because of his dad.'

'Right,' Kelson said.

'He knows. His dad does. But he thinks people take advantage of Scott. We keep it quiet.'

'I see.'

'I don't think you do. You followed us on the night when that man was shot at in the alley—'

'Alex Kovacic.'

'We were going to talk to Scott's dad at the hospital.'

'But then you turned around,' Kelson said. 'You went up Lincoln Avenue—'

'Scott called the hospital, and his dad wasn't there,' Vargas said. 'He's never there when you think he is.'

'Why did you want to talk to him? Why did you go up Lincoln instead?'

'You really don't know, do you?'

'I'm asking you to explain.'

Vargas stared at him. Then he stood up from the chair. 'No.' He looked weary.

'Why?'

'*You* can't help. You have no idea.'

'I know one thing. You act like you're broken up over Frida, but all you want is to figure out how much of a threat I am to you.'

'No,' Vargas said. 'My feelings about Frida are real.'

'I know another thing. You're scared. How long did you wait here for me? Was the door really unlocked, or did you break in? What are you afraid of me finding out?'

Vargas went to the door, stopped. 'There are things about Scott's family that would blow you away.'

'You mean like the sexual abuse?'

That jolted Vargas.

'Huh,' Kelson said.

But then Vargas surprised him. 'Do you know what that family does?' he asked. 'They take care of each other. That's called love. Not the puppy love you think you felt for Frida. Not the kind I have for Scott either. This is the real thing – hardcore love. I'll tell you something else. There's nothing more dangerous than that kind of love. It's the kind you kill for.'

FIFTY-SEVEN

When Vargas left, Kelson called Ed Davies and said, 'I need to talk with Scott Jacobson.'

'Won't happen.'

'I've heard he has a team of, like, ten lawyers. You must know at least one of them.'

'Sure, I know Diane Manning. Her specialty is making opposing witnesses cry.'

'What would it take for her to get me in?'

'More than you have to give – more than you'd be willing to give even if you had it.'

'What if I could get the charges against Scott Jacobson dropped?'

'You can't,' Davies said. 'No one puts ten players on the field unless they're guilty as hell and trying to chip at the prosecution.'

'Call her and tell her I'll meet her at the county jail.'

'She'll rip my head off.'

'I'll buy you a new one,' Kelson said. 'Tell her I've got the inside from the arresting detectives.'

'She'll still rip my head off.'

'She can take my head instead if she doesn't like what she hears. I'm used to it.'

Two hours later, Kelson walked into one of the five-story brick and concrete bunkers that served as jail for Chicago and the surrounding suburbs. The big gray, open reception area smelled of disinfectant and sour, unwashed bodies, a stink that got stronger the farther in Kelson went.

Diane Manning stood by the security checkpoint in a navy-blue jacket. She ignored Kelson's offer of a handshake and said, 'Eddie says you always tell the truth.'

'*Eddie?* No one calls him that.'

'I do. He says you play straight.'

'I haven't bent since getting shot in the head three years ago. I also talk too much.'

'Eddie says that too. We'll see.' She nodded at the guards. 'They'll want to look in your pants before they let you see my client.'

'I've been here before,' Kelson said.

'That's what Eddie says.'

The guards took Kelson into a separate room, where they searched him for weapons, pills, and other contraband. Then they led him and the lawyer to a gray room with a bolted-down table and chairs.

A couple minutes later, guided by another guard, Scott Jacobson came in. His hair looked matted, as if he'd been sleeping, or slapping himself in the head with an open fist. He wore a black nylon smock – sleeveless, open wide at his neck, squared off below his knees. No shoes, no slippers, no socks, belt, or laces.

Diane Manning told him, 'Mr Kelson says he can clear you. Based on a reference he's received, I think you should talk with him. But if any of his questions make you uncomfortable, don't answer. If he asks questions I think you'd be ill advised to answer, I'll tell you. Do you understand?'

Scott showed no sign he heard her. But he went to the table and sat.

Kelson took a chair across from him.

Diane Manning stood at the table like a referee.

'Hey there,' Kelson said.

Scott stared through him.

'Me too,' Kelson said, and leaned in enough to smell the fear and pain that clung to the other man. 'According to the police, you set up a series of killings so complicated almost no one realized they were happening at the time. I don't think you did them. I don't think you're smart enough.'

The lawyer gave him a warning look. 'Mr Kelson . . .'

'You aren't complicated that way. Nothing wrong with that. You're a fairly simple guy. The only killing you look capable of – Frida's – you couldn't have done since you were already locked up. The cops won't worry about getting you for her if they can nail you for the earlier killings – which takes us back to them being too complicated for a simple guy like you.'

'Get to the point, Mr Kelson,' the lawyer said.

'For instance, the Wendy Thomas angle. She's a perfect

scapegoat. Even if she didn't have direct access to the epinephrine that killed Patricia Ruddig, Josh Templeton, and Daryl Vaughn, she could work out a way to get it. And she knew what to do with it – how and when to administer it so no one would suspect it. That's knowledge a simple guy with no medical training wouldn't have, even if he spent a lot of time lurking around a hospital. But this is where it gets interesting. The police think you maybe blackmailed Suzanne Madani to get the epinephrine – she got you the drugs and you kept her secret about unauthorized admissions of homeless men—'

Diane Manning said, 'I don't see how this helps.'

'But even the blackmail is too complicated,' Kelson said. 'If you were ripping off Xanax or amphetamines – something you could share with your friends at Club Richelieu – that would make sense. But epinephrine? No. That's too tricky and you'd have no use for it – unless you got it for someone else, someone who knew how and when to use it. I don't think you did any of the killings. I think your team of lawyers will figure that out on their own, sooner or later, and if they're worth what your dad must be paying them, they can convince a jury. So if you don't succeed in killing yourself first, you'll walk out of jail free, with or without my help.'

The lawyer said, 'You might underestimate the challenges we face in this case.'

'I don't overestimate your ability, though,' he said. Then, to Scott Jacobson, 'That takes us back to the beginning. What did Patricia Ruddig really see when your mother died? I mean, the driveway in front of your house is narrow. The hedges on the sides are big. Unless Patricia Ruddig was standing on your front porch, she must've seen only the rear of your car as you backed out. Hard to imagine she saw much at all.'

Scott started to keen, from deep in his throat.

'That's what I thought,' Kelson said.

'Enough,' the lawyer said.

But Kelson said to Scott, 'On the night that the Lincoln Avenue alley got shot up, you and Jeffrey Vargas wanted to talk to your dad at the hospital. But you called and he was gone. What made you think you'd find him on Lincoln? What did you think he'd be doing there?'

Scott keened more loudly.

A guard peered into the room through wire-mesh security glass. Diane Manning said, 'No more,' and signaled to the guard to come in.

'Did your dad diddle you when you were a kid?' Kelson asked. 'Did Rick? Why would you want to protect whoever did it?'

Scott keened.

The lawyer told the guard, 'Get my client out of here.'

After the guard did, the lawyer glowered at Kelson. 'You scumbag.'

'Are you going to rip my head off?' he asked her. 'Do you want to make me cry?'

FIFTY-EIGHT

Wendy Thomas called Kelson at his office a little after four p.m. When she calmed down enough to talk straight, she said Jose was home – beaten badly but alive. Kelson needed to come. Right away. Jose would explain.

'Who had him?' Kelson asked. 'Where was he?'

Jose needed to tell the story, she said.

'Put him on the phone.'

'Please come.'

Kelson hesitated. 'Is someone making you say this?'

'No, Jose's scared—'

'The bull rider's scared? I never thought I'd see it.'

'Please come.'

'A half-hour,' he said, and hung up. Then he dialed Rodman and said, 'Something's up at Jose's house.' He described Wendy's call and said, 'Meet me there?'

'I'm walking out the door,' Rodman said. 'If you get there first, don't go in without me. I'll bring Marty too.'

Kelson stuck his KelTec in his belt, went down to the lobby, and walked out to the sidewalk. A thick stream of rush-hour cars moved through the street. The wind was rising. He crossed toward the parking garage. He saw the stream of cars – saw the pedestrians around him – saw a sheet of newspaper that the wind picked up and slapped against the side of a city bus.

But he didn't see the shooter.

And he didn't hear the gunshot.

He felt a massive fist slug him in the shoulder – on the same side Gary Renshaw had shot him less than a month earlier.

The blow spun him.

He seemed to dance.

The people around him stared, astonished.

He lifted off his feet – rising from his toes.

What did ballerinas call that move?

Then he was falling – always falling.

He crashed against the freezing pavement.

'Dammit,' he said.

Astonished eyes stared down at him.

Hands reached for him.

'Don't,' he said. 'Don't . . .' He groped for his pistol.

The eyes saw the gun. The hands drew back.

The eyes receded.

He was no longer a victim but a threat.

The cold wind blew, and he was cold.

Then, with impossible speed, an ambulance siren neared.

'It doesn't work this way,' he said.

No one was listening.

The eyes, the hands, seemed miles away. He was alone.

The freezing wind licked at his neck.

He was a step behind, a minute late.

The ambulance came and idled on the street.

Fingers touched him. Latex gloves. Containing the damage of his wound.

Eyes stared at him. Impossibly close. Magnifying-glass eyes.

'I'm not a lab rat,' he told them.

'Stay calm, sir,' said a paramedic.

Kelson made a noise.

'You're going to be fine.' Prodding fingers. Reassuring voices. The paramedic cut off Kelson's coat, exposing the wound. It was bloody – the bullet went in but never came out.

'I'm OK,' Kelson said. 'I'll be . . .' He tried to sit up.

The gloved fingers held him down. 'We're here to help.' The paramedic held a compress on the wound.

'I'm OK,' Kelson said. 'I need to get to Jose—'

'Did someone shoot Jose?' the paramedic asked.

'Not that I know.'

'Then Jose can wait.'

Kelson struggled. 'I . . .'

The hands held him. 'Sedate?' another paramedic said.

'No,' Kelson said.

'Do it,' the first said.

A syringe injected him. 'You need to stay calm, sir. Everything'll be all right if you stay calm.'

Like a paralytic dream, the drug took the fight out of Kelson. He said, 'I need to . . . I need . . .'

'You need us to take care of you right now,' a voice said.

They put him on a stretcher and strapped his wrists, his waist, his ankles. The crowd crept close. Eyes, so many eyes – hungry for the sight of a wounded man. They kept their hands to themselves. 'Which,' Kelson said, 'is something. Better than tearing off pieces of my flesh.'

Other sirens approached, responding after a delay one might reasonably expect for a thing like this.

Kelson gazed at the eyes in the crowd. He gazed at the paramedics rushing him to the ambulance. 'It doesn't work this way,' he said.

'It'll be all right,' one of them said.

The other reached to open the back doors. Kelson read the letters on the ambulance.

A   *Z*   *T*

'Goddammit,' Kelson said, and struggled against the Velcro restraints.

'Calm down, sir,' the paramedics said. 'Calm down.' They shoved him inside.

On the way to Clement Memorial, Kelson told them the danger he was in. They listened with the boredom of men used to dealing with the ramblings of the incoherent or mentally ill. When one suggested another sedative, Kelson swore he'd try to stay quiet. He failed but they hooked him to a saline IV instead and wrapped his uninjured arm in a blood pressure cuff.

'I need you to call one of my friends and tell him where you're taking me,' Kelson said. 'And my lawyer.' He gave them Rodman's and Ed Davies' numbers.

'Sure,' said the one who wanted to give him the sedative, 'you can take care of that at the hospital. Right now let's make sure we get you there in good shape.'

'How'd you come so fast?' Kelson asked. 'I hardly hit the ground before I bounced into your hands.'

'We're very good at our job,' the other one said.

FIFTY-NINE

When the ambulance pulled into the emergency bay at Clement Memorial, two men in scrubs came and, together with the paramedic who liked sedatives, guided Kelson's stretcher through double glass doors. They wheeled him down a corridor to a triage room, where a tall Asian doctor was waiting.

Kelson tugged against the Velcro. 'Would you please unhook me?'

The doctor – whose ID called him Akira Handa – ignored the question. He scanned Kelson's vitals. He shined a penlight in his eyes. He asked him his name, his age, his address. He peeled the compress from the wound and inspected the point of entry. He looked disappointed. 'What's the rush?' he asked the paramedic.

'A gunshot. We understood—'

'Is there major blood loss?' Dr Handa asked. 'Do you see evidence of cardiac or respiratory distress – anything beyond the trauma to the shoulder?'

The paramedic said again, 'We understood—'

'Put him in non-critical care.'

'Could you unstrap me?' Kelson asked.

Dr Handa looked at the paramedic, who gave a little headshake. 'Will you behave yourself?' he asked Kelson.

'I need to get to Little Village.'

'Meaning?'

'Unstrap me and I'm out of here.'

'Oh,' the doctor said, and left the room.

Kelson shouted Rodman's and Ed Davies' names and numbers after him.

As the others guided his stretcher into the corridor and toward a non-critical care room, the paramedic said, 'You work against your own interests, buddy.'

'That's a correct diagnosis,' Kelson said.

He lay on the stretcher alone in the non-critical room for nearly an hour. They kept him hooked to the IV drip and a couple of monitors. Sounds came from outside the room – a screaming child, a hollering drunk, rushing footsteps, a siren from beyond the walls, more footsteps. Kelson spoke to them all, but none replied. Twice a nurse poked her head into the room, the first time saying nothing, the second asking, 'Are you comfortable?'

'Nope,' Kelson said.

Then the door swung open again, and Dr Jacobson came in.

'Huh,' Kelson said.

The doctor gazed at him warmly. 'When I arrived this afternoon, I heard we had you back with us, but I had to see for myself.'

'And *I* heard you took a leave of absence after your son's arrest.'

'You heard right,' the doctor said. 'I lasted two days before coming back. I've always found that work gives me solace. It was true when my wife died, and I'm finding it true now. How are you feeling?'

'Like a target,' Kelson said. 'Like I'm standing at the wrong end of a gun range. Like you're standing at the other end.'

'Well, then . . .'

'And I'm more than a little pissed off about it. Will you take off these restraints?'

'Do you need something to ease the pain?' the doctor said. 'I'll be happy to give you something.'

'I need to get out of here. No problem with the pain, no desire to stick around.'

'I'm ordering X-rays of the shoulder. Let's see where the bullet is and decide from there. We'd hate for you to walk out and collapse, if for no other reason than that the board of directors would worry about our public image.' He smiled easily. 'I'm joking, of course.'

'Not at all like a man whose jailed son tried to kill himself last night,' Kelson said.

The doctor's manner remained easy. 'The truth is, when I walk into the hospital, my only concern is for patient wellbeing. I leave the rest of my life behind. That's necessary to providing good care – the only way I know how to do it.'

'That must make your patients feel good.'

'To tell the truth, it makes *me* feel good. It's nice to know that whatever's happening in the world outside, I can do something valuable while I'm here. But the patients benefit, yes.'

'I've heard you started off rough, when you were young – before you had your family.'

'That's what they say. To tell the truth, I don't remember so well. I just know the man I've become. Should we see about those X-rays?'

'I'd rather go.'

'In all likelihood, we'll leave the bullet in. There's little chance of infection – did you know that a fired bullet gets so hot it self-sterilizes? But we'll prescribe you antibiotics to be safe. Otherwise, we'll go in for it only if it threatens a significant vein or artery. If it causes problems with a joint or nerves, we can worry about it later.'

'I'll sign any papers you need me to,' Kelson said, 'and I'll do the X-ray later. But I'm leaving now . . .'

'Then there's also the matter of your talking to the police. I understand that when you were shot, you had a gun – with which you threatened bystanders. I'm certain the police will need your explanation – your version of events. I understand you became violent with the EMTs?'

'No, I told them what I'm telling you – I need to go.'

'I have the paramedics' report on my desk. They say you became belligerent. They felt threatened.'

'I never threatened anyone.'

'I'm sure the bystanders will support your account,' the doctor said. 'In the meantime, I'll do my best to keep the detectives away from you until we finish the X-rays and determine you're in no danger. With that in mind, I'd like to give you something more to keep you calm. The EMTs just took the edge off. If you're heavily sedated, the police will be unable to use anything you tell them against you or, for that matter, anyone else. That'll be an incentive for them to wait to interview you until after we've finished together.'

'I'll pass,' Kelson said.

'Of course, I'll give you nothing without your consent.' The doctor's fingers found the flap to his lab coat. He pulled out a plastic syringe case. 'Have you ever had an adverse reaction to barbiturates?' He opened the case, removed a full syringe, and flicked it with his middle fingernail. 'I believe the EMTs took all the precautions that were practical at the moment – a man shot, violent, potentially causing himself and others serious harm. I believe no one will question their judgment.' He hovered over Kelson. 'Do you question it? When faced with either the small possibility of an adverse reaction or the near certainty of irreparable harm, how should a medical professional act? Should he address the circumstances as best he knows how?'

Kelson struggled against the straps. 'What irreparable harm are you thinking about?'

'Only the most irreparable,' the doctor said. He held the syringe for Kelson to see.

Kelson yelled at the door.

'A lot of people make noise around here,' the doctor said. 'They scream from pain, from fear, from insanity, from all three at once. The nature of the place. It takes special conditions for anyone to come running – particularly if a patient is already being attended by a doctor known for his comforting manner.'

'You abused Scott,' Kelson said. 'You abused him and screwed up his head so bad he killed your wife.'

'No, you stupid bastard, *I* didn't abuse him.'

'Rick did?'

'You're a damned fool.' Pain showed on the doctor's face. 'My wife did. From the time Scott was twelve until he was fifteen. Then I found out – and she died. You're right, though – the abuse screwed him up. You don't recover from that. One thing the therapists succeeded in – Scott stayed gentle. He was a gentle boy. He's a gentle man. He's a shattered soul, but he never lost that gentleness.'

'A gentle mother-killer,' Kelson said.

'No,' the doctor said. 'Not him. Not Scott ever.'

Outside the room, there was another rushing of footsteps, louder than before – loud enough for Dr Jacobson to stop.

'The cavalry?' Kelson said.

The doctor smiled. He'd heard such noises in the hospital before, often enough to know he shouldn't worry about them. He said, 'Let's do it in your good arm.' He brought the syringe to Kelson.

Kelson yelled again.

The door swung open. Rodman and Marty rushed in, followed by two uniformed cops – a woman and a man – with their guns drawn.

'Huh,' Kelson said.

Dr Jacobson held the syringe – looking unsettled for the first time since he came into the room. He seemed to try to speak, but no words came. He seemed to be about to inject Kelson with the syringe, but he froze. He eyed the cops as if he feared they would shoot him.

But the cops aimed their guns at Rodman and Marty.

The woman cop said, 'On the floor.'

The man said, 'Now.'

Rodman lowered himself to the floor, favoring his injured leg, but kept his eyes on Kelson. 'You all right?'

'No,' Kelson said. 'Not in the least. Not at all.'

The woman said to Marty, 'You too – down on the floor.'

Marty narrowed his eyes at her.

'Get on the floor – *now*,' she said.

Marty looked like he wanted to tear her apart and eat her. He lay down on the floor.

Dr Jacobson set the syringe on a table and smiled. 'What's this about, officers?'

The woman gestured at Marty. 'This one came into the building and threatened a nurse.'

'You're nothing but trouble,' Rodman said to Marty. 'I told you to let me talk.'

'Shut up,' said the other cop.

'Yeah,' Marty said, 'shut up.'

'You too,' the cop said to him.

The woman said, 'One of your security people called it in. When we confronted them, they ran this way.'

'We walked,' Marty said. 'DeMarcus limped.'

'Shut up,' the other cop said.

'Is that your job?' Marty asked. 'The lady explains things, and you're the fucking idiot who says, "Shut up"?'

'Marty—' Rodman said.

'I didn't fucking bargain for this,' Marty said.

'I still don't understand,' Dr Jacobson said.

'*This* one,' said the woman, meaning Rodman, 'thinks his friend's in trouble. He got a call from one of your people here—'

'A paramedic,' Rodman said.

'He got a call,' she said. 'He says it's life or death.'

'Mostly death,' Kelson said.

'He claims it's an emergency,' she said.

Dr Jacobson smiled. 'Ahh.' As if this kind of thing happened all the time. 'May I speak with you outside? I can show you an incident report from the EMTs who brought in the patient – and some other records involving his medical background. He has a history of neurocognitive disorders—'

'Guilty as charged,' Kelson said.

'It seems that, along with his current injury, he may have suffered further psychological—'

'Nope,' Kelson said.

'He must have asked an EMT to contact these men,' Dr Jacobson said. 'We have a misunderstanding – based on a miscommunication from . . .' He gestured at Kelson. 'May I show you?'

The woman cop looked at her partner, uncertain. 'You got this?'

The other cop pointed his service pistol at Marty's back. 'Sure.'

'Could you unstrap me first?' Kelson said.

Dr Jacobson led the woman out of the room, saying, 'He's mostly a threat to himself.'

Marty eyed the remaining cop and said, 'You little fucker.'

'I'm warning you,' the cop said.

Then Rodman sat up on the floor.

The cop jerked his gun so it aimed at his big chest.

Rodman touched his thigh. 'Bum leg.' He raised his hands. 'It's cramping.'

'Back on your belly,' the cop said.

'Because you're going to shoot an unarmed man for sitting in a hospital room?' Rodman said. 'A man who never threatened you?'

'Epinephrine,' Kelson said.

'I'm not screwing around,' the cop said, gripping his pistol with both hands.

'What?' Rodman said to Kelson.

'Epinephrine.' He nodded at the syringe on the table.

'Holy shit,' Rodman said.

'On your belly – now,' the cop said.

Marty grinned at him. 'You're pissing in your pants, aren't you?'

Rodman gazed at the cop with half-closed eyes. 'I'll tell you what I'm going to do.' His voice couldn't be gentler. 'I'm going to stand up. You should back away a couple steps so you're sure of yourself. If I come after you, you do what you've got to. If I try to leave the room, shoot me in the back. But I'm not coming after you, and I'm not leaving. I just want to help out my friend, you understand?'

The cop aimed his gun at him. 'Don't move.'

'Nice and easy now.' Rodman lowered his hands, gazing at the cop's scared eyes. 'No reason for more blood – this place has enough.' He got up, slowly straightening his legs. 'You a religious man? I never did know what it meant to part the Red Sea.'

Marty said from the floor, 'What the fuck are you talking about?'

'But now I think I've got an idea,' Rodman said. 'It's wading in where you don't belong because you've got no choice. You think you're going to drown if you step in that water, but you go in anyway – no way back, no other direction. That's what we've got here. Our own Red Sea. Are you going to shoot me now? Do we need that blood?'

He turned his back on the cop, went to the table, and picked up the syringe. He took it to the sink. He shot the drug into the drain. He looked around the room, avoiding the cop's eyes.

He gestured at the bag connected to Kelson's IV. 'What's that?'

'Saline, I think,' Kelson said.

'Let's hope so.' Rodman punctured the top of the bag with the needle, dipped the tip into the solution, and drew it into the syringe. He snapped the cap over the needle and set the syringe on the table again.

He looked the cop in the eyes. 'Our secret, right? You don't tell, I won't.'

He lowered himself to the floor and lay on his belly.

Dr Jacobson and the woman cop came back, laughing. 'No,' the doctor said, 'you scared me but not as bad as the first two did. Any time you want to chase trespassers into a room where I'm working, you're welcome.'

'Ha fucking ha,' Marty said from the floor.

'I'm sorry for all of this,' the cop said. Her gun was back in her holster. 'You understand . . .'

'Of course,' the doctor said. 'I wouldn't have you do any differently.'

Kelson said to her, 'Did you figure out Jacobson's a lying psychopath?'

The cop walked over and looked down at him. She seemed amused. 'I don't know what the technical term is, but I figured out *you're* a nut job.'

'That's technical enough,' Kelson said.

She turned to her partner. 'Everything all right here?'

The partner seemed shell-shocked. 'Yeah,' he said, 'no problem.'

The woman pointed a thumb at Kelson. 'This one – three years ago, a kid shot him in the head. Blew out a piece of his brain. He's like a walking wonder – except he isn't so wonderful since he keeps ending up in the hospital.'

'Isn't that confidential medical history?' Kelson said.

She grinned at him. 'Nothing's confidential when your friends threaten a nurse.'

'They wouldn't've hurt anyone,' Kelson said.

'I missed that change in the law,' she said. 'When did they switch *threat of physical harm* to *threat of physical harm but didn't really mean it*?'

'No harm done,' Dr Jacobson said.

'Guess not,' she said. Then, to Rodman and Marty, 'Up.'

Rodman and Marty got up from the floor. Rodman looked at peace with the universe. Marty looked like he wanted to rip the universe apart. Marty said, 'Can we go?'

'What world do you live in?' she said. 'Put your hands behind your back.'

* * *

When the cops took Rodman and Marty from the room in cuffs,
the doctor gazed at Kelson on the stretcher. 'That, I'll admit, was
unexpected,' he said. 'One plans for every contingency, or tries
to, but life is like this, isn't it? Throwing a knuckleball at your
head when you expect a slider.'

'Those guys are good friends,' Kelson said.

'But ultimately ineffectual, aren't they?' The doctor took the
syringe from the table and removed the cap. 'Your breathing will
become labored,' he said. 'You'll have a heart attack or stroke
maybe. Maybe your lungs will fill with fluid and you'll drown
the way Josh Templeton did. You know who surprised me? Daryl
Vaughn. I expected him to go out quick with a heart attack, but
the man was a fighter. He went comatose and his kidneys got
him.'

'No wonder Scott's in such bad shape,' Kelson said. 'Whatever
his mom did to him, you did worse.'

The doctor smiled. 'I'm sorry to say you'll feel some pain –
quite a bit really. This isn't an easy way to go. When it hits,
you'll be unable to call for help.' He squirted a drop from the
syringe on to Kelson's cheek. 'Not that calling for help would
do you any good.'

'Once you do something like this, there's no taking it back,'
Kelson said.

The doctor leaned in, as if to share an intimate secret. 'I'm a
man of complete commitment.'

Then he stuck the needle into Kelson. He took his time, then
drew blood back into the syringe barrel and reinjected it.

'I wasn't there for the others,' he said. 'I regret missing their
deaths, but practical considerations dictated that I be
elsewhere.'

He gazed at Kelson expectantly – at his face, his chest.

'Do you feel it?' He touched Kelson's wrist. 'It should come
as an incredible rush to your brain, right about . . . now.'

Kelson laughed at him.

The doctor looked baffled. He watched Kelson. He checked
the monitors, which recorded Kelson's steady breathing, the
steady beat of his heart. For a moment, the doctor seemed tiny
in his lab coat.

Kelson laughed, as if laughter could turn the vicious man to
ash.

A raking sound came from the doctor's throat. He rapped on the heart monitor, as if willing it to register distress. When it didn't, he looked as if he would break apart. But he had an insight. He was the kind of man for whom clarity always comes.

He drew air into the empty syringe. He held the needle to Kelson's neck.

Kelson stopped laughing. 'No.'

The doctor was torn. He seemed to like the way the needle dimpled Kelson's skin. 'No, you're right.' He pulled the needle away. 'That won't do. Every contingency.'

Kelson let out his breath. The last syllable of a laugh – sucked in when the doctor threatened him with the needle – escaped. 'Good choice,' he said.

'It was a necessity, don't you see?' the doctor said. 'Well, we'll try again, won't we? We have goddamned cabinets full of the stuff.'

'Contingencies,' Kelson said.

The doctor smiled again. 'You do understand.' He went to the door. 'I'll be only a minute.'

But once more there was a rushing of footsteps in the hall – voices shouting – and this time Dr Jacobson backed away, drifting toward Kelson on the stretcher.

The door burst open. Venus Johnson and Dan Peters came in, pistols in their hands.

The doctor seemed to relax. 'Hello, officers,' he said. 'We're having quite an afternoon. Can I help . . .?'

Then Rodman and Marty came into the room.

'Ah . . .' the doctor said, as though the mistake was theirs. He turned and touched the syringe of air to Kelson's neck again. He held his thumb over the plunger.

'You don't want to do that,' Johnson said.

'One of the advantages of age,' the doctor said, 'and one of the prerogatives of being an authority in my profession, is I know exactly what I do and don't want to do.'

'Move away from him,' she said.

The doctor dug the needle into Kelson's skin. 'You seem to misjudge the situation,' he said.

'I don't think so,' Johnson said, and she shot him in the chest.

SIXTY

The X-rays showed the bullet lodged against a muscle in Kelson's shoulder. A safe little lump.

'We'll leave it,' Dr Handa said. 'You won't notice the difference when you step on the bathroom scale. But I want you to stay overnight anyway. You've been through a lot. Treat it as a mini vacation.'

'Bring me a bottle of Bacardi Limón?' Kelson said.

'Tonight's menu is beef stroganoff,' the doctor said. 'Open bar but a limited selection – cartons of milk or cartons of apple juice. You can live it up.'

They put Kelson in the same room they'd put him in after releasing him from the ICU when Gary Renshaw shot him three weeks earlier. They shut the window shade, but Kelson could hear the news vans outside. One reporter got halfway down the corridor, dragging a camera crew, before guards turned him away. Kelson remoted the TV, flipping through the channels. The news showed the front of the hospital, forty or fifty feet from Kelson's window. The reporters, bundled against the cold, talked into microphones, so close Kelson could throw rocks at them. He turned up the volume when a Clement Memorial spokeswoman went out to give a statement.

A nurse came in with a dinner tray. Beef stroganoff.

'Look, Ma, I'm on TV,' Kelson said.

'How's the pain?' she said.

'It's a throb.'

'We can give you something to manage it.'

'I like the throb,' he said.

She set the tray in front of him, then produced an airline bottle of Bacardi Superior from a pocket. 'Dr Handa's gift,' she said. 'We all feel so awful.'

'Open the shade, please,' Kelson said.

Instead, she took the remote from him and turned off the TV. 'No news is good news while you're recovering.'

So he unscrewed the cap from the two-ounce bottle, downed the rum, and said, 'Cheers.'

As soon as the nurse left, he turned on the TV again, got out of bed, and went to the window. He peered out through the slats. The spokeswoman was talking to the reporters from a platform below his room. If Kelson opened the shade, he could wave like a king.

'Nah,' he said, and went back to bed.

Venus Johnson came in while he was eating his chocolate pudding cup. She watched him spoon a mouthful and said, 'You're a pain in the ass, you know that?'

'I've been told,' he said.

She touched her lips. 'Wipe.'

He wiped off a smear of pudding.

'You're like a baby,' she said. 'Falling off ledges. Sticking fingers into outlets. Drinking bleach from under the sink.'

'I hate the taste of bleach,' he said.

She smiled. He liked her smile more than Dr Jacobson's. 'I like your smile,' he said.

'We visited Jose Feliciano at his house,' she said. 'He's banged up pretty bad, but he won't talk. He doesn't like cops. Doesn't trust us. Would rather suffer than give a statement. I don't have a lot of patience with guys like him.'

'That could be the problem,' Kelson said.

'I don't want to hear it.'

'Yeah, that could be the problem.'

It seemed for a moment that she would tear into him. Instead, she said, 'Looks like Jeremy Jacobson took Jose. We have a team at the doctor's house now. We found two pistols in his bedroom. One looks like a good fit for the bullet that killed Frida and the ones we picked up in the Lincoln Avenue alley. We'll know in a day or two. The better stuff was in the basement – a couple of metal brackets ripped out of the wall. A concrete wall. Someone kicked like a horse to get out of that one. Went out through the window well. Plenty of glass – broken from the inside out.'

'Sounds like Jose Feliciano.'

'That's the theory. We have prints – and some blood. We'll figure it out, whether or not he wants to admit what Jacobson did to him.'

'He's a proud man,' Kelson said.

'Far as I'm concerned, he's a fool.'

'What about Rick Jacobson?'

'Yeah – what about him? We have him at the station, and he's still somewhere between denial and anger. How much did he know about his dad? How much did he participate? How much did he choose not to know? How much did he run away from? We'll keep him as long as we can. We'll appeal to his better nature – if he has one.'

'Give him Scott,' Kelson said.

'What do you mean?'

'The doctor convinced himself that everything he did, he did out of love for his boys. He protected them because of love. He punished other people because of love. Who knows, maybe in some terrible way it was true. He wanted life to be different for Scott. But instead of creating a better world for him he tried to destroy the one Scott already lived in. Rick has a lot of his dad in him. Give him hope that Scott can have something better.'

'That's the dumbest suggestion I've heard in a long time,' she said.

'Yeah,' Kelson said, 'typical of me.'

At ten p.m. the nurse came and offered him pain medicine again.

'I still like the throb,' he said.

'Whatever floats your boat.'

'It reminds me,' he said.

'Of?'

'Of all I probably should want to forget, though I'm afraid that if I did there'd be nothing left of me.'

She considered that. 'Personally I prefer Demerol.'

At 10:30, he turned off the TV. He went back to the window and looked through the blinds. The earlier chaos of news vans and reporters had assumed a kind of order, as if everyone was settling in for an all-night party.

Kelson turned out the lights and pulled the blanket to his forehead. That reminded him of Frida lying dead under the white body sheet on the parking lot outside his building, and he yanked the blanket down.

He closed his eyes – then snapped them open. 'Afraid to dream,' he said.

He pulled the blanket to his forehead again, stared at the threads, and breathed the fabric until he started to sweat. He pulled down the blanket. 'Shh,' he said. He closed his eyes – opened them when the fear came – closed them again – opened them – and, without crossing a discernible line, fell into a hard, hard sleep.

During the night, someone opened the shade, and when Kelson woke the next morning, bright sunlight shone into the room. It warmed the bed and made him think of faraway places.

A new nurse brought a tray of overcooked scrambled eggs, a muffin, a sealed plastic cup of orange juice, and watery coffee.

'No rum?' Kelson said.

The nurse frowned. 'I've double-shifted since eight last night – so don't start.'

'Back to the real world,' Kelson said.

Rodman tapped on the door as Kelson finished breakfast.

'Hey,' Kelson said.

'I brought a pal,' Rodman said, and Jose followed him into the room.

The bull rider's left eye was swollen nearly shut. The skin around it, extending down his cheek, was purple. His right eye matched the left. His lips were scored with rivulets of dry blood. The skin on the bridge of his nose was cracked.

He grinned through his broken lips. 'Amigo,' he said.

'Hey, you look worse than me,' Kelson said.

'No, amigo, I'm always handsome. Ask Wendy – she'd never marry an ugly *cabrón* like you.' Grinning like that must've hurt.

'We both got bucked this time.'

'Nah, I rode to the buzzer.'

'Tell me about it.'

Jose told him.

Two days ago, Jeremy Jacobson came to his house and asked to talk with Wendy. 'When the boss rings your doorbell, you let him in,' Jose said, 'even if you think he's a son of a whore.' Once inside, Jacobson drew a gun. 'I'll fight a fair fight against any man,' Jose said. 'I'll fight an unfair fight against four legs and horns. But I don't like to get shot – I'm not stupid.'

'What are you implying?' Kelson said.

The battered man grinned. 'Nothing, amigo. *Nada.*'

Jeremy Jacobson seemed convinced that Jose had evidence of his secrets. He'd long known that Jose hired Kelson to investigate the patient deaths at Clement Memorial, and he'd learned about Wendy's records of the events surrounding her firing. So instead of killing Jose, he tore apart the inside of the house, finding only Wendy's notebook. Unsatisfied that he'd gotten what he needed, he hit Jose in the jaw with the gun butt. Jose spat at him, and the doctor hit him again. The doctor hit him and hit him, but Jose told him nothing. 'I didn't know,' Jose said, and his grin was gone. 'I didn't know anything.'

Jeremy Jacobson forced him out of the house and took him across the city to his basement, where he continued to brutalize him. He seemed sure Jose had something that could either save his family or destroy it. 'I fought him, man, I did,' Jose said. 'But I would've given him anything he wanted if I had it.'

'Then you broke free,' Kelson said.

'Yeah, I did.' The bull rider didn't look especially proud of himself for it.

'Did you see Rick Jacobson while you were at the house?'

'Never,' Jose said. 'If he was there, he must've heard – he must've known – but I never saw him. I only saw that son of a *puta* doctor. If the cop didn't kill him, I would've, my friend.'

There was another tap on the door, and Venus Johnson came in. She looked at the bright window, seeming to see the same illusion Kelson did, then glanced at each of the men. 'Gentlemen,' she said, though she nodded only at Jose, the way strong rivals acknowledge each other with wary respect.

She went to the window and shut the shade. 'That OK? I thought you deserved an update. It'll be in the news tonight or tomorrow. You should have it first.' She frowned at Rodman, but she didn't ask him to leave. 'We agreed to release Scott Jacobson into a residential treatment program – in Arizona.'

'That was fast,' Kelson said.

'We worked out a deal with Rick Jacobson.'

'Ahh . . . in exchange for?'

'Rick admits he knew much of what was happening. His dad confided in him, and Rick let it happen. He'll testify that much. He claims he had no active role. We'll keep digging. Either way, he fills in some blanks.'

'Such as?'

'Such as Terry Ann Jacobson's death. Rick says his dad did it because of the abuse. Then he put it on Scott as an accident because Scott was fifteen and could take the blame without a lot of punishment – but, you know, Scott ended up on the lakefront with a razorblade and then a visit to Camp Nutso. So maybe the doctor misjudged.'

Kelson took that in. 'Could Rick be lying?'

'Maybe, though I don't know that anyone gains from it now. Rick says that when Daryl Vaughn was doing jobs for the Jacobsons, he saw Terry Ann touching Scott in ways no mom should touch her son. Jeremy Jacobson wanted to scrub that memory. Vaughn was so far gone by the time the doctor found him on Lower Wacker, it was hardly worth killing him, but Jacobson had other ideas. Patricia Ruddig nosed into everyone's business. Chances were she didn't see anything clearly when the car hit Terry Ann, but the doctor wanted to be thorough.'

'Terry Ann Jacobson died six years ago. Why wait so long?'

'I guess Scott was finally growing up and coming into his own. Rick says his brother was tired of being a victim – tired of his dad insisting he act like one. Over the last year, Scott started confronting him about his mom. On the night the Lincoln Avenue alley got shot up, Scott and his boyfriend – Jeffrey Vargas – planned to confront him again. In the meantime, the doctor was heading up Lincoln to take care of another target he saw as a danger to him and his boys. Alex Kovacic. He went from fancy drug cocktails to drive-by shootings. Rick admits sending Scott after him – because, he says, he thought Scott might be able to stop him. Funny, but Rick still swears Jeremy was a loving father. Says he'd do anything for his kids.'

'I guess he did too much,' Kelson said.

'The doctor planned the deaths of Patricia Ruddig, Josh Templeton, and Daryl Vaughn so no one would connect them and no one would even see that they were killings. But *this* guy' – she nodded at Jose – 'saw it. That's something.'

Kelson said, 'But the doctor's plans felt apart. So he hit Suzanne Madani and Deneesa Smithson with fentanyl and then whipped out a gun and started shooting.'

'That was plan B, apparently,' she said. She turned back to Jose. 'No ribbons for this one, Mr Feliciano. No prize money. The hospital will fight to survive now that one of their top doctors is down. They'll get ugly – try to throw dirt on everyone else to keep it from clinging to them. They'll like the look of you for some of that dirt – you know they will. We'll try to keep you out of it – that's all we can do.'

Jose stared at her, cold. 'Do you expect thanks?'

'No,' she said. 'No, I don't. Even if I thought I deserved them, I wouldn't expect them.'

Jose considered that. He looked like he wanted to fight. But then he thanked her.

The hospital discharged Kelson at noon. Rodman was waiting for him in his van when a nurse brought him out in a wheelchair. Kelson stood and breathed the freezing air deep into his lungs. He didn't care if summer ever returned to Chicago.

'I don't care,' he told the nurse.

'That might make it easier,' the nurse said.

Kelson climbed in on the passenger side, and five minutes later, he and Rodman barreled up Lake Shore Drive toward the northside as a freezing wind buffeted the van.

'I don't care,' Kelson said to his friend. 'For today, I don't.'

'What difference would it make if you did?' Rodman said.

A gust snapped at the van and made it rock.

'Tomorrow,' Kelson said. 'Or the next day. Soon enough, I will, even if it kills me. But not today.'

'Doesn't hurt to breathe a little,' Rodman said. 'No harm in that.' He rolled down his window.

The icy air pummeled the van and stung their faces. It battered their clothes like flags and made their hands hard to grip.

Kelson rolled his window down.

He breathed in. 'Everything's cool,' he said.

Rodman grinned at him. 'Good for you, man.'

Kelson exhaled and breathed in again. He had a bullet in his shoulder, another bullet wound inches away from it, and a piece of his brain blown away by a third bullet. In the coming days and weeks – maybe from time to time for the rest of his life – he would cry for Frida, and for himself. But at the moment, he would speed along an icy road in the city he loved, alongside his closest friend, and he would refuse to see or hear the ghosts of the dead or of the man he'd once been. At the moment, he would insist to anyone listening – even himself – that all was cool.

ACKNOWLEDGMENTS

Many, many thanks –
    To Julia for reading first, second, and third.
    To Philip and Lukas for all.
To Kate and the great people at Severn House for everything else.

To Dr K for talking with me about disinhibition. The license I take and any errors I make are my own, not his.

To Julie, Isaac, Maya, and Elias for putting up with my own less-than-inhibited self.